FATAL DIAGNOSIS

Myra looked alarmed. "What about other ways it could spread? What about food?"

"I don't know. Remember, this is only a theory now. You'd have to be a cannibal before—"

"What about protein synths? What about the liver the girl was eating? Maybe that's how she got it."

Payne's head started to buzz. "That would depend," he said weakly, "on whether or not the bacteria was aerobic."

"And if it is?"

He looked at her. "Then we have it."

A DEATH OF HONOR

Joe Clifford Faust

A Del Rey Book

BALLANTINE BOOKS • **NEW YORK**

Library of Congress Catalog Card Number: 86-91386

ISBN 0-345-34026-4

Manufactured in the United States of America

First Edition: February 1987

Cover Art by David B. Mattingly

for Connie

The drug is the dance
And the Danse is the drug...

—KITSCH

Friday Night

▓▒▓▒▓▒▓▒▓▒▓▒▓▒▓▒▓▒▓▒▓▒▓▒▓

*T*he girl was sprawled out on the floor in the living room of his apartment. He shook his head and blinked and looked again to see if she was still there.

His second thought was one of disbelief. *What Kelce won't do for a laugh.* Where would he be hiding? Behind the couch? Sure. And he would come out and say, "Caught you, Payne! Should've seen the look on your face!" And then he would force his high-pitched nasal laugh and say, "You can get up now, Karol."

You can get up now, Karol. He rolled the words around in his head. He wanted to ensure that they would put the quick wrench to Kelce's plot. Yes, that would be quite amusing. Ready, aim, wrench.

Instead, he put his grocery sacks on a table near the door. He paced toward the girl until he realized that he had left the door open. What would the neighbors think? He retreated and closed it. Now, onto the problem at hand.

He found himself staring at the girl's breasts. Familiar with Karol's, he determined by the lack of a mole that it wasn't she. And Karol tended to jiggle at the slightest provocation. The ones he was watching were much too still. If this was Kelce's doing, he had gone too far.

He walked to her, knelt, and sank his fingers into the soft flesh of her neck. It was warm. He found some solace in that. He probed her neck, trying to find the carotid artery.

A new thought chilled him. *You can't find the pulse because there isn't one*. He rose slowly, wiping his hand on the cuff of his jumpsuit. He and Bailey were supposed to go to club tonight. Now he would have to wait for the removal squad, which would be hours in coming. It didn't seem fair.

He stamped his foot on the floor next to the girl's ear and shouted, "Come on, damn it. You can't hold your breath forever."

He trotted to the kitchen and took the ice chest from the top of the refrigerator. Popping off the lid, he rummaged through the ice for his last beer. He walked back, wiping the moisture from the bottle on the sleeve of his suit.

As a test, he held the dried bottle to his lips and exhaled slowly. Fog crept across the glass. He knelt again and held the bottle centimeters from the girl's face. Nothing. Not even a snicker from Kelce, who was surely hiding in the bedroom. He licked his lips and held the bottle until his fingers numbed. When he could take no more, he sighed and sat back on his heels.

"Okay, Kelce," he said. "You win. You've scared the hell out of me. Come on. It's time you end this thing." He rose to face his tormentor.

Nothing.

"Damn it, what more do you want?"

He glanced around the living room. The telephone caught his eye.

"All right. If you want me to make a fool of myself, I will." He crossed to the phone and put the handset to his ear. "The lines are even up. I'm going to call the law now." His fingers flitted over the heat-sensitive pads once, twice, three times, with no result. Part of the city had browned out and had taken a major trunk line with it. He tried again.

"Precinct Nine," said a sexless voice.

"Homicide, please."

"Thank you." There was a click.

"They're on the line, Kelce," he said loudly.

"Homicide." The synthetic voice came from a maze of printed circuit boards deep in the Precinct Nine building. "All of our lines are busy right now. Please hold and you will be connected with the first available dispatcher. Thank you for waiting." There was a click, and the line switched over to music, a dreadful canned version of an early Oldfield symphony. He pulled a chair close and sat.

"I'm on hold, Kelce," he said, no longer expecting an answer.

Eighteen minutes went by before he talked to a dispatcher. During that time he moved to the couch, occasionally glancing at the blonde on the floor, still half waiting for her to sit up and ask for her clothes. The minutes dragged, and badly arranged music played to one ear. Kelce's joke showed no signs of life. Payne retrieved the beer from the floor and drank it.

"You were pretty," he said to her. "Did you work? Maybe you were just out in the world having fun." He sipped the beer.

The handset clicked, and the music cut off. The voice said, "Transferring." There was another click.

"Precinct Nine Homicide." This voice was real and pleasantly female. "Do you wish to make a report?"

"Yeah."

"Location of body?"

"I'm looking at it."

"Location of body?" The voice was impatient.

"The Plus Fours Apartments Southwest. Number seven-thirteen."

"Cause of death?"

"I don't know. She was dead when I got here. I didn't

see any marks on her." He hadn't thought that she might
be oozing blood all over the cheap carpet.

"Victim identity?"

"Unknown."

"Approximate time of discovery?"

He thumbed his watch and listened. How long had it
been? "1820 hours," he guessed.

"Did you witness the event?"

"I wish I had."

"Can you approximate the time of death?"

"It wasn't too long ago. As of twenty minutes ago she
was still warm."

"Your name?"

"Payne." He spelled it and added, "D.A. Payne."

"Thank you, Mr. Payne. Pickup will be in about four
hours."

"Four hours!"

"It's a busy night. Friday, end of the month, full moon.
A perfect three out of three."

"Right," he said dully. "See you in four hours."

"Thank you for reporting."

Thanks for reporting? Thanks for another body to add
to the count? Did they get paid by the numbers? Piece-
work, perhaps? Had things actually come to that?

He decided that such questions were inconsequential.
The body was on his living room floor, and he had four
hours before someone picked her up and tagged her and
read him his rights. He had no plans to take the Thirty-
First. All he wanted was the body out of his apartment
and perhaps a confession from Kelce that the whole business had been his doing.

The telephone bleeped, and he jumped. This was it.
Kelce was calling to say what a fool Payne had been, and
the cute blonde would sit up and laugh. He grabbed the
handset and tried to speak, but the greeting came out in
a dry croak.

"Payne?"

"Yeah?"

"Where are you? You were supposed to be down ten minutes ago."

He checked his watch. 1912. Time had gotten away from him.

"Payne, are you okay?"

Payne cleared his throat. "No, Bailey. There's been some trouble here."

"Trouble?"

"I've got a dead girl lying next to my couch."

Bailey whistled. "Anyone you know?"

"I don't even know how she got here."

Bailey sounded exasperated. "I guess this means we can't go club tonight."

"We can go. We'll just have to come back early."

"Shouldn't be a problem. I thought I'd do some procreation tonight. If I get tied up, you may have to leave without me."

"I thought you weren't into that," Payne said dryly.

"Into what?"

"Forget it. You can stay if you have to. What are you wanting to buy now?"

"Nothing in particular. Things are slow at the plant right now, and there's rumors of layoffs. I thought I'd get a little money built up, pay the rent in advance, that sort of thing."

"If you're still working in nine months, you'll have a nice bonus coming."

Bailey laughed. "And if not, then I've literally laid aside some money for the future."

Payne ignored the joke. "Are you all clean and approved for your evening's entertainment?"

"Got my Bill of Health this morning."

"Give me fifteen minutes and I'll be down."

"Fifteen minutes!"

"I'm still in work clothes."

"Very well. Tempus fugit."

"Lighten up, Bailey." He spoke sharply, having lost his patience. "It won't take that long."

"Sorry. It's just that I'm stirred and ready. Aren't you?"

"I'm going gray tonight."

"You always go gray. You ought to sow the seed once in a while."

"The longer you keep me on the phone, the later we'll be in getting to the club."

"Gone. See you in fifteen."

"Make it ten," Payne said, but the line was dead. The power had failed before Bailey could finish.

He gathered the groceries and carted them into the kitchen. The perishables went into the ice chest with the new beer. The canned goods went into the refrigerator. He felt the bottom of the freezer compartment while it was open. Cold. There had been no brownouts on his block today.

The suits came last. He'd purchased three of them in off shades of green, blue, and brown. Walking into the bedroom, he tore the cellophane and pulled out the green one. With a flick of his wrist, it neatly unfolded. Payne took a hanger from the closet and hung the suit, dusting off bits of lint.

With a spray bottle he began to mist the suit, starting at the bottom and working his way up. As the fibers absorbed the water and expanded, the wrinkles and folds neatly disappeared. Payne set the bottle aside and glanced at the package. OLYMPIC TEXTILES, it read. TWO MIL RE-INFORCED TREATED PAPER SUIT. SLOW BURNING, SELF-IRONING. The self-ironing part made him laugh. He did all the work of spraying the thing, but they made it sound as if the suit did it on its own.

He peeled off the old suit and tossed it into a box with the other discards. Next he sprayed his face with water. The more the evening dragged on, the less he felt like accompanying Bailey to a club. He would invariably end up drinking alone while Bailey wandered into a private chamber to make a shot at a government check. Still, that was better than spending the evening with a cooling corpse.

He pulled the new suit from the hanger, stepped in,

and zipped it up. It was baggy, but that was nothing that wouldn't be cured as it dried. He slipped his loafers on and headed for the door.

Scarf.

He had forgotten the scarf. Returning to the bedroom, he threw open a drawer and rummaged until he found his gray scarf. He wrapped it around his neck, pulled on a ring fastener, and tucked the ends into his suit.

As he left the apartment, he found his keys dangling from the deadbolt lock. Had he not left them there, he would have walked out without them. He slipped them in his pocket.

It was a short trot down to Bailey's apartment. He knocked, and the door opened on a man wearing a bright green scarf around his neck.

"What's your hurry?" Bailey asked. "You're the one who didn't want to go anywhere."

"I'm the one who has to be back early. Tomorrow's my Saturday in."

"Now you tell me. Let's get going, then." Bailey locked his door, then led the way down the remaining stairs to the main doors.

"If you don't mind spilling the secret," Payne asked, "where are we going tonight?"

"The club over on Lancaster Boulevard. It's my lucky club."

"On a Friday? Lots of luck."

"Why?"

"The Lancaster is everyone's lucky club."

"Cynic."

"Flatterer."

They walked down the middle of the street, stepping around the rusting hulks of automobiles.

"What are they calling the club this week?" Payne asked.

"Danse."

"Still?"

"Twelfth big week. Biggest single United Media has had all year."

"Biggest of the year, sounds like."

"Kitsch is getting rich."

"Undoubtedly."

Six blocks later they found themselves across from the club. It was unlike any other in the city. The others had been built within the decade and were slick and stream-lined. What this week was called "Danse" had been the last of the giant motion picture theaters from decades long forgotten. Coaxial cable, laser technology, the digital pro-cess, and narrowcasting had dealt the death blow to the theater system.

Then came the refugee. The man from Great Britain had a compassion and a nostalgia for an era that was already history by the time he was born. He took pity on the aging, abandoned beast. He kept the screen, upgraded the projection and sound systems, removed the seats, leveled the floor, installed a bar and a glass dance floor, and the theater became the club. By the time the govern-ment moved into child rearing it was no problem to buy the two adjacent buildings and install the privacy cham-bers. Office space was made for the government clerks who were responsible for keeping track of who had impregnated whom. The icing on the cake was the floating name: that of the week's number one song. It had the right chemistry, and it worked. The club was one of the most popular in the city, even flaunting itself during power breakdowns by using solar collectors by day to store the needed power for the night.

Payne and Bailey stared at the oasis of light on the darkened avenue. A giant liquid crystal display took the place of the theater's once grand marquee, letters heralding STILL DANSE! which melted into TWELFTH WEEK! which in turn dissolved into YEAR'S BIGGEST HIT!

"The time is right," Bailey said, stepping into the street. Payne stayed behind to watch the huge melting letters. It was only after Bailey prodded him that he broke his gaze and crossed the street.

"Packed yet?" Bailey asked the admissions clerk.

The clerk smiled insipidly. "Plenty o' room."

"Admit two."

"Ticket class?"

"I'm loaded. My friend here is going gray." Bailey laughed. "He's tired."

Payne said nothing but held out his scarf so the clerk could see the black onyx stone in his ring.

"I wouldn't be so generous in laying it on your friend," the clerk said. "He's probably your father. Seven-fifty for you and four for him."

Bailey flipped over a plastic card. The clerk shoved it into a console, keyed in the amount, and returned it.

"He stole that ten-prole ring, you know. He just goes gray so he can get in cheap."

Payne laughed and followed Bailey into the lobby. "Want a drink?"

"Too early. Hinders performance." He adjusted his scarf. "Let's dance."

They walked into the ballroom and were assaulted by heat and overpowering bass notes that rattled the bones in their chests. The air was thick with smoke. Lasers danced on the ancient movie screen. With the exception of the bar and the booths lining the walls, the floor was a mass of tightly packed bodies, jumping and twisting, losing themselves in sound and scent.

"Plenty o' room," Bailey said sarcastically.

"Lots of seating at the bar," Payne offered.

Bailey checked his watch. "It's only 1940." He shook his head. "The real rush doesn't start until around 2100."

"In which case we'll never find our way out."

"This is all your fault. We were late."

"You were the one who wanted to come here on a Friday."

Bailey sneered.

They fought their way to the bar beneath the screen

by cutting through the tangle of bodies on the dance floor. An entire song played through before they got there, and Payne took an elbow in the kidneys somewhere in the middle of the fleshy maze. The blow caught him off guard, and his legs buckled, but the people were packed in so tightly that he hovered with the crowd.

His reverie was broken by a dishwater blonde with a badly scarred nose. "What're you on?" she asked.

"I'm sorry?"

"Blueskies. That's it. You're doing Blueskies."

Payne shook his head and winced. "I'm doing a ruptured kidney."

The girl turned, drawing attention to her flaw. She tilted her head toward the chambers. "Want to bed down?"

Arms pinned to his sides by the crowd, Payne motioned to his scarf with his chin.

The girl flushed. "Oh. Sorry. Well, how about a dance, then?"

He shook his head politely. "Maybe later. Right now I want first aid."

She forced a smile. "Sure." And somehow in that mass of bodies she turned and floated away.

A veteran, Payne thought as he dropped his feet and continued to squirm through the crowd. He twisted his head, trying to get his bearings. Regaining his sense of direction, he pressed on, emerging from the crowd feeling as if he had accomplished something. He looked for Bailey, who was nowhere to be seen.

One song later, when the crowd thinned to applaud a four-song set, Bailey appeared, weaving easily through the crowd as if he had done it all of his life.

"You make it look so easy. I couldn't do that when I was your age."

"They didn't have the Danse when you were my age."

"It was just the Lancaster Club back then. Where were you?"

"Groping." Bailey giggled. "A man has to get warmed up. That's the purpose of the dance, you know."

"Are you looking now or are you going to wait a while?"

"Who knows? I feel like a champ tonight. I may go for two. Why?"

"Ran into a girl." He paused and stared into the crowd, which had congealed for the next set. "She was ready."

Bailey was interested. "In money?"

Payne shook his head. "Pleasure."

"Was she nice?"

"I thought so. Kind of cute, but she has a screwed up face."

Bailey touched a finger to the side of his nose. Payne nodded.

"She's bad news," Bailey said. "Can't hold her babies. Some guy got upset after one of her miscarriages and tried to tear her face off. Lucky for her he'd tried it right outside of the Satyr on a 31st. The doormen came over and beat him to death."

"They didn't shut the club down?"

Bailey shook his head. "This guy had a rep, too. A bad one. A real piece of garbage. Everyone looked the other way. A crowd of fifty people gathered around, and not a damn one of them saw it. Nobody would touch his Thirty-first."

Payne swallowed. "So why doesn't she plastic her nose?"

"Beats me. Maybe she's proud of it. Maybe she thinks it's a Purple Heart."

Purple Heart. Payne licked his lips.

"Let's get a seat," Bailey said. "If I'm going to try tonight, I've got to get some alcohol on my breath."

Payne followed Bailey to a booth and sat down. "I thought you didn't want to drink. Performance, you know."

"Think back to your own career, father of ten. Ever try to bed down when you were squeaky clean with anti-septic breath?"

"All of mine were done at home. My place or hers."

Bailey shook his head. "I'm only having one, for the taste and smell. You want anything?"

"The usual."

Bailey nodded and disappeared. Payne sat back and listened to the music. The song playing was old, something from last century, something nonirritating. Unlike the hits of the day it was melodic and was recorded with antiques: guitars, primitive keyboards, and acoustic percussion. He closed his eyes and smiled.

Suddenly the power of computer drumming slammed from the speakers at full volume, and a tumultuous roar of approval broke from the crowd.

"Top of the hour!" a coarse voice shouted. "You know what time that is?"

Baited, the crowd screamed.

"The number one song in the nation!"

"Danse!" the crowd screamed.

A dissonant synthesizer cracked over the drumming, and a voice screeched. The people did the dance, which consisted of turning as fast as one was able, shaking one's head and throwing one's limbs in random directions. The object was to keep up with the song's breakneck pace without collapsing before it was over. It was no easy task. After thirty seconds the maladroits were already on their knees, giggling for mercy.

Others became dizzy and collided, falling into each other's arms. More often than not, it resulted in a pair that invariably would repair to the chambers. Payne mused that this was the reason for the song's runaway success. It was nothing more than a mating dance, and the ones still on their feet at the end of eight minutes were worthy of passing their genes on to the future. The song was more fun than the crowd would ever know. He was very, very amused.

And then his eyes fell on the girl with the flawed face. Still on her feet halfway through the song, she carried a stealth unlike any other on the dance floor. As she spun, her hair swirled across her face, creating a veil, and suddenly her defect no longer mattered. Coming down, she gracefully landed on her feet and shot back up into the air, arms spread wide. She gleamed with sweat, and the shirt clung to her body. She didn't move. She flowed. And if to no one but herself, she was proving that she was one with her body.

"Should've worn a green scarf," Bailey commented.

Payne started.

"I see those looks you're making." Bailey slapped a glass on the table. "Which one is it? The redhead?"

"Reliving a lost past," Payne lied.

"Yeah," Bailey replied, as if nothing were hidden from him. "It's the redhead. You should've gone green."

"You're right. Lend me your scarf."

Bailey scrutinized him. "It must be a memory. And a nice one at that."

"Why do you say that?"

"The redhead isn't *that* great."

Payne laughed and took the drinks that Bailey had brought.

"This one's yours, too." Bailey pushed a third glass to him.

"You're not having two?"

"I'm not even going to finish this one. It's got to look like I'm drinking a lot. There's an art to this, you know."

Payne sipped. "I know."

"When you finish one of those, put the glass on my side of the table." He gulped his drink so fast that liquid ran down his chin.

"Are you going to drink that or wear it?"

"Both." He wiped his chin with the palm of his hand and patted his face. "It's the smell, remember? If you smell of alcohol, they think you've been drinking more than you really have."

"Times have changed."

"You have an easier way?"

"I'd show you, but I'm grayed out."

"Excuses." Bailey drained his glass. "Have fun drinking. I'm going to go test the water."

"Don't get in too deep."

If Bailey caught the humor, it went unacknowledged. He glided to the choked dance floor and let the crowd absorb him. Payne shook his head and laughed. It was so much trouble now. When things had first started, it was so easy. There were nice touches; you took the girl to your place or went to hers, you talked before acting, if you decided to act at all, and you didn't need the chambers or the mating dance. He looked out across the dance floor.

The first two drinks went quickly. By the time the third was almost done, an alert barmaid supplied him with more. He slid the three empties to Bailey's side of the table along with one of the fresh glasses and started on his fourth. Midway through number five, Bailey returned to the table with a redhead on his arm. Payne wanted to laugh but checked himself. Playing gentleman, Bailey let her slide in first.

"Payne, I want you to meet my friend . . ."

"Glory," the girl said. Her head bobbed about as if nothing were inside.

"Short for Gloria," Bailey said. "Glory, this is my friend Payne."

"Pleasure's dubious," Payne said, smiling wryly. Bailey glared. Glory blushed.

"Oh, thank you." She shook Payne's hand and turned to Bailey. "You were right. He is a nice guy." She arched her eyebrows. "Maybe we all should've come in red tonight, huh?" She shifted her gaze from man to man.

Payne coughed to cover a laugh. "No," he said. "I don't think so."

"Just as well. I need the money."

Payne rolled his eyes. Bailey gave him an evil look.

"Your drink is getting warm," Payne said, trying to salvage the situation. He held up the last remaining drink. "I got an extra, just in case."

Glory took the glass. "Oh," she said, exactly as before. "Thank you."

Bailey looked down at his side of the table and shuddered in astonishment.

"Something wrong?" Glory asked between sips.

He picked up an empty glass. "I drank . . . all of these?"

Payne nodded and winked at the girl. "Bailey here is a drinking fool. Once he gets the first one down, the rest just pour in."

Glory flushed and snuggled closer to Bailey. "So tell me," she said to Payne. "Why is such a nice person like you grayed out tonight?"

"I'm being celibate."

"Oh, how very nice."

Payne was ready to burst by the time the man in house uniform stopped at their table.

"Excuse me," he said, leaning into Bailey. "Your chamber is ready."

Glory squealed with delight and produced her Bill of Health. Bailey yanked it from her hands.

"Not yet!"

Payne twisted in his seat and bit his lip. The usher took the note.

"Excuse me," he said. "I distinctly remember you saying that this would be a chamber for two, not three."

Payne cleared his throat and waved his scarf.

Glory sighed loudly. "I guess we all wore the wrong colors tonight."

His resistance worn away, Payne began to laugh. Bailey rose and grabbed Glory by the arm, towing her across the tabletop as the laughter came. The usher made a mental assessment of the woman and began to laugh as well. Bailey shook his head helplessly.

"Nice to meet you, Mr. Payne." She patted him on the shoulder and winked. "Maybe next time."

Payne lost his mind to the laughter. Laced with the alcohol, the laugh convulsed him, leaving him gasping for breath. He finally calmed enough to finish his drink, promising it would be the last of the evening. As he drained the glass, his eye caught the dishwater blonde in his edge of the crowd. Time to make good.

He set the glass down on the table and rose to meet

the crowd. She had disappeared again, dancing and bobbing in the wake of music. Payne worked his way into
the crowd and began jumping and twisting, a utility dance
used to see over and into the crowd. In two minutes he
had worked his way into the center of the mob but had
no luck in finding his quarry. He tired quickly. What alcohol there had been in the drinks was finding its way to
his brain, and his calf muscles ached. He ground to a stop
and let the crowd move around him.

The song ended in applause. He turned to get his bear-
ings and found her wandering aimlessly through the crowd.
He worked his way over and laid a hand on her shoulder.
"I believe I owe you one."

She turned and looked as if he were the last person in
the world she had expected to see. She blinked rapidly
and looked down at the floor.

"Unless you're busy with someone."

"No," she said suddenly. She smiled wearily. "No, I'm
alone."

"You've been dancing all night."

"By myself. I like the dance, you know." She closed
herself off by embracing her shoulders. Before she could
retreat any further, the music had started and Payne took
her hand.

"Let's do it, then."

They jumped and swayed, bounced and collided, leaped
and twisted. There was an abandon to their movements,
Payne's from the alcohol and hers from the pleasure of
dance. They made their way through two sets, and at the
top of the hour when "Danse" ripped through the speakers
and Payne tried to leave the floor, she caught him by the
back of the neck and made him stay. His attempt lasted
twenty seconds, ending with his fall to the floor. She kept
dancing with an intensity that he hadn't noticed before;
it was as if she had blocked out everyone but him, and
her dance was a gift, an offering. He gave her his complete
attention, noting every hair on her head, the way the lights

fell across her body, her smile when she knew he was watching.

The crowd cheered at song's end. She looked down at him as she caught her breath. He nodded in approval. She took his hand and helped him up.

"I like watching you," he said, trying not to sound trite. She took the compliment, brushing the hair from her eyes and looking down at the floor.

"Play something slow!" shouted someone in the crowd. Others shouted in agreement. The air filled with echoes of the idea. "Play something slow!"

The lights went down, and a soft electronic melody drifted from the speakers, drawing a collective sigh from the crowd. The girl turned to leave, but Payne stopped her.

"I tried the 'Danse,'" he said. She smiled softly. Payne looked into her brown eyes and became lost. She wrapped her arms around his neck in calm complacence. He drew her close and held her, beginning the slow, wide circles that she faithfully followed. The song faded into another and then another. If the thronged dancers were pleased by the slow set, they were too involved to voice their approval.

A minute into the third song Payne noticed the girl tighten her grip on his neck. He brought her closer.

"My name is Payne," he whispered into her ear. There was no reaction. Her head remained pressed into his chest. They continued dancing, turning, holding. The third song faded into a fourth. The girl shifted slightly, and a pair of soft lips brushed against his ear. "Myra," they whispered.

Payne closed his eyes and hugged her.

The song faded out. The lights stayed down, and the crowd gave the DJ a muted round of applause for his work. The speakers remained silent. The dance floor slowly emptied as couples went off to the chambers.

Payne took Myra by the arm and escorted her to his table. "Buy you a drink?"

She shook her head, keeping her eyes away from his. He gently took her chin and turned her head to face him.

"I know I'm grayed tonight," he said, "but I want to take you home with me."

"Why?"

"I chose you out of everyone here, and you wonder why?"

"If this was normal, you'd have gone to the lobby to buy a green scarf and we'd be in a chamber. We'd finish and leave and never see each other again because we weren't even trying. But you want to take me home."

"Maybe this isn't normal."

"Do you mean it?"

"Follow me home." He smiled. They could stop at a Handi-Mart for an extra toothbrush. A pleasant conversation, walk her up the stairs, open the door for her, let her find the body on the floor—

He grimaced and cursed.

Myra turned away and bit her finger.

He took her hand. "Myra, I'm sorry. I've just remembered that there's something I need to take care of tonight."

"You've got another woman at home."

Laughter peeked out. If only she knew.

"No," he said. "A friend of mine is taking the Thirty-first tonight, and I've got to be there for moral support."

"I see." She was pouting.

"Tomorrow night. 1900. This table." She had to take that in earnest because of the early hour. "I'll meet you right here. I'll reserve it tonight before I leave. We can stay around and dance, go for a walk, whatever. Coming home will be up to you. Maybe we'll go our separate ways—"

"No," she said hesitantly. She set her lip and repeated the word, this time trying to make it sound like a stern refusal.

Payne pulled the ring from his scarf and pressed it into the palm of her hand. "I've got to show up tomorrow. I'll have to get this back." She stared at the ring and then into Payne's eyes, blinking. Her lips parted.

"Bloody hell!"

Solid red and in high dudgeon, Bailey stormed to the booth and plopped down beside Myra. "That woman was crazy! Do you know what she wanted to do?"

Payne nodded at Myra. Realizing the presence of a woman, Bailey flushed again. When he realized who she was, he did a double take.

"I'm sorry," he gurgled. "Bad experience. People get so carried away." He looked at Payne incredulously.

"I told you not to get in too deep," Payne taunted. "I didn't think you could. Not with Glory. Didn't think she had the mind for it."

"Don't you start in on me. I'm wired enough as it is."

"You've got two hours yet." Payne waved at the dance floor. "They've just finished a slow set. The chambers should be emptying out by the time you splash on another drink."

Myra smiled.

"As if I could function," Bailey shouted. "You expect me to try under these conditions?"

Payne smiled at Myra, who was again solemn. "I'm afraid I've got to go. I should see that my friend gets home safely."

"Well," she said, clenching his ring in her fist, "thanks for the advice."

Payne leaned over and kissed her on the cheek. "Any time." He smiled. Bailey rose from the table, and Payne clapped him on the back. "Now, Lawrence," he said paternally. "Tell the coach all about your problem."

The instant they were out the doors, Bailey turned on him. "What's *your* problem, Payne? I told you that girl is bad news. Did you bed down with her?"

"Calm yourself," Payne reassured him. "I was only giving her some friendly advice."

"On what?"

"How to handle men."

"What about the kiss? That wasn't from any self-defense video I've ever seen."

"Bailey, do I interfere with any of your activities? No. I let you walk off with the first airhead you see, even though I know better, even though I should have been righteous enough to warn you. If she and I were going to try, it would be none of your affair, would it? If I can let you screw up, then you can grant me the same courtesy. True?"

Bailey nodded sheepishly. "True."

"As it stands, it was your basic counseling session, okay? A pep talk and a list of places to hit a man other than the groin."

"You still haven't explained the kiss."

"I kissed her," Payne said, "because she's had a hard life."

The rest of the walk home was quiet and uneventful. As they walked through the main doors of their building, Bailey suggested that Payne come to his apartment until the Pickup Squad arrived. There was no sense in being alone with a corpse any longer than necessary, and he had a couple of new videos that he thought Payne might enjoy. Touched by the offer, Payne accepted.

Inside the apartment, Bailey found a flashlight and took great joy in showing off the solar collectors he had installed outside the bedroom window. The installation job was excellent. The cords from the panels to the batteries were tucked neatly into corners, and the remote plug-in unit was draped from a clothes hanger, the attaching cord neatly coiled around it. Bailey strung the extension out into the living room and plugged it into the master power jack.

"What's with all of the boxes?" Payne asked.

"Boxes?"

Payne motioned to a corner of the closet. Stacked in a corner were a multitude of flattened boxes, the largest of which was half as big as he was.

"Oh, those. They were the shipping crates for the video

equipment and collectors. I save them in case I have to ship them out for repairs."

Payne nodded. "Method to your madness. All this time I thought you were a pack rat."

Bailey grinned. "No, not me." He clicked on the monitor, and the room filled with a bluish glow. "People think I'm crazy. They tell me if they had solar collectors, they'd use them to run the refrigerator. I say that solar is for running something you want when the power's down. When power is up, I use it for other things, but my video always runs off the sun. That way I don't feel like I'm wasting what power the city gives me." He slipped a small silver disk into the transcriber. "I think you'll like this one. I picked it up last week."

Payne did. Bailey had judgment enough to show something light—a British comedy—that took his mind from the unpleasant fact upstairs. Under the circumstances, he found it very relieving to laugh.

"I don't mean to sound horrible," Bailey said when it was over, "but the invasion of England was one of the best things that could've happened to us. Our culture was stagnating, and the refugees who came were like a transfusion of fresh blood."

Payne was so impressed by Bailey's collection that he asked if it would be an imposition to return later in the week to watch more. Bailey was honored. It would be no imposition at all. Payne again gave his thanks at the door.

"Do you want me to come with you?" Bailey asked. "Would you like a friendly face there for support?"

Payne smiled. "Thanks for the offer, but it should be no trouble. The Health Department will probably be the ones making the pickup."

"Just thought I'd ask."

"I appreciate it. Thanks." He closed the door and went up three flights to find a small handful of uniformed men wandering the hall and muttering.

"Seven-thirteen?" Payne asked. They looked at him,

puzzled. "Are you looking for apartment seven-thirteen? Are you the Pickup Squad?"

"What's it to you?" a fat cop asked.

"I'm the man who called." He extended his hand to the group in a general invitation. "I'm Payne."

A dark-haired officer with a ruddy complexion stepped forward and shook his hand vigorously. "Sergeant Delgado. City P.D. P and S Unit."

"Glad you're here. Follow me." He led the group down the hall and unlocked the door, letting them step in first. "I decided to step out until you came. I hope you don't mind."

Delgado removed his cap reverently and looked at the girl. "A waste," he said. "Why in hell'd you do it?"

Payne was stunned. "I didn't. I just found her like that." He looked at her. The fat officer was snapping photographs as two others examined the body. "I checked for pulse first thing. She was dead."

"How long ago was this?"

Payne checked his watch. "About five hours ago. What did I say on the phone? 1830? She was still warm then."

"If she was still warm, why didn't you try to revive her?" He made notes on a stenographer's pad. One of the examining officers was trying to LaserLift a fingerprint from the corpse, and the other was checking elsewhere in the apartment, also for prints. The fat man supervised and chewed a chocolate bar thoughtfully.

"I thought," Payne sighed, "that she was a practical joke." He felt mindless. He hadn't even tried to revive her.

"Explain."

"I've got this friend at work. More of an acquaintance, actually. Name of Kelce. A real nuisance. He traded in his common sense for a twisted sense of humor."

"A joker?"

"The worst kind. He's outgrown spring snakes and exploding cigars. He's into the painful practical joke."

"Example."

Payne scratched his head. "Hiring a girl to take off her clothes and play dead is just his speed. I stood around for ten minutes waiting for him to jump out from behind the couch and yell 'boo.'"

"When did you check for a pulse?"

"I figured that he wanted me to play into his hands first. That would be five, ten minutes after I came in."

"And then?"

"And then I called you guys. What else? I waited twenty minutes to talk to a dispatcher. That's how I spent the first half hour with her."

"Where'd you check for pulse?"

"Carotid artery."

"Did you touch her in any other way?"

"Can that question," one officer said. "The initial shows no sexual contacts in at least twenty-four hours."

"Question withdrawn," Delgado said politely. "Where did you spend the remaining time?"

"Until you came? A friend and I went to a club. We were there until a little before 2200, and then we went to his place to watch video."

"Do you have witnesses to place you at the club?"

Payne thought of Myra. "Yes."

Delgado turned to the examining officer. "Cause of death?"

"Hard to say. The initial shows no marks, bruises, open wounds, broken bones. No recent needle tracks. This one's got to go in storage until we can get a chemical analysis of the blood and tissues."

"Ha!" The fat cop sneered.

Delgado glanced at his wrist. "I've got to wrap this up. We only get thirty minutes now."

"What do you need?"

"First, assuming you're innocent, how do you think the body got in here?"

"I don't know. My door was locked. Force of habit."

"Does anyone have a key besides yourself?"

"No."

"You're sure?"

"Positive. I installed a new lock myself: Even the landlord would have to pick it."

"Isn't that against house rules?"

"The landlord here doesn't give a damn as long as you get the rent in on time."

"What kind of lock did you install?"

"Wesco's Pikprufe III."

"Ha!" the fat cop repeated.

"Shut up," Delgado snapped. He waved at an officer, who began to examine the lock with an optical device. "Now, what about this Kelce character. Does he go off the deep end very often?"

"Quite often. But this is a record low." He pointed at the girl, who was being covered with a sheet.

"You know this guy from work. Where is that?"

"Biotech Industries."

Delgado looked up from his pad. "Sounds familiar. What do they do?"

"Biological engineering. We're the company that came up with Cannabis Blight."

Delgado smiled as if he had met a celebrity. "Always nice to meet one of the good guys. What's your relationship with Kelce?"

"Coworkers. We're both level E-6. That's a supervisory position."

"No signs of picking on the lock," said the officer with the optical device.

"Document it," Delgado said. He turned back. "You have any grudges with Kelce?"

"Only that he sometimes carries a joke too far. Other than that, I can get along with him. Not the kind I'd club with, though."

"Fine. Your name again."

"Payne. D.A. Payne."

"What do the initials stand for?"

"Don't ask."

Delgado looked confused, then laughed. "Fine." He

reached for his metal clipboard and produced a bright yellow card adorned with black print and a rubber band fastened through one end. Payne felt his heart pounding.

"There is currently a nine-month waiting list on homicide investigations, so you have until January of next year to leave the country. If you can." He fastened the rubber band around the big toe of the girl's right foot. "If you don't want to leave or can't leave, I would suggest you take the Thirty-first. Things don't look too good for you at this point." He tore the perforated stub from the tag and held it out. "Your claim tag."

Payne swallowed hard. "I don't need it."

"By law you have to take it."

Payne took it numbly.

"By law I am required to read you the provisions of the Thirty-first Amendment." He looked at a sticker on the clipboard. Payne realized he was looking through it rather than at it and was reciting from memory.

"As a private citizen who is a victim of a major crime as defined by the Carlton Act, you have the constitutional right to use your own personal facilities and talents to conduct an investigation into the circumstances surrounding said crime in the event that conventional law enforcement agencies cannot do so within a sixty-day period. In order to do so, you have the right to obtain from your employer a leave of absence not to exceed the draw time of said conventional law enforcement agency." He looked up from the board. "Your draw time in this case is nine months. Do you understand your rights so far? Am I going too fast for you?"

"Go on," Payne said.

"During your investigation period you have rights, protections, and privileges similar to those given law enforcement officials. Any abuse of said coverage will result in immediate suspension of your rights under this amendment.

"At the end of said draw time, if your investigation is incomplete, you may turn your findings over to said conventional agencies for completion. You may also, in the event your investigation is completed before draw time, present your evidence in a court of law, which will then take appropriate action. Do you understand these rights as I have read them to you?"

"Yes."

"Do you wish to go on record as accepting the terms of the Thirty-first Amendment to the Constitution of the United States?" Delgado's delivery had a stiff and formal stature, cultured from years of saying the same words at the end of every pickup.

"No," Payne answered, just as stiff.

"You understand that by law you have thirty days to accept the option?"

"Yes."

Delgado stood silent, never knowing what to say after the reading. He waved a finger, and the fat cop moved out the door, flanked by the two carrying the stretcher. Delgado took up the rear, closing the door behind. Payne stood alone and watched as it reopened.

"Payne," Delgado said, eyes sympathetic. "Think about it. Please."

Payne nodded. "I will."

Another nod and Delgado was gone. Payne didn't move. He let his ears fill up with quiet. He inhaled until he thought his lungs would burst and then exhaled very, very slowly.

Turning the bright yellow tag over in his hand, he noted the three-letter, three-digit code number that would correspond to the half on the girl's toe. He looked at the number of Legal Council, the people to notify in the event he decided to take the option. And he stared hard at the spot on the floor where the girl's body had been.

"There," he said. "I've thought about it."

He tossed the card onto the table next to the telephone

and, letting his thoughts turn to his current lack of Myra, padded into the bedroom in anticipation of a good night's sleep.

It had been a long evening.

Saturday Morning

Payne slowly became aware of the ticking of his alarm clock. Inside his head, disjointed music played and a girl with hair tossed across her face danced. Then the alarm stabbed him in both ears.

His hand shot out and struck at the clock until the ringing stopped. He lay in silence until it threatened to swallow him, then found the energy to sit up. He looked around the room blankly and tried to remember where he was.

Home. Yes, that was it. And he needed to work on the ritual. He swung his legs off the bed and planted his feet firmly on the floor. He took the alarm clock and wound it tight, checking its time against his watch. Replacing the clock on the nightstand, he ran his tongue across the inside of his mouth. It was stale and tasted of smoke. He coughed and rubbed the crust from the corners of his eyes. He rose and padded to the bathroom, deciding he was too old to keep up with the likes of Bailey.

He splashed himself with cold water to take the tingling from his loins. Then he looked at his face in the mirror and for the first time saw the name that came with the sensation.

"Myra."

He could feel the tingle returning. Instead of succumbing, he worked against it, continuing his ritual until he had washed the last bits of toothpaste down the drain and pulled the green jumpsuit from the hanger on the bathroom door. He sniffed it cautiously. It smelled of smoke and alcohol. Shaking his head, he hunted down the brown suit, unwrapped it, and ironed it.

Should know better than to drink so much when you've a Saturday in, he told himself. Even as watered down as the drinks had been, the amount he had consumed would be lethal to today's clearheadedness. It made him dream about a girl with a scarred nose and about finding nude bodies on his living room floor.

"Give it up," he said hoarsely. "Got to give this up." Suited, he stepped into the living room. There was no corpse. He was very much relieved. Another good excuse for giving up the vine: those damned dreams. They had been bad before—the apartment on fire, lost the job, caught something virulent at the lab—but none had been as disturbing as the one last night.

Kelce would die when he heard.

In the kitchen he found a can of CitruSlush and poured it into a glass. He stirred until it was thick and icy, then began to sip it. His watch said he had time to catch the news if there was power enough to run the monitor.

He returned to the living room, snapped on the receiver switch, and plopped down on the couch.

Something crackled under his weight.

He shifted and, feeling with his free hand, produced a crumple of paper. He blinked in confusion at the message it held. Against a gold background, red block letters heralded CHOCORATION PLUS!!! and below that in smaller, black print: PACKED WITH FLAVORS!!! On one flap the message continued: "Sugar, Milk Synthate, Chocolate Synthate, Sorbate III flavoring, crushed peanuts, almonds, and cashews, coconut flakes, chopped raisins, Poly-Vitamin Enrichment Complex (PEC), Fructose suspen-

sions, Artificial Colorings (FDA Safe Level IV), and less
than one-half of one percent presence of LTN as a preservative."

Payne was mystified. He didn't like chocolate, and he
couldn't imagine who had left the wrapper behind. Kelce
again? No. The wrapper was familiar; he just couldn't
place it. He recrumpled it and tossed it across the living
room. As he watched it fly, he noticed something out of
place.

It was on the table by the telephone, fiery yellow,
broadcasting a message of urgency. Payne walked over
and was racked by nausea.

Sitting on the table was the claim stub for a body.

Things suddenly fell into place. The Chocoration Plus
had been stuffed into the face of a fat, critical cop whose
one comment on the state of anything was "Ha!" Payne's
heart sank as he realized he couldn't write last night off
as a dream.

He looked at the time. He needed to get to work. The
monitor was switched off. The wrapper and ticket stub
fluttered into the refuse bag in the kitchen. He drained
the last of the citrus drink—too fast. His hard palate took
the cold and angrily gave him a blinding headache. He
rubbed his scalp, and his eyes watered.

Taking his key ring, Payne set the door to secure behind
him. He stepped out and pulled the door shut. There was
a sharp, metallic click. He pushed on the door. Solid. He
tried to turn the knob. It wouldn't move. He stood and
stared at the door. *How did she get in?* He ran his finger
down a seam in the wall. The door had been locked. He'd
had trouble getting it unlocked, in fact. *How did she do
it?*

He turned away and took the stairs. There were other
questions to consider. What had killed her, for one. Who
had killed her was another, unless it had been some sort
of bizarre suicide. Why his apartment? Why not Bailey's?
Why not one of the other tenants? It seemed so random,

so senseless. And it would be at least a year before he got any answers.

He crossed the street and fell into the flow of morning traffic. It was a quiet, still morning, and things were slow. The nice thing about Saturday was that traffic was low and he didn't have to listen to the slapping of leather on asphalt that on a busy day sounded like water boiling. The hissing of the bicycle tires was something else, and the ringing of their bells. And the buzzing of the occasional ElectriCart.

Adopting a leisurely pace, Payne kept to the sidewalks—one less obstacle for runners and those who had wheels. He could also move freely around the bottlenecks, the places where automobile carcasses choked the lanes of traffic.

Biotech Industries was three kilometers from Payne's apartment and, along with the Plus Fours and the club on Lancaster, was classified as being downtown. It was housed in a squat gray stucco building that at one time had been a tenement hotel. The rest of the neighborhood had crumbled along with the outside of the Biotech building. The streets were spotted with cheap lounges, greasy spoon diners, fast-food outlets, and run-down department stores.

This neighborhood had been considered dangerous the year Biotech had moved in. But Biotech had started the example of putting their branches where they were needed, and other corporations followed suit. As they did, renovation began. The lounges became more reputable or turned into small clubs. The greasy spoons cleaned up, proud once again to be feeding clean businessmen. The neighborhood improved from the inside, while the outside, though crumbled looking, took care of itself. And the block leaders tipped their hats to the company that had started it all.

Biotech Industries had become more than just a corporation. It had become synonymous with innovation, excellence, and concern for community and country. The rewards for its efforts were prosperity long after the passing of its founder, who was buried on the dairy farm from which Biotech had sprung. Biotech was unlimited effortless energy and pride in human spirit. Its success could be found in the words that had been chosen to accompany the corporate logo on buildings around the world:

IMAGINATION IS THE KEY

Payne stared up at the words, sensing a quirky oddness about them, as if they held the answer to questions yet unasked. They mocked the man on the decaying street below.

IMAGINATION IS THE KEY

Payne shook off the feeling and walked through revolving doors into a lobby that had been preserved from the original hotel. He strolled to the front desk and was greeted by a toothy blonde.

"Morning, Payne."

"Hello, Karol. Any mail?"

Karol turned from the cubbyholes with a handful of envelopes. "Mostly departmental updates and a few memos. Looks like you've gotten a letter from someone."

Payne took the items from her hand, staring.

She cocked her head. "Are you undressing me again?"

He smiled wryly. "Ever since New Year's..."

She hissed at him.

"A dentist can fix that," he said soberly.

She glared. "You've obviously been running with Kelce too much."

He smiled back. "No, the problem is that *you've* been around him too much. Anyone lacking in sufficient wit comes off sounding dry to you."

She scoffed, friendly again. "You probably see him more than I do."

He laughed again. "I only work with him. You're the constant companion."

"That's what you think."

"Don't tell me you've moved on."

"Want to bed down after work?" She leaned toward him provocatively.

"You're kidding."

"I'm not kidding. After work. You name the place."

He almost refused, but he had entertained some thoughts about Karol, and on a slow night she had been good for a couple of fantasies. "Your place."

"Keep it detached, please. How about one of the clubs?"

He stared. The fun was gone. "You're not kidding."

"Of course I'm not."

"When did you move out?"

"About two months ago. Where have you been, Payne? I thought everyone here knew."

Payne shook his head. "Sorry. I hadn't heard."

She clasped his hand. "Don't get apologetic. It was all my doing. He'd always liked unlimited access, and I think it's gotten to him. He'd become manic by the time I'd left. He was starting to get into some red-scarf stuff. I went along with some of it because I didn't mind being tied up, but he started to get really disgusting.

"So I figured, why stick around? If the thrill in me is gone, there's no sense in my living in. He'll find someone who'll put up with his atrocities. I'm certainly not doing him any good."

Payne shrugged. "I hope you're over it."

"These bones will break a few more times. There's no love lost from Kelce. You'd think I'd never moved in."

Payne pocketed the letters. "I hope things pick up for you."

"Thanks." She smiled brightly. "I'm sure they will."

He nodded and headed for the staircase. As his foot hit the first step, Karol called.

"My offer still stands," she said. "You pick the place. If you're not too timid, I'll show you some red-scarf tricks that are real toe curlers."

"Sounds interesting."

He walked to the top of the stairs and faced a white wall. He pushed his hand against a black square, and warm blue light scanned it. Words appeared across the top.

IDENTITY CONFIRMED.

PAYNE, D.A.

RANK E-6.

These words vanished and were replaced by more.

YOU'RE LATE, PAYNE.

6 MIN. 23 SEC.

Payne looked sourly at the square. "I've been here for ten minutes, but I was down talking to Karol."

There was no reply.

He sighed. "Okay. Put it on my account."

Hydraulics hissed, and the wall lifted. Payne stepped through. The computer informed him that he was one hour and seven minutes to the good, and the door slid shut.

In the locker room beyond, he got out a silicon fiber oversuit and clumsily slid into it. He tightened the drawstrings around his wrists and pulled the hood over his head, sealing it so only his face was exposed.

At the far end of the locker room he stepped into a small cubicle flooded with orange light. Again the door closed as he passed through.

"Close your eyes, please," the computer instructed.

Payne obliged, feet shoulder-length apart, arms outstretched. When the sound of rain on his oversuit stopped, he shook the drops from his face and walked into the Wind Tunnel. Three steps in, hot air blasted from all directions. By the time he reached the end, he was completely dry.

In the next room he looked in the mirror. His face was cast in a yellowish pallor and was spotted with droplets of iodine-colored liquid. A few hairs had strayed from under the hood and had become coated with disinfectant. A drop of the deep brown strayed and ran down the side of his face.

He took a clipboard from the wall and leafed through the project sheets. About a dozen people were working in today. With any luck he could have the initial rounds done by 1200 and could devote the afternoon to studying for the E-7 boards. He passed his right thumb over a smaller version of the black box, and a monitor reprised his name and rank, then allowed him access to the labs.

On a normal workday there would have been a din, with workers filling all the individual carrels and bolts of conversation charging the air. Saturdays in were subdued. There was less clatter from the computer terminals. Talk was at a whispered minimum, and there was a mutually agreed upon musical selection playing at low volume.

Most of those in today were there to check on cultures and growth patterns. A few were inoculating, and one was composing a final report. Payne drifted back and forth, offering advice, chatting pleasantly. At one point he heard a song that had played at the club the night before, and he drifted off, trying to separate last night's dreams from the reality.

"How quickly they forget."

Payne looked up from his clipboard and into the face of Trinina Rueben. She smiled at him.

"Are you deliberately ignoring me?" she asked.

"Off in the ozone." He set the clipboard aside and hugged her. "How have you been?"

"Wonderful. Yourself?"

"I can't complain. What brings you down here?"

"I got tired of Advanced Concepts. I was never crazy about working in a think tank. They're too theoretical. All talk and no do. I decided to get some lab work in."

"Anything special?"

"The Biotech Challenge."

"Cellulose?"

She nodded. "There's got to be a way we can use it."

"Any leads?"

"This time I'm working on a mutated gut bacteria. What I'm trying to do is get an established one that will learn to break down cellulose for use in the human system."

"That idea sounds familiar."

"It was yours," she said softly. "Before I could pursue it . . ."

"They pulled you upstairs." Payne looked her over. She was a little heavier than when he had last seen her but still attractive. "Heard anything about Nathan?"

This troubled her. "Aren't you reading your mail?"

"I moved about three years ago, and things got screwed up. They still aren't straightened out."

"Well," she sighed. "The last report said that he's showing a tendency toward electronics and composition."

"A musician?"

"A composer."

Payne smiled. "Maybe for his twelfth we should buy him a Composition Board."

The thought entertained her, and she flashed the smile that had attracted him years ago. "It's early. He's just turned six. Kids change their minds a lot. Did I ever tell you what my sixth-year initial painted me as?"

"Assembly-line work."

She nodded. "That's me, don't you think?"

"I don't know," he teased. "I'd always thought of Advanced Concepts as an assembly line of ideas."

She shook her head and bade him farewell, explaining that she'd left something cooking in her lab space. He stared wistfully as she walked away, a bit sad that things had come to an end. When she was out of sight, he returned to his rounds.

By 1130 he had finished and was in the lunch room buying a CitruSlush. He sat at a deserted table and fished the mail from the breast pocket of his jumpsuit.

He spread the envelopes out before him. A couple held Biotech updates and company newsletters. There was a subscription renewal form from *Bioengineering Today* and the electric bill. Karol was right—there was a letter from someone, an old college roommate who was now working on an Oil Farm in the Arizona desert. And there was an official government letter. He opened this first, knowing what it was.

Out of the envelope came a computer printout and a green plastic government check. He ignored the check and opened the printout. Below the agency masthead was the headline CHILD DIVIDEND STATEMENT. What followed was a list of a dozen names, ages, and a dollar amount beside each, listed from oldest to youngest. He ran his finger down the list until he found what he was looking for:

NATHAN RUEBEN-PAYNE   5 YR 11 MO

He smiled. The boy had come from one of the better moments in life. Payne had met Trinina at a Biotech convention and found that she was in the process of transferring to his branch. They shared a suite for the balance of the convention, and when she got to town, she moved in with him. When she became pregnant, Payne looked after her until Nathan was born and weaned and ready to leave for Mother America. He had never before stayed with a woman during pregnancy, and it fascinated him. It would also be the last time he would do such a thing. Their hearts were broken when it came time for Nathan to leave. Less than a month later their relationship fractured.

Payne swallowed the lump in his throat and read down the rest of the list. He totaled the figures in his head, then looked at the check. A nice tax-free windfall of about 3000 new dollars. As he tucked everything back into the envelope, he noticed the form at the bottom of the printout.

ARE YOU GETTING YOUR QUARTERLY REPORTS? it asked. No, thought Payne, and he didn't really care to. IF NOT, FILE THIS FORM WITH YOUR NEAREST GCR OFFICE. He stared at the form and thought of his conversation with Trinina. Wasn't there a GCR office on the way home? He would file for reports on Nathan then.

He opened another letter and was unfolding it when a short, pale man appeared at the far end of the cafeteria.

Pulling the hood from his head, the man ran a hand through his thick blond hair, shaking off sweat, and paced nervously toward Payne.

It was Lol Winthrop. He hadn't been there when Payne had started his rounds.

"You're E-6, aren't you?" Winthrop asked. Payne noticed his thick accent. Winthrop had come from Biotech London on a two-year information exchange program. Toward the end of the tour, Russian troops crossed the channel and Britannia was under siege. Winthrop was one of the displaced.

Payne stuffed the letter into his jumpsuit. "What's up?"

Winthrop shook the hair from his eyes. "I'm having trouble with some new culture samples."

Payne stood. "You're the one doing the research in atherosclerotic breakdown, right?"

"Right." They walked back through the disinfectant shower. In the Wind Tunnel, Winthrop continued his narrative. "I've been working on a bacteria that could live in the human bloodstream and feed on the fatty deposits in the vessels, keeping them clear. A nice Nobel-flavored project, wouldn't you say?"

"Doubtless," Payne agreed. He knew Winthrop wasn't after the glory. The money would buy his way out of the United States and put him on the next boat to Sydney.

"My first attempt was a disaster. It was more of an inoculation. I tried a vaccine that would create antibodies to attack and destroy the stuff. It worked great on the P.V.'s. Cleared the vessels in about nine weeks. The problem was—"

"The problem was the antibodies had been trained on human tissue," Payne said. "And when the deposits were gone, you had a bunch of hungry little critters that were raised on veins and arteries, so they went to work on them next. All of your volunteers probably died of massive internal hemorrhaging."

"Unfortunately, not all of it was internal."

"Still. Pasteur had the same problem with his rabies

cure. Early efforts used the brains of animals that had died from it. That worked great until the people started making antibodies to fight their own brains."

"I guess I'm in good company."

"So where are you now?"

"With bacteria. The first cultures were gobbled right up by the defense systems. So I did a little splicing and came up with a nonoffensive bug that does the trick quite nicely. There's only one problem."

"It's developed an appetite for brain cells?"

"I'm wondering." Winthrop was dead serious. "That's not it, but it looks frighteningly close." They stopped at Winthrop's work carrel, cluttered with test tubes, beakers, stirring rods, and petri dishes. Floppy disks were scattered around the computer console. A Union Jack hung from the ceiling. Winthrop brushed aside scribbled-in notepads and tattered textbooks, urging Payne to take his seat. He clicked a switch, and the computer screen winked. When he had a cursor, he leaned across Payne and typed in a command.

"This was the hot subject. We had him all ready for a nice big MI."

The screen showed a view of a blood vessel—if one could call it that. It was a narrow path that wound its way through clusters of fatty matter.

"We kept this guy on a high-cholesterol diet. Salts, red meats, saturated fats, the whole bit. Then we introduced the culture. Here's a week into the test."

Another view: The tunnel looked different.

"Two weeks." There was a flicker. The pathway widened. "Three weeks. Four weeks. Five."

The path became a tunnel, gradually widening, the deposits thinning and clearing out. By twelve weeks the vessel was smooth and clear.

Payne smiled. "Good job."

Winthrop took the views through twenty-five weeks to show that there was no change in the vessel's condition.

"Looks excellent," Payne commented. "What's the catch?"

Winthrop typed a new command. "Part of the battery was a weekly I.Q. test." The screen changed to a graphic of a downward-sloping curve. "As you can see, things were stable for about the first six weeks. Early on there were some minor fluctuations in scoring, but that's to be expected." He traced the falling slope with his finger. The scores slanted down into the low seventies and then dropped sharply to zero. "We had a marked decline before we had to quit giving the tests. His mind suddenly gave out. He's a vegetable now. I'm thinking of having him euthanized so we can take a look at his brain. The problem is I'm not sure what to look for."

"What kind of waste products do these bacteria make in breaking this stuff down?"

"A series of salts and minor acids that the kidneys catch and eliminate. Nothing major. The urine smells pretty strange for a while, and it leaves a scum on the top of water. Disconcerting at first, but a small price to pay."

He keyed in a new command, and the screen flickered to a video of a man sitting at a table scattered with pegs of assorted shapes and colors. To the left and out of focus was another person. Winthrop tapped the screen.

"That's Jill McKulty, the tester. E-1." He turned up the volume. "This is the very first interview."

The man, clad in Prison Orange and sporting a three-day beard, glared at McKulty. "Are you some kind of a wiseass or what?" he snarled.

"Please," McKulty said. "This is important. We want you to match each peg with the shape of the hole and the color of the hole. If you have a black cube, it goes into the black square. A red cube would go into a red square."

He stared angrily. "You're screwing with my brain. When I signed up, they promised they wouldn't screw with my brain."

"This is a test that everyone takes," Jill said patiently.

"All subjects have their IQ tested prior to and during the experiment."

"I told you my IQ," the man hissed. "My word ain't good enough for you?"

Jill turned away from the camera. "Clark, would you get me another volunteer?"

The man tossed his hands in the air. "Don't pitch a bitch, lady. I'll take your damn test."

He quickly matched the pegs. A timer superimposed in a corner of the screen ticked off 111 seconds for the series.

Winthrop fed another command into the keyboard, and the tape sped forward. "The last test."

The man was back, now with a full beard. The clock's readout slipped over the 5000-second mark. The man looked helplessly at a red cylindrical peg and turned it over in his hands.

"This is about an hour and a half into the test."

The subject tried to fit the cylinder into a small blue square. It wouldn't go. He grabbed a beige pyramid and tried to pound the cylinder into the slot. The cylinder splintered and snapped. The man shouted obscenities, tossed a cube at the camera, and burst into tears.

Payne shook his head. "Jill's slipping. She should have known better than to let it drag on this far." He turned the volume down.

"She tried to stop it after a half hour. He insisted he could do it. It went on for ten minutes more before she convinced him to quit."

Payne shook his head.

"Of course, nothing happened with the controls. The subject you saw was the best example of the effects without getting too grisly. Of the five P.V.'s, he's about the middle of the road. One man died. His heart just stopped. Another had a massive stroke. This one lost his mind and went into quiet catatonia. The fourth became violent and had to be restrained. The last one beat his brains out on the walls of his cell. I have video on all of them. Not pretty stuff."

Payne stared at the monitor. "You've got a problem." He sighed. "You've got five brain dysfunctions from one probable cause. Do you realize how many more subjects you'd have to run in order to get a categorical breakdown?"

"Too many. That's why I came to you. I thought you could suggest what to look for, maybe order up some tests for me. Do you have any ideas on what we're seeing here?"

Payne drummed a pencil on the desk top. "Death," he said. "Insanity. Mental deterioration. Stroke." He snorted. "Ironic, isn't it? The very things . . ." He drifted off.

"Something wrong?"

"Stroke. Stroke and heart disease. Atherosclerosis. You wanted to prevent all of that and created it instead." He sat up suddenly. "That's the pattern! Call up the views of that subject's artery again."

Winthrop hunched over the console and typed.

"That was from a fiber-optic transmitter in the aorta, right?" Payne asked.

"Yeah."

"Six-hour samplings?"

"One-hour samplings."

"A watchdog. Run the series by at high speed."

The monitor fluttered, and they watched the choked tunnel melt down to the walls of the aorta.

"Again."

The congestion evaporated, melting like March snows.

"Again."

It was like watching a candle melt.

"No good. It's too fast. Try medium speed."

"It's tedious, Payne. Thirty-minute running time."

"Let's try it."

After ten minutes they gave up.

"The slow speed runs two hours," Winthrop said.

"Out of the question." Payne tapped the pencil. He

took it in his fist and snapped the eraser off with his thumb. "That's it." He sat up and typed.

"What have you got?"

"We're going to let the computer watch for us. I'm calling up some good old E-4 graphics." He stopped to look at Winthrop. "What level are you, anyway?"

"E-3."

Payne shook his head, disgusted. "With the work you're doing? Remind me to put you in for a bump. Someone of your caliber should be at least E-5. I'll try and get it for you."

Winthrop smiled. "Thanks."

The screen flickered. COMMAND GRAPHICS READY. Payne leaned back from the keyboard.

"Feed the whole series into it. Give it thirty seconds of the first three views to orient the program, then feed the rest at high speed."

Winthrop keyed. The first view appeared. The computer drew a green outline of it. Winthrop fed it the next two. It quietly sketched.

"Okay. Let it go."

They watched. The tunnel widened, the deadly plaque melting away, dissolving. The computer watched.

The screen went blank.

Green letters appeared.

READY.

Payne called up the menu of graphics options, then placed his order.

"This is the computer's view of the survey."

The outline of the view appeared. They watched lines shrink to a drawing of the aorta.

"What we do now is have the computer look at this sequence and identify anything out of the ordinary." He put the word NORMSCAN on the screen. They watched the melting again.

Suddenly the screen flashed, and letters across the top blinked: PATTERN BREAK. The screen showed nothing but a sketch of the deposits. Payne's fingers darted over the keys. The scene replayed in a jerky slow motion.

And they saw it.

Part of the plaque in the middle of the screen broke off rather than melting away. A chunk of crystalline fat cut loose, floating in the bloodstream, drifting along, perhaps still being melted away by Winthrop's bacteria.

If it took a wrong turn, it would find its way into the brain and become lodged in one of the millions of capillaries inside.

Causing a stroke. Death. Mental deterioration. Madness.

They worked with the graphics display, changing modes and reprogramming until they found the problem. After a week of lying on the surface of its food source, Winthrop's bacteria began to burrow inside, making microscopic wormholes that weakened the structure of the deposits. Battered by the flow of blood, tiny pieces would break off and rush through the body. Many ended up in the brain, where they created the afflictions chronicled by Winthrop.

"Back to the lab," he said dejectedly.

"Not really. I think a little work might take care of the burrowing. All you'd have to do is take samples and lase out gene pairs. One of them would destroy that tendency. You'd have to make sure the organism could function without it, though. Maybe you'd have to splice something in. Have you checked the cultures lately?"

"No."

"It could be that they're mutating. We'll take samples from your friend and check. Remember, we're encouraging adaptation here. Some strains get so used to it that sometimes they take the initiative. Do you have a master brew?"

"In the fridge."

"We'll need samples for comparison. Let's have a look."

Winthrop thumbprinted the fridge lock, and there was a hum, followed by a metallic click and a green light. He opened the door, and his face knit into a frown. He cursed and shook his head.

Payne looked into the frosted compartment to see a five-liter jug filled with clear golden liquid.

"What kind of suspension are you using?"

"Kelp and plasma," Winthrop said. "It should be a cloudy gray. I don't know why it looks like that."

Payne removed the bottle and held it against the light. "Can I open this?"

Winthrop nodded. "It's administered by injection."

Payne pulled the safety ring, and the seal gave with a hiss. A scent ran up his nose and turned to taste on the back of his tongue. His mouth watered. He moved his nose over the bottle, and before Winthrop could protest, he sniffed.

"Are you crazy? What if that had been aerobic? It's semimalevolent."

"It's beer."

Winthrop stared.

"Take a whiff if you don't believe me." He put the cap back on the bottle. "You've been had."

"Would you mind explaining what's going on?"

"It looks like you're another of Kelce's victims. He probably switched jugs after you left Friday and hadn't counted on you coming in today. Monday you would have gone to him for help. He would have made a big production out of checking the jug and then taken a swig from it. You'd have fainted, and he'd have laughed. It's one of his favorite pranks."

Winthrop fumed. "This whole thing was his doing?"

"Just the beer."

"Then where's my master brew? How did he get into my storage?"

"He's an E-6. He pulled rank and got into the security override program so he could make the switch. I'll bet he's even got justification on record for doing it." He returned to Winthrop's console and began to type. "Chances are it's in his storage slot. I'm accessing it now."

"You'll be put on report."

"I'll tell why. They might chew my ass, but then they'll turn right around and kick his." The wall throbbed behind the closed door. When it stopped, Winthrop pulled it open and cold steam rolled to the floor.

"It's not in here."

Payne looked. Kelce's storage was a clutter of test tubes, beakers, petri dishes, syringes.

He cursed and stalked to a telephone, Winthrop at his heels. He found a book labeled *Employee Directory Biotech Branch #101* and leafed through it, then picked up the phone and dialed.

"Hullo?" In the background was noise, talking, and music.

"Kelce?"

There was no response.

"Kelce?"

"I'm sorry. I can't hear you."

Payne shouted. "Try turning your music down."

The level of the noise dropped. People were shouting Kelce's name. Another extension of the phone clicked.

"Kelce here." The voice was hoarse. Background noise was picking up again. He shouted an order to close a door, and it subsided again. "This is Kelce."

"Payne here. Where's Lol Winthrop's master brew?"

There was another sound from the phone, low and guttural, from deep in the throat. Kelce was laughing.

"It's not funny," Payne said. "Not tampering with someone else's project. Where'd you hide it?"

Kelce snickered. "Hide what?"

"You know what."

"Where do you think I hid it?"

Payne rolled his eyes. Kelce was drunk. "It's not in your storage," he said firmly.

Kelce's laughter choked off. "You accessed my storage? Why?"

"To find Winthrop's bottle."

"You son of a bitch. You have no right to do that. You're going on report."

"Keep up the threats," Payne said. "I left the door open."

"On my cultures? You didn't!"

"Winthrop's bottle, Kelce."

"In my locker. Where else?"

Payne slammed the handset into the wall. "It's in his locker."

A cry slipped from Winthrop's throat, and he raced out of the room. Payne shouted into the phone.

"That's great. What kind of bacteria are running your brain? The locker room is a free area, and Winthrop's culture is malevolent. What if you've caused a breach?"

"You left the door open!" Kelce cried.

"That's *my* little joke, Kelce. I didn't leave the door open. Now tell me what you're going to do if there's been a breach."

"His lot was lab-safe, wasn't it? There's no way it'd survive outside a sterile environment. You should know that."

"Beside the point. I think the lot is highly mutagenic. The fact that you—" He looked up from the phone to see a tearful Winthrop bringing the bottle to him. The suspension had separated at room temperature. The bottom of the jug was coated with gray sludge. Above that was a layer of gray-green, and above that a serum-colored fluid.

"It's ruined."

"You've destroyed Winthrop's culture," Payne yelled.

"Good riddance if it was malevolent," Kelce hissed back.

"You've just ruined a lot of work for your own entertainment. I'll see you busted down for this."

"No can do. We're both E-6."

"We'll see what the board says. I'll see you put back in the D's. You'll have to sign a paper every time you want a test tube."

"See you in hell." Kelce hung up.

Payne shouted and beat the handset against the wall, sending plastic shards flying. He looked numbly at the shattered phone and slowly hung up what was left.

Winthrop set the jug on a table. He said nothing.

"Is it totally ruined?"

Winthrop exhaled. "I'm not sure. The suspension is really important, but I may be able to skim a few surviving organisms from the bottom and introduce it into a cholesterol base. That should get it going again."

Payne's hands were shaking. "I'd stay here to help," he offered, "but I think my nerves are shot."

"No offense, but this is something I think I'd rather do alone."

"Is there anything you need? Any program I can requisition for you?"

"Not that I can think of."

Payne wrote on a pad, tore the page off, and gave it to Winthrop.

"The top number is the E-6 call-up. Type that, my name as I've written it, and the number that follows. That'll access you to anything in my level."

Winthrop took the paper and smiled. "Thanks."

"No problem. Now, if you'll excuse me, I've got to get out of here." He shuffled to the commons door, suddenly very tired.

"Payne?"

"Yeah."

"What's this bottom number?"

"My telephone."

Winthrop stuffed the paper in his pocket.

"I'll probably be at the Lancaster Club from seven until around midnight," Payne told him. "After midnight call at your own risk."

"Lancaster Club?"

"You know. The song title place."

"You mean Danse? Why didn't you say so?"

"I thought I did."

By the time Payne reached the locker room he had the oversuit peeled off and wadded into a ball. He stuffed it into his locker and headed for the door.

Down the stairs and in the lobby, Karol had gone home for the day.

He stepped out into the evening air.

Saturday Night

░█░█░█░█░█░█░█░█░█░█░█░█░█░█░█░█░█░

*T*he walk home did him good. He was calm by the time he got to the apartment. He stepped through the doors and caught the building's musty smell. As he looked at the rickety flight of stairs, something not entirely pleasant began to creep up his spine.

He decided to take the elevator. In his pocket, his fingers crossed, hoping for power enough to run it. He hit a button.

The doors slid open right away, and he stepped in—his foot came down on nothing. Vertigo gripped him. He pitched forward, hands darting out and catching on the edges of the door. His head bobbed out over the edge of the brick and steel cliff, eyes wide open.

The top of the elevator was four meters below. His stomach rose to this throat.

Above him was angry crackling. He looked up and saw blue flashes at the very top of the shaft. There was a new smell here—ozone. The servos were burning out. There was electricity enough for the old beast, but it was dying of old age. In its desperation it was trying to swallow him up as a blood sacrifice.

Payne backed out of the jaws. He left the doors open

to warn the next hapless tenant. He would have to face the stairs, after all.

By the third flight he could feel the wear on his muscles. The fourth floor was Bailey's floor. He thought of Bailey at the club on Lancaster—and Myra.

Halfway to the fifth floor it struck him hard. There was death in his apartment. He stopped and considered the stairs. A good thing the elevator hadn't been working. He'd be going mad by now, trying to claw his way out of the rising room with his bare hands.

What if there was another one up there?

No. It couldn't happen. Lightning doesn't strike twice. Not like that. He continued up the stairs.

By the time he reached his door he was shaking so badly that it took him five minutes to fit the key into the lock and open the door. His stomach pushed against his throat. He bit his lip and shoved. The door swung wide open.

Nothing. Nothing wrong at all. No new bodies. Not even a reminder of the first one. Payne closed the door and had a good laugh.

He turned on the monitor and sat for a long time, letting his mind wander, trying to escape the agitation he had felt since waking. He took slow, deep breaths and rubbed his face. He was suffering from sensory overload. The run-in with Kelce, seeing Trinina again, the encounter with Karol, Myra...

Finally he began to make plans. Should he feed her when she came in? Should he wait until later? Perhaps food shouldn't be a consideration at all. He could always open a can of something.

He pulled off his jumpsuit and sniffed it. There was a faint trace of beer, and the sweat in the fibers had the sharpness of rage and frustration. He pulled out the green suit from the night before. Its scent was different. It reminded him of Myra. The prospect was exciting. Perhaps Bailey was right to wear alcohol on the dance floor. He put the suit on a hanger and ironed it.

When it was dried and fit, he looked in the mirror. He wondered if Nathan would get his wiry frame, his dark eyes, his intent stare. Closer to the mirror, his eyebrows knit together. Nestled into the jet-black was a single thread of platinum. He singled it out for pulling but at the last minute spared it.

Now his breathing was becoming irregular; it was only intensifying the closeness of the rendezvous time. He fought for control. The tingling from morning was back, the one that clouded his thinking. An ancient saying popped into his head: *Who knows what evil lurks in the hearts of men?* He laughed, remembering how he had run up the stairs. Nothing evil about it. He knew exactly what he wanted to do.

The gray scarf was where he had left it the night before. He put it on and checked how it looked. There was a difference he couldn't describe. He squinted at the mirror and decided to go green.

The telephone rang, disrupting his thoughts. He walked into the living room and put the handset to his ear. "'Lo?"

"Payne? Something wrong?" It was Bailey.

"No. Just lost in thought."

"Sounds like you should give your brain a rest."

"It's been a long day."

"Has it, now? I've got the perfect diversion."

Payne winced. He hoped Bailey's plans didn't involve the Lancaster. "What?"

"I thought we could taxi to the 'Flesh and Blood' over on the east end. Sit around, do some serious drinking, watch the dancing. You know."

"I didn't know you were getting into assimilation."

"Not a bad idea. It pays more. If we get bored, we could bring home a couple of strays."

"I'd love to, Bailey, but I'm afraid I've already made plans."

"Going to the Lancaster for the redhead?"

Payne rolled his eyes. "Yeah. You bet."

Bailey laughed. "Don't worry. I understand. But if you strike out, you're on your own."

"Fine." Being alone was not in his plans. He clicked the handset and returned to the bedroom. Thumb to watch told him it was 1807. He had to get moving. He glanced around the apartment. How does the place look? Fine, she'll love it.

He had one foot out the door when he realized he had forgotten his scarf and keys. It took him two more minutes to fumble the green into a passable knot, wishing he had his ring to hold it on. By the time the door was locked and he was in the hall, the anxiety was back.

He chided himself for being so nervous and descended the stairs. He glided easily out of the Plus Fours, down the street, through all the proper connections to Lancaster Boulevard.

He stood and stared at the club until he realized that he was stalling.

It made him think. This was supposed to be a pleasurable meeting, but he felt as if he were facing exile. Whatever was causing his unease, it was time to be a man and face up to things. Myra would be waiting.

He walked across the street and fell into queue at the ticket booth. Two greens ahead of him were already all over each other. They'd be in a chamber all night. The line slowly dwindled until his turn came. He paid his money and went inside.

Bass from the ballroom rattled the fixtures in the lobby. He wandered to the concession stand and looked at the selection of scarves and contraceptives.

A pretty brunette smiled from behind the counter. "Can I help you with something?"

Payne looked at her blankly. "I'm sorry?"

"Do you need something?"

He exhaled. "Just looking."

She twitched her eyebrows. "We've got some new red-scarf aids at the other counter."

"Maybe later," he said, wondering if she gave demonstrations.

"Well, if you need anything, let me know."

His stomach tightened. An offer like that from her was going to be hard to resist. He had an impulse to pick something kinky and ask to see how it worked, just to hear her pitch. Instead, he moved on.

The ballroom was dark. What light there was came from the lasers on the screen. The crowd was not dancing. They were mesmerized by the tangle of pure colors on the screen. They sparked and bled and oozed and cracked the screen in sync with a product that blasted from the speakers.

Payne tried to listen. The music was merely frantic drumming and a bass part that wandered the limits of the register. A coarse, muted whisper was pinned beneath the floor of the music, its message indistinguishable. All he could sense was a cool malevolence that sent shivers into his spine. Payne covered his ears to keep it out. The light from the screen had begun to hurt his eyes. He stumbled to a corner and waited for the assault to end. The bass quit kicking, and a roar went up from the crowd. The song had made them insane.

He turned to the person next to him, a kid in his early twenties wearing a sharp black jumpsuit with a bright red scarf knotted around his right arm. He was screaming at the top of his lungs. Payne tugged at his sleeve.

The kid looked at him. "No thanks. Not into that."

Payne glared and flagged his green.

The kid laughed. "Sorry. What do you want?"

"I want to know what the excitement is all about."

There was a broad grin. "What do you mean?"

"What's the big deal with the music?"

The face he was looking into showed pure, unadulterated joy. "It's a test run."

"A test run?"

"The new single from Kitsch. First time it's ever been played."

"Kitsch?"

"Ever heard 'Danse'?"

"Yeah."

"That's Kitsch."

Payne nodded.

"Wasn't it great? That man is a genius!"

"What was so great about it?"

"Couldn't you feel it?"

Payne stared. "What was I *supposed* to be feeling?"

"The song. You feel the song. Didn't you feel the knives?"

"Knives?"

"That's what the song's called. 'Knives'."

Payne thought about the song's effect on him and nodded gravely. "I can see why." He moved away, weaving through the crowd.

"Thank you!" a voice cried from the speakers. "Thank you very much!"

Payne looked back at the DJ's booth. A figure was standing in the window, arms outstretched to the crowd below.

"My next single. Thanks for your time and thank you for making 'Danse' number one!"

The crowd went mad.

"Take it, Bobby!"

Drums kicked through the speakers, and the dancing started. Payne was now trapped in the middle of the crowd. It all seemed so darkly familiar. Bumped and shoved by the dance, he jumped into the air to get his bearings.

Then it came to him. This was their song.

He calmed, no longer worried about the future. All he had to do was meet her at the table and things would take their natural course.

Table.

He had promised to reserve a table. He cursed and ground his fists into his temples. He fought his way to the wall and found the table he wanted occupied by another

couple. Perhaps it wasn't too late. He'd bribe them with
the sexual aid of their choice from the concession stand.

As he watched, a barmaid brought them drinks. Two
sets of doubles. The Happy Hour had just ruined his life.

Thinking quickly, he made his way to the lobby and
flagged down the brunette.

She gave him that smile. "Decide on something?"

"Yes. Is it too late to reserve a table?"

"Not for tomorrow."

He slapped the counter. "Great."

"Will there be anything else?"

"No. No thanks."

He wheeled away, cursing. He had forgotten, and Myra
was the checking type. When she found that no table had
been reserved, she would probably get mad enough to
buy a yellow scarf and go off with the brunette. He mas-
saged his temples and tried to think. There had to be a
way out of this.

The most obvious solution was to leave the club and
never, ever come back. That was too full of holes; he had
to get his ring back, and what would he tell Bailey the
next time he wanted to come? Sooner or later he'd run
out of excuses. Most importantly, he didn't want to compound Myra's problems any more than he had to. Things
had been rough enough for her.

The real solution was easy enough. He had to stay in
one spot and wait for her to show. If he did nothing else
for her this evening, he'd tell her the truth. He looked
out across the dance floor, hoping for a glimpse of her.
The time was 1850, and the place was quickly filling. At
this rate, waiting might take forever.

Then the scales tipped his way. Two red-scarved couples abandoned their booth for the chambers. Things were
back under control. Payne had the table by the time
"Danse" pounded the club.

The music melted the time away. The third time the
barmaid came by he broke down and ordered a drink. By
the time it arrived, the ice had melted and it was warm.

The barmaid looked forlorn. He laughed and thought about pouring it on his suit. There was still no sign of Myra.

"Danse" played again. He was getting restless, but figured this was his penance. He yawned. When he opened his eyes again, Glory was peering down at him, palms on the tabletop.

"Hello again," she said.

"Hi," he said unenthusiastically.

"Looks like we've got the wrong colors again." She waved a red scarf.

Payne looked down at his green. "Looks like."

"What the hell. The night's still young."

"Going to be crowded."

"Well," she said, smiling numbly. "I'm going to go get tied up."

Payne waved. "Have fun."

She disappeared into the crowd. Things were getting too complicated. One had to wear the right scarf, have the right look, carry the right scent—and listen to Kitsch.

The next drinks he ordered were quicker in coming and were still cold, the ice chattering in the glass, beads of perspiration forming on the outside. He took one for himself and placed the other where Myra would sit.

The club was too loud to hear his watch, so he looked instead. 2028. She wasn't going to show. His evening was wasted.

He looked sullenly at the drinks. Might as well kill them and set the pace for the rest of the night. He picked one and knocked half of it back. It went down with some difficulty, warming and burning, and he shook off the initial effects.

Myra, indeed.

He took a mouthful of ice and crunched it. He'd been taken. He felt like a fool. There was nothing in the world he hated more than being taken for a fool. She probably had a cigar box full of prole rings at home. He took another large gulp.

"You shouldn't drink alone."

He looked up and saw her.

"They say it's very bad, psychologically."

"Nice to see you," he said sheepishly.

She smiled coolly. "May I have a seat?"

He stood. "By all means."

She slid in across from him.

"Your drink is getting warm."

"How did you know what to order?"

"I didn't."

She gracefully picked up her glass and sipped, smiling at his thoughtfulness.

"Do you want something else?" he offered.

"No. I'm just passing through."

So that was that. There was nobody to blame but himself. He decided to go home after she left.

But Myra was not about to leave. She took another sip of her drink. Her hair was different this evening. It was pulled to the back of her head and knotted in a ponytail. Perhaps that was why he hadn't spotted her earlier.

"You look nice tonight," he said.

His ring hit the surface of the table. "Where in hell were you?"

He cleared his throat. "At this table. Since 1900."

She jerked a thumb over her shoulder. "That table. That was our table last night."

"I forgot to reserve it. I was busy with Bailey."

"Do you want me or not?"

Payne stared. She had been so vulnerable last night. Why the change? Was she doing Blueskies? Is that what the popular drug did to a person? "I got a table, didn't I?"

"Not that table."

"A table is a table."

"You promised." He saw last night's face for a fraction of a second. She began to bang the ring on the lacquered surface of the table. "Your problem is obvious. Why don't you take me to a chamber and get it over with?"

Payne slammed his glass. The ice rattled nervously.

"I'm sorry you have no faith in people. I admit that I forgot, but at least I tried to make it up. I did get a table, even though it wasn't reserved, and I've waited for nearly two hours. For most people that would be enough." He stood and turned toward the dance floor.

"Payne."

He glanced back.

"Your ring."

"Keep it." He moved into the crowd, trying to remain calm. That was important now. He couldn't let things get to him. He'd do something stupid, something foolish that he'd regret.

His initial impulse was to get a red scarf and look up Glory. It was impulse, which he had to fight. Anger and frustration would take the place of reason and result in something he would regret. Two of the twelve names on his GCR report were impulses; one had been three days after Trinina had moved out.

Payne crowded though the mob, pushing to the lobby exit. Squeezing through a last cluster of dancers, he reached the door and threw it open.

He found himself standing toe to toe with Myra.

"I'm sorry," she said through moist lips.

"Sorry." He tried to force it as anger but failed. The word came out stilted and wooden.

Her eyes went to the floor. "I've been here . . ." A wisp of hair had come loose from the ponytail and fell across her face. "I've been her since 1900. I've been watching you."

All he could do was stare.

"After you left last night, I checked to see if you'd really reserved a table. You hadn't."

"I forgot. It was an honest mistake."

"I thought you were like all of the others. I wasn't even going to come tonight." She raised her hand, a glimmer of silver twinkling in her palm. "But you left this with me. I wasn't sure if you'd come back for it, and when you did, I figured that you wouldn't wait long. So I just watched." She looked back into his face. "You really do want me."

He took the ring from her hand. "Yes."

Her eyes filled with tears. "I shouldn't have done it. I just wanted so to be sure . . ."

He kissed her hand.

She abruptly pulled away. "No. I should leave you alone." She took a step for the lobby, and Payne caught her by the arm.

"Myra." He held the door open with his free hand and nodded into the ballroom. The lights were subdued, and gentle tones were drifting their way. "Slow dance."

She tried to pull away.

"Just one. No obligations."

"I suppose I owe it to you."

"No." Payne dropped her arm. "If you come, you'll do it because you want to."

She managed a smile.

"Is that a yes?"

She nodded.

Payne extended his hand. Hers was there to meet it.

They walked into the blue-flooded room and slipped into the desperate clutching perfected the night before. They turned around each other and meshed with the crowd. Low blue footlights circled the floor. Thick fog poured in from ports placed high in the walls, and laser light formed a blue ceiling inches above their heads. In the middle of the set red light was introduced, warming the hues to purple. The effect was staggering. The darkness, the fog, the laser ceiling. The crowd compressed around the center of the floor, crushing tighter, making room for those pouring in from outside.

Payne was suffocating even though the air was chilled. At one point he swore his breath was coming out in a vapor. His skin was thick with gooseflesh, but Myra was so warm. He tried to pull her in, to absorb her, absorb her warmth. Her head pressed against his neck, and her fingers worked the muscles of his shoulders. He melted around her.

"Tense," she said softly.

"Bad day." He nuzzled behind her ear.

They pulled and held and turned and swayed. They separated and studied each other's faces in the blue and shadows. Their feet shuffled in slow grace.

There was a sensation in Payne's ear that made him raise his head and look around. Silence. The lights were pure, crystalline blue. No music was playing, but the crowd was still embracing, slowly turning. In the light it looked like a congregation of pale ghosts, those who had danced as the ship slipped under the waves and had not yet been told of their icy fate. He shivered.

Myra's head lifted from his shoulder.

"I'm okay," he said. "It's over."

"What?"

"The music."

"Oh. Yes. So it is."

Payne scanned the room. The scene was remarkable.

"This is so nice," Myra said. She pulled his head down and bit his ear. "Stay."

But the silence was bothering him. He became self-conscious, too aware that he was moving to nothing. Myra's fingers worked his shoulders.

"Tense again."

He shrugged.

"You don't like the Quiet Dance?"

"I feel like people are watching."

"They're not."

"How long does this go on?"

"Until it breaks up. They'll warm the lights to let the stragglers know."

He moved away from her. "I seem to have lost track of time. The deal was for one song, not one set."

"I didn't mind."

"I'm glad you came."

She nodded. "My pleasure."

"I'll let you go now."

She looked hurt. "You're sure?"

"I won't force anything on you."

Myra's face formed a wicked, feline grin. Her hands wrapped around his neck and pulled his head to hers, her nose and lips brushing his face. "But I'm forcing *you*."

She moved away with the grace of falling silk. At arm's length, her hand slid out to him, fingers brushing the palm of his hand. A tremor numbed first his arm, then the rest of his body, leaving him fighting for breath.

She was slinking toward the screen, her body flowing through the fog as if it had never done anything else. He followed helplessly, the moisture leaving his throat.

They stopped at doors perpendicular to the screen. Beyond would be a corridor to government offices and chambers. She gave him a new look, happily in control. Her hand dropped his, then flowed to the back of her neck. A twist, and hair cascaded to her shoulders, neatly framing her face.

He fought the knowing grin that wanted to surface, afraid of smashing the moment with the look of an adolescent going in for his first Bill of Health. Instead, he let his eyes flicker. That was all she needed.

Their hands joined. There was darkness on the other side of the door. She flowed in, and he stepped after.

"Payne!"

He took another step. Something registered in his subconscious.

"Hey, Payne!"

He choked. It was the voice heard a thousand and one times during a lifetime—the voice of being called out of a dream on a sweltering summer evening. His hand twisted around Myra's, and he stopped. She looked back, not understanding.

He turned and greeted Lol Winthrop.

Winthrop returned the salutation and nodded apologetically at Myra. "I'm sorry if I'm interrupting things, but I need to have a word with you. Shouldn't take too long."

Myra looked frustrated.

"This is Lol Winthrop," Payne said. "He's a colleague from work. I wouldn't ordinarily do this, but it's important. I'll be right back."

She slipped through the door.

"What's up?" Payne asked.

Winthrop started an eccentric pace. "My table's over here. Buy you a drink?"

"Pass." He slid into the booth.

Winthrop plopped down solemnly. "I wouldn't bother you at a time like this, but I wanted you to know."

"The cultures?"

Winthrop grimed. "Salvaged. I took some samples from the bottom of the master brew and found some organisms that were still alive. I've inoculated them into a series of mediums and should know something within forty-eight hours. If they're still growing, all that remains is to toss them into a new jug of suspension and things should be fine."

Payne scratched his chin. "Why are you telling me this, Winthrop?" He studied the blond's face. "That's not the reason you pulled me aside."

Winthrop avoided Payne's eyes. "I came because I'm turning the project over to you. It's all yours."

"What's going on?"

The smile came. This was the happiest Payne had ever seen him. "I'm getting out, Payne. I've got passage to Sydney on a ship leaving at midnight."

Payne took Winthrop's hand and pumped it. "Congratulations. When did you get your clearance?"

The speakers cut the silence, and "Danse" resurrected the crowd. Winthrop glanced at his wrist. "In one hour," he shouted over the music.

"An hour?"

"I'm meeting the guy here." He tugged a yellow scarf

that dangled from his neck. "You don't think I'm fool enough to wear one of these bloody things, do you?"

Payne's mouth dropped open. "The black market? Oh, Winthrop..."

"I had to, Payne. I'm losing it here. You've a nice country, but it's not home." He swallowed from a glass, eyes clouding. "I'm sure you'd feel the same were the positions reversed."

"I'm sure."

"At 2200 I'm meeting the guy in a chamber. I got word at work and left a message in your mail, but when I heard the rendezvous was here, I figured I'd tell you in person. You were hard to find in that tangle of bodies."

"If you don't mind my asking, what's this little venture running you?"

"Fifty thousand dollars."

"*Fifty thousand?* That's extortionate!"

Winthrop shook his head. "It's worth it. I'm getting a letter of transit, steerage ticket on a ship, and twenty-five hundred dollars Australian. Enough to get the job done."

"That must have cleaned you out."

Winthrop shrugged. "Opportunity knocked. I couldn't wait any longer."

"Don't get stung."

"Not bloody likely. I made sure of that. I don't pay until the papers are in my hand."

"How do you know they exist?"

"I called Port Authority. They confirmed my reservations for midnight. It's really going to happen."

"What are you going to do when you get there?"

"I haven't decided. Isn't there a Biotech in Melbourne?"

"Sydney."

"Close enough. I thought I'd see if they'd take me on."

"I'm certain they would. Going back to cholesterol?"

"I'd be happy analyzing range grasses."

Payne tapped the table. "Tell you what. I'll put you in

for a transfer and mode it to Sydney. I'll put you in as an E-5. It'll be waiting when you get there."

"Would you?"

"Certainly. Cable me when it's confirmed and I'll cold pack your cultures and ship them."

Winthrop emptied his glass, hands trembling. "That would mean so much to me."

"It's good as done." Payne stood. A lump was forming in his throat. "Forgive me for not sticking around."

"I understand."

They fell into an embrace. He patted Winthrop on the back.

"Godspeed."

Winthrop nodded, eyes brimming with tears.

Payne turned his back and walked away.

Myra was waiting where he had left her, calmly leaning against the doorstop, her face a mask of controlled calm. Payne slowed as he neared her. He knew what it meant.

"The moment's gone."

She nodded.

"This hasn't been my night."

"Our night," she added. "The chambers are full."

Payne led her away from the door. "This is ridiculous. I've been acting like a fool for two nights running."

She was silent.

He stopped and turned her to face him. "If we were destined to get together, it would have happened by now."

Her look melted. "You don't like me?"

"I like you just fine. It's just not working."

"I'm a problem?"

"There's nothing wrong with you. It's me. I'm not being a sane, rational creature about any of this. Understand that I'm under some pressure right now. I've got problems with work, and I was under the influence of a crisis last night. When I get like this, I do things that I ordinarily wouldn't."

"Am I an impulse?"

"I don't know. I don't want to find out. If I do, the

magic will disappear, and I'm afraid of that." He let go
of her. "I don't want you to get hurt."

"You seem rational enough."

Payne shook his head. "I'm sorry. It's not the right
time."

He took her by the shoulders and put his lips to hers.
Her arms moved up to grab, but he held them back. Pulling away, he gave her a soft smile and vanished into the
crowd.

He pushed through the doors, fighting the incoming
stream of people. He briskly paced past the concession
stand and the knockout brunette, not even noticing as she
held a leather mask to her face for a red-scarved customer.

The door swung wide, and he stepped onto concrete,
a cool breeze wrapping him as he went. He didn't stop.
He walked out into the middle of the street and set course
for home.

Payne's shoes made a click on the pavement that he
couldn't keep from counting. It had a rhythmic quality,
and even though he felt sullen, there was a brightness and
energy in his walk. It was springy and alive. Record it,
add a bass track, and they'll name the Lancaster after it.
He counted out time and tried to improvise a bass part,
but something was wrong. There was something in the
numbers that staggered the gait and threw off his timing.
He counted again: one-two, two-two, three-two, slip. He
tried to pace the walk and couldn't keep up.

That was when he realized that he was being followed.

Fear started to fill him. He decided that it was time to
come face to face with things, lest he spend the rest of
his life cowering at shadows and strange sounds from the
street. He launched a step and snapped his foot down.
As he raised up for the next step, he kicked and spun,
planting his other foot and stopping.

It was Myra.

She was walking a quick pace, shoe heels clicking
crisply. Occasionally her left foot gave out, causing the
skip in his timing.

"I've got to get this heel fixed," she said calmly.

"What are you doing here?"

"You invited me."

"That was last night."

She unshouldered a satchel and handed it to him. "Would you be a gentleman and carry this?"

The bag caught him in the stomach. He wrapped his hands around it. "I told you to forget it."

"There's no need to."

He tried to hand the satchel back, but she put her hand on his chest. "I was playing games, but I'm through now. I promise. I just wanted to find out where you stood."

"Where I stood?"

She looked down again. He swore to break her of that habit. "I'm not really very trusting." She touched the scarred side of her nose. "I don't like surprises. I realize I might be an impulse to you, so if things get a little ragged, I'll understand."

"You're making this sound permanent."

"That's not what I mean. I'm referring to getting booted out of somebody's place without breakfast or good-bye. Home is always anticlimactic after meeting in the clubs. Especially one like the Lancaster."

Payne looked down the street, resistance fading. "Well, we're four blocks away, and you're still appealing."

She wrapped an arm around his waist. "Take me home."

"You're asking for trouble."

"I know."

He let an arm fall around her. "Let's go."

The walk to the Plus Fours was pleasant. They exchanged small talk and opinion, and exchanged impressions of their meeting the night before. Feeling relaxed, Payne asked her why she had followed him.

"I wanted to find out what the magic was," she said.

"Magic?"

"When you thought I was an impulse, you said you were afraid the magic would disappear."

"I said that?"

"You did."

He thought about it. "I'll explain later."

"Tell me now."

"No."

"Why not?"

"It's too heavy-handed. I'll tell you about it when things get intense."

"Intense?"

"*If* they get intense."

He held the door for her, and they glided up the stairs, not noticing the line of milk bottles outside Bailey's door.

"How far up do you live?"

"Seventh floor."

"This is a jog for me. I live on the twelfth."

"Where?"

"The Hanging Gardens."

"You're a long way from home."

"I think Danse is worth it. You're lucky to live so close."

"I rarely go there," Payne confessed. "But that may change."

They crested the seventh floor landing, and he took her by the hand. Laughing like adolescents, they walked down the darkened hall to Payne's apartment.

"Do you have any plans for when we go in?"

He stared. Her eyes were shining through the darkness. "I thought I'd give you the dollar tour."

She moved close. "You mentioned things getting intense."

"As an option."

She rose up on her toes, and her mouth surrounded his for one stunning moment. "Something to consider."

"Inside," he said. He gently reached past her and twisted the knob. The door cracked open. He pushed it open and let her in. "After you."

She took a step, and he froze.

Had he left the door open?

His eyes shot to his hand, still on the knob. By the

time he looked up, she was three steps into his living room.

"Myra..."

A giant hand shot from behind the door and struck her in the back. She staggered across the living room, collapsing at the kitchen entrance.

Payne took another step. "*Myra!*"

The door slammed him into the apartment. A hand grabbed him by the lapels, and another sank into his stomach.

"Where's the ticket?"

Payne tried a glance, but his eyes weren't working. He inhaled loudly, trying to recover the air punched from his lungs. His nose caught smoke and sweat and the sharp tackiness of acetone.

Then he fell to the floor. When he looked up, a heel snapped across the side of his head. He flopped over and looked again. The face that looked back was hard.

His lapels jerked, and he rose. Coughing, he stared at cyanotic lips that blew the scent in his face.

"I said, where's the ticket?"

"What ticket?"

Payne slammed into the wall. He felt the toss and threw his arms back to break the impact. He dug his heels into the floor, awkwardly kicking to stay on his feet. A man that big and that sick wouldn't move that fast. He had the advantage if he could outmaneuver him.

From the corner of one eye he saw Myra slipping for the door. He jerked his head and shouted.

"*Myra! No!*"

His ruse worked. The giant turned for a split second. Payne pushed off the wall and planted his foot squarely in his attacker's groin.

There was a roar of annoyance, and the man stumbled into the table by the door. The legs cracked and shattered under the burden, tossing their oppressor down.

The big man stirred. Payne leaped for the door and

slammed it into him, knocking him back down. He slammed it again and bolted into the hall.

Myra was shaken but safe, standing by the stairs.

"Down!" Payne shouted. "Four twenty-nine!"

"What about you?"

"I'm right behind you!"

"Payne?"

"Go!"

And suddenly he was crushed. He was biting the hard varnished floor and gasping for breath. Acetone was creeping down his neck. The weight on his back was massive.

"Ticket, please."

"What ticket?"

He was pulled up by the hair and smashed down into the varnish.

"Okay!" Payne cried. "I give!"

The weight rolled from his back. He was picked up by the collar and moved into a bear hug.

"Easy," he gasped.

"Nothing doing. I got your breathing, and I don't let up until I see the yellow."

"Yeah." Payne wet his lips. He lifted his legs and began to slide down. The giant shifted. Payne dropped his head. The sudden dead weight was too clumsy for the man to handle. He took a step and relaxed his grip for a fraction of a second.

Payne filled his lungs with air and threw his head back as hard as he could. It connected with something solid, which gave with a sharp crack. The hold was broken. Payne dove for the floor and rolled away.

It was an ugly scene. Hands moved away from the hard face, now twisted in agony. Thick red was pouring from the nostrils and running across the stubble on his cheeks. He took a wobbling step toward Payne and collapsed as if his legs had been kicked out from under him.

Payne ran after Myra on rubber legs. "He's not down for long." He pushed her to the stairs, and they scrambled down. On the last step Payne's ankle buckled, and he twisted to the floor. Myra, halfway down the next flight, stopped.

"Go!" Payne screamed. "Four twenty-nine! Get Bailey!" Myra turned and fled. Payne pulled up, tried a step on the ankle, and fell. He grabbed the banister and tried to limp down the stairs. He imagined Myra screaming and pounding on Bailey's door, oblivious to the milk bottles at her feet. Inside would be Bailey, his back bent over some strange and clawing woman, her shouts of admiration drowning out the sounds from the hallway.

There was a blow to his back, and he tore loose from the banister and tumbled down the rest of the stairs. He turned in time to be lifted and tossed down the next flight.

He tried to break his fall, but couldn't time the bumps. His hand shot out and grabbed a banister rail. His arm was nearly jerked from its socket, but it brought him to a stop.

Almost.

There was a crack, and the scent of rotted wood filled his nostrils. He felt another jolt—then he was again falling, the support rail clenched in his hand.

Flat out on the landing, he crawled to the railing and pulled to his knees. The stairs above shook under the weight of what approached. Pushing with his good leg, Payne stood. The giant looked at him and smiled, then began to spring down the stairs.

The timing would be crucial.

The man's lips split and spilled out an evil cackle. Payne leaned over the banister and swung the piece of railing with both hands. It connected with a kneecap. The force of the blow took the wood right out of his hands, and the giant fell with such force that dust rose from between the planks of the floor.

Ignoring his throbbing ankle, Payne hobbled down the stairs as fast as he could. At the foot he stopped to rest, leaning against the wall. He cast a glance over his shoulder. The big man wasn't moving.

He gingerly stepped out into the hallway. Out of the corner of his right eye, he caught Myra ringing for the elevator.

"No." He stumbled and shouted for her.

She turned to face him. "We'll be safe in here. We can lose him."

"No. You don't understand—"

The bell sounded, and the elevator doors opened wide. Myra waved him on and stepped in. From deep inside, Payne found strength enough for a wild leap. His hand lanced out and caught her by the wrist as the shock of no floor below her heel registered on her face. She let out a squeal and locked onto his arm, then plunged over the side.

Sinking his fingers into her skin, Payne hit the floor and slid helplessly toward the waiting jaws. He rolled sideways and slammed his legs and torso against the wall. They stopped, but his arm was bent down over the edge, holding Myra. His hand was beginning to convulse and go numb. With her weight on the other end, his brachial artery was crushed against the edge of the brick, depriving his arm of blood.

"Climb," he gasped through clenched teeth.

"I can't."

"You're pulling my arm off."

"Help me."

"I can't."

"What do I do?"

"Climb. Kick. Scream. Do *something*!"

She froze. He was getting dizzy, and nausea filled his bowels. Something had to be done.

He slipped enough to move the pressure from his upper arm to his armpit. Spines of fire took his arm as blood rushed back to his fingertips. Myra screamed at the jolt and climbed up his arm, hands wrapped above his elbow, now clawing at his shoulders, trying to find something to clench on the smooth surface of the floor. She found something, and her face came up over the edge. Payne saw it was ashen. Her free hand grabbed his collar and pulled, and her foot kicked up and planted near the ledge. She looked at him, face smeared with sweat and dirt, and smiled.

Suddenly the smile dissolved. Payne looked to his left. It was too late. Myra's saving handhold, the pillar on the gritty varnished surface, was a leg.

A swollen and bloody face leered down at them. The big man leaned against the opening of the shaft, weight resting on the outside leg. Blood was puddling on the floor, seeping from high on the inside leg, which was swollen to bursting against the restraints of the jumpsuit fabric. He twisted his jowls and spat. A molar struck Payne's forehead and clanked to the floor. The giant laughed and grabbed Myra by the hair. She clutched helplessly for Payne.

"Don't." He looked the man in the eye.

The man gave a bloody smile. He was enjoying this.

Payne grabbed the inner leg and twisted it at an impossible angle. There was a moist tearing sound, and the man grunted. He shook Myra over the open shaft.

"Let her go."

The man laughed. Payne squeezed and twisted.

"Let her go, you bastard!"

She hit the floor.

It was all over. Payne was shaking and would vomit at any moment. He was tired, more tired than he had ever been in his life. If he quit now, they would both end up dead.

He held the leg stupidly, numbly, at the compromising angle. Seconds clicked off as the Goliath tried to catch his breath.

Payne reached. There was nothing there, nothing at all, not even the tiniest spark that could be tapped for that last instant. He didn't have strength enough to draw breath. The man looked down at him, eyebrows twitching, a low grunt escaping from his throat. He seemed to be fighting a look of satisfaction. His eyes blinked rapidly, then closed for a moment. When they opened again, he was smiling.

And then help came as Payne's advantage began to fade. Immaculately manicured hands that were stained with grease and blood took the swollen limb from him and continued to twist. And then came a push, up and out into the middle of the shaft.

The giant reared back his head in an openmouthed scream. There was a precarious moment when he took in a wet suck of air, and then he silently pitched headfirst into the mouth of the shaft. If a crash followed, it went unheard.

"Thanks," Payne said.

Myra nodded and wiped her mouth with a sleeve. "Friend of the family?"

Payne lifted his head from between his knees. "I think I have some explaining to do."

"I should hope so."

"You're not mad?"

"Mad? You saved my life. I should reward you, lover boy."

Payne shook with nervous laughter that hurt from head to toe. "I've had all of the intensity I can handle for one night."

Myra looked to the ceiling and wrapped herself in a schoolgirl's giggle.

Eventually they helped each other to their feet and began a slow ascent of the stairs. Payne's ankle was still tender, but bothered him less with each step he took. By the time they reached the apartment he was walking without Myra's support.

"I lied to you," he told her. "I was the one optioned for the Thirty-first last night."

"I should have figured as much."

"How so?"

"Your friend was babbling about wanting a yellow ticket."

Payne nodded. "I should have known. You're still not mad?"

"It depends. What's your case disposition?"

"On the Thirty-first? I didn't take it."

"You know you're a fool for that."

"Not for much longer," Payne said. "As soon as we get to my phone, I'm changing that."

Sunday Morning

Myra woke him with a kiss and a smile. Delgado and company had arrived, and she was raiding Payne's kitchen to cook breakfast. He rolled out of bed, frightfully sore from the night before. He stumbled into the bathroom to shave and check his wounds.

He looked as if he had been through the mill. There was a gash above his left eye, and his cheek had raised a small but impressive welt. There were miscellaneous cuts and bruises from his shoulders to his heels; scrapes at the knees, elbows, and upper back; and a large knot had formed on the back of his head. The twisted leg was black and blue from midthigh to scraped shin and was swollen at the ankle. There were blisters on both hands, and his arms were bruised and scabbed from where Myra's nails had dug in. He was bruised along the left side of his ribs and had a large tender spot just below his diaphragm. He felt amazed to be alive. He washed his face and slipped on a fresh jumpsuit.

Delgado was torn between shock and amusement when he saw him. "Looks like you had fun last night."

A female assistant snapped photographs of the ransacked apartment while Delgado and Payne went over the details of the assault. On a cue from Delgado, she put down her camera and examined the locks with the optical device.

"Fresh pick marks on the lock," she said.

Delgado nodded. "Make note. There weren't any Friday night. See if you can lift any prints."

"Don't bother," Payne said. "I covered the knob with my hand. Anything there is probably ruined."

"We're still going to fog for prints. We'll be making lifts of you and your girl."

"That's fine."

"We'll also need to get pictures of your injuries. The girl, too." Delgado waved at his subordinate, who went into the kitchen. In a moment she and Myra repaired to Payne's bedroom and closed the door.

"So," Delgado said. "Will you be taking the Thirty-first on the assailant?"

"No need to. I killed him. That should be retribution enough."

Delgado looked troubled. "My call card says—"

"I can guess what your call card says. I'm taking the Thirty-first on the girl. If I find who killed her, I'll know who hired our friend in the elevator shaft."

"You think there's a connection?"

"I know there's a connection." He tossed the yellow stub on the coffee table. "He was after this. That's why he ripped the place apart. When he couldn't find it, he tried to beat it out of me."

"What did you do, hide it?"

Payne nodded sheepishly.

"Where?"

"In the garbage. Under a candy wrapper."

Delgado clucked his tongue. "Well, Payne, it looks like you're off the hook."

"What do you mean?"

"A bit obvious, isn't it? This guy killed the girl and

dumped her in your apartment. He came back yesterday for the yellow so you couldn't take the option."

"Wait a minute. What makes you think I could have caught him? I'd never seen the man before."

"There's always that chance."

Payne leaned forward. "Two days ago you were begging me to take the option. Now you're trying to palm it off on some lackey who's nothing more than a convenient excuse. Well, I've got some questions that I'd like answered, Sergeant, so maybe you'd like to answer them for me. Why did he leave her in my apartment? How did he get in on Friday without picking the lock, and why did he have to pick it last night? Who was this girl? She had to have friends or family. Why did he kill her? You can't just write it all off."

Delgado shrugged, and the front door opened. An officer entered, shaking his head.

"Problems?" the sergeant asked.

"Couldn't find him."

"What?" Payne was up from the couch.

The officer shook his head. "Someone came in and cleaned up. I found samples of blood in the cracks of the floor near the elevator entrance, but they were spoiled by antiseptic."

"The landlord?"

"Doesn't work weekends. Made him mad enough that we hauled him out to get to the elevator."

"Don't tell me he's still alive," Payne said.

"Shouldn't have to worry about that. I got on top of the elevator car and took samples. Lots of blood and viscera. Whoever it was got impaled on the bolts of the pulley assembly. If he is alive, he won't be for much longer."

"Left under his own power?" Delgado asked.

"Doubtful. There were drag marks to the emergency hatch on top of the car. I also found contaminated blood samples in the carpet. Whoever took him out did a sloppy job. He accessed the car, opened the rescue hatch, dragged him out, then went back and mopped up. Didn't even think to check the top of the car."

"Did the landlord see anybody down there last night?"

"Landlord's a Sneeze addict. Doesn't even know what day of the week it is."

"Anything else?"

"That's it. The others have gone to the van for the print fogger."

"Fine. I want you to look for a section of banister with a missing support rail between floors five and six. Part of this man's story is that one tore loose and he used it to crack the assailant's kneecap."

The assistant winced.

"If you find it, bag it. Also put out word to the Trauma Treatment Centers. Have them keep their eyes open for a great big guy with a punctured gut." He rubbed his chin. "This building's ancient. That shaft'll be damn filthy. I'll bet the pulley assembly was caked with that great industrial grease they used to make. If our boy is still alive, he's going to have one hell of a case of peritonitis. Give a bolo to the Storage and Disposal Centers and have them watch for the same thing."

"Right." The officer twisted on his heels and left. As the door closed behind him, the women emerged from the bedroom.

"Thank you," Delgado said to Myra. "Hope we didn't put you out."

"No. I'm used to posing . . ." She trailed off and blushed.

Delgado took the camera from his assistant. "Now it's Mister Payne's turn."

Delgado shot a roll of 3d/1000X of Payne's injuries, then took him and Myra into the hall as officers brought in the print fogger.

"The fog will clear in about two hours, so you might want to go for a walk or something."

While green mist pumped into the apartment, Payne and Myra retraced their steps for Delgado. On their way

to the sixth floor they passed an officer who waved a large
plastic bag. Inside was the splintered rail.

"Good job," Delgado said. "They're fogging now. Tell
them to shoot Flat 36X if any prints turn up."

Once the path was traced and clear in Delgado's mind,
he escorted them to the van, where they filled out statements and took prints. Once this information was col-
lected, Delgado slipped film rolls, statements, print lifts,
and tissue samples into a cardboard box, sealed it with
plastic wrap, and attached a bright orange card to the
side.

"This is your case box," he said. "As we don't seem
to have a body, we're going to cheat and file it as an
aggravated assault."

He tore the orange stub and handed it to Payne, then
read him the Thirty-first Amendment. Before accepting
it, Payne asked if he had to work the assault separately.

"No," Delgado answered. "I'm filing this as being
related to the homicide. Your case for their connection
looks good, so I'm letting you have it that way."

"What happens if the guy's body turns up?"

"I can assure you that it won't. If someone went to
the trouble of pulling it out of the elevator shaft, it's not
going to show. Not unless the guy lived to see a Trauma
Treatment Center."

"I'm taking the option," he said.

"Very good."

There were forms to fill out and statements to sign.
Delgado was the supervising officer, and Myra witnessed.
They were given a booklet detailing private investigation
because, according to Delgado, most people didn't
remember the basics from high school. As he went over
it with them, the crew returned from the apartment.

"Is there anything else you need before we take off?"

"Lab hours," Payne said. "When can I get in for samples?"

"Name it. They never close." Delgado tucked his clipboard under an arm. "The labs were getting backed up

on regular hours." He looked at his watch. "I've over-
stayed my welcome. The chief'll be after me for taking
so long. They give us ninety minutes if someone takes
the option, but I'm here to do it right, not fast. The case
will be held at Warax Substation until you're ready. You
know where that is?"

"Near where I work. Thanks again."

Delgado shook Payne's hand. "Good luck, Payne."

Payne took Myra to the sidewalk as the crew piled into
the van and revved it up. There was a crackle, and the
engine stalled. Ozone filtered through their noses. At the
passenger window, Delgado shook his head.

"Dynamo's going bad. Don't build them like they used
to."

The van geared to a purr and slowly lurched away from
the curb. It glided silently into the morning.

"Well," Myra said. "What's your first order of business?"

"Getting something to eat. I suppose you left breakfast
out to get covered by their incendiary fog."

She shook her head. "It's covered and in your refrigerator."

"I've got an ice chest for the cold stuff."

"It'll keep. Trust me."

Payne rubbed his face. It was covered with stubble.
He probably looked terrible. "Tell you what. Let's go for
a walk."

"The park?"

"Work. As long as we're exiled, I might as well put in
notice that I'm on the Thirty-first. We can also go by the
Warax Substation and get the preliminaries out of the
way."

"That's going to take a while. You buying breakfast?"

"I thought you were cooking."

"You heard the man. It's two hours until the fog clears."

He took her to a small streetside cafe—the only one
they could find open this early on a Sunday—and bought
her a breakfast of toast and egg synths. Half an hour later

they stood before the Warax Substation. Built before renovation became the standard, the building was an entire city block of gleaming glass and chrome. Although its five stories were stunted by the surrounding brownstones, it outshone anything near.

"How are you going to handle the investigation?" Myra asked as he opened the door.

"I've got some ideas."

They stepped up to the receiving desk, and Payne produced his ticket.

"May I help you?"

Payne waved the stub. "I'm here to begin an investigation."

The clerk pointed to the floor. "Match the color of your stub to the color on the floor. Follow the line to its end."

"Thanks." He looked at the floor. A rainbow of colors flowed from under the desk and branched off as they streamed down the hall.

They took the yellow line until the other colors disappeared. When they did, the walls and ceiling turned the same color and led them to yet another desk. Payne flagged down a clerk and let him see the stub.

"Taking the Thirty-first?"

Payne nodded.

"Have a seat, please. A counselor will be with you in a few minutes."

They sat only a short time before a short, balding man with a pleasant smile and an absentminded look in his eyes approached. He shook their hands and introduced himself as Louis, stating that their wish was his command. Payne handed him the stub, relieved to get it out of his hands.

Louis turned the stub over and checked the number. "Oh, yes. QRG898. A pretty one." He pronounced the letters with a flourish, as if they were actually a word.

"You know her?"

Louis nodded. "I know them all. I have the gift of

association. There's a face behind every damn one of these numbers. This way, please."

He led them to a cul-de-sac framed by elevators. "Take your pick." He waved his arms like a carnival barker. "It's a Sunday. Nobody dies on a Sunday."

"Bets?" Myra commented.

"Homicide humor," Louis said. "Our big day is Thursday. Nothing ever happens on a Thursday, so that's when everyone comes in for the slicing and dicing." He noticed that Myra had paled. "Sorry, ma'am. Slab humor. Have to keep your guts together when you work around here."

"I understand."

"Of course, Thursdays are offset only by Fridays. That's when they really come rolling in. You get a good hot summer night, and it's standing room only around this place. We get them stacked up like cordwood." The elevator door hissed, and Louis herded them into the car. "Your ticket, QRG898. She came in on a Friday."

"Yeah," Payne said.

Louis thumbed a button, and the car dropped. Payne swallowed hard and Myra grabbed for the rail.

"Sorry. Some of the 'vators here have a mean streak. Don't like to work on a Sunday. Not like me. Give me a Sunday duty anytime. This precinct rarely gets bodies on a Sunday, I don't know why that is. Guess they'd rather let them ripen another day than call P and S."

"Would you mind keeping your theories to yourself?" Myra asked weakly.

"Sorry. You work here long enough and you get cold. You talk all the time so your brain doesn't have to think about what it's doing. When you get so you toss off death, you're going to offend someone."

Myra looked stern and nodded.

"So," Louis said tenuously. "Are you QRG's family?"

"Family?" Payne repeated. "No."

The elevator lurched to a stop. Louis stared at the door, then gave it a swift kick. It opened.

"Car nine," he explained. "Should have warned you

not to pick this one." Payne and Myra followed him out to find they were no longer surrounded by the nervous yellow walls.

"What made you think we were relatives?"

"The fact that you came in so quickly. It takes about ten days for someone to work up the fortitude to come in. That's for a homicide. You get a good grand larceny and more often than not they come in with the scene squad."

"If I knew who she was, things would be much simpler."

Louis stopped cold. "You don't know her?"

Payne shook his head.

Louis clapped his hands. "Poor thing. It's good that she wasn't listed as a Jane Doe. Some of the guys take the lookers, shoot them full of Alamex, and rent them out to frat house parties."

Alamex was a compound that protected cells from outside intrusion; it kept a body warm and alive-looking.

Myra bit her lip. "You don't . . ."

"No," Louis said decisively. "I don't. But some of the guys here do, and I believe they're going to burn in hell for it." He started back down the hall. "So what approach are you going to take—" He checked the stub. "Mr. Payne?"

"First I need to find out who she is. That could make things easier all the way around."

Louis nodded. "I'll warm up the 'face' program."

"And what killed her, of course."

"No traces on the body?"

"It was an inside job."

Louis laughed. "I think I'm going to like you, Mr. Payne." He stopped before a large metal door. "She's in here."

Payne extended his hand. "After you."

"What about the lady?"

Myra shrugged. "I've come this far."

"You're sure?" Payne asked.

"Until I change my mind."

"All aboard." Louis yanked the latch, and the door lumbered open. They walked into a garish white corridor lined with rows of drawers set four high into the walls.

"She's down this way." He led them through a maze of walls and drawers. They walked long stretches and turned corners until they were dizzy.

"How do you find your way around this place?" Myra asked.

"My mother was part lab rat."

"You know right where her body is?"

"I'm one of three here with the curse," Louis replied. "I've got it the worst. I never have to use the Green Line."

"Green Line?"

Louis pointed to the ceiling. "If you'll look, you'll see a row of bulbs between the fluorescents. There's a computer terminal by the door that you feed the stub number to, and it lights them in a path to the drawer. It's an experience that most civilians would like to forget. Because of the preservatives and suspensions we use, those lights make the dead look alive." He stopped and slapped a drawer at shoulder level. "Here she is. You ready?"

Payne looked at Myra. He could tell she wasn't, but she nodded for the go-ahead.

"Let's see her."

Louis dug his fingernails under the rim of the handle and pulled. The drawer slid straight out, cold smoke pouring from the opening.

Myra stepped back.

The girl was lying on her back, eyes wide open, naked except for the claim tag on her toe. Her skin was cast in gray, her lips had blued, and the skin under her nails was black. She was covered in gooseflesh, and her areolae had puckered and tightened, thrusting her nipples straight up.

Payne choked and swallowed.

"A waste," Louis said.

Myra closed her eyes and leaned against Payne.

"You going to be okay?" he asked.

"Let me catch my breath."

"It's chilly in here," Louis said sympathetically. "You're not really dressed for it."

"Yeah." Myra swallowed.

"The gray cast you see is Solari. It's a decay-retarding antibacterial suspension that works well with cold. Alamex would've kept her warm, but it's more expensive." He checked a plastic card mounted on the table. "We used Solari because the reporting officer rated you low on response probability."

Payne shook his head. "Should have figured," he said. "It's my own damned fault. Well, it shouldn't affect the outcome of tissue analysis, though some journals say that any suspension may alter the postdeath blood chemistry shifts."

Louis looked at Payne and blinked in astonishment. "Civilians don't talk like that. You're a bio boy."

Payne smiled. "I try to keep up."

"Which precinct are you with?"

"I'm not. I work for Biotech Industries."

"You in on the development of Alamex?" Louis clapped his hands again. "I feel like such an idiot."

"I'm in another division. Bioengineering."

"In that case, I can skip the list of options. You probably know them all. What'll you have, then?"

"A rundown of toxins in the bloodstream. Take a long look at the brain. There may have been a buildup of something that caused the death."

"What about a run of major organs?"

"That'll be fine, but don't waste too much time on them. There wasn't enough discoloration or deformity to implicate one, which is why I suspect the brain."

Louis grease-penciled notes on the plastic chart. "You going to want a slab shot?"

"Slab shot?"

"Sorry. That's what we call it. A photograph of the

victim in state. In case something comes over on a face or print run."

"Might as well."

"Anything else?"

"A cursory exam of the trachea to make sure it wasn't crushed or blocked. There wasn't any outward bruising to support the former and no signs of struggling for the latter, but it doesn't hurt to be on the safe side."

"Great." Louis slipped the grease pencil into his breast pocket. "And I thought today was going to be slow. This'll keep me busy for a couple of hours."

"You mean this'll be done today?"

"You bet. Sunday is our day of rest. That is, when we're caught up on what we're behind on. Most of the guys jack around on Sunday, but I prefer to stay busy. It helps that you know just what you're after. We get people in here who have no idea of what they want, so we have to keep going until we find a cause of death."

"Sounds like it should be easy."

"It's not. More often than not we have to run a victim profile because we don't know the circumstances of death. If you've got a distraught family to contend with, it can take a long time."

"So how long should I give you?"

"Try coming back around 1430. I should have things wrapped up by then. That'll give you a chance to clear your heads."

"Sounds excellent." They shook hands, and Louis marched them back through the cold maze.

As Payne and Myra stepped out the door, they heard Louis shout. Payne looked back to see him climbing onto a cart with front-end lifts. He steered into the maze as if leading a cavalry charge and shouted something about avenging the honor of the Great Sword.

"He's strange," Myra commented when they were out in the hall.

"He has to be. If you don't distract yourself, you start

to crack. Imagine having to cut into strangers every working day of your life."

"I can't."

"A lot of them can't, either. The average service time in Homicide Pathology is just under seven years."

"That can't be right. What about morticians?"

"A different line altogether. The same with standard pathology. Homicide Path is something in an unwanted league, and Louis is in it up to his elbows."

Myra shivered. "Did you have to put it that way?"

"That's how the point is made."

"And how do you know so much about the field?"

"I almost went into it."

Once out of the elevator, they followed the bright yellow until it brought them to heat and a different kind of light. The closer they got to the main lobby, the more alive things seemed.

Electronic chirping filled the lobby as they walked in. Payne looked to the main desk. A man was leaning against one corner, screaming and holding a blood-soaked rag against his head as streams of thick red ran down the side of his face and stained his jumpsuit. Two men in deep brown, summoned by the chirping, appeared from another door and grabbed him under the arms.

"Get him to med," the clerk shouted. The officers dragged him out another door.

Payne and Myra stood frozen as the chirping stopped and the man's screams subsided. Finally, Payne called across the lobby to ask if it was safe to go out.

"It is now," the clerk said. "It's all over for another couple of months. They just blew up the Emigration office down the street. It happens every now and then."

"Why don't they move into this building?" Myra asked.

The clerk smiled. "Because we won't let them."

Outside, they saw the smoke curling from a jumble of splintered wood and shattered rock at the other end of the block. Firemen milled around the site, washing it down and ducking falling debris.

"Another blow for renewal," Payne said.

"Too bad they couldn't have just blown the inside," Myra replied. "I'm more for renovation."

"You are? You're going to love where I work."

He was right. Already fascinated by the design of the urban area, she loved the lobby of the Biotech building. She spent the fifteen minutes required to get a visitor's clearance wandering around and examining the furnishings from the last century. After much discussion, he was able to pull her away. He took her through the decontamination room, past the main work room, and stopped at his work carrel.

"This is it," he said.

"This is what?"

"This is where I work."

She looked over the carrel. With the exception of a few papers scattered across the desk top, it was neatly organized. In a corner she noticed a brown jar marked with a skull and crossbones. From the mouth of the jar peeked the tips of pens and pencils. "This is it?"

He pulled a chair from the next carrel and invited her to sit. "Not entirely. There's lab space available for hands-on, storage facilities, and we can pretty much get what we need to work with provided we've got an idea worth pursuing."

Myra looked around. "A playground for the intellectual."

"Not so much the intellectual as the curious."

"Curious?"

"A Biotech catch phrase. Curiosity is what stimulates the imagination. Imagination is the key."

"You sound like a brochure."

Payne shrugged. "Can I help it if they have a point?"

"Curiosity," Myra said, "killed the cat."

Payne sat back in his chair and folded his arms. "Satisfaction brought him back."

She gave him a smile that he had never seen before: It was warm and sincere. She was interested in what was going on. "Isn't it dangerous working with all of these mutations? Doesn't it worry you?"

He shook his head. "What we work with are lab-safe until we can determine whether or not they're totally benevolent. If a bug got loose and started making for the door, it would die before it got through the downstairs lobby. They can't live outside of a sterile environment."

"How do you fix it so they can?"

"Genetic engineering."

"I see. So what do you do here?"

"Play."

"Seriously, Payne."

"I am serious. Right now I'm on break from playing. I'm supervising others who are playing. By virtue of past work, I'm allowed to help out the newer personnel."

"You're losing me."

"I'm the man with all of the important toys."

"Okay. Do you have any big projects now?"

"Not now." He stopped and thought about Lol Winthrop. "I take that back. I am helping with one that might be very big. Would you like to see it?"

"Sure."

He turned on his terminal and keyed into a program. "Remember the guy who interrupted us last night?"

"Barely. I was pretty upset."

"This is his."

The terminal screen flickered cool green. Letters at the top winked MAIL WAITING. "That'll be from him." He keyed in RETRIEVE MAIL DAP E-6.

The screen went dark, then filled with green letters.

DEAR PAYNE,

MY LUCK HAS TURNED. BY THE TIME YOU READ THIS I WILL BE ON MY WAY TO AUSTRALIA. THROUGH NEFARIOUS MEANS I HAVE OBTAINED TICKET AND LETTER OF TRANSIT. BY THE TIME YOU READ THIS I SHALL BE ON MY WAY TO A MORE DESERVED WAY OF LIFE.

"So that's what the big secret was," Myra said. "You're really in the export business."

"Winthrop's the exception."

ON TO THE CULTURES. NOT ONE TO CAST MY WORK ASIDE, I AM LEAVING YOU THE LEGACY OF WINTHROP CULTURE # 11. I TRUST YOU AS MUCH AS ANYONE ELSE HERE, AND KNOW THAT YOU WILL SEE THE PROJECT THROUGH TO FRUITION.

THAT BRINGS ME TO THE NEXT BIT OF GOOD NEWS. I WAS ALBE TO LOCATE ENOUGH ORGANISMS TO START THE CULTURES OVER AGAIN. THE FIRST CAME FROM THE BOTTOM OF THE JUG THAT KELCE HAD HIS FUN WITH. SO YOU WON'T HAVE TO GO THROUGH THE ORDEAL THAT I DID WITH THE P.V.'S, I STARTED A CULTURE FROM TISSUE SAMPLES TAKEN OUT OF OUR FRIEND IN THE VIDEOS. I HAVEN'T CHECKED AT THIS WRITING, BUT I SUSPECT THAT YOU'LL FIND AN INDEPENDENT MUTATION IN THE WORKS.

"What's a P.V.?"

"Prison Volunteer."

"You do that here?" She grew quiet.

SPEAKING OF OUR FRIEND IN ORANGE, IT LOOKS LIKE YOU WERE RIGHT AGAIN. I HAD HIS HEAD OPENED AND SCANNED THE SAMPLES. GUESS WHAT? TINY BITS OF CHOLESTEROL WERE BREAKING OFF AND LODGING IN THE BLOOD VESSELS IN HIS BRAIN, CAUSING A SERIES OF MINOR STROKES. PAYNE HITS THE NAIL ON THE HEAD. I GOT SUSPICIOUS AND WENT BACK TO CHECK THE REPORTS. I FOUND HE HAD BEEN COMPLAINING OF NUMBNESS IN THE EXTREMITIES—FINGERS, TOES, ETC. GUESS THE BITS WERE BLOCKING CAPILLARIES AND THE TISSUES WERE DYING. COME TO THINK OF IT, OUR HEADBANGER WAS COMPLAINING OF SHORTNESS OF BREATH. LOOKS LIKE YOU PEGGED IT.

Myra covered her mouth and shuddered. "Opened his head?"

Payne nodded.

"What for?"

"He was dying."

"You killed him? You killed him so your friend could check for bugs?"

"We euthanized him," Payne said. "It was necessary. Winthrop's strain was malevolent."

"What made Winthrop's strain necessary?"

"Life and health."

"What about *their* life and health?"

He looked Myra straight in the eyes. He tagged ESCAPE, and the writing cleared from the screen. She had seen more than enough. She would never go for the details of the others in the test. "They all knew what they were getting into. They were volunteers." He turned away and keyed into a new program.

DISCIPLINARY ACTION REQUEST.

"I'm sorry. We didn't come here to fight."

Payne shrugged it off. "It's the way that some people feel. You can't make everyone happy."

REQUESTING ACTION AGAINST:

Payne typed. KELCE, DEREK BARTHOLOMEW. E-6.

"What are you doing now?"

"Getting ready to hang somebody."

GIVE REASON(S) FOR REQUEST:

1) VIOLATION OF PRIVACY RULE.

2) MISUSE OF AUTHORITY.

3) BREACH OF STERILE AREA WITH MALEVOLENT CULTURE.

"What did this guy do?"

"Caused us a great deal of trouble."

"Anything serious?"

"Could have been." He abruptly stopped entering information and stared blankly at the screen, tapping his finger on the desk top.

"Something wrong?"

"They want a date for the hearing."

"What's wrong with that?"

"There's a conflict. The Thirty-first Amendment."

"I'm sorry."

"That's okay. You didn't know. Under the circumstances, I think this is the least important of the two. We were able to reverse most of the damage, so there's only been a minor setback. Besides, Winthrop's out of the country by now."

"Could it have been bad?"

"It could have been very bad. Kelce could lose his job if I press the issue."

"You're not?"

He hit ESCAPE. "Not right now. There are other things that need to be done." Payne typed REQUEST FOR LEAVE OF ABSENCE. He looked at Myra, who managed a smile.

She watched silently as he typed responses to the computer's questions. She thought it would be simple enough: One pleads the Thirty-first, shows one's stub to the boss, then walks out the door. Such was not the case. When Payne typed that he was exercising his constitutional rights, the computer stopped to think about it, then gave him form after form to fill out.

At long last he finished. He rubbed his eyes and stretched.

"I didn't realize there was so much you had to go through," Myra said.

"I'm afraid this hasn't been very exciting for you."

"Things go wrong."

"I've got to take a look at Winthrop's cultures to see how they're doing. If you're interested, I'll show them to you, politics aside."

"How long will it take?"

Payne thought. "About as long as getting a Leave of Absence."

She glared.

"I never said things would be fun."

Myra smiled. "Who says they have to be dull?"

"Unless you're really into biology, microscans are rather boring."

Myra was out of her chair and moving toward him. "Who said anything about microscans?"

"That's what I'll be using to check Winthrop's culture."

She wrapped her arms around his neck and straddled his lap. "We were discussing how to prevent boredom. I've got something that could be very, very exciting." She kissed him deeply.

Payne tried to push her away. "Not here. It's a sterile area."

"Relax." She tugged at the zipper of his oversuit. "We've both got Bills of Health, don't we?"

"That's not the point . . ."

It was useless to fight. She was all over him like a vampiric animal. He tried to push her away, to reason with her. There would be plenty of time later. He gave one great shove, and she started to fall. She snaked her arms out and grabbed him. Smiling coyly, she pulled.

They tumbled to the floor.

Sunday Night

*I*t was 1500 when they returned to the Warax Substation, and Payne was feeling fairly content. He felt he was doing the right thing by taking the Thirty-first, and he was certain that things would fall into place in a matter of hours.

The visit with Louis changed all of that.

The desk clerk directed them to a room that was done in gentle shades of green rather than the harsh yellow that permeated the halls of Homicide. It wasn't long before Louis stepped in, clad in a fresh smock. He smiled and shook their hands. "Mr. Payne," he said.

"How did it go?"

He looked at them. "Sit down. Please."

They did, and Louis took his place behind the desk.

"Why is it that I don't like the way things sound?" Payne asked.

Louis folded his hands and stared down at the thick file he had carried in. "What you have here," he said, "is an interesting pathology."

"I don't like the sound of that."

Louis nodded. "I hate to say it, but we've been running across more than our share of this lately. Nothing alarming

yet, but it could get that way. I've been trying to find a
pattern so I can figure out what in hell is going on."

"The cause of death?"

"I don't know."

"You've got multiple cases, and you don't know what's
causing them?"

"It's a hell of a note. I have the sick feeling that I'm
getting in on the ground floor of something bad."

"What does it look like?"

Louis pulled papers from the file and spread them out
for Payne. "I couldn't find a damn thing wrong with her.
Her airway was clear, and there was no unusual buildup
of toxins."

"So what made the death interesting?"

"Ah, yes. The features." He shuffled the papers. "Your
friend had a great hunger for liver. Her stomach was full
of it. Almost burst when I cut into it. There was even
more in the intestine. I traced it through until it became
indistinguishable. What was undigested came to nearly
two and a half kilos."

"Two and a half kilos?"

"The last few meals, I'd say. There were some liquids
present, mostly alcohols. She had a noticeable blood alcohol level but nothing of significance. She'd devoted the
last few days of her life to the consumption of liver."

"Don't tell me she was anemic."

"On the contrary, blood iron levels were above normal."

"Was she starving?"

"She didn't die of hunger, I'll put it that way. She
wasn't eating enough of the right things."

"Malnutrition?"

"Not at the time of death. Liver is mostly protein, but
there are fats and sugars enough to keep you going for
quite a while. Her diet didn't kill her, but it may have
been a contributing factor." He tapped a graph. "You'll
notice that everything in her blood is nearly depleted.

Blood sugars, fats, acids, and especially blood-soluble oxygen."

Payne looked over the graph. "These levels remind me of something. The first thing in the morning, when the body is running out of everything. Time for breakfast."

"You ready for the real killer? Check the protein level."

Payne ran his finger across the chart. The bar wasn't where it should have been. He dropped his finger to the bottom of the page. "There's nothing left. No wonder she binged on liver."

"Something was taking it right out of her. Some of the protein chains in her cellular structure were starting to break down as well. I had to dig to find it, but once I knew what to look for, I found signs of it all over. Most of it was in her own liver, but it was also evident in the brain and bone marrow. It's lucky she died when she did. It could have been very unpleasant."

"What could have happened?" Myra asked.

Louis looked at her. "She would have disintegrated from the inside out."

She bit a knuckle.

"That's what *would* have killed her. Toxins would have built up in her body as the major organs shut down. Her adrenal glands had already collapsed. That's not what killed her, and I don't have a clue as to what did."

Payne drummed the tabletop. "Let's take what we've got and work it. Is there anything that would have caused the condition you found?"

"Yes and no. There are toxins that break down protein chains, but none of them have the pathology found in her body."

"Something outside? Radiation? Unusually strong magnetic fields or electrical currents?"

"You're thinking job hazard?"

"Exactly."

"I ran her pathology through the computer and drew a blank. The closest thing I could find was electrolytic toxemia, but that leaves a mark, a buildup of salts in the blood. Whatever this is, it's damn unique."

Payne cursed and slapped the desk. "Did your computer identify her?"

Louis shook his head. "I'm not much use to you today. Nothing all the way around. I went five years back in missing files. Facial, retinal, and fingerprints all zeroed out."

"So we're back to square one."

"I'm afraid so."

The three of them stared at the papers on the desk. Payne found a pencil and tapped it. His job wasn't going to get any easier. The government employees had given him a fileful of papers that added up to nothing. He had a body with no apparent cause of death and nothing to work with but a handful of symptoms. At best he would end up on a street corner with the other desperate cases, waving a laminated photograph of the girl at passersby.

"Did you make a slab shot?"

"Yeah. Made a couple of copies." Louis handed him a portfolio with a series of large stills inside. The girl looked surprisingly alive, although her stare was somewhat glassy.

"Looks good."

"That's the lighting. Our photographer really knows how to warm them up." He flipped over to the last page. "There's a list of vital statistics: height, weight, etc. She didn't have any distinguishing scars, marks, or tattoos. You lucked out again."

Payne leafed through the photographs and then stopped suddenly.

"What's wrong?" Myra asked.

"Symptoms," Payne said.

"Pathology," Louis corrected.

"No," Payne insisted. "Symptoms."

"Only if she was alive."

"Perhaps that's the mistake we've been making."

"Are you saying that a disease could have caused this?" Louis asked.

"It's a possibility. After all, we were blaming some pretty strange things before."

"I've never heard of an organism that would do a thing like that."

"Neither have I," Payne said. "But that doesn't mean that one can't exist."

"You're looking at one hell of a lot of work. I'm not sure I can swing it."

"You don't have to. I've got the best lab in the city at my disposal."

"You're going to try and culture it?"

"Why not? The solution may be as simple as getting some sample organisms for an Identiscan."

"If it was an organism, what makes you think it'll be there now?"

"I've got to try it, anyway. It's all I've got to go on."

Louis nodded sympathetically. "I'd be doing the same thing if I was in your position. What are you going to need?"

"A lot. I've got plenty of ground to cover." He looked at Myra. "Looks like I'll be buying you dinner, too."

"Back to the lab," she said.

"How much blood?" Louis asked.

"About a liter. Tissue samples, too."

"Liver, bone marrow, brain," Louis recited as he wrote. "How badly did you dice the brain?"

"Not too. We took core samples from key areas to determine toxin buildup. I also took a few scrapings when I noticed the protein breakdown. For the most part it's still in one piece."

"I'd like it sent to the Biotech building tomorrow morning. I'll need the blood as soon as possible."

Louis jotted notes on a pad. "I can get it for you right now. It'll be later today for the tissues."

"As long as I can get moving on this," Payne said.

Louis had him sign a series of forms, then disappeared.

"I think I see your point," Myra said.

"About what?"

"About losing your mind to Homicide Pathology. If you haven't noticed, Mr. Louis is using your shoulder to cry on."

"I disagree. He's showing nothing but professional enthusiasm."

"Professional enthusiasm?"

"Certainly. For example, you said you'd done some modeling?"

Myra looked at the floor. "I didn't think you'd caught that."

"What do you do when you get together with other models?"

"Bitch."

"About what?"

"The stupid stuff we have to wear and the poses the faggot photographers bend us into. How we're all probably getting cancer from the lasers."

"Do you have a good time bitching?"

"I have a great time."

"Why do you suppose that is?"

She smiled. "Do you always answer questions that way?"

"I try to."

In another ten minutes Louis reappeared, a small Styrofoam ice chest dangling from one hand. It bumped his leg, and the foam squeaked, setting Myra's teeth on edge.

"Here it is," he said, setting it on the desk top. He flipped up the lid, and cold steam boiled out. "I took the precaution of packing it in dry ice. I haven't seen the weather in thirteen hours, so I'm not sure what you're up against."

"This'll be fine."

"Be sure and let the samples warm a little. The Solari will keep them from freezing up, but you might get some clotting if the temperature changes are too rapid."

"You shouldn't have gone to all the trouble. As soon

as I get to the lab, I'm going to throw in some Alamex to get things stopped."

Louis peeled a thin pair of gloves from his hands. He went to toss them in the wastebasket but noticed they were bloody and shoved them into his pocket instead. Seeing that Myra was staring, he said, "There's a proper place for everything. Including used gloves."

"I wasn't noticing that."

Louis checked his fingertips. For the first time Payne noticed the purplish nails.

"Oh. That." Louis peeled the color from one nail. "It's paraffin." He seemed almost embarrassed. "I've got candles that I melt over them before doing any cutting. I'm a nail-biter, and the wax keeps the blood and viscera out from under them."

"Don't the gloves keep your hands clean?" Myra asked.

"No," he said decisively. "No. No matter how careful you are, the feeling always seeps through to your skin. After a bad day you can take your gloves off and scrub with whatever you want for as long as you can stand it, and you never feel as though you've gotten it off."

"We do what we have to do," Payne said, glaring at Myra. "Not all of it is pleasant."

"There's a lot that isn't," Louis amended.

"Sorry," Myra said. Payne took the ice chest and thanked Louis for his help. Louis said to think nothing of it, that it was a pleasure to work with someone from Biotech.

"If I find a new strain," Payne said, "I'll credit it to you."

"Nonsense. You were the victim."

"Tell you what. You discover something and we'll share the credit."

"Agreed. Good luck, Payne."

Once they were down the hall, Myra asked, "Were you serious about giving him credit for the discovery?"

"If this is something new, yes."

"What for?"

"If he gets his name in the journals, it'll be enough to get him out of here."

"Do you realize what you're doing? You're giving up notoriety. You're willing to toss it off to help out someone that you don't know."

"I don't think you see the whole situation."

"I think I do. You're giving up the benefits that notice would bring."

"Would you stop acting like it's the Kane fortune? You forget where I work. I have my name on three new strains of bacteria. I share credits on five more, six if Lol Winthrop has his way. Two of those are shared with more than one other person. There's nothing to this so-called notoriety. It's another line on my résumé, but it could be enough to get Louis out of Homicide Path."

"I suppose you're staking him out for Biotech."

"Does everything I do have to have an ulterior motive? If he applied at Biotech, I'd pull for him, but he'd have to be qualified."

"I can't see giving credit to a complete stranger."

"If you were walking down the street and saw someone about to step in front of an ElectriCart, you'd do something to help, wouldn't you?"

"Yes, but..."

"Same principle. This guy is going under for the third time, and I've got something that might float him. I've got a moral obligation."

"But Payne, he's a total stranger."

Payne glared at her. "And by contrast, I've known you all of my life?"

She snapped her jaw shut. He had taken it too far, but this time he felt justified. Unlike her objections to the P.V. program, this wasn't a legitimate argument. It was greed.

Myra quickened her pace as they walked. By the time he reached the end of the block, she was across the street. By the time he reached the Biotech building, she was a full block away. He stepped up to the door and stared as she walked away, her image becoming fluid as the midday heat rose from the concrete walks.

He pulled at the door and strolled to the front desk, setting the chest on the counter top and ringing the bell. A short girl with close-cropped black hair and a huge smile emerged from the back office.

"Hello, Payne."

"Hello, Billie. I've got some blood that I need shuttled up to the lab area for culturing. Can you arrange it?"

"What level are you working on?"

"They've got me on two right now, but my heart's on five. I'll take it up there."

"Fine."

"Thanks, Billie."

He took the stairs with a quick stride and thought about Myra while he went through decontamination. He tried to get something profound out of what had happened with her but could come up with nothing. He tried to explain to himself what had happened, but the reasons weren't there. All he knew was that it was all over. Myra had walked into the horizon while he stood and watched.

The elevator door opened and pulled him out of his trance. He blinked at the corridor and then started to walk, stopping when he came to an office marked "Central Processing." As he entered the office, his mouth fell open in surprise."

"Trinina!"

Her dark hair was neatly rolled up and pinned to the back of her head, and she was peeling rubber gloves from her hands. He half-expected to see wax covering her nails.

She saw his face and looked alarmed. "What happened to you?"

His hand moved to the scrape. "This? I fell down some stairs. What are you doing here?"

She wadded the gloves and stuffed them into a disposal chute. "There was a malfunction in my freezer section, and I came up to check the cultures. It turned out to be a glitch in the readout."

"Relieved?"

"To say the least. What brings you up here?"

"I'm having some tissue samples brought in from outside. Have you seen them?"

"No. Errol needed to step out, so I said I'd watch things while he was gone."

"Who's Errol?"

"He's new. They moved him from—" She stopped and scowled playfully. "You know who Errol is."

"Do I?"

"Of course you do." She looked him in the eye. "That's not what you're asking."

He feigned ignorance. "I don't know what you're talking about."

"You're trying to see if Errol's special to me."

"Would I do something like that?"

"What do you think?"

He grinned. "I think I want to know who Errol is."

She turned her nose up. "He's very special to me."

"How so?"

He had read her, and she knew it. "I see him every bit of once a month—he brings in the leaves and grass clippings for my P.V.'s."

"You should be tied and beaten," he said with mock sternness.

Trinina gasped and went red. "Watch your mouth."

Payne lost his breath. "I'm sorry." He could see a smile forming on her face. She was trying to hold it back. "I take that back," he said decisively. "I'm not sorry at all."

The smile surfaced. "I'm not sorry, either. I haven't heard that in a long time."

"A long time?"

"Not since—" Her eyes broke their hold on him. "Not since I left."

"I haven't said that in a long time," he answered. "Not since."

She looked back at him, eyes moist. "Payne . . ."

"I need to retrieve my tissue samples," he said quickly.

"I've got a lot of work to do." He turned to the receiving area, and she called his name again.

"Yes?"

"About Nathan."

"What about Nathan?"

Her eyes were blinking. "His—" She cleared her throat. "His sixth-year initials are over, and he's allowed a maternal visit. As of tomorrow I'll have him for a few days. I was thinking that you might want to . . . to . . ."

"I'd love to." He smiled. "What night do you want me?"

She blinked again, and tears spilled down her cheeks. "Doesn't matter."

"Tomorrow."

She wiped her eyes. "I'm glad. I so wanted you to come. I wanted him to meet his—his—"

"Father," Payne finished. He pulled her in and hugged her. "I want to meet my son."

Trinina sobbed. He held her until she stopped.

"I've got to go now," he said softly. "I've got important work to do."

She loosened her grip and backed away, nodding.

"You going to retrieve my samples?"

She bit her lip and shook her head.

"That's okay. I've got clearance to get them myself. You leaving?"

"Yes."

"Errol may never forgive you."

She gave a weak smile. "Who's Errol?"

"I'll cover for you."

Trinina gave a final nod and slid out the door. A lump formed in his throat as he watched her leave, as he remembered the first time she had left, after Mother America had taken their infant son. It would be nice to see Nathan again. Very nice.

He slipped behind Errol's desk and powered up the keyboard that fed the dumbwaiter. He stabbed at keys until he got a cursor, then again until he got a prompt.

STATE REQUEST.

REQUEST RECEIVING CLEARANCE FOR EXTERNAL SAM-PLES.

SAMPLE TYPE?

HUMAN TISSUE—BLOOD.

REASON FOR INDUCTION?

RESEARCH.T/CRIMPATH.CODEEU/31.

STATE CLEARANCE.

PAYNE,D.A./E6.

NAME RECEIVING/PROCESSING AGENT?

STAINTON-MEYERS, BILLIE/D9.

The screen blinked off, relit full of random characters, then went blank again as if lost in deep thought. When Payne's patience began to fray, letters returned.

CONFIRM   TISSUE   SAMPLES.MEYERS-PAYNE.(E6). HUMANHEMO.BTY/B+.XMTCH CODE/QMEQ101*BBB+BBA +998991*BAL00701*RXS*.RSCODE/AM31.

Payne sat back and sighed. The hard part was just beginning.

SECURITYCLASS/HERMETICALLYSEALED.QXS8-14.

It was talking to Billie now, getting her side of the story. Billie answered.

CONFIRMATION HERMETIC SEAL.STAINTON-MEYERS, BIL-LIE.D9.

ACCEPTED.LABSPACE CLEARANCE?

PVT LABSPACE/PAYNE,D.A./NEG(-)PRESSURESEAL.

He nodded. He would have to take a private working booth and seal himself in while working. His girl might have a nasty trait that could be passed on to the other bugs in the lab.

The screen blinked at him. His turn again.

PAYNE CONFIRM LABSPACE CONDITIONS, it asked.

PDAE6.PVT. (-)PS, he acknowledged.

CLEARANCE CONFIRMED CLEARANCE GRANTED.

Payne turned to the dumbwaiter. A row of amber lights went green, followed by a steady hum from below. Red LEDs advised STANDBY. He drummed his fingers. Hissing was followed by a sharp click. The seal on the dumbwaiter popped. READY, said the lights. He pulled the door open, revealing a row of clear plastic bags filled to plumpness with dark red fluid. He gathered them into his arms, counting off ten. Billie had a penchant for dividing things symmetrically. Ten was a good number, the best of numbers, she said. It was a nice, neat job. She had even sealed the package of photographs and charts from Louis.

He located a carryall and placed everything inside, checking his watch and hoping that Errol wouldn't be much longer. He couldn't leave the station unattended, but he needed to get moving before any further changes occurred in the blood, with or without Solari.

In five minutes he was on the verge of panic. As it took hold, Trinina reappeared, her face clear of the earlier sadness.

"Did I give you enough time? Errol isn't going to be back for a while."

"Now you tell me. I was starting to worry."

"Sorry. I'd forgotten how fast you work."

He looked her over. She was in good health. She still had the spark that had drawn him to her. He clutched the carryall. "I'd like to stay . . ."

"Get out of here." She smiled. "Your tissues are going to spoil."

"As long as you understand."

"Tomorrow," she reminded him as he left.

He gave her a thumbs-up and crossed to the back of the building, where he checked a wall-length chart of available lab spaces. Most of the larger ones were silhouetted in red, indicating their occupation. This was of no consequence to him. All he needed was a small cubicle where he could sort the samples into groups and use them to inoculate a variety of environments, one of which might produce an organism that could be blamed for the girl's death. He found what he was looking for in a far corner: little more than a wall closet with seating for one and room for another to stand. The smallest cubicle in the building, it was stocked with a bare minimum of equipment, including three Variset incubators. Payne laid the samples on the workbench and used his thumbprint to seal himself in. His ears popped as the pressure dropped. The safety indicator lit. He pulled his hood off, kicked off his plastic slippers and street shoes, sat down at the chair, and propped his feet up on the desk.

And cursed. "Where to begin."

He drummed his fingers, then picked up a clipboard and scratched with the pen until the ink was flowing. Discarding the scribbled sheet by wadding it up and tossing it over his shoulder, he wrote on the next page.

PROTEIN.

He looked at the word. It sat on the page, alone and not saying anything. Its silence mocked him. He wrote the word again so the first wouldn't be lonely. It did nothing for him. He wrote it a third time, then a fourth and a fifth. He stopped when he had covered the page. He tore out the sheet, and it joined its crumpled companion.

PROTEIN.

He wrote it on a third page, heavily underlining it. Below that he sketched a protein chain, molecule to molecule, hydrogen, oxygen, carbon, nitrogen. He started off with a small peptide and gradually expanded it into a monster that covered the page. He stopped again, this time imagining it escaping from its test tube and devouring half of the city until consumed by some errant but equally monstrous enzyme. Then he tossed the sheet.

Now he felt ready. His mind had played enough. He sat at the keyboard and began typing out a list of things that needed to be sent up: more dishes and beakers and stirring rods and inoculation loops and expansion racks for the incubators. He needed a whole series of suspensions—from whole blood in kelp to a complex medium that could be altered to fit almost any purpose. He ordered quantities of high-protein materials.

He pecked at the keyboard until the joints in his fingers ached, and Billie cheerfully acknowledged it all. By the fifth page, the dumbwaiter was humming regularly, giving him an excuse to stand up and stretch. The best thing about working on Sunday was that he could get all the equipment he needed in a short amount of time. The lobby staff, a skeleton crew on weekends, was invariably bored, and Payne's orders gave them something to do without being the burden that his requests might have been on a weekday.

In half an hour he had the desk and floor of the lab space so cluttered that when he rolled back in his chair, it crushed several petri dishes. He mopped up the glass with a wet paper towel and started on his work.

He bent over the beakers, stirring liquids and powders together until they began to congeal. He measured out amounts and coated the dishes with a precise and deliberate method perfected while he was still in school. One by one, he removed the bags of blood from the cooling unit below the desk, propped them in a beaker, and slashed out the bottom with a scalpel. The first sack was the last of the samples that Billie would have prepared. The fluid inside trickled out in spite of the cut Payne had made. He squeezed the top, and something gave. Blood plopped into the beaker, flowing like curdled molasses. He bit his lip and poured the thickening mass down the steri-sink, cursing his lack of enthusiasm with Delgado on Friday night. The difference between the Solari and the Alamex might make all the difference in the world over the next few days.

The next sample was better. It flowed smoothly into the beaker, as did the remainder of the bags. After the last bag was done, he checked the time. 1600. He rose from his chair and unplugged the clock, a trick he had learned at the university. Setting up for a lab run could be tedious and tiresome, more so if you were looking a timepiece in the face. Now he was free to work, his only worry the gnawing that had started in his stomach. In a while he would have Billie send up a CitruSlush. There was too much to do now.

The lots of blood were divided into four groups and treated accordingly. The first was left alone. The second was treated with Solari neutralizer. Solari neutralizer *and* Alamex were added to the third. The fourth was treated only with Alamex. Samples from each lot were inoculated or smeared into the various environments that he had prepared. There were three of each environment, and these were divided and placed into the three incubators, the temperatures set at 34.0°, 37.0°. and 40.0° Centigrade. He sealed the incubator doors.

Then he laid his head down on the desk and closed his eyes, forcing them open when he began to tip over the edge into sleep. There was still much to do.

He sent down for a cold drink, then poured a small amount of each of the four lots in a thin film across the bottom of its own clean petri dish. One by one he placed them under the laser light of a Microscan and squinted into the stereo eyepieces. He didn't know what his search would bring. This was a last effort, a cast out in hopes that the line would bring something back in.

He saw nothing out of the ordinary. The first lot he studied was the one treated with both Solari neutralizer and Alamex. There was nothing that wouldn't have appeared in a grade-school biology textbook: blood platelets, white cells, occasional tissue fragments, and parasite bacteria. He removed the plate and placed it in the rinse. Next went the fourth lot—Solari intact with Alamex. It went down the sink after revealing nothing more than what he had already seen, save for the Solari chemical crystals glittering back at him like microscopic jewels.

He drank two cans of slush as he scanned the straight sample, more interested now in the fortifying qualities of the drink than in what was under the scope. Then he dumped the last lot and replaced it with number two— Solari neutralized—pausing to type in a request for another can of slush. Two dots of white light stabbed his tired eyes. He backed off, retrieved the third can of cold slush from the dumbwaiter, and sat back, guzzling the frosty liquid.

He looked again. He exposed his eyes for another five minutes, then clicked the visual scanning head onto hold. This tack wasn't giving him anything at all; the image was the same under the needle-thin lance of light. These were the platelets, the tissue, the vigilant defenders, and the diamond Solari crystals.

He stopped.

This sample had been neutralized, or so he thought.

He peered back through the lenses. Solari prisms winked back.

Payne cursed. The lot beaker held the heavy petrol smell of the Solari process. He poured another dish and switched it with the current sample. He glanced in at a fuzzy image. No problem. Fine-tune the head.

He backed away from the eyepieces. "You stupid son of a bitch."

He had been forgetting to fine-tune the heads. Their adjustment was sensitive, and they had to be reset with each sample because of variations in their thickness. He thumbed the remote in his hand, and the optics began to shift, slowly clearing the picture.

He gasped, and his stomach tightened into a hard knot. The blood left his head, and he could feel his heart pounding in his throat.

What he was seeing wasn't a Solari crystal, at least no Solari crystal that he had ever seen before. The sharp focus melted away the edges of the prism to reveal a stretched egg shape among the tissues—a stretched egg shape with sharp spines that radiated out at every angle. It reminded him of a weapon he had seen in Bailey's British comedy, a spiked metal sphere mounted on a wooden handle. Bailey had called it a morning star.

Payne fought to breathe and gulped down the rest of the warming drink. Jaw trembling, he looked a third time.

There it was—the fierce head of Bailey's morning star, ready to puncture anything that came near.

His hand reached out for the remote and knocked it on the floor. He fumbled it back to his lap and reduced magnification.

There were dozens of them. As the theater broadened, he could see them, sitting quietly like mines in a harbor, patiently waiting to be challenged.

He tapped on the handset. An amber light advised RETRIEVE READY. Back in the scope the inoculating loop appeared. Forefinger and thumb to a small knob, he guided it to an area where five of them were grouped in a guarded cluster. His thumb clicked another button.

RETRIEVE.

The loop fell into the film, and there was a hiss. Smoke curled up from the plate. The five had been captured with a small amount of blood, held in the loop by surface tension.

He grabbed one of the remaining environments and shoved it into the Microscan's secondary theater. He clicked his remote until he got the desired results: INOC-ULATE READY. Another button switched the view to a clean, organism-free plate of medium. The loop fell to the surface, meticulously pushing halfway into the suspension.

TRACE. Payne ordered.

Cross hairs appeared in his sights. He marked off areas north, south, east, and west of the inoculation sight.

DROP TRACE.

The Microscan hummed and, in the locations marked, dropped microscopic silicon chips.

And so he continued, making several inoculations into each environment, marking them out for future reference. Soon the Microscan ran out of the silicon slivers, and he sent down for more. They came up with a note from Billie: *When are you coming out of there?* He sent one back with the three empty cans of CitruSlush: *Maybe never*. She replied with a fresh can: *On the house*.

When this last group was in the incubators, he rechecked the other lots of prepared blood. The strange shapes he had seen were present only in the samples free of Alamex.

He wrote in the notes he had been accumulating: *Possibly destroyed by Ala.?*

One more tour through his notes, a final check on the environments, and he was ready to leave. He leaned back in his chair and surveyed the lab space. It was littered with soiled beakers and stirring rods and blood-caked petri dishes. The lab bench was crowded with half-used bottles of suspensions, powders, and solutions. Glassware reflected back at him from every inch of cabinet space.

SECURE PREMISES, he typed.

Lights flickered on the storage areas, cooling cabinets, and incubators. He sealed the doors with his thumbprint.

OPEN DOOR.

A jet of air tossed his hair and his ears filled. The door opened slightly, and he crept out, sealing the lab behind him. On his way out, he stopped to check the lab space chart. There was his space, the small one in the back, now outlined in red. Payne rubbed his face and headed for the main elevator.

He was held at the lobby level an extra two minutes while the lights lining the elevator walls decontaminated him. Finally released, he emerged to receive a cheerful greeting from Billie.

"He's back from exile."

He rubbed his neck. "Don't tell me what time it is."

"2135. Do you realize how long you were in there?"

He looked at her in disgust. "I told you not to tell me."

"Five hours, forty-five minutes."

"You're acting like it's never been done before. Some spend days in a lab space."

"In a big lab space," Billie corrected. "Nobody using that little one lasts more than three hours."

"I don't want to hear about it." He pushed on the main door and let the cool night air bathe him. "See you tomorrow."

"Mr. Payne? Wait!" Billie was out from behind the counter, a scrap of paper in hand. "I almost forgot. This came while you were locked up."

He took the slip and moved out at a slow pace, reading as he went. It was a telephone message from Trinina. Struggling to decode Billie's scrawl, he came to the conclusion that Nathan had been released a day early and that he was more than welcome to come over, should the hour accommodate it. He smiled and put the message in his pocket.

2140? Not late, especially for Trinina, who always seemed to get by on a minimum of sleep. He checked the note again. The apartments she lived in were in the opposite direction from where he lived. It would be a long walk home, but he didn't mind. He didn't feel like returning to an empty apartment, and she just might put him up on the couch. He changed course, a fresh spring in his step.

He knocked lightly on her door at 2200.

"Who is it?" he heard her whisper.

"Payne," he whispered back.

There was a snap, and the door opened to reveal Trinina wrapped in a robe, her hair combed down below her shoulders.

"Sorry. Am I too late?"

"For Nathan, yes. Not for me." She stepped to the side and allowed him to enter.

"I didn't think he'd be awake."

"Then why did you come?"

"To see him asleep, I guess. I knew you'd be awake." He saw that the couch was folded into a bed and stopped. "Expecting me?"

She smiled and shook her head. "Not really. I gave up around 2100. Billie said you were busy."

Payne tossed his packet down on the bed and sat down in a nearby chair. "You said Errol didn't mean anything to you."

She stared him down. "He doesn't. This is a single-bedroom apartment. I put Nathan in my room so he wouldn't be disturbed by visitors."

"You *were* expecting Errol."

She sat on the edge of the bed. "I was expecting you."

"What made you think I'd show up?"

"You got my note."

"What if I hadn't?"

"Then I would have been asleep. Someone would have come in to replace Billie, someone less efficient who wouldn't have seen that it was delivered. If you had gotten it that late, you wouldn't have come over."

"Clever. Using Billie as a barometer."

"After you learn the way people think, you begin to use it to your advantage."

"Does that include me?"

"It especially includes you. For example, I know that you're impulsive and you like spontaneity. You like planning only when it's for a set purpose and only to achieve direct results. So I knew you'd come over if I left a note. It appeals to that part of you."

"I feel used."

Trinina fingered the information packet. "Hardly. I just thought you'd want to see Nathan."

"He's really here?"

"Of course. What did you think?"

"I'm not sure."

"Another thing about you," she said, rising. "You tend to jump to conclusions." She took him by the hand and led him into her bedroom, where a small figure was lying in the bed, curled into a tiny ball. "Surprised?"

"No." He looked at her. "That's one thing about you. You work in patterns. Once I catch the pattern, you can't fool me."

"Not even for an instant?"

"Perhaps for a small instant. A very small instant." She returned his stare. "You haven't changed."

"Neither have you."

They moved into an embrace and kissed, his mouth pulling at the softness of her lips. She was warm and firm and clung to him with a conviction he hadn't felt in years.

They ended the kiss, and she took his hand again. "Come meet our son."

He followed her to the side of her bed. Nathan was sound asleep, his arm tucked up under the pillow, the other held under his chin. He had the delicate slope of her nose and the shape of his head. The way his eyes closed and forehead knit was all him; the way his lips curled down in a nocturnal pout was hers. The curly body of the hair was hers, its dark color his. The boy had her high cheekbones, Payne's strong chin. The skin tone was a perfect blend of his ruddy peach and her smooth almond. Payne felt a lump in his throat. Nathan was a perfect carbon copy of them both.

"Look at the set of his jaw," he said. "He's going to be stubborn."

"He already is."

"Is that from your side of the gene pool?"

"I'm sure it's yours. You get determined looks like that."

Nathan stirred slightly and sighed.

"Better keep it down," Trinina said. "It was an ordeal getting him to bed." She stepped to the door and turned back. Payne was still looking at Nathan. She returned to his side. His arm crept around her waist, and her head came to light on his shoulder. Together, they stood vigil.

"He's beautiful," Payne said.

Slowly they moved out the door, holding desperately to each other.

Payne checked his watch. "It's late. I should go."

Trinina nodded.

He put his hand to the doorknob. They moved together, embraced, and held.

Trinina raised her head from his neck. "Thank you for Nathan," she said.

He pulled her closer. "Thank *you*."

And then they were all over each other, grasping and stroking and kissing and touching. Suddenly they were on the sleeper, their clothes having magically fallen away, and they were moving together as if they had never been apart.

Later, he reached out and covered them both with a sheet and held her close, her head resting under his chin. One of her hands was tucked under the pillow, and the other rested on his chest, just under her chin. He stroked the length of her back with his hand. She took in a large breath of air and sobbed. He wrapped his arm around her.

"I want to keep him."

He pulled her close.

"I want to keep him, Payne."

He squeezed his eyes shut. "So do I."

He held her, sheltered against the world, until they were both asleep.

When he opened his eyes again, it was dark and he was still holding her close. He slowly unwrapped from around her. As he did, she stirred and reached for him.

"Don't go."

"I don't want to go," he whispered, "but I think I should."

"Why?"

"I need to get an early start tomorrow."

She pulled him. "Start from here."

"My things are at home."

"Handi-Mart down the street."

He kissed her on the cheek. "I don't think it would be proper for Nathan to find us like this."

She pecked him back. "Have to change that."

"We will."

He slipped from bed and hastily pulled on his clothes, pocketing his watch so he wouldn't see the late hour. There was no reason for him to know how much sleep he would be losing.

Another kiss for Trinina, a final check on Nathan, and he was out the door, making sure it was secured. He found his way down the hall and out into the middle of the night, marveling at the number of stars that were out. A quick glance gave him the reason; the area was blacked out.

He inhaled. The air was fresh and sweet. It had rained,

and the clouds had rolled off in time for his departure. Night always made him feel good. He got his bearings and began to make for the Biotech building, a confusing swarm of thoughts buzzing his head.

He pushed against the concrete, the sound of his own footfalls his only company. The darkness sidled up next to him, got under his skin, and he became a part of it, skulking across the sidewalks in an attempt to keep sleep and the tides of thought away.

When he rounded the corner and the lights fell on his face, they frightened him back into an uncomfortable state of reality.

"Hey, mister," a penitent voice said. "I didn't mean to scare you."

Payne's first attempt at answering came out in a croak. He cleared his throat.

"You okay?"

"Fine." He stepped around the light and found the source to be the front beams of an ElectriCart, its magnetics and brushes softly humming.

"Helluva night to be out."

"It has its charm," Payne said.

"I'm sorry?"

"I said yeah. They must have lost a whole plant."

"I think so. The whole city seems to be out. What I've seen of it, at least."

"A burden they pass on to us."

The man laughed. He was leaning against his cart, puffing a cigarette and scratching at his beard. He thumbed over his shoulder to bright yellow lights that spelled TAXI. "Need a lift?"

Payne looked at the driver and then at the taxi. A weariness was settling in his bones, and he hadn't even made it as far as the Biotech building yet.

"You talked me into it," he said, and climbed into the back of the cart. The driver, babbling thank-yous and gratefuls as fast as he could spit them out, clambered into the driver's seat, revved the dynamos, and lurched out into the street.

The cart gently rocked, and Payne closed his eyes, which ached from the taxi's bright lights. He rolled down a window and dangled an arm into the moist air.

There was an abrupt jolt, and more light poked his eyes. He brought his hand in to make shade and was jolted again.

"Mister," the driver said. "Sorry to bother you, but we're there."

"Already?" Payne asked groggily.

"Not really. You've been asleep. Good thing I found you. You might have spent the night at the Curbside Hilton."

"Very good," Payne said. He fished out his Bancard and handed it to the driver. As he stretched out of the cart, the driver asked which floor he lived on.

"Number seven."

The driver groped under his seat and pulled out a tube, which he twisted between his hands. The interior of the cab was bathed in a sickly green light. He reached out the window and handed the glowing rod to Payne, along with the card.

"Complementary light," he said. "It'll give you about ten minutes. More than enough time unless you doze off on the way up."

"I won't." Payne laughed. He thanked the driver and watched the taxi pull away, then turned to the task of dragging himself up to the seventh floor.

It took far less time than anticipated. The strange, twisting shadows cast by the light stick motivated him to move quickly up the stairs.

At last he had the key in the lock. He gave a twist and pushed. The door held fast. A sick feeling came over him. This was how the door had behaved Friday after his shopping trip—the Friday of the discovery. He pulled the key out, examined it, and tried the lock again. This time the door gave. He held a deep breath and looked in.

Nothing. The living room was immaculate. He heaved in relief and secured the door. Each step he took left clothing on the floor.

He wandered into the bedroom, tossing the stick onto the bed, where it lit the room. A rustling sound caught his ear, and his eyes followed it. There was an odd lump in his bed, and it turned over and sat up, picking up the green glow and squinting at it through sleepy eyes.

It was Myra.

Monday Morning

*P*ayne was up before the alarm rang, lying in bed and listening to the ticking of his clock. He reached up and clicked the knob to spare himself the alarm, then rolled out of bed and wandered into the bathroom to stare in the mirror. Bagged and bloodshot eyes stared back. He was running on adrenaline.

He splashed cold water on his face half a dozen times, trying to wash away the worn appearance. He looked hard at himself, the water running off his features, then found a razor and began to scrape.

It wasn't until he noticed the smell of Myra on his robe that his mind began to sort things out. From the kitchen came the sound of running water and clanking glass. He followed the sound and found Myra at the sink washing dishes.

She stacked a plate and smiled at him. "Good morning."

"Morning." His voice was thick and foggy.

"The power hasn't been on long enough to heat the water. You should get Cold Cleanse. It's made to work in cold water."

"It's made by our competition."

She shrugged. "Just a thought."

Payne licked his lips. "You came back."

"It was too late to go all the way back to my place."

"You should have taken a taxi."

"Who can afford a taxi? Besides, I kind of like it here."

"I'll tell my landlord."

"You must have missed me," she taunted. "You didn't come home until late."

"I didn't come home," Payne growled, "because I spent the night up to my elbows in blood."

Myra swabbed a plate. "So how did it go?"

"You're so curious, you should have stayed around."

She stacked the dish and moved his way. "I know. I'm sorry about last night." She wrapped her arms around his neck and kissed him, her lips massaging his. He stood solid. Her hands fell from his shoulders, found the knotted cord of the robe, and began to undo it. He caught her hands and pushed her away.

"You're changing the subject," he said.

She backed off and pouted. "You got your apology, didn't you?"

"Maybe I wasn't looking for one." He shuffled into the kitchen and pulled the ice chest down.

"There's coffee on the Sterno."

Payne took a CitruSlush from the ice and opened it. He sipped and recoiled at the tartness. The next taste was easier and cleared his throat.

"What do you want from me?" he asked.

"What kind of question is that?"

"Why did you come back? What are you doing here?"

"I came back because I wanted to be with you. You weren't worth tossing off just because our views differ."

"Granted."

"Besides, you were the one who invited me here to begin with. What did you want with me?"

"I wanted a lot of things," Payne said, not missing a beat. "I wanted to see if you'd be warm when I woke up next to you. I wanted to find out what made you dance."

He paused. "You looked vulnerable. You looked like you needed to be taken care of. That appealed to me. I wanted to bring you home and take care of you." He took a long swallow from the can. "I have since discovered that you are more than capable of taking care of yourself."

Myra crossed her arms and thought about it. "Is that it?"

"You want more? You want it to rhyme? Are you looking for a sonnet?"

"That's not what I meant. Are you throwing me out?"

"That depends on how much cooperation I get from you."

"What's that supposed to mean?"

"You're manipulative," he said. "You've got to make sure that I'm always where you want me. Like having me explain this to you. You knew full well what I was talking about—you were just trying to force my hand, maybe get me backed into a corner so you could throw one of your little temper tantrums and get me back where you wanted. It's not going to work. I believe in an even relationship, which means that I'm going to have some control."

She frowned. Her eyes found the floor. Her hand crept to her neck and found the tab of her zipper. She caught it and pulled it down below her navel.

"Zip it up," he said, not looking at her.

She pulled it down the rest of the way.

Payne emptied the can and dropped it into the garbage. He stepped within arm's length of her, grabbed the zipper, and jerked it to her neck. "I said put it away."

"It was your idea. That's why you brought me here."

"That was one of the reasons, but you're using it as a reward, to change the subject, to make a point. For once let it be for mutual enjoyment."

"I was doing it for you," she protested. "I was doing it because I thought that's what you wanted."

"Yes. I did want sex, but I didn't want *just* sex. I wanted it with you—there's a difference. You don't do it because you're with a man and you think that men run

on sex. It's no good that way, and it won't always work
for you."

"You wanted sex with me?" Her eyes lifted to his. She
was blinking again. "You're different. You have a strange
attitude."

"I'm getting too old for clubbing."

"I didn't say it was bad."

"Neither did I."

They stood and stared. He waited for her to speak.
When he was sure that she had nothing to say, he pulled
the zipper down to her waist. She grinned and pulled it
back up, then turned to the sink.

He walked to the bathroom, where he lathered and
took a proper shave. Even before he soaped his face, he
thought he looked better than when he had awakened.
Then he had looked unresolved. Now he looked to be
more at peace. There were still questions to be dealt with,
but for the first time in days he felt as if he had accomplished something, and that there might actually be an
end to the confusion his life had become.

He washed the remnants of his beard down the sink
and splashed his face. He was starting to wear down,
something he couldn't afford. He needed to get moving,
to check on his samples, to show the slab shots around,
and to visit Trinina this evening.

His thoughts were instantly scrambled when he opened
the door to his closet. His clothes had been pushed to
one side to make room for more. Dangling from hangers
and taking up the right-hand side of the closet was an
assortment of Myra-sized jumpsuits. He ran a hand over
them and examined a few at random. Most of them had
been worn at least once. There were a couple of new
ones, but a quick check of the tags showed that only one
had been purchased yesterday. The others were several
months old. She *had* made it all the way home. All of this
surely hadn't been carried in the bag she had brought
from the Lancaster Club. He ground his teeth.

He would have been content to burn over this point,

but it brought up something else that needed to be answered. He pulled a gray suit from a hanger, slipped it on, and walked back to the kitchen.

"I have a question."

Myra was rinsing out the sink. "Why do I have this feeling of impending doom?"

"How did you get in here?"

"You invited me, remember?"

"I'm not talking about that. I'm talking about last night after we parted company. You got to your house and decided that it was too quiet, so you arranged for a little surprise."

"How'd you find out?"

He held up one of her jumpsuits. "It doesn't take a genius to figure some things out."

She shrugged. "I lied a little."

"It all goes back to manipulation," he said firmly, "but I believe we've already had that discussion. That part should be resolved. What I really want to know right now is how you got into this apartment."

"I opened the door and walked in."

"Don't get cute with me, Myra."

With a firm twist she shut the water off. "It's the truth."

"It's not all of it. Somebody had to open the door for you."

"I did."

"You know what I'm talking about. Somebody had to give access into this place. A landlord with a key or someone who can pick a lock without leaving scratches."

"What makes you so sure someone helped me?"

"Because I always lock up when I leave."

Her look showed fire in her eyes. "Well, maybe you didn't lock the door," she said through clenched teeth, "because you weren't the last person out of here."

The breath left his lungs, and his shoulders slumped. "The Pickup Squad."

"You've got it. When I left you, I came here to get what I'd brought over. I'd assumed that the door was locked, and like a fool I sat in the hallway and waited for you to come and let me in. After a while I figured that things weren't so bad and that I should give you another chance."

"You went home to pick up a few things."

"When I got back, I rattled the knob, and the door popped open. When I caught the funny smell of the fog, I realized what had happened."

Payne held his hand out. "Friends?"

"Friends."

They shook hands, slowly moving into a kissing embrace. Myra ran her finger down the seam of his zipper.

"Do you want to go to bed?"

He shook his head. "I'd only sleep. I've got too much work to do."

She pulled away into the kitchen. "Not until you've had breakfast."

"I've had breakfast."

"You call that frozen pulp a proper breakfast?" She wagged him out with a finger. "Go. I'll be done in five minutes."

Forty-five minutes later, he left the apartment after giving Myra a gratuitous peck on the cheek, her meal sitting heavily in his stomach.

At the sixth-floor landing he stopped and looked up the stairs, half expecting to catch her following. It was getting to be too much. He felt that he now had control over her but had lost control of himself. Perhaps he should talk to Bailey. His friend might seem single-mindedly libidinous, but there was an insightful side to him that could be tapped if one knew the incantation.

Bailey answered midway through the first volley of knocks. The sunlight had been blocked out of his apartment with thick blinds, the glow from the video system its only source of light.

"What brings you by?" Bailey asked, turning the sound off.

"Guess," Payne said. He flopped on the sofa and tossed his packet on Bailey's coffee table.

Bailey pointed his finger to the side of his nose. "Her."

Payne was shocked. "How did you know?"

"I stopped by yesterday and caught her cleaning your apartment. Ended up doing most of the work, too."

"I'm sorry," Payne said, embarrassed. "I should have warned you."

"No. I should have warned you."

Payne half smiled. "As I recall, you did. I didn't listen."

"It could have worked out for the best. Until yesterday, all I knew about her was hearsay. You know how talk goes around the clubs."

Payne nodded.

"What's she like?"

"I can't tell. She goes through moods like jumpsuits."

"She seemed okay yesterday. She did tell you that I dropped by?"

"Not a word."

"Don't worry. Nothing happened."

"I trust you, Bailey. Besides, if she's going to try and manipulate anyone, it's going to be me. And she's so damned good at it."

Bailey sighed. "No offense, Payne, but I guess I shouldn't have listened to all of those rumors."

"If you hadn't, you'd be upstairs talking to me right now."

"Payne, are you sure that you have things in their proper perspective?"

"What other perspective is there?"

Bailey grabbed the information packet. "Are you sure there's not something else on your mind? Something that's tainting the way you're seeing things?"

Payne looked at the plastic-wrapped papers, his mind falling back to the day before. He had put in a long day of work, but that certainly wasn't what had colored things. It was Trinina and Nathan, tucked into their respective beds, holding their pillows for lack of something that had

long since been taken away. He pointed at the packet.
"That's not it."

"You're telling me that you didn't put in a few extra
hours working with the blood samples from this girl? Myra
said you were."

"I did put in a few hours, and it probably is a contributing factor, but there's something else—or perhaps I
should say some*one* else."

Bailey nodded. "I didn't think it was the Thirty-first.
Not with the way you were talking on Friday."

"It's Trinina."

Bailey looked at him. "You've got a problem."

"Yes."

"What are you going to do?"

"I don't know yet. I'll probably have to wait and see
how things turn out."

"Will you dump Myra, then?"

"She may dump herself."

"You're thinking she'll find her own way out?"

"Yeah."

Bailey laughed. "With your luck, Myra will find her
way out about the time that Trinina tells you to drop dead.
What'll you do then?"

"Call you up and invite you to go club."

"I think you're going to come out of this, Payne. You've
got a good attitude."

"I have no doubt that I'll come out of it. It's the waiting
that kills me."

"Congratulations. You've come to terms with yourself."

Payne rose from the sofa. "Thanks for the help, Bailey.
Occasionally I need someone to show me the obvious,
and you've done an exemplary job."

Bailey held out the packet. "Don't forget this."

Payne stopped. "I wanted you to take a look at the
girl's picture. If you don't mind."

"No. Not at all." He drew back the plastic zipper.

"I doubt if you'll know her, but I've got to start some-where."

Bailey slid the thick photographs out of the sleeve. He held it out to the light of the video set and tilted it back and forth to get the three-dimensional effect.

"I don't know who she is," he said, still staring.

"That's what I thought. Thanks." He reached for the packet, but Bailey was still studying one picture.

"But I've seen her before."

"You have?"

Bailey nodded. "And the funny thing is, it's been under this same kind of light. The way the video is flickering set it off. I don't think I would have recognized her other-wise."

"Someone you brought home?"

"Not that familiar. This is a face in the crowd, one you get used to seeing again and again. Like Myra was to me, only Myra had gone to the next step. This girl is a face with nothing tied to it."

"You've seen her at a club, then."

"Probably. I don't know where else it could have been."

"The one on Lancaster? Flesh and Blood?"

"Definitely not Flesh and Blood. They don't have the right lighting there, and the blacks are the only ones that go out to dance and proposition. The rest of us go there to watch and make do."

"So you may have seen her at the Lancaster?"

"There, or Eve's Apple. Or ImoGenes. There's a pos-sibility it may have been Dresden's, but I don't go there that often."

Payne took the packet and reassembled it. "Would you go with me to show this around tonight?"

Bailey shook his head. "I've got other plans. Be glad to later in the week."

"No offense, but I don't think I could wait that long."

"None taken. It'll give you an excuse to take Myra dancing."

Payne grinned. "Or Trinina."

"She's not the type and you know it."

"You're right. I'll have to take this in small steps. Thanks, Bailey."

"What are friends for?"

"Leaning on." Payne stepped out the door, feeling good about his start. His reinfatuation with Trinina would more than likely resolve itself, probably about the time that Nathan went back home. Most importantly, he had a lead that might produce the identity of the girl.

The only problem was showing the slab shot in four different clubs. With turnover in clientele, it might take weeks to get a name. If he went through management for their cooperation, it would still take time to make contacts. He had to narrow the choices to one club.

When he got to work, he showed the shot to Karol. She had no idea of who the girl was, nor was there a glimmer of recognition. She disclaimed her information by saying that she never remembered a face unless she slept with it, which Payne knew was not entirely true.

"One more thing," he asked. "I need to know which clubs you've been frequenting."

Karol looked down. "How recent?"

"Past couple of months."

She didn't look up.

"For process of elimination," he explained. "I've got too many leads, and I need to narrow them down."

"There are three," she said. "Cousins and Dresden's. But I haven't been to either of those in about six weeks."

"That eliminates one. What's the third?"

Karol's voice faltered. "I've been at the Threnody a lot..." She shrugged. "There's no excuse for it, really. I don't go in for any of the hard stuff."

"Discipline?"

"Mostly."

"Kelce?"

She didn't answer.

"It was Kelce, wasn't it?"

She nodded.

"It's not your fault. Kelce's behavior was more than you could tolerate, so you bailed out. There's nothing wrong with that."

"I keep thinking that if I'd been more of a woman, maybe he wouldn't have gone that way."

"You're fine as a woman, Karol. Kelce was coming apart long before he moved in with you."

"But I can't help thinking that I had something to do with it."

"A natural reaction." He watched her face. "You were starting to fall for him, weren't you?"

"Yeah," she said hesitantly. "I think so."

"It's going to hurt for a while. I went through the same thing with Trinina."

"But you've got a chance of getting her back. Billie told me about your note."

"The note doesn't mean a thing. Nathan's here on maternal visit, and she thought I'd like to see him. That's as far as it goes." He wondered if she could read the lack of conviction in his voice. "Thanks for the help, Karol."

She waved as he left the lobby.

Upstairs, he showed the photograph to others with prospering night lives. In doing so he eliminated Dresden's as one of the clubs in question. One employee insisted that he had bedded her, but none of his clubs matched any that Bailey had mentioned. He noted them but discounted the lead as its source couldn't remember his name after the fourth and fifth reminders.

Finally, he sat at Winthrop's carrel and stared at the photographs. He had narrowed the choices to the Lancaster and Eve's Apple. He had once been big on the latter, spending a lot of time there with one of the girls from clerical. In fact, he had introduced the club to Bailey, who was tiring of ImoGenes at the time.

He tapped the girl's nose with the eraser end of a pencil. For a moment it was Myra, and he tried to erase the scar on the side of her nose. *I wonder why she never had it repaired? Bailey had said it was a Purple Heart. Why*

*don't you get it fixed, Myra? The better to manipulate
you with, my dear...*

His thumb snapped the pencil in half.

He hadn't asked Myra, yet, she had more to go on
than a photograph. She had seen the body, and hadn't
talked about knowing the girl.

He drew a line through "Lancaster," but reconsidered.
He left Winthrop's carrel for the nearest telephone, pray-
ing for the lines to be up. His fingers pounced on the
pressure pads and brought a ring.

She wasn't answering. He let it ring five, six, seven
times. Perhaps she was out. Perhaps the lines there were
dead. Perhaps she had moved out.

She caught the telephone on the ninth ring, answering
with an insecure, "Hello?"

"What took you so long?"

"Payne?"

"Yes."

"I wasn't sure if I was supposed to answer."

"Of course you were. Listen, I've got to know which
clubs you frequent."

A long silence. "What for?"

"My investigation."

Another silence. "Are you checking up on me?"

"No. I'm checking up on the girl. I've got a list of clubs
she may have frequented, and I need to narrow it down."

Nothing.

"Don't be embarrassed. I've discovered that one of my
colleagues is a regular at the Threnody. It can't be any
worse than that."

"This is rather sudden."

"You're not selling secrets to Russia," Payne growled.
"Look, you're not a regular at The Catherine Wheel, are
you?"

"Of course not," she snapped defensively.

"Then I know you won't castrate me in the name of
militant lesbianism. Where do you usually go?"

"Sometimes," she said tentatively, "Cousins."

"Where else?"

"The Metropolis."

"Any more?"

"Lastly and mostly, Danse."

"The club on Lancaster Boulevard?"

"The club on Lancaster Boulevard," she confirmed.

"That leaves Eve's Apple."

"I'm not following you."

"Bailey's seen the girl before, and I had it narrowed to Eve's Apple or the Lancaster. If you didn't recognize the girl, that eliminates the Lancaster."

"But I have seen the girl."

Payne was struck dumb.

"Did you hear me?"

"You knew her?"

"No. I've just seen her around."

"The Lancaster?"

"Yes."

"Why were you so quiet at the morgue?"

"I was about to throw up, Payne."

"Your silence..."

"Was recognition."

"I'm sorry," Payne said.

"Is that all you wanted?"

"No," he said abruptly. "How would you like to go dancing tonight?"

"Tonight?"

"You're not going to work, are you?"

"No..."

"Great. We'll leave around eight and go at it until you're ready to call it quits. How does that sound?"

"Okay, I guess."

"Fine. I should be home soon."

"Payne," she said in a bewildered tone. "Are you—"

The phone went dead in his hand. The lights in the building flickered into the imperfect supply from the emergency generators.

He clicked the recovery switch, but it did no good.

The power was gone. Payne laid the handset in the cradle and returned to Winthrop's carrel, where he sat and pored over the notes that had been left behind. He would photolink them to Sydney when he sent the other information.

Just as he was beginning to decipher Winthrop's exquisite scrawl, his concentration was broken by a tap on his shoulder. He turned, and the electric blue of the visitor's clean suit hurt his eyes. A familiar face peered through the elastic-bound hood.

"Delgado?"

"Mr. Payne. You're rather hard to track down."

"I've been here all morning."

"So I've heard. They had me waiting on the fifth floor for over an hour."

"I've appropriated a lab space up there for doing some work on my Thirty-first."

"Must be nice to do the lab work yourself."

"Better wait until you see what kind of results I get."

"And leads?"

"I'm looking for traces of disease in her blood. I may know where she spent her last few hours, but I'm not talking yet."

"I don't blame you."

"So what brings you up here? Business or pleasure?"

"Business, I'm afraid." He motioned to a chair across the aisle. "Do you think they'd mind?"

"Of course not."

He pulled the chair into Winthrop's carrel and sat. To Payne's horror, he opened a hermetically sealed bag and produced a photograph.

"What's wrong?"

Payne eased his breath out. "Other than the fact that you've just breached a sterile area, nothing."

"I hope I haven't caused any trouble."

"People have been fired for less."

"The lady with the teeth sealed everything into this damn bag. I told her I wouldn't be able to get to it, and she said, 'Rules are rules.'"

"That's Karol for you."

"I won't get you in trouble, will I?"

Payne took the bag and hid it under a stack of Winthrop's papers. "What can I do for you?"

Delgado handed him the photograph. "Do you know this person?"

Payne twisted it under the light. "It's Lol Winthrop." The picture was a bad representation. His hair was in disarray, and his eyes were glazed. He looked as if he'd been doing Fairlights. "You guys arrest him at the docks?"

"He's dead."

The picture fell to the astroturf floor. "What happened?"

"I was hoping you could tell me."

"Me?"

Delgado reached across Payne for the plastic bag. From inside he produced a small slip of paper. "Recognize this?"

Payne took the paper. His stomach turned. "You found this on the body?"

Delgado nodded.

"Breast pocket?"

Another nod.

"I gave this to him."

"I figured as much. That's your telephone number on the slip."

"In my handwriting." Payne looked at the photograph on the floor. Winthrop stared back up. Now he recognized the style of the picture. The glaze of the eyes was Alamex. It was a slab shot.

"What happened?"

"We found him in a pile of trash by the docks. I find it strange that you knew he was there."

"He told me that he was going there."

"Did he?"

"Yes. Saturday night at the Lancaster Club."

"Did he say what he'd be doing there?"

"He was—" He stopped. Winthrop was planning to leave the country illegally. Payne had known and had failed to report it. Impeding the flow of justice, they called it.

"Yes?"

"I suppose I'm suspect in this."

"That depends."

"Do I have any rights in this matter?"

"What do you think?"

"Are you going to Mirandize me?"

Delgado looked around the room. "If you want it, Mr. Payne. If you think you really need it. Otherwise, I think it can be disposed of for the esoteric piece of bullshit that it really is. If you're guilty, we're going to have you, with or without your constitutional rights."

Payne swallowed. "Forget it."

"Good. I lost my Miranda card years ago and never bothered to replace it."

"What do you need to know?"

"What was he doing at the docks?"

"Getting ready to leave the country."

"Legally?"

"What do you think?"

"I think if he was doing it legally, he would have made it. Alive."

"What else do you need?"

"Something else on that paper I'd like to know about. The string of numbers and letters."

Payne checked the sheet. "That's easy. It's a testing code."

"For what?"

"In this company, you prove competence in different areas of research and development. As you do, you move up a scale so you have access to more and more materials, which in turn stimulates creativity—or so the philosophy goes. Winthrop was gifted, but the project he was working on required computer programs that he couldn't get to. To help him out, I gave him a higher access code. Or so he thought. That's a special number given so the computer can monitor the user's competence. The user thinks that he's getting away with something, but he's actually being tested."

"For promotion." Delgado laughed and rubbed his forehead. "We need something like that where I work."

Payne returned the paper. "The rest of the writing is Winthrop's. This was his carrel, if you'd like a sample."

"Do you know what the rest of this means? 'Danse' 22, Fifty K. Circled and underlined."

"Under the circumstances, yes. The last time I saw Winthrop alive was Saturday night at about 2100. We were both at this club on Lancaster that names itself after the top-selling song of the week. He was going to meet somebody at 2200 and pay him fifty thousand dollars to get out of the country."

"He got as far as the docks before he ran into trouble. Did he give you any more details? Who was he supposed to meet, where the exchange of money was to take place?"

"He didn't give me any names. He did say that the money bought the papers to get him out and passage on a ship. He'd already seen the reservation forms."

"What about the exchange?"

"He didn't say, but it probably took place at the club. He was going to meet the guy by playing gay and going into a chamber with him. That's probably where the final details were worked out."

Delgado had pulled a pad from the bag and was making notes. "From there he was probably escorted to the docks under the guise of making sure he got on the right ship. Once there, your friend was killed and the murderer took the papers from him. From there I'd say he turned the reservations back to the travel agent the next day and got his deposit back. A neat little job." He looked up from the pad. "What you've given me is help, but it's not enough. You didn't hear the name of a ship, the number of a dock, anything?"

"He didn't offer it," Payne said. "He was too excited about going home."

"Winthrop was Australian?"

"British. He was living for the day when he could get to Australia. I was going to forward some work to him so he could finish it up." Payne flipped through Winthrop's notebook. "It doesn't matter now. He's gone on to a better place."

"Do you you believe in God, Payne?" Delgado asked after a long pause.

"I don't know. I'm tempted to." He looked at Delgado, who was putting his notes away. "Why do you ask?"

"Your reference to a better place."

"That's not saying a lot. It doesn't take much to wish someone to a better place."

"Times change, Mr. Payne. Wishing a better place on the dead is archaic. Any more, people wish each other a better place as a matter of greeting. It's a wish for the living. That's why I asked."

"Character reference?"

"More insight, really. If you want my opinion, I think you do believe in God. In fact, I think you're rather devout about it. You just don't know it yet."

"What about you?"

Delgado rolled the plastic under his arm and stood. "I believe in God, and I know it. And every night I pray to him that when the bullet finds my brain, he won't turn me away."

Payne stood. "I don't think he will."

"Good-bye, Mr. Payne."

"What about my being suspect in this case?"

Delgado shook his head. "You aren't."

"What about the girl in my apartment?"

"She's your problem." He started to turn away, but Payne grabbed his shoulder and spun him around.

"What did you say?"

"I said the girl in the apartment is your problem."

"What do you mean by that? What gives Lol Winthrop priority over Jane Doe? Is it because Winthrop was British? Is somebody's embassy putting pressure on your department? Winthrop was my friend, and I'd like to see his killer brought in, but what puts him ahead of my case? What puts his ahead of anyone else's, for that matter?"

Delgado looked back with tired eyes. "It's because Winthrop isn't alone."

Payne released Delgado's shoulders. "There were others?"

"I'm not supposed to let this out, Mr. Payne, but I will, just to ease your soul. If word of this gets out, you'll land in jail. Understand?"

Payne nodded.

"Your friend's death raised the body count to eleven. In every case the pattern was the same. Refugees wanting to get out of the country, and no friends or family to carry the Thirty-first. All found at the docks, all killed the same way." He pointed to the back of his head. "One blow with a crowbar to the skull, right where it joins the neck. Leaves a nice, deep puncture, and if they survive, they don't do a lot of talking. We've been groping for clues, but nothing has been as useful as what you've just given us. It's a matter of time now. One thing about people who use a pattern is that they get sloppy. The killer struck your friend four times before he found the right spot." He shook his head solemnly. "For that we're going to nail him."

"Soon, I hope."

"Not soon enough. Don't feel like you should apologize, Payne. You've helped immensely. If you think of anything else, get in touch."

As Delgado walked out, Payne sat numbly at Winthrop's desk, not knowing what to do. He shuffled the stacks of papers and leafed through the notebooks, but he lacked the motivation to get on with the work. He knew that he should check on the recovery of the cultures, but it now seemed futile. Winthrop was dead. Perhaps he should let the cholesterol project die with him.

No, he thought. That's not what Winthrop would have wanted. Had he known what was coming, he would have made arrangements for the work to be completed. Payne

may not have been first choice to do it, but for now he
was stuck with it.

He sat up straight and stared at the mess he had made
of Winthrop's carrel. He needed to tighten his resolve and
get to work, straighten what was there, and trace the
direction in which Winthrop had been headed.

But first he had a few other details to get out of the
way. If he could identify the girl, the rest would fall into
place. Once that was done, he could see Trinina out of
her crisis. All that remained was Myra.

His head started to ache. He realized that he had promised to take Myra to the Lancaster tonight, but another
promise had been made—to Trinina and, most importantly, to Nathan.

He slammed his fist on the desk top. Which was the
most important? An unfair question, perhaps, for surely
it was Trinina and Nathan. But the body, although it was
lying dissected on a cold slab, was a constant pressure
that might put a damper on things. By this time tomorrow
he could be free of that obligation, free to enjoy their
company without the specter of death hanging over his
head.

He began looking for Trinina, his story rehearsed so it
wouldn't come out in a jumble when he tried to explain.
It was a simple matter of setting their date back a day.

In the lobby, he hailed Karol. "Have you seen Trinina?"

"Didn't she come in?"

"I thought I'd check with you. Nobody upstairs has
seen her."

Karol looked at a screen and typed. "I'm not showing
her in."

"I'll bet she took a few days to spend with Nathan."

Karol shook her head.

"Did she call in?"

She struck a key, and the screen cleared. "Nothing.
I'm not showing the boy in day care, either, though she
did give notice that he'd be attending for a week."

"It's not like her to do this."

Karol shrugged. "Maybe something happened on the way to work." She saw Payne's face fall. "I'm sorry. I'm not being much help."

"You're doing what you can," Payne said, patting her hand. And then he was running to the door, still in his sterile suit, his fingers tearing at the plastic that formed a ring around his face.

He ripped the hood off, fed it to a trash barrel, and ran down the street. He weaved in and out of the Monday ped traffic until he decided to take his chances against the bicycles and ElectriCarts in the street. It paid off, and he moved around the clogged sidewalks at a good clip, drawing annoyed stares from those he passed.

He turned off the main thoroughfare and on to the back street that led to Trinina's. At a beep from behind, he jumped to the sidewalk. Something caught on the edge of the curb, and he plunged to his knees, rolling off one shoulder and ending in a sitting position in the middle of the sidewalk. He checked his feet. The plastic outers had tattered into long tangles that had tripped him. He tore them off and stuffed them into a pocket, noting that a hole had been torn in one knee of the protective suit.

At the base of the stairs he stopped, doubling over and grabbing air for the final ascent. He made a last swallow and sprinted, taking the stairs two at a time until he stood before her door. He caught his breath and rapped his knuckles on the wood synths.

"Trinina?"

There was no answer. He knocked again.

"Trinina!"

Another series of knocks.

"Trinina!"

There was nothing but silence in return.

He lowered his hand to the doorknob, pressed his palm to the flat of the knob, and twisted.

His sick feeling returned. He was afraid it would haunt him for the rest of his life, and it was all the fault of a girl

who probably had no idea of where or why she was dying.
It was a useless and paralyzing feeling, and the only way
he would ever overcome it was to walk through doors
with the same abandon that he once had. He pushed the
door, and it drifted open. He took three steps and called
her name.

Nothing.

Closing the door, Payne checked the apartment. The
couch was still broken into the bed, and the sheets were
rumpled from where she had slept. A light on a coffee
table shone. The only change since his departure was that
the video terminal had been left glowing, the sound
switched off.

He moved into her bedroom. The bed had been made
by a childish hand, and a small selection of toys and easy-
read books were scattered across the top. The curtains
were open, and light streamed in. On Trinina's dresser a
small suitcase lay open, disgorging its ill-packed contents.
He opened the bathroom door. A child's toothbrush, soap,
and toothpaste adorned the counter top; a small stepping
stool sat before the sink. The toilet lid and seat had been
left up. The sight of this in the obviously feminine bathroom was enough to make Payne smile.

The kitchen was empty save for the smell of fresh
coffee. The brewing pot was three-quarters full. Dishes
were stacked neatly in a sink full of water: large plate,
knife, fork, two spoons, large glass, small cup, cereal
bowl. The burners on the stove were cool. He checked
the cupboards and found the usual assortment of staples,
the only addition being a large box of VitaKrunch cereal,
a gaily colored box that was clearly out of place. A check
of the refrigerator was similarly uneventful with the
exception of a six-pack of CitruSlush in the corner.

Back in the living room, Payne stared blankly into a
decorative mirror. He still wore the shredded clean suit.
He peeled it off and pitched it into her garbage.

On the way out, a Big Chief tablet caught his eye. He
stared at the chief, all solid cheekbones and perfect nose,

the safety goggles around his neck like some kind of ornament, the collar and shoulders of the lab coat looking freshly pressed, eyes staring intently at something direly important. It took him back to his own school days, carrying an identical tablet tightly under his arm, laboriously copying the names of bones and muscles and organs onto the grainy paper. The memory made it all the more urgent that he spend some time with Nathan. Perhaps he could take some time off and convince Trinina to do the same.

He opened the tablet, expecting to find the pages filled with Nathan's handwriting. They were blank. He checked the date on the price tag. It had been bought with the cereal and the Slush. He sat on the edge of the bed and took a pen from his breast pocket.

TRI—
Some last minute complications with the tissues—
I can't make it over tonight. Tomorrow and nights
following are a promise. Can't wait to meet Nathan
(awake). Take care and REMEMBER TO LOCK
YOUR DOOR.

—Payne

He folded the note and stood it on top of the tablet so it could be seen from the door. It was a sad substitute for actually being here tonight.

He sighed, and the sigh brought in the smell of the place, and the smell was of Trinina. It was as warm and soft as she had been on the countless nights they had shared a bed. There was a trace of her sweat, from work, from tears, from sex. It was a scent that she took great pleasure in wearing because of its effect on him. The smell froze him in time and brought it all back to him more vividly than the Big Chief had. Each tender and terrible moment was so real that he reached out as if to touch them, only to see his hand pass through air. The sight stabbed him in the heart, and he felt he could die for the want of having it all back.

When he left, he locked the door—not so much to keep the undesirables out as to keep the memories in.

Monday Night

*T*he building was trembling down to the concrete foundations. The beast in it had wakened and was clamoring for another blood sacrifice. Payne tried to swim out of the black, clutching his chest to find his heart pounding wildly, beating so hard that it would surely crack his ribs and burst right out of him. The thought of opening up like that sickened him, and he pushed his eyelids open.

"Take it easy. Calm down. Calm down. Just relax, Payne. Relax. You're okay. You're okay."

He filled his lungs with air and looked around. He was sitting up in bed. Myra was holding him by the shoulders, her voice calm and cool.

"Are you awake?"

He swallowed. His throat was dry and cracked.

She pried his hands from her upper arms. "Must have been some dream."

"I don't remember," he said, gasping. "You woke me up too fast."

"If it was that bad, it's better off not remembered." She rubbed her arms. "I think you bruised me."

"Sorry." Payne rubbed sleep from his eyes. "What time is it?"

"1915, as per your request."

"Thank you." He swung his legs off the edge of the bed and planted them on the floor.

She rose gracefully from the bed. "Do you want to eat before we go?"

Payne worked his fingers through his hair. "I don't think so. I'll grab something when we get back."

"Going to shower?"

"Yeah." He stood and picked up his robe. "And shave."

"I thought you shaved this morning."

"I disciplined myself this morning," he said, closing the door as Myra walked out.

He stared hard into the mirror and shook his head sadly. Had he actually faced the public looking like that?

He brushed the soap to a lather and spread it across his face. The stubble soon yielded to the blade. Next he stepped into a scalding shower. The wash cut through his sweat and sent it cascading down the drain. Before finishing, he turned the hot water down until the cold drove pins and needles into his skin, shocking him awake.

He wrapped up in a warm, thick towel and wiped fog from the mirror. He now looked alert, but his eyes lacked their usual spark.

"You're putting a lot on this trip tonight," he said aloud to himself. "It'd better bear fruit or you're going to lose it. If getting the girl out doesn't clear things up, you've got some serious thinking to do."

When he opened the door to the bedroom, he found that Myra had ironed a brand new jumpsuit for him. He blessed her under his breath and stepped into it. The suit was metallic gray, a new color he had spotted in a store near Trinina's while on the way home. The color complemented him, making him look stern and well postured. There was even evidence of that spark back in his tired eyes. He felt a new energy as he draped the scarf around his neck, the happy green contrasting with the neutrality of the suit. The ring slid to his neck, the black onyx winking as if trying to tell him something.

"Oh, no," he told the ring. "Not her. She's not the—"

"Something wrong?" Myra stopped in the doorway to look him over. "The color does you justice."

"Justice." Payne laughed. "That's a nice abstraction."

"Something's got to bring justice into this world," Myra said.

Payne took the fabric between his thumb and forefinger and rubbed it, feeling the softness. "Maybe it'll bring me luck. If it does me that much justice, maybe it'll help me find more."

"You don't look like the type to believe in lucky charms."

"I'm not, but I won't ignore free help if it's there."

Myra shook her head. "And you call yourself a detective." She took him by the hand and led him out the door. "Now, if you'll excuse me, I've got to change."

Payne wandered into the kitchen and checked Myra's job of restocking the refrigerator. A vague scent twitched at his nostrils. He checked the kitchen table. One of the chairs was pulled back, and a steaming bowl of soup rested on a mat. On the side were crackers and a freshly opened can of his vice. He smiled at this, then sat down and crushed the crackers into the soup.

By the time Myra had finished changing, he was rinsing dishes. He stacked the bowl and spoon and turned to see her standing in the doorway. He blinked.

"You like it?" she asked.

"Yes," he said, taken aback by the suit she was wearing. Her feet were resting on the latest of the foam wedge designs, her toenails painted a silver that would absorb and reflect the lights in the club. The cuffs of the bright red suit had been cut and frayed into soft fuzz. The outseam of each leg had been slashed from hip to knee, likewise the arms from shoulder to elbow. A tear-shaped section had been cut out of the suit's midriff from between the breasts to just below the navel, into which she had put a small jewel. Her hair was combed straight behind her ears. Her eyes were painted dark; her lipstick was black. The green scarf was knotted tightly around her slender neck, the two loose ends straddling her right shoulder.

"I do my own customizing."

"You do a good job."

"No sense in paying the fashion plates to do it. Every woman should know how to run a pair of scissors."

"You should have done something to mine. I suddenly feel undressed."

"It's not your job to be flashy." She kissed him on the cheek.

"What is it, then?"

"To choose and pursue." She turned. The back of her suit had a tight V cut from midshoulder to the small of her back. He slowly followed her out of the kitchen.

"I thought the male was supposed to be the one with the plumage." He moved through the living room, extinguishing lights.

"That's in the animal kingdom, dear. We are very different from them."

"You're right. Their main concern is mating."

She smiled from the door, teeth shining against her darkened lips. "So is mine." She slid out of sight.

He followed her out, taking care to lock the door. He took her arm, and they made their way out, the packet with all that remained of a girl's life clutched tightly in his free hand.

They approached the club, and all at once things seemed to buzz with blue sparks of life. He was overwhelmed by emotion as surely as if he had been struck by lightning. The breath cut short in his lungs, his nose and throat went dry, and his eyes stung. A ringing tore his ears, and his extremities were covered with prickling numbness. He stopped in midstride, staring at the building across the street.

"What's wrong?" Myra asked.

Payne blinked to moisten his eyes. "I'm scared."

"Of what?"

"I don't know." He looked at her concerned expression. "Silly, isn't it?"

"I don't know. You look sick."

"Is it that bad?"

"Your palm went clammy. What does it feel like?"

"Electricity," he said.

She gently caressed his hand. "It'll be okay."

They walked across the street to the ticket booth, and Payne tapped the glass to get the clerk's attention.

"May I help you?"

Payne held the slab shot up to the window. "Have you ever seen this woman?"

"Yeah." The clerk grinned. "But never like this."

Payne's face soured. The clerk's eyes were riveted on Myra. He banged the picture against the glass. "Not her. This picture."

The clerk turned his head and focused on the shot. His eyebrows knit, and he squinted; then he abruptly looked at Payne.

"It depends."

"On what?"

The clerk tapped the list of admission prices.

Payne slapped his Bancard on the counter.

"Ticket class?"

"Pair of greens."

"I wish," the clerk said under his breath.

"Take twenty for yourself," Payne said, still tapping the picture. The clerk locked eyes with those of the dead girl.

"No," he said firmly, sliding the card back under the glass.

Payne checked it. He hadn't taken the money.

"Take a bit of friendly advice," the clerk said. "This is the kind of place where people come to have a good time. They come to forget their troubles and get mindless.

You go poking a pic of a dead slice under their noses, and they're going to get resentful. People got a lot to forget nowadays."

"You think I don't?"

"Just a warning. You're taking your ass in your own two hands."

Payne nodded curtly. "Thanks."

"I mean it!" the clerk shouted as they entered the club. "I wouldn't go showing that around..."

Myra gripped Payne's hand. "You're trembling."

"She's here."

"How do you know?"

"The cashier knew her."

"Are you sure?"

"I'm positive. He was lying to me."

"How could you tell?"

"He got unnerved when I showed him the picture. When he looked at it, his pupils dilated. He was concentrating on it. And he was fighting to keep a poker face."

"So how do you get him to break?"

"I don't. If he knows her, somebody else will, too. Hopefully an employee."

He stopped in the center of the lobby and looked around. He nodded with resolve, then pulled Myra to the concession stand and flagged down the fabulous brunette.

"Hello again." She smiled.

"I need some help."

"What'll it be, dears?" The brunette looked at Myra. Her face twitched for a moment, then she smiled. "Handcuffs, right?"

Payne set the photograph down. "Have you seen this woman before? I think she was a regular here."

The brunette stared. "I have to be honest," she said, shaking her head. "I've been here two weeks, and the number of people I do recognize can be counted on both hands."

"You're certain?"

She picked up the picture and tilted it against the light. "I'm sorry."

"Thanks, anyway." Payne grabbed the packet and Myra's hand, and they made for the ballroom.

"What about her?"

"She was telling the truth."

"The eyes?"

"The picture didn't move her. The cashier was shaken by what he saw."

"Old partners?"

"Could be. He's certainly in the position to set himself up. A few free admissions and he's set."

They stopped at the ballroom. Payne stepped back to let a huge, muscular man pass, then held the door for Myra. When she didn't appear, he turned to find her tapping on the big man's shoulder.

"This man's a bouncer here," she explained.

"This guy giving you trouble?" the bouncer asked with a familiar accent.

"He needs to talk to you."

Payne fished the packet from under his arm. "Do you recognize this woman?"

The bouncer took it from Payne's hands and looked, his eyes narrowing into slits. He shoved it back with a massive hand. "I wouldn't be showing this around if I were you."

"You knew her?"

"You heard what I said. Don't show it around."

"Are you infringing on my constitutional right of personal investigation?"

"I'm discouraging it. Any time you exercise your rights, you step on someone else's. Practicing your freedom of speech may move others to practice their freedom of expression, which might entail beating the hell out of you."

"Relax. I'm not going to put it up on the screen."

"Beside the point. People come here to have a good time."

"So I've heard."

"Remember that the others here have a right to pursue happiness."

"Pursuit means just that," Payne said. "They can try. They may achieve nothing."

The bouncer glared. "Watch your step." He turned on the ball of his foot and stalked off.

"Friendly place," Myra said.

"She was here, all right."

They pushed through and stopped to scrutinize the activity on the dance floor. Payne was amazed. Monday night, and the place was as packed as it had been on the weekend. He shook his head at the sight and the sounds that drove it. "Doesn't this place ever close?"

"Mornings," Myra said. "They get the last of the stragglers out around 0500. They clean up and let the sound equipment and lasers cool down. It starts again around noon."

"Noon," Payne echoed.

"Except weekends," Myra amended, "when they reopen at 1000."

Payne took her elbow and led her across the dance floor, through a path that opened up before them. He found a table in a corner and sat her down, then slid in beside her and placed the packet on the table.

"How romantic," she said sullenly, turning the picture face down.

Payne gave her a dirty look and opened the packet, spreading out the contents. He stacked the papers by information type, keeping the photographs close to the edge of the table. Myra took one of the stacks and began to read.

"This can't be right." She tapped the paper.

"What's that?"

"Weight at death, thirty-five kilos."

"You don't trust Mr. Louis?"

"Payne, she was a hundred seventy-one centimeters tall."

"I know." He continued sorting.

"She didn't look sick, Payne. I saw her, remember? If she was that underweight, it would have shown."

"Not if something had been eating her from the inside out."

Myra slapped the papers down. "She wouldn't look like that. She'd be skin and bones. I have friends who are anorexic, and they look worse in life than she did in death."

"You're not taking one thing into account. Your anorexic friends are purging themselves of body fat. This girl had plenty of body fat."

Myra looked at the papers. "Is it what Louis said about the proteins?"

Payne nodded.

"And that's where the girl's liver comes in?"

"And her brain. And her bone marrow."

"Something was *eating* it?"

"In a manner of speaking."

She bit a knuckle.

"I think I may have a lead," Payne said. "I found something in the girl's blood that looks like spore cases."

"*Spores*? Is this like the old video of the plants in people's basements?"

"No. You're thinking of plant spores. These are different. They're called endospores, and they're what's left of some microorganism."

"I don't understand."

"Go back to grade-school biology. Disinfection theory. Some microorganisms are resistant to attempted disinfection. You can boil them, you can hit them with whatever you want. When they start to die, they form a little case that contains their DNA—enough information to build again when the conditions are right."

"What kind of conditions do they need?"

"It varies from organism to organism. With this one I suspect protein environments, since that's what was depleted. It may have been serving as food. Body temperature may also have something to do with it."

Myra looked alarmed. "Then it could spread."

"There's a possibility that a spore case could get in through a cut. I wouldn't worry about it, though. That's why Mr. Louis wears gloves and wax on his fingertips."

"What about other ways? What about food?"

"I really don't know. Remember, this is only a theory right now. You'd have to be a cannibal before—"

"What about protein synths? Could it get into those? What about the liver the girl was eating? Maybe that's how she got it."

Payne's head started to buzz. "That would depend," he said weakly, "on whether or not the bacteria was aerobic."

"Speak English, Payne."

"If the bacteria could live in the open air."

"And if it can?"

He looked at her. "Then we have it."

Myra became pale.

"This is all theory," Payne said. "It might be something totally different."

"And if it's not?"

"Then it can't be that simple." His throat went dry. "There'd have to be more to it than that."

"Of course there is!" She knotted her hands and held them under her breasts. "It eats proteins, right? What else is made of protein? Hair, Payne. It could be spreading to stylists." She twisted a handful of hair for emphasis. "You know what else is made of protein, Payne? Remember *your* grade-school biology?"

He closed his eyes. He knew what would be next.

"Sperm. Correct me if I'm wrong. They're just protein and DNA." Her voice was quivering and rising in pitch.

Payne turned away. He looked out at the dance floor and listened to the beat of the music, watched the people twisting and leaping and sweating.

Tears were flowing down Myra's face. "She was from here. She was a regular. She probably did the same as everybody else."

Now Payne was shaking. He gripped the tabletop until

his knuckles were white. He blinked numbly out at the floor and watched a couple heading for the chambers. His jaw trembled.

Myra reached out and turned his head to face her. "*This whole place*," she said in a cracking voice, "*could be a bloody factory.*"

"I can check you," Payne said. It was all too much for him. His eyes were burning, and his brain was weak from the possibilities.

"What good will it do?" she shrieked.

He pulled the scarf from his neck and dabbed her tears away. "Because I think I know what kills it."

Her eyes became wide.

"Alamex," he lied. His visual examination of the processed blood had been cursory. Even if Alamex destroyed it, it would not have done any good. It was a toxin that killed by blocking chemical exchange between cells. What made it deadly to the living made it the perfect preservative for the dead. If indeed they had the disease, there was nothing that he knew of that would stop it.

"Let's go now," she whispered.

"I have work to do."

"Please."

"We'll go as soon as I'm done, I promise."

"Now."

"No. We haven't been exposed for long. Another couple of hours shouldn't make that much difference."

"Are you sure?"

"Yes," he said. Another lie.

She managed a weak smile. "I guess this means you're being the aggressor."

"For a change."

She sniffed and nodded.

"Do you want a drink?"

"Please. A Fallen Angel."

"I'll pick one up for you. Meantime, if someone offers you a steak sandwich, turn them down."

She nodded. New tears fell from her eyes.

He kissed her. "I'll be right back."

He kept watch on Myra as he left her with the revelation. If the morning star heads turned out to be spore cases, there was every possibility that he and Myra could be contaminated. He tried to comfort himself by punching holes in the theory. Perhaps it was just a fluke. Perhaps what he had seen were crystals of some other kind, something that did cause protein depletion and death. If it was a disease, and if it was spreading, there were bound to be symptoms. People wouldn't suffer a massive protein breakdown without exhibiting symptoms. As the liver collapsed, there was bound to be jaundice unless something masked it.

No matter how he tried to push fear from his mind, the arguments defeated themselves. Perhaps cases weren't showing up in hospitals yet because this was the ground floor of the disease. Perhaps this girl was the first in what would be a long succession of victims. Or perhaps the victims weren't in hospitals because they had died before they could get there.

Perhaps they didn't make it because they didn't know they were sick.

The thought chilled him. He fought the urge to grab Myra and drag her to Biotech to draw blood for immediate testing. If they were contaminated, it wasn't going to matter. Anyone making the discovery now would have a head start on a cure and would have it out before things got serious—but not before the first wave of victims would be claimed. He and Myra would be among that first wave, and they would go down as martyrs in the Age of Biological Superiority, their names scribbled in a lab technician's notebook and forgotten.

By the time he reached the bar his stomach was as hard as a rock. He flagged a barman.

"What'll it be?" the man asked cheerfully.

Fool, Payne thought. Don't you know you're working in a biological hothouse? "I need a Fallen Angel," he said. "And what do you have for a rough stomach?"

"Hair of the dog?"

"Nervous tension."

"How about a Peppermint Smooth?"

"With double vodka."

"You got it."

Payne leaned against the bar and surveyed the floor. He tried to find Myra through the crowd, but the people were mobbing and blocking his view.

Then he had a vision.

It was nothing hallucinatory or mystical, although the way it happened made it seem as such. The crowd parted to form a path no more than a meter wide. It cracked into an angle, but a piece broke off and moved across the open space, straightening it. The path went completely through the crowd and finished near their table, where Myra sat patiently. She saw the break, too, and she saw Payne leaning against the bar, elbows propped against the padded armrest. She smiled and waved.

But Payne didn't see her. His line of sight hadn't made it that far. His eyes were nailed to a spot just beyond where the flow of people had straightened the path. He was staring at the dark-washed profile of two people standing toe to toe: a tall female with her head down, the split in her customized jumpsuit running the entire length of her side, and the second half of the silhouette, a small skinny man, hair askew, nose too big for his face, a yellow scarf knotted tightly around his neck.

He was sure it was Kelce.

He paused for a second, his mind swimming in suspicion. What was Kelce doing here, why tonight, and who was that woman? He tried to clear his head. Like the ticket clerk had said, people came here to forget. If Kelce had gone to work this morning, he had been anticipating the worst. Perhaps he was celebrating his continued employment with Biotech after spending the weekend sweating out the prospect of suspension.

But who was to say that he remembered the phone call at all? From the way his apartment had sounded, Kelce's mind was likely to have lost most of what had transpired over the weekend.

Well, he thought. You're not going to get any answers leaning on the bar. Why not take a stroll and find out why your friend is trying to chew that woman's lips off? She seems to be enjoying it, which isn't bad considering he's yellowed out.

He moved away from the bar and took two steps in Kelce's direction. He was brought back by a shout. He turned to see the barman, two drinks in his hand.

"Done already?" Payne commented in surprise.

"You thought that was fast?"

"Fine service."

"I won't tell you how I screwed up, then. Do me a favor, though."

Payne flipped his plastic to the counter. "Name it."

"Before you leave, tell my boss that I'm fast."

Payne laughed. "Sure." He took a sip of the Peppermint Smooth. It went down by name and went to work, softening what Payne had forgotten in pursuing Kelce. He sipped again, and the barman returned his card.

"I'll also tell him that you're good with recommendations."

The barman smiled. "The drink's okay?"

"Perfect. Thanks."

The fissure in the crowd had healed. Better that it had—it would keep him from confronting Kelce with his hands full. It meant he could get back to Myra and pick up the packet, sparing her the experience of meeting Kelce. It would be better all around to walk up and shove the picture under his nose. There was something to be said for shock value.

He took the long way back to the table, moving around the crush of bodies and taking sips from both drinks to prevent spills. On the first taste of Fallen Angel he screwed up his face. Like the Peppermint Smooth, the drink tasted according to name. From the kick it carried, it was clear that tonight Myra would be trying to forget as well.

By the time he reached the table, Myra had sobered and dried her eyes. She met him with her trademark shy smile.

"They played our song," she said.

"I noticed." He placed the Fallen Angel before her and gathered the contents of the packet. "I'll be back."

"Payne?"

He stopped.

"I don't like to drink alone."

"I won't be long. I just need to shake someone up."

He started to turn, and she called him.

"I don't like to dance alone, either."

"I'll hurry."

He walked away, trying to track Kelce. It was no use. The crowd had congealed, and the only way to see in was to become a part of it. He looked to the doors and watched the stream of people. From this point on, things weren't going to get any better.

He moved in, the packet clutched tightly to his chest. It was slow going as he tried to elbow gently between people, tried not to break locked-up couples. It was easier between sets when people thinned out to regroup.

Midway between the bar and his table he spotted Kelce. He lurched that way, but on arrival found no sign of the other man. It seemed impossible that someone could move through this crowd with such agility.

The speakers issued a familiar banging. The crowd raised their voices as if the song were something marvelous that was being played for the very first time. The intro went through all the familiar paces, giving time for the crowd to thin to the number who could do the "Danse." Couples broke, and people spread out and started to spin. Payne took advantage of the sudden spread and made for a neutral corner of the ballroom.

He delicately wove between the spinners, ducking his head and jumping out of the way to avoid collisions. He was nearly out when a girl with bluing lips and a twisted, agonized smile went down where his next step was to be.

He lost his balance and wobbled, pushing out with his grounded leg to get the extra distance he needed to keep from stepping on her stomach. He brought his other leg up and over, then planted it back on the shining floor. Close, he thought.

Then someone's fist caught him in the side of the head and sent him to the floor, the packet spinning out of his hands and skittering across the dance floor until it stopped to be trampled by dancers.

A girl was immediately at his side, arms sliding under his and lifting.

"I'm terribly sorry."

"Not your fault," Payne mumbled, stunned.

The girl looked at Payne's bruised face. Her hand went to her mouth. "Did I do that to you?"

He worked to his feet and tried to shake off the blow. "No," he reassured, "I got this at the Threnody."

The girl dusted off the sleeves of his jumpsuit. "You know," she said, "the right girl could probably straighten you out."

Payne rubbed the side of his head and looked at her. A red scarf dangled from her neck.

"But I'm not the right girl." She grinned evilly.

"Later," Payne said, staggering toward the packet. He caught up with it ten meters from where it had originally landed and, upon retrieving it, collided with a man who was enthusiastically jetting through the air.

"If you can't do the step, clear the floor," the dancer grunted.

"I'm working on it."

He cleared the crowd, trying to rub the dust and scuffs from the surface of the packet. He surveyed the area and saw nothing. He might as well go back to Myra.

Then he saw Kelce. He was still with the tall woman, and there was enough of a view to make a positive identification. His arms were wrapped around the woman, and he moved from chewing on her lips to chewing on her neck. They broke their clutch and took the five steps necessary to pass through the double doors that led to the chambers.

"That's wrong," Payne said. They should have known club rules as well as anybody. Kelce would be turned away for lack of an appropriately colored scarf. He'd have to go to the lobby and buy one.

He moved quickly toward the double doors in the hope of catching them before they got to the desk. Better yet, he could wait at the door and catch Kelce alone when he came back to buy a scarf. He looked through a window. All he could see was wall; the hallway ran parallel to the ballroom. He cracked the outside door and looked down the darkened hall. Near the front of the club, the hallway made a sharp right. The desk would be around that corner.

In the dim light he could see two figures halfway between the doors and the turn, crouched tightly against the wall. A tall woman and a short man with a light scarf. It had to be them. The sight reminded him of a scene from Bailey's British comedy, the one in which a prostitute led the unwitting hero into a filth-strewn alley, put her back to the bricks of a decaying building, and tried to entice him by slowly raising her dress.

He opened the door farther and squinted against the lack of light. What in hell were they doing? Trying to get around the price of a new scarf? That wasn't likely. The hallway was too big of a risk.

The time was right for a confrontation. As he pushed on the door, a hand appeared from behind him and caught its edge, jarring it to a stop.

"Going somewhere?" It was the bouncer. "Where's your date?"

"She dumped me. I'm going to masturbate in a chamber."

"There's lots of leg on the floor."

"This one was special." Payne pushed the door. The bouncer held it fast. "If you don't mind, I've got an appointment to keep."

"You certainly do." The bouncer grabbed the packet

from Payne's hand. "The owner wants to have a word with you."

Payne extended his hand, fingers outstretched. "Tell him I'll be there in five minutes."

"You'll go now." The bouncer planted his hand between Payne's shoulder blades and gave a shove that sent him stumbling through the doors and into the far wall. He turned and looked back to see the bouncer tugging his sleeve. "This way."

They went straight down the hall. Kelce and the woman were gone. He took solace in the fact that he might see them at the desk.

But when they rounded the corner, the pair was nowhere to be seen. The bouncer laid a hand on Payne's shoulder to stop him, then leaned over the desk and showed the receptionist a plastic card.

"This gentleman is a guest of Lyndon's."

The secretary nodded and typed on a keyboard. Something behind them hissed. A wall raised, turning the L intersection into a T. Behind the sliding wall was a well-lit section of stairs.

"You're about to see a part of this club that few people get to see," the bouncer said.

Payne started up the stairs, the bouncer following. The door hissed ominously behind them.

At the top of the stairs, they stopped for a closed door. The bouncer slid his card into a slot, and the door opened.

Payne was stunned by the size of the office. The largest desk he had ever seen was tucked back in one corner, a large L-shaped affair that held stacks of papers, a computer console, and small silver music disks. The far wall by the desk was a floor-to-ceiling bookcase filled to capacity with books, disks, videotapes, and looseleaf-bound manuals.

The rest of the office was furnished with overstuffed couches and chairs, small tables, and a wet bar. The corner opposite the desk was cluttered with exercise machines, which nearly blocked a small door.

"Where's Lyndon?" the bouncer asked of the others loitering in the room.

"In the shower. He'll be out in a couple of minutes."

"Have a seat," the bouncer told Payne.

"No, thanks." He walked to the window and looked down on the ballroom. He could see the crowd to the edge of the main hall, and for the first time he could see the elaborate patterns the lights made under the clear glass dance floor. The sight amused him, and he became lost in thinking what people might say if they knew they were being watched. He checked the table where he had left Myra. It was hard to tell because of the dimness of the lights, but it looked like she was on her second drink.

"Where's our guest?" The voice carried a British accent thicker and more undecipherable than that of the bouncer's. Payne turned away from the window to see a man emerging from the small door, wrapped from neck to ankle in a thick, black robe, rubbing his hair with a towel.

The bouncer nodded at Payne. The man moved immediately in his direction. Payne met him halfway, and they shook hands.

"Andrew Lyndon-Smith," the man said, his accent now trimmed for an untrained ear. "My enemies call me 'that bastard' or Mr. Lyndon-Smith. Those who don't know me just say 'Mr. Smith.' Friends call me Lyndon. My parents called me Andrew or Andy." His eyes met Payne's with an icy stare. "But they were the only ones."

"Nice to meet you."

"And what might you be calling yourself?"

"Payne."

"Payne-what?"

"Just Payne. That's what everyone calls me. Some call me Mr. Payne, but they're few and far between."

"What about your Christian name? Your mother's maiden name?"

"I don't like them."

"So they call you Payne?"

"When they're not calling me 'that bastard.'"

Smith threw his head back and laughed. The blue in his eyes softened, and his stern look dissolved into amusement. "Get you a drink, Mr. Payne?"

"No thanks. I've got one getting warm downstairs."

Smith laughed again and crossed to the bar. "It's a shame, Mr. Payne, that you forsake the names your mother and father gave you. They gave them for a reason, you know. Worked very hard at it."

"That's a matter of opinion."

Smith fetched a glass from the bar and was using tongs to fill it with ice. "The British have been using the compound last name for centuries. You Yanks always got such a kick out of that. Always such a laugh. The shoe's on the other foot now, Mr. Payne. Used to be that only some of us had them, but now all you Yanks carry them. Matter of law, I hear. What do you think of that?"

"Not much. But then, I wasn't one of those who were laughing."

"And that gives you the right to toss off your mother's surname?"

"Nobody's complained."

"Payne. One syllable. Goes by awfully fast. You need something to stretch it out. People won't remember you."

"Being remembered is for people with egos."

Smith sighed. "I suppose you're right. You can be called what you wish, I guess. Names are just a matter of the law. That should be all you have to use them for if you're so inclined. Have to keep the bloodlines straight and the gene pool clean."

"Something like that."

"I'm a fine one to talk." Smith laughed again and took a long swallow from his drink. "Having tossed off my own Christian name."

"That was my next point."

Smith took a mouthful of ice and crunched it. He set the glass down and stalked to the bouncer. "Enough of the formalities. Do you know why I brought you here?"

"I have the feeling that you want to have a heart-to-heart talk about constitutional rights."

"Something like that." He grabbed the packet from the bouncer, twisting the picture and squinting. "You're upsetting a lot of people with this."

"The only people I've upset seem to work for you. I've shown that to three different people here, and he's one of them. The others are that treasure you've got working the S and M counter, and that shaved mammal you've got in the ticket booth."

Smith said nothing. He opened the packet and pulled out the contents, fanning them for a quick look, ignoring the technical papers. He walked to his desk, examining as he went. He plopped down in his chair and spread the papers out, shaking his head.

"These pictures aren't very flattering."

"You know her?"

"She's my sister."

A wave of relief passed through Payne. The Peppermint Smooth burned in his stomach. Sweat beaded across his forehead, and his brain numbed as the blood rushed back to his heart. *It's over*, he thought. He started to smile but saw that Smith looked grim.

"Where is she?"

Payne blinked. Of course. Smith couldn't know.

Smith put his palms flat on the desk and rose. "Where is she?"

"She's—" The words caught in his throat. "She's dead."

Smith slumped back into the chair. "When the Soviets were crossing the Channel and we were making our plans for escape, my parents decided that they were too old for such a trip. They wanted to stay behind and fight for Mother England. I had decided to stay, too, but they wouldn't have it. We'd already lost almost half the family—my two older brothers died in France. Father told me that I *had* to go. I had two jobs, he said. I had to carry on the family name, and I had to watch after Honor until she was capable of looking after herself. She was the favorite, you know. Father's pet, the only girl. I thought she was smart enough to take care, so I turned her out when she wanted to go. I guess I was wrong." He turned to the papers and stared, going from page to page and shaking his head. "These don't mean a damn thing to me. How did it happen?"

"I'm not sure," Payne said. "I have a few theories."

"Were you her companion?"

"No."

"Then why are you doing this?" He shook the papers at him.

"Her body turned up in my apartment."

Smith said nothing.

"I'd stepped out to buy a few groceries. When I came back, she was lying on the floor. I don't know how she got there. My landlord denies giving anyone access to my apartment."

"Why didn't you get in touch with me sooner? What you've done is in very bad taste, Mr. Payne."

"I didn't know who she was. I'd never seen her before the night she turned up in my apartment. I'd determined that she was a regular here, and I was showing the pictures to your employees in the hope of finding who she was."

"Why should I believe you, Mr. Payne?"

"There's no reason you should. All I've got to show is what you've got spread out on your desk and a room full of tests running at Biotech."

"Biotech?"

"My employer. A bioengineering firm. Your sister showed no outward signs of being killed, so I was running some tests on tissue samples."

"Poison?"

"I can't say for sure. There were no physical manifestations left by common toxins. I think I may have it narrowed down to a couple of things."

"What?"

"I found something in her blood that may have contributed to her death. There might be some kind of bacteria that was breaking down the proteins in her body. I've got to go back to the lab tomorrow and check on the tests."

"What else?"

"Perhaps a complication of the disease. The levels of blood sugars, soluble oxygen, and so on, were severely depleted. Her liver and bone marrow were breaking down, and her adrenal glands had collapsed. It's got to be tied in to that."

"And if it isn't?"

"Then you're back to square one."

"*I'm* back to square one?"

"The case is yours now."

"Like hell it is."

Payne closed in on the desk. "My role in this was as secondary victim. The only reason I was on the Thirty-first was because your sister was a Jane Doe at the time of discovery. That's all changed. She's your blood, and that makes you the primary victim. I'll give you what I've come up with, including the results of the tests cooking at the lab. Beyond that, I'm done. She's your responsibility now."

"You can't do that."

"I certainly can. It's covered in the Amendment."

"Very well then," Smith said. "I'll take your Thirty-first and report that a Mr. Payne of Biotech is responsible for my sister's death."

Payne shook his head. "Oh, no you don't. I can prove myself clear. What we're looking at may turn out to be a new form of bacteria. Your sister was one of the first victims of a new epidemic."

"An epidemic that you started."

"Wrong."

Smith pulled up from the chair. "No, Mr. Payne, quite right. After all, who would be more qualified to come up with a new source of infection? What kind of a grudge made you do it? I'll bet you hated your mother. That always seems to be the reason. Another victim taken from the breast by your beastly government. That's why you refuse to be called anything but Payne, I'll wager. Anything else conjured memories of your mother."

"You'd never make it stick."

Smith gestured at the others in the room. "I have in this room four besides myself who will swear before a judge that you are a known malcontent and have been ejected from this establishment on a number of occasions. I can get others who will swear that your tastes did not run in accordance with the charter of this club."

Payne stared in disbelief.

"Look at your face. You're quite obviously the sort who frequents the clubs of lesser repute."

Things suddenly clicked. "You knew," Payne said. "You knew that your sister was dead."

"Please don't change the subject, Mr. Payne."

"I'm not changing the subject. *You knew, you bastard!*"

"Would you mind explaining this little outburst?"

"You had to know she was dead. You sent a bouncer to get the claim ticket from me. When he didn't get it, he tried to kill me. The only thing is, you didn't count on him dying."

Smith looked past him and at the bouncer. "What makes you think he was a bouncer?"

"Because he was big and ugly," Payne said, pointing. "Like him."

"Kingman," the bouncer said.

"Mr. Payne, would you remember this man's face if you saw it again?"

"Don't get cute, Smith."

"If you would hold your temper, I may have something that could be mutually beneficial." Smith opened a drawer and produced a packet identical to Payne's. He held it out, and Payne took it with trembling hands.

"It's him." It was out of his mouth before he looked at the picture. His hands shook as he tried to study it, but there was no need to. It was the man with the acetone breath. He could taste fear in his mouth. "It's him," he repeated.

"Mark Wilson-Kingman," Smith said coolly. "Your assessment was correct. He was a bouncer, and he did work here. Saturday night he disappeared from work. Early this morning I received a call from a Trauma Treatment Center—"

"Massive internal injuries."

"How did you know?"

"It hasn't been long enough for peritonitis to set in."

"Would you please stay on the subject?"

"I am. I killed your bouncer in self-defense. I pushed him down an elevator shaft. Law Enforcement already knows about it."

Smith exhaled and shook his head.

"There's a point that remains," Payne continued. "Somebody had to carry him out of the shaft because he wouldn't have been in any condition to leave under his own power. And somebody had to put your sister's body in my apartment."

"You think they're related?"

"I'd put money on it." Payne turned away from the desk and walked to the door. "Were I a gambling man."

"Aren't you forgetting something?"

"Not that I know of. I solved your mystery, Mr. Smith. Time for you to solve mine."

"I'm a very busy man."

Payne stopped and spun. "You think I'm not?"

"I've a club to run."

"I've a life to run. No offense to your sister, but I'm glad to be rid of her. She was compounding other problems that are not so easily dealt with." He jerked the door open. "You can tell the law your little story about my being the murderer if you want, because that'll give me the chance to share mine about your having known all along."

"Fifty thousand dollars," Smith said.

Payne caught the door and looked back. "*What?*"

"Would fifty thousand dollars change your mind?"

"You're not serious."

"I am quite serious."

"You'd hire me out to finish your case? I'm not licensed. I'm not even in law enforcement. What you're talking is illegal."

Smith sighed. "It wouldn't be the first time that I was involved in such."

"The answer is no."

"You'll have complete cooperation from me."

"Give it to yourself. I'm not interested."

"If that's the way you feel about it."

"That's the way I feel about it."

Smith turned to the bouncer. "Giles, what do you think Mr. Rodrigues will do when he hears that Mr. Payne was showing around a picture of Honor?"

Giles thought about it. "Kill him," he said emphatically.

"Yes. That's what I thought, too."

Payne froze. "Who's Rodrigues?"

"I'm sure you'll meet him soon enough."

"How does he tie in to all of this?"

"I thought you were no longer interested in this case."

"You're making it sound as if I should be."

"It's something to consider."

"Why?"

"Because Mr. Rodrigues is going to be rather upset when he finds you've been showing a slab shot of my sister. He's a very impulsive person. I wouldn't want to know how he might take news of her death."

"He might take it out on the messenger," Giles suggested.

"On the other hand," Smith said, "I could arrange for his complete cooperation."

"Perhaps you should." Giles nodded. "It'd be a shame to lose someone like Mr. Payne."

"Would you mind telling me what's going on?"

"Planning our strategy. We'd hate to see a repetition of the ugly incidents such as have happened at places like the Satyr or the Threnody. I'd dearly hate for the reputation of this place to be tainted."

"Rodrigues will have to be restrained," Giles said.

"Who is Rodrigues?" Payne repeated.

"The missing link in your chain. But you're no longer interested in the number Thirty-one. You've made that quite clear."

"It's different if my life is in danger."

"I didn't say it was."

"But it might be," Giles added.

"There is a man," Smith continued, "who runs a few rackets out of this place. A fairly harmless lot. His name is Rodrigues, and his temper tends to run a little hot. My sister was living with him until about a month ago. I don't know who she was with at the time of her demise, but I wager Rodrigues would know. He was rather fond of her. He's got that Latin blood, and you know how they are about their women."

So much for Smith's support of assimilation, Payne thought.

"As I said, I don't think he's going to like hearing what's become of our Honor. Even if you were a victim of her killer, I don't quite think he would see things in the same light."

"He's killed men for less," Giles said.

"Maybe he was the killer," Payne suggested.

"Not a chance. To him it would not be logical. To kill her would deprive him as well as whoever he was with. He would much rather see that her companion met with some unfortunate circumstance."

"Like falling down an elevator shaft," Giles said.

"You think he was the one?"

"I don't know."

"It's his style," Giles said.

"You could ask him if you wanted," Smith added, "but I wouldn't recommend it. If, however, assurances were made..."

"What kind of assurances?"

"He wouldn't take kindly to the prospect of exile."

"What if he's the guilty one?"

"That's where I come in."

Payne looked from Smith to Giles and back. Between the two of them, they could probably wrap things up, but they wanted a runner, someone to do the footwork. "Okay," he said. "What's the game?"

"Mr. Rodrigues must be assured that he will not be punished for whatever sins arose from this involvement with my sister. He obviously will not listen to a complete stranger. He will, however, listen to me."

"Has to," Giles said.

"What will you tell him?"

"That he is to give you complete and unadulterated cooperation in this matter, even if he's the guilty party."

"How do you know I'll get it?"

"If you don't," Giles said, "he'll lose his franchise."

Payne wanted to question what Giles meant but thought better of it. From what Smith had said about his checkered past, he didn't want to know any more than he absolutely had to. "What if he's the one who killed your sister? You'll be assuring him that he won't be turned over to the law."

"He won't be," Giles said.

"If he's the son of a bitch who killed my sister, he'll be punished."

"What about me?"

"You'll have your case solved. And you'll have fifty thousand dollars on top of that."

"It'll be taxed the minute I try to initialize the card."

"That'll be taken care of. A forty-five percent buffer will be added to satisfy the government."

"I want half in advance."

"Greedy," Giles said.

"I've got expenses."

"I've foreseen that." Smith slid a stack of materials to the edge of his desk. It was the reformed file on Honor Lyndon-Smith, the file on Mark Wilson-Kingman, and two plastic cards. He reached down.

"Touch them and you've accepted my offer."

Payne looked again. One card was drawn on a local bank. The metallic maroon stripe across the middle showed that it was unused, unassigned, and worth the full amount. The second was a passcard similar to the one Giles had used to get past the desk.

"That second card is an unlimited-access pass to the club. You can go anywhere you want, including up here. It can't be questioned by any of my employees. They're to give complete cooperation to anyone carrying one at the expense of termination if they don't. It'll also cut your expenses. It'll get you in the door free, regardless of ticket class. You'll get your drinks free, and you don't have to change scarves to get into the chambers."

"Does that go for a companion?"

"Of course."

Payne picked up the cards. "How will I know Rodrigues?"

"Giles will point him out to you. From then on, it's your show. You arrange for any confrontations."

Payne walked to the windows and looked down. Myra was on the bottom of her third drink. He thumbed his watch and listened. It was getting late. He turned to Giles.

"How will I know it's not some drunk you're tossing?"

"You'll know," Giles said.

Payne walked back and took the packets from the desk. "I've a better idea."

"You've sealed the deal already."

"Arrange a meeting," he said to Giles. "Tomorrow night at 2100. The hallway to the chambers."

"What'll I tell him?"

"Nothing."

"He won't take that."

"Tell him that I need to have a private chat with him."

"And then?"

Payne waved the passcard. "And then we repair to the chambers."

Giles laughed. "You don't look the type."

"I'm not."

"Don't do anything stupid," Smith advised. "Rodrigues will eat you alive."

"I'm not worried about Rodrigues. He isn't the one we're after."

"How do you know?"

"I can feel it."

Smith laughed. "A psychic. Who are we after, then?"

"When I find out, you'll be the second to know."

"You're sure you don't want me to point him out?" Giles offered.

"Certain. Just give me time to get back to my table and get out."

Smith nodded. "Whatever you say."

Payne left the office, giving the door a solid shove. He stopped and listened as the slam reverberated down the staircase, then cocked his ear and listened for any conversation that might come from the other side. He could discern voices but no words. He descended the stairs, turning the passcard over in the light and looking for the slot to open the door. He needn't have worried. Five steps from the bottom the door raised, letting him into the dim light of the hallway. He turned at the desk and made for the doors, wishing that he would again find Kelce and his mystery woman crouching in the hallway.

As he moved through the doors and into the ballroom he was struck by a wave of heat so powerful that it staggered him. The dancers were in the middle of a fast set, and there was so much airborne sweat that the place smelled like a sick and evil soup. Smoke was rising from the glassed floor as if being ignited by the dancing feet, the lights below strobing oranges and ambers to the illusion that people were spontaneously bursting into flame. Overhead, red and yellow lasers bolted inches over their heads, bright phosphors of liquid light that reminded Payne of color photographs he had seen of night battles in the last century.

He carefully weaved through the casualties, the lights

making them bleed as well as burn. The sound from the speakers that gashed the crowd was familiar, frantic and fast-paced, probably something from the biggest artist of the year. A phrase caught his ear and he recognized it as "Knives." That man wasn't a musician, Payne thought, and he certainly wasn't an artist. He was an industry.

He found Myra precariously slumped in her seat and staring uncertainly at what would be her fourth drink.

"Took long enough," she slurred.

"I didn't take that long."

"Four drinks."

"You're not supposed to throw them down like there's no tomorrow." He grabbed her and pulled her from the table.

"How do you know there's tomorrow?" she screamed above the music. "How do you know we're not going to end up like that girl, all opened up and gutted by Louis?"

He snapped his wrist and jerked her close. "You want the truth? Fine. I can't say that we won't end up just like her. I can't make you any promises."

She tried to focus on him. Her glazed eyes wandered. "See?"

"That's not saying that we will end up like her. We may not even have it. I told you I'd check. You can't run away from this because it looks bad." She started to pull away. He stepped into her and cranked her arm up between her shoulder blades. "You've got to show a little courage, Myra," he breathed in her ear. "You can't get weepy or drunk because things look dark. If everyone did that, we'd be an extinct race."

"You don't understand."

"I understand more than you think. Thanks to your behavior, you're going to have to wait twenty-four hours before I try a blood test. Your blood alcohol level could screw things up. If you've got it, how much damage do you think those little bugs could do in that time?"

Myra's face collapsed. Mascara flowed down her

cheeks, and lipstick smeared across her chin. "Alcohol kills germs," she said, as if reading an advertisement.

"Not this one," Payne said deliberately. "Our girl had been drinking long before she died. Who knows? Maybe alcohol speeds it along."

He let go, and she fell into the booth. He looked at her and shook his head.

"Is there a problem here?"

Payne turned and saw their barmaid. He pulled his passcard and flashed it. Recognition lit the girl's eyes.

"A small one. This lady has overindulged."

"I'm sorry. Had I known . . ."

"Not your fault. She didn't realize her limits."

"How can I help?"

"Would you summon Giles and have him assist me in escorting this lady to the door?"

"Certainly." She nodded politely and was gone.

"Bastard," Myra spat as Payne reorganized his materials.

"What's your problem now?"

She looked up, and contempt burned in her eyes. "You're having me thrown out of here."

"No, I'm not."

"Yes you are. I know who Giles is. He's the head bouncer."

"He certainly is. He's going to assist me in getting you out of here."

"See? I told you."

"I'm leaving with you. You shouldn't be alone right now."

"I sure as hell don't want to be with you."

"Fine. If that's the way you feel about it, you can leave as soon as we're done at Biotech."

She blinked at him, trying to cut through the fog in her head. "Why are we going there?"

"To give blood," Payne said.

Tuesday Morning

*P**ayne* was not surprised to find Myra gone. It was something he had all but predicted in dealing with her drunken behavior the night before.

Giles had helped get her out the door. They tried to walk her out, but she balked and slid to the ground. Exasperated and driven by humiliating stares from those who found it amusing that a great big man couldn't handle a frail little woman, Giles grabbed Myra by the waist and tossed her over his shoulder. With Payne leading the way, they got as far as the sidewalk before Myra threw up. Giles shouted and dropped her in the gutter. She glared and spat vile oaths at them. Payne apologized to Giles, who shook it off, saying it was a job hazard. It wasn't the first time that had happened, and it certainly would not be the last.

Giles returned to the club, and after Payne coaxed Myra to her feet, she managed a wobbling gait down the sidewalk toward his apartment. The magic numbness from the alcohol was beginning to lose its glitter. Her hair strayed from its precision combing and jumped out in random directions, completing the disastrous state of her face.

She looked an utter wreck and was growing weepy and penitent.

"I'm sorry," she sobbed. "I don't want to die yet."

"You're not going to die," Payne growled.

"How do you know?"

He watched her trying to keep balance on a sidewalk that couldn't have been any flatter or straighter. "Because I'm the bioengineer," he said. "I'll pick it apart and find something that kills it."

She shifted her gaze to the night sky and embraced her shoulders. One sleeve of her jumpsuit drifted into the street.

"Hold me," she said. "I'm cold."

"Hold yourself."

"What's wrong with me?"

"You vomited all over yourself."

When she saw it was true, the weeping started again. She tried to tear away the offensive part of the jumpsuit but realized that doing so would leave her uncovered. She sniffed miserably and held the garment over her breasts.

"You going to throw me out?"

"We'll talk about it in the morning."

"Don't you want to talk about it now?"

"I'll wait until you're sober. You won't remember any of this tomorrow."

"Oh, yes, I will," she muttered.

They walked to his place in silence. Once there, he tore off what was left of the jumpsuit and shoved her into the shower, letting cold water pound her skin. She howled in distress.

"You're waking me up!"

"I need you awake." He cut the water and handed her a towel.

"I want to go to bed."

"Not yet. We've work to do."

"But you think I'm too drunk."

Payne tossed a clean jumpsuit in her face. "Not to give blood."

"You said I was too drunk for that, too."

"I lied."

"Bastard."

He filled her with coffee, and they left. Much to Payne's relief, he found Billie working the late shift. He obtained Subject Clearance for Myra, and the trio crossed the lobby and descended stairs that Myra believed led to a chamber of horrors.

Twice she tried to escape, and twice they talked calm reason and got her to lie on a cot. On the third attempt she made it halfway up the stairs and was carried back. This time she was tied down, and Payne slid a hollow tube under the skin of her arm. She fainted as the first thick drops spilled into the half-liter bag, and she remained unconscious through the remainder of the ordeal.

Now free of the burden of Myra, Payne relaxed and lay on a cot while Billie put a needle in his arm. A half liter later, they carried Myra to a recovery room and put her to bed. He thanked Billie for her help and went to his lab space, where he put their blood through the same tests that Honor Lyndon-Smith's now endured.

It was 0300 when he staggered out of the lab, free for what would be too short a time. He went to the basement and pulled Myra from her deep, troubled sleep. She woke to the point where she could walk, and they left; she leaned on his shoulder and engaged in small talk to keep from drifting off.

Both were exhausted by the time they returned to the Plus Fours. He carried her up the stairs and placed her in bed still dressed. After tucking her in he stopped to stare. Her sleep was not at all like Trinina's regression into infancy. Rather, her furrowed look reminded him of someone who was running from something, as if rest carried the realization that something ominous was steadily gaining. He stroked the bridge of her nose to melt the troubled look. It faded, but only for a few seconds. A shift, a sigh, and it returned.

Payne left her in bed and trailed clothing into the bathroom. He turned the shower hot and soaped off the day, letting the water melt him into drowsiness. He slowly toweled off, anticipating sleep before his head hit the pillow.

But when he opened the door to the bedroom, Myra had pulled off her jumpsuit and was sitting up in bed, waiting.

"No," he said without waiting for the question.

She inched to his side of the bed. "Why not?"

"We've been through this once. I don't want to go through it again."

She patted the bed.

"No."

"Give me a reason."

Payne blinked. If he left his eyes closed, he would be asleep.

"It doesn't have to be deep," Myra said. "Give me a reason and I'll leave you alone."

"I'm too tired, and if you had any brains, you'd be asleep, too."

"I won't buy it. I want to know why I'm not attractive to you."

He stood solid. This would probably go on all night if he didn't do this right. He looked past Myra at the bed. Sleep was calling, and he wanted nothing to come between their meeting.

"I like women who are on terms with themselves. The ones that know it's all right to be a little feminine. You're overpowering. There's no mystery to you at all."

"But you told me—"

"I know what I told you. I was wrong. You're female, but you're not a lady."

Myra pulled the sheets up to cover herself. "Why do you say that?"

"Ladies know that men have egos and like to be on the chase once in a while. Ladies carry themselves with grace under stress. They might break down and cry, but they don't hide in a bottle. Ladies show discretion in everything they do and believe in moderation. They don't have to be carried screaming out of clubs."

Myra broke eye contact. "Is that all?"

"Ladies don't throw up all over themselves." It went quiet. He could hear the air in the room freezing. "I'm sorry," he said quickly.

She said nothing but turned her back, curled into the bed, and went to sleep.

When he realized she was asleep, he crawled in next to her and watched her breathe, then turned away and went to sleep, wishing as he went that she would make that pilgrimage to his side of the bed and indicate that all was forgiven.

It didn't happen. When he opened his eyes the next morning, he was lying in the middle of the bed. He bolted up and made a quick check of the apartment. Breakfast was not cooking on the stove. Dishes left in the rack to dry had not been put away. Myra was nowhere to be found. He checked the bedroom closet and found that while half was still taken up with her clothes, some of the garments were gone along with her satchel. No doubt she would come back for the rest when she was certain he was gone, talking the landlord into giving her access with some fabricated story about what an ogre he was. As long as she didn't turn up dead on the living room floor, he could tolerate it.

The thought of the body brought him back to immediate concerns. He needed to check on the cultures to see what they had produced. He also needed to see if the cultures from the Warax Substation had arrived. He had forgotten to check yesterday, and Karol hadn't mentioned them when he was at the desk.

He picked up the telephone. It was dead. The video set worked, but the stations were down, giving him a choice of 200 empty channels. He turned it off and dropped the phone into the carpet. The last time both had gone out, it was three weeks before things were restored. There had been a bombing, and the repair work had been slow.

He walked through his morning routine and was out the door in an hour. The hallways looked brighter, and the staircases didn't feel as threatening as they once had. He felt optimistic and was filled with an energy that he thought had been lost over the weekend. He was in control of his world once more, something that felt very, very good.

On the fourth floor, Payne knocked on Bailey's door. Much to his surprise, a familiar redhead answered.

"Why, Mr. Payne." She grinned. "What a surprise!"

Payne dropped his gaze to the floor. Three milk bottles stood vigil by the door. "A big surprise," he answered.

"This is an informal visit, I hope?"

Payne cleared his throat. "I'm afraid it's formal. Is—"

"Bailey? He's fixing breakfast. Come on in."

"I haven't long."

"Then I'll get him."

Bailey's voice carried from the kitchen. "Who are you talking to? I told you not to answer—" He emerged wiping his hands on a towel, a bib apron hanging from his neck emblazoned with the words I HATE HOUSEWORK. He looked as if he had been caught in flagrant delicto and forced out a muted hello.

"Finally caught up with her, I see," Payne said.

Bailey cleared his throat. "Ran into her at ImoGenes."

"Such a coincidence," she gurgled.

Bailey laid a hand on her bare shoulder. "Go watch the stove for me, would you?"

She pecked him on the cheek. "Certainly."

"And put something on." He stepped out of the apartment and pulled the door shut. "I really did run into her. I swear it's the truth. She got all apologetic about the other night and followed me home like a lost dog."

"Cooking her breakfast, Bailey?"

"I'm playing gentleman."

"I'm never going to let you live this down."

"I was afraid of that. What's up?"

"I won't take long. You have things you need to do."

"Give me a break."

"I wanted to thank you for helping me yesterday."

"You get the case solved?"

"I found out who she was. Does the name Honor Lyndon-Smith mean anything to you?"

Bailey shook his head.

"She's the sister of the guy who owns the Lancaster."

"No lie? How'd he take it?"

"There was some grief, and he swore vengeance, but he had a funny attitude..."

"Like he was expecting to hear the news?"

"Exactly. Like he thought it was inevitable. Why do you ask?"

"After you left yesterday, I started thinking about that face, trying to remember where I'd seen it. I had seen her at the Lancaster in dark corners, secluded tables, hallways, poorly lit corners. She was always with some guy, and it looked like they were doing business."

"Smith said she was the constant of the guy who runs their rackets. I thought he was talking about the S and M concession, but pharmaceuticals would certainly fit into the picture."

"If she was his constant, he might have been keeping her strung out. Is that what killed her?"

"I don't know yet. I'm on to something, but I'll certainly keep drugs in the picture."

"What've you got?"

"I'd rather not say until I know for sure. I do have a favor to ask, though, but I can't explain it to you. You'll have to trust me."

Bailey's face showed concern. "Go on."

"I'd like you to stay away from the clubs, especially the Lancaster. Maybe even postpone your attempts at making an investment. Be really careful for a while."

Bailey nodded. "I will. Thanks." He cracked the door.

"Don't let it get out."

"You've got my word."

The door opened to reveal Glory in one of Bailey's old jumpsuits. She had cut away the bottom half and was wearing it like a nightshirt.

Payne said his good-byes and left, wondering how he would handle Rodrigues that night. He was certain that Rodrigues wouldn't kill him, even if he was the murderer. Too much of his future would hang on whether or not Payne stayed alive. If Payne turned up dead, even as the product of an ex-lover's jealous rage, it would play as an admission of guilt. Rodrigues would have to be calm. Smith would be watching.

Trinina and Nathan. He suddenly realized that he had forgotten his promise to see them tonight.

He bit his lower lip and hurried down the street. If the case didn't clear tonight, he would put it on hold until Nathan's visit was over. It was already the third day, and Payne had seen him for all of two minutes, during which time the boy slept. It wasn't right, and he knew it. Trinina needed his support, and he had denied it. After all, he had nine months to work the case.

There was no good news waiting for him at Biotech. Trinina wasn't in, and she hadn't called. They had tried calling, had tried the pager, and had sent someone by her place, all to no avail. They had also checked with the law. She hadn't turned up dead, for what solace could be found in that. In another day or two Biotech would assume that she had jumped with a patent and assign one of their agents to a Thirty-first. Until then she was merely truant.

To make matters worse, there weren't any parcels from the Warax Substation. He would have to pay Louis a visit, but first he needed to check the cultures.

He wandered up to the fifth floor and thumbed into his lab space. He had left it in a mess: Broken glass was swept hastily into a corner; dirty glassware filled the sink, and clean was scattered haphazardly across the desk and computer console; crumpled wads of notebook paper sprouted like mushrooms from every available flat surface.

It was time to clean up. By habit he would become so immersed in his work that he would let the lab go for the sake of progress. Then something would snap, and he would be unable to do anything constructive until the place was back in order.

He rinsed out the dirty and contaminated glassware and sent them down on the dumbwaiter for sterilization. He sorted and stacked what was still usable on the appropriate shelves and cupboards, and cleared the area of wastepaper, broken glass, and CitruSlush cans, sending them down the InciniChute.

Now in a decent environment, he could get to work. He powered up the computer console, established his security level, and added the word LINK.

IDENTIFY EQUIP DESIRED LINK-IN.

BASCO 101 MODEL/MICROSCAN, Payne typed.

LINK ESTABLISHED.

OPEN SECONDARY LINK.

OPEN.

BASCO 1211 MODEL/ELECTROSCAN TRACKER.

LINKED.

READY PRIMARY LINK.

READY.

Payne left the console and opened the incubator. He looked at the dishes one by one, studying the spots and smears that were sprouting across the medium. He could identify most from the colors and growth patterns. They were common parasite bacteria or low-grade infections that didn't produce symptoms. He shook his head. He wasn't looking forward to doing visuals of each dish, not with the assortment of common organisms present.

Instead he went directly to the inoculations made of the suspected spore cases. A visual examination showed nothing out of the ordinary. He removed the lid and slid it under the microscan.

LOCATE MODE, he typed. GRID COORDINATES.1(−/−).2(+/ −).3(−/+).4(+/+).

Blue laser scanned the plate, making it glow like a

cathode tube. The glow died, and servos lowered the nosepiece to a scanning position midway between the four microchips he had planted.

POSITION LOCATED.

Payne put his eyes to the lenses and manipulated the nosepiece in a tight scanning pattern, the computer keeping him in bounds with a series of beeps.

There wasn't much to see. The medium loomed before his eyes like a great gelled desert. It didn't look right. Something should have been down there, but there was nothing to see.

He found the O-shaped crater left by the inoculating needle and a dot of blood, but there was no sign of anything in the crater. He reduced magnification until he could see the whole circle. Nothing. He increased magnification and slowly scanned the surface inside the crater, his fingers cramping around the mouse. Still nothing. He looked up from the microscan, white circles burning into his brain.

Look again.

He knuckled his eyes into their sockets, the image of what he had seen still visible.

Something's not right.

Again he peered into the scope. There was a random scattering of black dots in the field of view. He decreased magnification.

The random order dropped into a pattern.

"I'll be damned," he said.

The pinpricks of black formed a thin trail that he painstakingly followed out of the crater.

Something was there, and it moved.

Once out of the crater he could see more than sparsely placed pinpricks. By studying the color and patterns in the medium, he could see areas that were thinner than others.

Something was there, and it moved. And it looks like it's been feeding on the medium.

His hand cramped again. He pulled it away, shook it, flexed it. He needed a can of CitruSlush, cool and wet in his throat, solid and cold to wrap his aching hand around. He took the mouse and scanned.

Then he saw it.

It sucked the breath right out of his lungs. Under magnification it seemed every bit as huge as a woolly mammoth. It darted in and out of his field of view so quickly that he wasn't sure what he had seen. He decreased magnification, trembling with anticipation.

There were dozens of them. They were wheeling and turning, swimming over and under each other, occasionally bumping.

They were clearly a cut-and-paste job. No god, no matter what his sense of humor or indignant wrath, could have seen fit to create something so haphazard. They were mushroom-shaped with a thick flagellum that erupted from the base of the stem and tapered to what looked like a razor-sharp point. They didn't so much swim as dart, cracking the flagellum like a microscopic whip. And here, where they were congregated, the medium was thinnest of all.

Payne was sweating and trembling, feeling as if he had looked death in the eye. He dropped the mouse, which smacked against the tiled floor. His other hand reached for the cover of the dish, fumbling it to the floor, where it shattered. He found a new dish and, breathing deeply for control, placed its lid over the culture and clattered it back into the incubator.

Then he fell to his knees and threw up in the wastebasket.

From there he collapsed, lying spread out on the floor like a dog waiting out the August heat.

He was right. They were endospores, and from them had come the things that had killed the girl or had been killing her when she died from something else.

But what?

He had to get out of there. The walls of the lab were closing in. The air was too thick, the temperature too hot. He had spent too much time there.

He crawled to the door and put his thumb to the pad. A wave of cold air slapped his face and put the sour smell of vomit behind him. He turned back and emptied the garbage down the InciniChute.

On the way out he grabbed a can of CitruSlush and had it down his throat before exit decontamination. He took the stairs two at a time, stopping at the desk before leaving the building.

"Anything on Trinina Rueben?"

"Nope," the girl replied.

"Have any cultures come in from Law Enforcement over on Warax?"

"Nope."

"Thanks."

He started toward the Warax Substation, his mind restless and wandering. It kept going back to the image of the thing in the microscope, the swollen head, the slender body, the malignant tail. Those things had to be responsible for the girl's death.

He stepped through the Substation doors and followed the yellow line until it gave way to yellow walls. He went straight to the desk and asked to see Louis.

Louis was busy at the moment, the clerk told him. Could someone else help him? Payne showed his stub. Mr. Louis was assisting him on a matter, and it was urgent that he talk to him. The clerk checked his schedule. Was he sure that nobody else could help? Mr. Louis was going off duty at 1200.

"Tell him Mr. Payne is here to see him."

"Very well, but you're wasting your time."

"Give him the message."

The clerk jotted it on a paper and handed it to a runner, who vanished down a corridor. Payne wandered to the waiting area and sat, unable to control the rush of thoughts in his head.

"Ahoy!"

Louis, clad in a bloody apron, was waddling down the hall peeling paraffin from his fingertips.

"You're late. I was expecting you yesterday."

"You said you were going to send the cultures over."

"I didn't send them because I knew you'd show if they didn't." Louis thumbed his office open and let Payne in, then took his place behind the desk.

"What did you find?" Payne asked.

"It wasn't me. After you left Sunday, I was in the lab doing the slice and dice on her liver, when a colleague came in. He was working some derelict from the McKimson Auto Apartments, so he pretty much knew what the Path was going to be. We get so many of them that you can do it without opening them up.

"Anyway, he saw me working her liver and asked why I was going to all of the trouble—thought I had a derelict, too. I told him the story about this case and how you were looking for a biological cause. Told him all about you, by the way. He wants to meet you."

"What did he find?"

"Well, Roddy—that's his name—has this big thing about the brain. Whenever we get stuck on one, we call him. You should see his office. All sorts of maps of the brain, models, preserved specimens. He offered to take a look. I figured what the hell, two heads were better than one, and I didn't know what your work would turn up.

"It didn't take him long to come up with something. We've got a way of taking apart organs so we can reconstruct them if the Field Expert wants a look. Roddy's our brain F.E., so I let him go to work. He noticed the breakdown in the brain tissue right away. I told him that was the angle you and I were working on, and he took it one step further. He figured what parts of the brain were being destroyed and developed a Path from that. It says that your girl died from exhaustion."

Payne blinked. "Exhaustion? Didn't he mean protein starvation?"

Louis slid a dingy green file folder across the desk. "I was thinking the same way you are. With the depletion levels the way they were, she was certainly headed that way, but it wasn't enough to be fatal. Her body did it for her.

"Whatever was breaking down the proteins had moved into the brain and was working on it. When an area of her brain went dead, she lost that function." He produced a page with a typewritten list. "The main damage was in the area of bodily regulation. Her sleep center was dead. The area that controls digestion was dead. Likewise the area that dictated her fuel needs. She had no sense of when to eat or drink. She had no sense of when to slow down, when to rest."

"She just stopped."

"That's about the size of it. The only other dead area was the one that produces the natural opiates, but it didn't fit into the pattern. It looked to be more from disuse than anything. Its condition reminded Roddy of samples he had seen of heroin addicts."

"Heroin? That hasn't been around for three decades."

"That's what Roddy said. He said that you guys took it out."

"My predecessors did."

"We even rechecked her blood. Couldn't find a damn thing."

"Anything else?"

"No other areas were lost, but a lot were on the way out." He checked the list. "Color and depth perception. Regulation of bladder muscles. Advanced linguistic skills. Sensitivity to cold."

"I wonder if the organism selected these areas or if it was random."

"Roddy said he'd need at least ten more cases before he could tell."

Payne became silent. He felt as if the office was suddenly very cold.

"Is there something you want to tell me?" Louis asked.

Payne sighed. "You may get your ten cases. You may get more."

"It's got to spread. Simple logic dictates that."

"It spreads venereally."

Louis paled. "Are you sure?"

"I haven't proof yet, but I'm ninety percent certain. This thing likes to concentrate where there's protein. One of those places would be the testes."

"Protein and DNA."

"I'm afraid so."

"At least that gives you another symptom to work with. Male sterility. But who's going to admit to it?"

"I would, considering the alternatives. The problem is, I don't know of any symptoms that would give us an early start in catching this thing."

"Where did this stuff come from?"

"It's a handmade. If you saw it, you'd agree."

"Can you trace it to the parent lab? Don't they microengrave a serial number on the nucleus or something?"

"Not without killing the organism."

"Isn't there some way to identify it?"

Payne thought of the Electroscan, turned on and waiting in the lab. "I've got a piece of equipment that analyzes cellular structures by passing electricity through them."

"Doesn't that kill them?"

"There's no amperage in it at all. It links in with a computer and analyzes the cell by measuring microchanges in the electricity running through it."

"Every organism would have a unique pattern, then."

"Exactly. But a trace would take forever. It puts the data into a binary machine code. There's a program available that could run the comparison and trace it, but I don't have the clearance to use it."

"Find someone who has."

"They'll take it out of my hands."

"Payne, you've got to do something."

"We have other factors to consider. What would happen if word got out that there's a new venereal disease that's fatal within, say, a month? Even if this thing turns out to be a fluke, there's going to be a panic."

"It would kill the clubs."

"Exactly. It wouldn't just wreck the economy. It'd tread on the government's toes as well. When the birth rate drops, they're going to wonder what's going on. If it does turn out to be a fluke, they're going to roll some heads."

"I don't go to the public executions," Louis said.

"I don't think either of us would like to be the guest of honor."

"Isn't there someone you can talk to about this? Someone with the clearance? Somebody you trust?"

Payne rubbed his face with both hands. Of course there was. There was someone with clearance who wouldn't turn the case over. Someone who, after all these years, would trust him implicitly.

"Yes," he said.

"Alive, I hope."

"Missing."

"You'd better start looking."

"Yes," Payne said, as if hypnotized.

"You've got to move quickly."

Payne stood and grabbed the report. "If I'm not already too late."

"And if you are?"

"I don't want to think about that yet. Thank you, Louis."

He returned to Biotech, no longer in fear of what waited in the lab space. It was a challenge that had to be met.

The girl at the desk smiled as he pushed through the doors. "Back so soon?"

"Any messages?"

"No, sir."

"Anything on Trinina Rueben?"

"Not yet."

"When was the last time her apartment was given a physical check?"

"Around 0930."

"Are the phones up?"

"Haven't you heard?"

"The station get bombed again?"

She shook her head. "Burned."

He nodded. "I'm going up to my lab space."

"You must be on to something. You've been spending a lot of time up there."

"You might say that."

"Karol says you're going to make yourself sick if you keep closing yourself in like that."

"Human endurance knows no bounds," he said, and raced up the stairs.

Minutes later he was on the third floor, looking for Trinina's carrel. She wasn't the type to commit something as trivial as a password to memory. She had once told him that she would rather use every available brain cell toward progressive thought, and he had laughingly chided her. After all, it had been proved that areas of the brain were structurally different and couldn't change jobs. A cell for holding memory was doomed forever, with never a chance to indulge in creative thought or mathematical calculation.

Her carrel was neat and well organized. The bookshelf was overflowing with textbooks on cellular structures, plant taxonomy, and digestive operation. He rifled through them, checking for notes on index cards or scribblings in book margins that might give the code away. He found nothing but endless notes and sketches of molecular and cellular structures of plants, and observations of the digestive systems of herbivores. The corners of the pages were cluttered with her renditions of cartoon cows. The recurring theme was encouraging, and when he saw a bovine dressed in a lab coat and peering into a Microscan, he knew that she was on to something. Aside from that, there was nothing that hinted at what he was after.

He could no longer wait. He would either bluff his way into the program or do without. If she didn't have the information on paper, then it was something so simple that it couldn't possibly be forgotten. He restored the carrel to order, then hopped the escalator to the fifth floor.

The first thing he did when the lab door sealed was

check the cultures based on his and Myra's blood, taking time to work the fine tuning on the scope. He checked each sample and found nothing. He replaced them and sat in the lab, staring at the wall. He and Myra were clear, which was cause for rejoicing. He wasn't going to fall apart and die as Honor Lyndon-Smith had done.

After sending for two cans of CitruSlush, Payne took the dish in which he had first seen the organisms and put it into the microscan's viewing theater. He shook his head in awe. The population had trebled since his last survey, and areas of the medium that had been totally eaten away were visible to the naked eye as pinholes in the surface of the gel.

He leaned over the keyboard.

PREPARE ISOLATION MODE.

Gears in the machine hummed.

READY.

He took the mouse from its cradle and looked in the scope. Cross hairs were superimposed on the field of view, and flat black letters across the bottom advised ISOLETTE READY. He manipulated the mouse until the cross hairs were over a half dozen of the creatures. He clicked the button, and the words changed.

ISOLETTE LOCK.

Payne clicked the button again, and the screen went dark. A servo arm reached out of the base of the machine and pushed into the surface of the medium. When the field of view returned, he could see that five of the things had been corralled by the white ring. He clicked again.

ISOLIGHT READY.

Isolight was a cute name for it. Everyone at Biotech called it the Death Ray. He rolled the mouse until the cross hairs were over one of the creatures, then clicked the button. The creature shriveled and died. There was no flash, no puff of smoke, not even a hiss from the plate. He rolled the cross hairs to another. A click on the button, and a flash from the base of the scope killed its target. Some of Payne's coworkers made a game of the isolation process, even going so far as to wager money on their prowess with the mouse. To Payne it was like shooting fish in a barrel. Without the Isolette ring it might be more of a contest.

He repeated the procedure until he had five rings, each containing a single organism. He transferred these rings into a separate dish and placed them in the incubator.

Now was the hard part.

He turned to the computer and told it Q-UP ELECTRO-SCAN LINK. When this was done, he stared blankly at the screen. He might as well try to get into the program on his E-6. For all he knew, it might have been declassified.

REQUEST PROGRAM ACCESS/ESCAN IDENTIFIER MK.III.

The screen winked. ACCESS DENIED PAYNEDA.E6.

REASON, he typed.

IDENTIFIER MK.III REQ L.F-1 +.

That's what he thought. He hoped that Trinina had gotten her promotion.

OUT, he typed.

OUT.PAYNEDA.E6/LOGOFF 1301 HRS.

He stared at the screen, the cursor blinking from the upper left corner. He thought carefully about what he was about to do. If he got caught, he might be put as far back as D-9, at which time Kelce would happily walk all over him. Even if he wasn't caught, he would have to reveal his work when he pinned down what had killed the girl. It wouldn't be as bad that way, perhaps only resulting in a severe censure. Either way he would have to try and break in to the program. He would have to be damned clever. If the computer caught him, he would be sealed in the lab space until a computer supervisor was on the other side of the door.

"Let's try it," he said.

IN.

LOGON READY.

ASHAHN-RUEBEN.TRININA.F-1.LINK.

ENTER CODE.

Payne sighed with relief. She had made the F's. Now

if he could remember her Social Identity Number. He put the numbers down and entered.

HAVE YOU FORGOTTEN AGAIN?

Payne looked at the numbers and cursed. Two were inverted. He reentered it.

PERHAPS YOU SHOULD CHECK YOUR SIN CARD.

He almost laughed. Trinina never remembered her SIN number. He could almost hear her talking back to the program. He tried another variation of her number.

ASHAHN-RUEBEN,TRININA.F-1.LOGON AT 1331 HRS.

Payne wiped sweat from his forehead and reached for the second can of drink. He cracked it and drank until his shaking stopped.

LINK, he entered.

IDENTIFY EQUIP DESIRED LINK-IN.

BASCO 1211 MODEL/ELECTROSCAN ID.

LINKED.

OPEN PRIMARY LINK.

READY.

He took a deep breath. Time to make or break.

REQUEST ACCESS PROGRAM/ESCAN IDENTIFIER MK.III.

ACCESS START ENTER CODE.

Payne felt ill. There was no turning back. It had to be something obvious. An undeniably simple logic to the identity of the number.

KLK2880. Her telephone number. The first three entries had to be alphabetic, so he used the equivalent.

The screen went completely blank.

That does it. I've been caught. The computer knows that she hasn't shown up today.

The cursor appeared in the upper left corner. He had been bounced off line. He reached over and thumbed the door. It unsealed. He canceled the order and settled back into his chair. He wasn't in trouble yet.

Try again?

He got her SIN number on the first try. When he reached the access code, he froze.

What was it?

Keep it simple, old boy.

He stared at the screen.

Well, don't just sit there like a fool . . .

The screen went blank, the cursor jumping home. There must have been a time limit on the damned thing.

Once more. His fingers darted over the keys until he was staring at that taunting phrase.

ACCESS START ENTER CODE.

When in doubt, the answer is always the simplest of those available.

Then it fell into place. He reached over and typed.

NRP0505.

PROGRAM ACCESS GRANTED. ENTER NUMBER OF ORGAN-ISMS.

Payne fell back in his chair and sighed. Nathan's initials and the first four digits of his date of birth. Good old Trinina. He told the computer to sample one organism.

MOUNT SAMPLE.

Now he was coasting. He pulled a prepared ring from the dish and opened a small cabinet adorned with high-voltage warnings. The interior was thick glass with two slender prods that rose from the base. He put the ring between the two prods, then plugged them into a terminal in the back of the cabinet. Sealing the door, he turned back to the computer.

MOUNTED.

SET LEVELS.

He spent the next few minutes setting the degree of analysis he wanted, requesting everything the program had to offer. When the levels were set, he told the computer to run the scan. High-voltage warning lights blinked, and the doors locked shut. He sat for ten minutes, keeping an ear tuned to the sounds the cabinet made and occasionally sniffing the air. If voltage was overestimated, the sample would incinerate, ring and all.

At the end of ten minutes a bell rang, the illuminated letters dimmed, and the cabinet doors unlocked. Payne took the ring from the cabinet and dropped it into a test tube full of Alamex, sealing it with a rubber stopper and paraffin.

The computer obliged his request for a readout, and for five minutes binary code rolled up the screen. He tried to pick out individual elements of the organism as the code flickered, but he had never mastered the language.

READY IDENTIFY MODE, he typed.

LOAD CODE.

He struck a button, and the code was dumped in thirty seconds.

HOLDING, the computer advised.

RUN IDENTISCAN.

RUNNING.

It was disconcertingly quiet. There were no timing beeps, no flashing cursor. Payne believed he had finally been caught, and when the computer finally did beep, he jumped.

That's it? he thought.

He looked at the screen. One word stared back.

LOCATED.

Payne touched the return key. Letters spilled out across the screen.

BIOTECH INDUSTRIES IDENTISCAN/ELECTROSCAN MK III LINK.

ORGANISM IDENTITY: BIOTECH INDUSTRIES LOT NO.90874353XYL.DBK.

ORGANISM TYPE: HANDMADE.

ORGANISM SOURCE: BIOTECH INDUSTRIES BRANCH 101.

Branch 101. It had come from this building. His stomach began to sink.

ORGANISM RATING: LABSAFE/MALEVOLENT TYPE IV.

CURRENT RESEARCH STATUS: ABANDONED.

PRESS RETURN FOR MENU.

The organism had been classified as useless, and research had been abandoned. A small sample would be kept in the archives for future reference, but would be carefully guarded. Somehow it had gotten out. He called up the menu and requested the history.

ORGANISM'S DEVELOPMENT WAS INSTITUTED OUT OF INTEREST IN NEEDS PRESENTED BY RECENT PROBLEMS IN LUNAR COLONIZATION.

ORIGINAL CONCEPT: DEVELOP HUMAN COMPATIBLE PARA-SITE ORGANISM FOR MORE EFFICIENT B'DOWN AND DIGESTION OF FOOD RATIONS BY COLONISTS.

SECONDARY CHARACTERISTICS: ORGANISM TO HAVE ABIL-ITY TO TAP HUMAN RESERVES OF STORED FATS FOR USE AS FUEL.

TERTIARY CHARACTERISTICS: ORGANISM TO HAVE ABILITY TO LIBERATE FAT-SOLUBLE OXYGEN IN BODY AND/OR TRAPPED IN FOODSTUFFS.

It was developed for a most noble cause: to make human digestion more efficient. If such was the case, more colonists could live on limited amounts of supplies. It could also be used Earthside in areas of famine.

REASONS FOR REJECTION: (1) INTOLERABLE MUTAGENIC RATE (26.25258%). (2) ORGANISM PATHOLOGY (Q.V.).

Now he knew how it could survive outside of the lab. One in four organisms would die or develop undesirable tendencies. It was entirely likely that it had overcome its lab-safe status. The problem was to determine how it had gotten out of the lab in the first place. He called up the organism's pathology. What he read terrified him.

The organism had been rejected because it had a tendency to break down proteins, which he already knew. The lot was inefficient because it refused to go after fats or soluble oxygen. Something the report had failed to mention was the fact that it would go after *any* proteins, not just those that were newly introduced. There was an excellent reason for this oversight, which Payne found as he continued.

In digesting the proteins for its own use, this organism produced a waste product that was inert until it linked with another compound in the body.

This other compound was the chemistry of memory.

The brain was responsible for producing a host of compounds that ensured its continued functioning. One set of these was manufactured when one of the five senses was stimulated. These were the compounds that caused brain cells to transmit their stored information: their memory. The waste product of the organism readily linked with this compound to form a third compound, which in turn stimulated a different part of the brain.

The pleasure center.

And it worked better than the brain's own chemicals did. The union produced an orgasm more overwhelming and intense than the brain's chemistry could.

Payne read the report through again to make sure he had it right, his chest tightening as if he were being crushed.

It was a drug.

But there were flaws. Stored memory might be tapped for the sensation, but it was hard enough to concentrate during a conventional orgasm. The experience the drug produced would shatter any form of concentration, breaking its own vicious circle.

Unless something else stimulated the memory.

The sense of smell was the strongest trigger of memory. He thought of the scent of Trinina's apartment and its effect on him.

Next was sound: music. They'd had a song, too. Hearing it after a long time did wonders for bringing memories, both good and bad, to the surface. And he would probably never be able to listen to "Danse" again. Not that he would want to in the first place, but the memories associated with—

"No," he said.

There's music at the Lancaster, and there's always some scent in the air—smoke, sweat, or the perfume of your partner—

This was the perfect drug for the Lancaster Club.

—and the more you dance, the more you sweat, which means that there's more in the air—

What was it Bailey said about wearing your alcohol rather than drinking it?

—and it sinks into your clothes, and you wear it home with you.

Was that what Kelce was doing in the hallway? A brief transaction conducted with a hypodermic needle? Was it really an accident that this lot had escaped from the lab?

It couldn't be that easy. He was running on guesswork. He needed proof, something solid, something concrete. Something he could hold in his hand and show to Sergeant Delgado.

He looked back at the display. His evidence was there, in a neat row of letters across the very bottom of the screen.

ORGANISM DESIGNER: DEREK BARTHOLOMEW-KELCE.

Tuesday Night

*P*ayne clenched his teeth and shook with rage, glaring at what the computer was showing him, trying to deny the words on the screen. But there was no escaping the truth. All the computer had done was confirm his darkest suspicions.

He had accessed a program used in making projections based on organism pathology. In a matter of hours he had entered Honor Lyndon-Smith's autopsy, the most outstanding feature of which was a protein breakdown curve that Payne had done using another program.

When he finished this task, he called for the projections. Even though based on the limited information available, they were bleak enough to throw Payne into depression.

The good news was that chances of aerobic contamination were less than one-tenth of one-hundredth of one percent. There was no way that he or Myra or anyone else would catch it by breathing the air in the Lancaster. That was the only good news.

Taking what little Payne was able to give and defining a "fully contaminated individual" as one beyond the point of medical help, the computer rendered the following projections:

Transmission by saliva from a fully contaminated person was a one in five possibility.

Transmission by a fully contaminated female was 62.1 percent.

Transmission by a fully contaminated male was 98.808 percent.

Once infected, a victim would become fully contaminated in three to seven days. After this, infection would prove fatal in fifteen to forty-five days. Depending on the organism's appetite and what organs it attacked, it could kill its host in a myriad of ways. The most grotesque of these was the disruption of the bond between cells in a soft organ. At any given moment, a random part of the body would cease to exist, melting and flowing with the pull of gravity. If that organ was the skin, the victim's insides would fall to his or her feet, still connected by tissue and viscera and nerves.

Yet none of this caused Payne's rage. He was sitting, face ashen, trying to absorb what he was reading, when the thought struck.

What if an infected woman is pregnant?

A discovered cure might help if she was partially infected, but if she was fully contaminated, the baby could be taken and surrogated or incubated until term.

Couldn't it?

He typed in one more command.

PROJECT MORTALITY RATES FOR EMBRYO/FETUS DURING PREGNANCY.

The computer complied and threw a curve on the screen.

Contamination probability was 99.09 percent.

The death rate was a slow curve: 100 percent fatal from conception to nine weeks, trimming down to 82 percent fatal for a term infant.

He threw open the incubator doors and grabbed a bottle of Alamex. He glanced over the warning on the label.

A nice, thick layer over all the cultures would do the job. From what he had seen in the girl's blood, the lot did not stand up to the compound. They would vanish without a trace, not even leaving a bladed spore.

He looked back at the incubators. Perhaps it would be easier to use the "purge" command and let heat and radiation do the rest.

No. It had to be the Alamex. He knew that would work. He uncorked the bottle and removed the first dish,

Then reason stepped in. He had to have something to show Delgado, and all the available information would be needed when the bodies started to pile up. It might be enough to avert a major spread. He recapped the Alamex and put it back on the shelf, closed the incubators, and made sure the temperatures were correct. When he was certain everything was secure, he policed the area, stacking notes and reports and tossing drink cans away. When all was done, he bolted out the door.

He went to the second floor, where he found Kelce's carrel and rifled the contents, looking for anything that might give him an edge. If he went before the board, anything he found would be thrown out as a product of illegal search and seizure, but at this point he didn't care. There were lives that needed to be saved.

He found nothing of significance. There might be something locked in the built-in safe, but only Kelce's thumb would open it. Disgusted, Payne stomped off, leaving his mess for Kelce to find.

The elevator to the main level was too slow and too long in decontaminating. He ripped the plastic from his body as he descended the stairs, handing the shreds to the girl at the desk.

"Toss these, please."

"You're being very wasteful with these suits, Mr. Payne."

"Put them on my account, okay? Where's Kelce?"

The girl checked the personnel board. "Mr. Kelce has left for the day."

"Give me his home address."

"I'm sorry, he wasn't going home."

"How do you know?"

"He told me not to forward any calls. He wanted me to take messages."

Payne's eyes narrowed. "Messages?"

The girl gave a coy smile. "Women are always calling for him. Some men, too. He's that way, you know. Karol told me."

"How many calls does he get in a day?"

"Some days it's real slow, but weekends it seems like that's all we get. I'll bet he's got his twenty-five-prole ring by now."

Payne clasped the girl's hand. "You've been very helpful. I'm sorry I was so short with you."

"That's fine. Mr. Kelce has been out of sorts, too. Do you want me to take a message for him?"

Payne thought about it. "Yes. Tell the son of a bitch that I want to see him."

The girl looked up from her pad in dismay.

"Those exact words."

"Thank you, Mr. Payne," she said, blushing. "I'll see that Mr. Kelce gets your ... message."

"Thank you."

He started in the direction of Trinina's. After three blocks he decided it was futile. It seemed she was missing, and not even the Biotech agents could find her. He would give her until 1900 to appear. He would show up as promised, and if she didn't make it, then to hell with her.

He detoured into a small deli whose solar panels were decorated with canvas to look like antique awnings. The inside was packed, a surprise because the prices were double that of anywhere else. Looking around, he saw the reason why: a sign above the counter proudly proclaimed "WE USE NO SYNTHS. ALL 100% REAL PRODUCTS." He thought about leaving but decided that he had worked hard enough to justify a reward. He took a number and fell into line. When his turn came, he ordered a roast beef sandwich with the works to go, a carton of real milk, and a whole tomato. The bill was over twenty dollars. Still, he was pleased. The sack crackled happily in his hands as he carried it home.

Once there, he opened the carton of milk and took a long swallow. It was fresh and cold and didn't have a plastic synthate aftertaste. He put the food on the coffee table, filled a tumbler with ice in the kitchen, and checked the bedroom closet on his way back. Myra's things were still there. She'd need a day or two to calm down and think things over.

He poured the milk into the tumbler and sat down to eat. The beef had a rich flavor that the beef synths lacked. The onions had a pleasant bite and were almost too hot.

He was polishing the tomato against his jumpsuit when the pounding came, startling him. At first he thought it could be Myra, but the knock was too forceful to have come from her hand. Perhaps she had brought a bouncer to help carry her things.

Checking the peephole, he saw a group of men in Federal Blue government uniforms, complete with sticks and fiberglass skullcaps. They pounded again.

"Payne!"

He retreated to the couch and answered. "One minute!"

The pounding came again. He gathered up the sandwich, tomato, and milk and rushed them into the ice chest.

"Payne! Open up!"

Brushing crumbs from his clothes, he hurried back to the door and turned the knob. When the bolt cleared the jamb, the door burst open, knocking him back into the living room. Five men in Federal Blue streamed in, blocking the path to the door as it closed.

"Mr. Payne? My name is Davis." The speaker tapped the lieutenant's bars on his shoulder. "I'm with Federal Enforcement. You don't mind if we take a look around your place, do you?"

Payne turned to watch the others swarming over the

apartment. "It doesn't look like I've got a whole lot of choice in the matter, do I?"

"Don't get smart with me, Mr. Payne."

"Don't get smart with *you*? You're the ones who burst in here like—"

Davis put his hand to his stick. "No unseemly comparisons, please."

"Would you mind telling me what this is all about?"

"You're under investigation."

"What the hell for? How about showing me a warrant—providing you have one."

An officer peeked out from Payne's bedroom, a gloved hand choking several of Myra's clothes. "Lieutenant. Women's clothing."

The lieutenant smirked.

"You don't have a warrant, do you?"

"Since when does the government need a warrant?"

"You're violating my constitutional rights."

"The Constitution's bullshit," Davis snapped. "Where is she?"

Payne held fast. "Who?"

"The owner of these clothes. Unless you wear them, faggot."

"Who wants to know?"

Davis jerked on his stick. It came out of its sheath and struck Payne in the solar plexus. He went down, gasping for breath. The Federals formed a barrier between him and the rest of the apartment.

"The girl's not here," one said.

Davis smiled. "I do hope we can get some cooperation out of you, Mr. Payne. You're in a fucking bit of trouble right now."

"If you want Myra," Payne wheezed, "she's gone."

"Myra? You're quite funny. We, however, are quite serious." He raised his stick, but one of the officers grabbed it by the tip.

"You interfering?" Davis hissed.

"He's telling the truth. Those aren't the girl's clothes. Some of the suits are tagged with that name—Myra."

Davis leered. "You get around, Mr. Payne."

Payne gulped, still trying to catch his breath. "Would you mind telling me what you're talking about?"

The intervening officer knelt beside him. "The lieutenant is a bit overzealous. We're trying to locate Trinina Ashahn-Rueben."

Payne sat up. "You're the good cop, right?"

The officer's look went from compassion to rage. He slapped Payne with an empty glove. Payne's finger went to his lower lip. When he drew it away, it was bloody.

"I guess pretend time is over."

Payne was shoved back into the floor. "We'd better get some cooperation or you'll fucking disappear. Get me?"

"She's not here," Payne said sourly.

"We know that, asshole."

"Have you tried her apartment?"

The officer slapped him again. "Don't get cute."

"You're the detectives."

The officer screamed and fell on him, hands leaping for his throat. Payne brought his knee up, which kept his attacker away long enough to be pulled off by his colleagues.

"The girl's apartment burned early this afternoon," Davis said quietly. "Started in an overheated coffeepot. Completely gutted her apartment, ignited the one above it, smoke damage to a bunch more. No bodies."

"Why do you want her?"

"She bolted with your child."

"You're with the Child Rearing branch?"

Davis nodded.

"You think she brought Nathan here?"

He nodded again.

"You're all stupid bastards. I don't know where she is."

"Prove it."

Payne laughed. "You're supposed to be more efficient than that. I'm sure you've been trained in cranial tapping."

"We don't like to mess up our uniforms."

"You want an alibi? Go check with Biotech Industries. They're looking for her, too. She's become quite popular lately."

"Get on with it."

"Ask the girl at the desk about me. She'll verify that I've been very concerned for Trinina's welfare. If I'd known she was going to cause me this much grief, I wouldn't have come home."

"How do we know you haven't hidden her?"

"I haven't seen her in five years."

"And you work in the same building?"

"Okay, I take that back. I saw her and the boy on Sunday. I stopped in to get acquainted but left after a few minutes because the boy was asleep."

"Anything else you'd like to share?"

"Yesterday I went to her place to visit, to see if I could catch Nathan while he was awake. The door was open when I got there, but she was gone. I thought she'd stepped out for a few minutes because there was coffee brewing. I locked the door as I left to keep someone from cleaning the place out."

"Why are you telling us this?"

"Think about it. Monday I lock the door on a live coffeepot, and today the pot catches fire and burns the place. Obviously nobody's been in her apartment since yesterday. Trinina's got a twenty-four-hour jump on you."

"You seem very amused by all of this," Davis said coldly. "Do you have any idea what's going to happen when she gets caught?"

"Does that count you guys getting together for a little gang rape? If you're trying to worry me, save your breath. You're not going to find her."

"You seem rather sure."

"I've got good reason. Trinina's smarter than I am, and she's certainly smarter than the lot of you put together."

Davis raised his stick.

Payne opened his arms. "Do you see her here? Did you find her by beating information out of me? You've been had, Lieutenant."

Davis looked at the others and holstered his stick. "Let me remind you of something. Child-stealing is a felony according to a rather liberal interpretation of the Twenty-ninth Amendment. If you're harboring Ms. Rueben, your sentence will likely be the same as hers. The GCR doesn't like to be screwed with."

"You're not scaring me. She has you beat, and you know it."

"We have a ninety-eight percent recovery rate."

Payne pointed. "There's the door, Lieutenant."

Glaring, Davis opened the door, and his men filed out, leaving Payne with his victory. He limped into the bathroom and checked his lower lip. It was split, but considering the other marks on his face, the wound didn't seem out of place. It might not be a bad idea to apply some Healing Wax before seeing Rodrigues.

The milk was still cold, and the sandwich tasted better after sitting on ice. The tomato was plump and juicy and stung his lip—a small price to pay for the real thing. With his stomach full, his mind was drawn to the fact that Trinina had bolted with Nathan. Had he not been so involved with other things, he might have seen it coming and been able to prevent her from doing it. But if her mind was made up, she would have done it anyway, no matter how much reasoning or bent-knee pleading he would have done.

Stubborn girl. Where did she think she could run? He hoped that she had a plan and that she would get away with it. Most of all, he hoped that when she got to wherever she was going, she would take the time to drop him a letter.

Enough of that for now. He needed to get to the Lancaster. It was well before 2100, but he wanted to sit and watch the crowd for victims of Kelce's bug. He wanted to get an idea of how widespread the infection was. The "locate" program had given him a list of observable symptoms, and he was hoping that these would explain some of the strange behavior he had seen in previous visits.

When he got to the club, he slid the new passcard under the glass partition. The clerk looked up sourly.

"What some people won't do for a freebie."

"What's your problem?"

"You blackmail the old man with your photography?"

Payne watched him move and listened to him talk. He didn't look contaminated. "Mr. Smith insisted that I have this."

"I'm sure."

"Give me the card back and let me in."

"Pushy, aren't we? My, my. Get a little leverage on the old man and you think you own the place."

"I wouldn't have it," Payne snapped, and reclaimed his card. He walked straight in and accosted the first bouncer he saw. "Excuse me."

"Need something?"

The lips looked okay. "Your name, please."

"Leonard."

"Leonard. Do you know Giles?"

He nodded. "My boss."

"How long have you worked here?"

Leonard scowled. "What's the big idea?"

Payne flashed the card. "Answer the question, please."

"Four . . . no, five months."

"Have you been puked on yet?"

"Why do you want to know?"

"How would you get the smell out of a new jumpsuit?"

Leonard's nose twitched, and he grimaced. "I suppose I would . . ." His face became cynical. "Are you selling something?"

Payne clapped him on the back. "Nothing at all. You've

been very helpful, Leonard. I'm recommending you for a raise."

He continued through the lobby. The bouncer was clear. His newness to the job had probably saved him. The old hands would be testing the merchandise and sampling the clientele when it was slow. Leonard was undoubtedly avoiding all of that until his probation was up.

His next stop was the S and M concession, where he flagged down the fabulous brunette.

"Hey," she said, "aren't you..." Her eyes blinked in rapid succession.

"Are you okay?" Payne asked. Her lips were covered with high-gloss red.

The girl blushed. "I'm sorry. What do you need?"

Payne waved the card. "Your name, please."

"Frannie," she said. "Frannie..."

"How long have you worked here?"

She blinked. "Uh...not long."

"Do you remember your senior year in high school?"

"Do I?" She giggled. "Oh..." She went rigid and arched her back, her nails clawing the glass counter top. Perspiration masked her face. "Oh..."

"Are you okay?" he asked again.

She broke out in gooseflesh and shook her head. She took a gulp of air and tried to regain her composure. "Yeah," she said unconvincingly. "Fine."

"Thanks for your time," Payne answered, and walked away. She was as good as dead.

In the lobby he asked casual questions of three more people. All were clear. At that point he decided to single out those who were exhibiting what looked like the secondary symptoms. Sampling in this manner was infinitely impractical but was less troublesome and more immediate than asking each individual for a sample of sperm or blood.

"What's your name?" he asked of a highly painted woman on a bar stool.

"You don't mince words," she said.

"What's your mother's maiden name?"

"You interested in babies or pleasure?"

She wasn't sick. He felt regret, wishing that he could warn everyone not tainted to leave, to refrain from sex, but he couldn't, lest a panic start. A more subtle approach was in order. What if he told people that the drinks here were watered down?

He bumped into another girl. She turned, and he caught the odor on her breath. It was thick with acetone.

"What's your name?"

"Alantha."

"What's your mother's maiden name, Alantha?"

"It's . . ."

"What's your Social Identity Number?"

She blinked and went into gooseflesh.

"What's the scent of your favorite cologne?"

A moan slipped from her lips, and she arched back.

"The words to your favorite song?"

She fell into him, sinking her nails into his arms. "Devil," she panted into his ear, "you know how to work it by talking. Ask me more."

"The first man you had sex with."

She gasped.

"The first woman you had sex with."

She yelped and fell backward, releasing his arms, hands twisting into knots. He let her fall to the floor like a stone.

"I give you a week to live," he said, and called for a bouncer.

He continued to look for the outward signs and followed up with a diagnostic interview. He became proficient at spotting cases and by the end of an hour had found eighteen in the swelling crowd. Three out of four people he approached were infected. The remainder thought he was a terribly forward sort who was looking for money, entertainment, or both. By the time he stopped, the bouncers were giving him the evil eye—four of his interview subjects had to be carried away. None, however, seemed to be as advanced as Alantha, which led him to believe that the disease was still in its first month out of the tube.

"Danse" pounded through the speakers, and Payne thumbed his watch. 2101. He was a minute late.

He rushed through the center of the crowd. The numbers of people who participated were beginning to dwindle as the top of the hour came and went. It looked as if the "Danse" was losing its appeal. He sidestepped as a man in the throes of something hit the Plexiglas.

Then the thought struck him. Was the crowd thinning because a growing number of people were incapable of dancing? Could they no longer control themselves on the floor? After all, what evoked more memories than a number one song?

He pushed on double doors and checked the corridor. Halfway down, a small man was leaning against the wall, cigarette dangling from his mouth. His arm was bent, and he was thumbing his watch.

"Twenty-one oh-five and fifteen seconds, mark," the watch was reporting. "Twenty-one oh-five and twenty seconds, mark. Twenty-one oh-five and twenty-five seconds, mark..."

"Rodrigues?"

The man looked up. He was smaller than Payne had imagined, and he didn't look dangerous at all. His eyes were two dark beads. When he sucked on the cigarette, light from the burn revealed a strong chin, a bent nose, and a thick mustache. "You're Payne?"

"Yeah."

"The Smith says you wanted to talk."

He nodded.

"What do you need?"

"Your Social Identity Number."

"What is this? A joke?"

"The first woman you had sex with."

Rodrigues took the cigarette from his mouth and stabbed it in the air. "I don't run with the clientele here, Mr. Payne."

"What kind of cologne was she wearing?"

He slid the cigarette back in his mouth. "I'm out of here."

Payne grabbed his shoulder. "Smith said you'd talk to me."

"He didn't say you were going to ask for personals. What are you, some kind of voyeur?"

"Answer the question."

"Which one?"

"The cologne will do."

Rodrigues knit his eyebrows. "Garlic. We were both in college. She worked part time as a fry cook. I went to see her one day when she was closing the place. She was all sweaty from cooking and smelled like garlic. We went back into the meat locker and—"

"That's enough."

"You asked."

"I wanted the scent, not True Confessions. Let's get a room."

"I thought you wanted to talk business."

"I do."

"You've got a funny way of breaking the ice."

"I have my reasons."

They walked to the desk, where Payne waved his pass-card. "Room for two."

Rodrigues put his hand on Payne's arm and leaned down to the woman. "The usual."

The woman nodded and gave him a magnetic key. Rodrigues turned down the hall toward the chambers, waving for Payne to follow.

The room they went to was in the middle of the honeycomb of chambers, fourth corridor, fifth room on the left. Rodrigues plugged the key, and the door opened. "After you."

Instead of the usual well-padded chamber and fixtures, they walked into a small office complete with computer terminal, desk, two small chairs, and a love seat. He turned back to Rodrigues. "They take things seriously here, don't they?"

"The Smith doesn't do anything halfway." The door closed tight behind him.

"I'm impressed. I expected something in a basic back alley."

Rodrigues sat behind the desk and tapped a box on one corner. "Smoke?"

"No, thanks."

Rodrigues produced another cigarette. "So talk," he said, lighting up.

"I want to talk about the rackets. Smith said you had the franchise on the rackets here."

"Perhaps."

"Spare me. You don't get a chamber converted to an office like this on good looks." He sat down in a chair.

"Is that a compliment?"

"What do the rackets entail?"

"What do you want them to entail?"

"Drugs."

"You're naive, aren't you?"

"I wanted a confirmation. What else?"

"Minor stuff. I fence things I might be able to use or unload. I arrange citizenship for immigrants or refugees on occasion. That's kind of rare, though, and rarer still when we can pull it off. Few people want to claim this country as their own."

"You could probably make a good concession out of getting people out of the country."

"If I wanted."

"You stick to small stuff. Drugs."

"Yeah. Do you mind telling me what this is all about? The only word I got was if I gave you my full cooperation, you wouldn't turn me over."

"That's right."

"Turn me over for what?"

Payne sighed. "I'm told you knew Smith's sister."

Rodrigues stared. "Yeah. What about her?"

"She's dead."

Rodrigues swallowed.

"I understand she was your companion. I'm sorry to have to break the news. I thought Smith would."

He shook his head. "Not his style. What happened?"

"I found her dead in my apartment. Smith wouldn't carry her Thirty-first, so I am."

"That bastard. He wouldn't." He calmly blew smoke. "Was it drugs?"

"Why is it that everyone I've talked to about her seems to have expected this?"

"It was inevitable. I just didn't think it would happen this soon."

"Tell me more."

"What's there to tell? You know how you get suckered in by a woman, Payne? They set you up so you're thinking you've really got something, then it turns out they're only manipulating you, that they've been after something all along?"

Payne nodded sympathetically.

"That was Honor. She was special, but she was so screwed up. She put the plays on me, and fool that I am, I fell for them. I don't know what her problem was. The only reason she put up with me was because I ran the rackets here. Being her brother's place, they didn't dare kick her out. She knew too much."

"You supplied her with drugs?"

"No. She helped herself. My inventories were always running short. If it did something different to her, she'd take it. Stimulac, Blueskies, Sneeze, even Alka. I don't know what made her do it. Could be she wanted to go home."

"England?"

He nodded. "I got the impression she left someone behind in the rush to get out."

"Drugging to forget?"

"Doesn't make sense, does it? Not if it's someone you'd like to keep alive in memory. Anyway, she was a walking chemistry set. She wasn't happy with me, so she threw me over for one of my suppliers."

Payne kept quiet.

"He was keeping her happy, last I heard. He was weak-willed and knuckled under to her."

"What was his name?"

"He wasn't the type to kill her, if that's what you're after. She was the one who took the fatal shot, the last pill, whatever it was. It was a long, slow suicide."

"I want the name of your supplier."

"It's really not necessary, Mr. Payne. You've got your answers."

"No, I don't, Rodrigues. You're supposed to cooperate, so damn it, start."

Rodrigues shook his head.

"Why are you protecting him? He's just a maggot, a parasite. He's the one who supplied Honor with the drug, he's the one who was with her when she died, and he's the one who left her in my apartment. He's a thief, Rodrigues. He's stolen from his employers, and he stole your woman. If he was working for you, you'd cut him out. But you're letting him walk all over you. Why?"

Rodrigues looked into Payne's eyes. "You know who he is."

"Of course I do."

He jumped from his seat. *"Then get off my back!"* he shrieked.

Payne stood and grabbed Rodrigues by the lapels, pulling him across the desk and knocking paper and cigarettes and money to the floor. "I've got to hear it from you. Quit being such a coward, Rodrigues. What would Smith say?"

Rodrigues blinked numbly. Payne could feel his strength. Rodrigues could easily reverse the situation and leave him dead with a broken neck, yet he was taking the abuse. Whatever he was hiding was important. He shoved him back into the chair.

"To hell with you. I'll get it from Smith. And he'll get an earful from me." He turned to the door.

"Kelce," Rodrigues spat.

Payne stopped. "That wasn't so bad, was it?"

"You don't know what you're doing," Rodrigues babbled. "You don't know what you're getting into."

Payne turned on him. "And you don't know what you've started, mister. If you think Honor's death was a bloody shame, wait until people start dropping dead on Smith's dance floor."

Rodrigues was trembling.

"Kelce is nothing. Kelce is garbage. Why does he have such a hold on you?"

"The house drug."

"The what?"

"The house drug. I don't know how familiar you are with club operation, but every club has something exclusive. It's a prestige thing. The club with the best drug gets all the business."

"And Kelce is supplying you with a house drug?"

"Yeah."

"The one that produces orgasms?"

He nodded.

"Did Kelce ever tell you what his house drug was?"

"Not really. He said he got it from his work."

"Do you know where he works?"

"A chemical supply house, I guess."

"You stupid son of a bitch. I hope you know your 'house drug' isn't going to be a secret for much longer."

"You can't," Rodrigues cried. "You can't break it. You don't know what you'll do."

Payne leaned across the desk. "Rodrigues, I don't have to tell anybody. You could kill me right now, and the law would still have this place shut down in thirty days. Kelce doesn't work for a chemical company. He works with me at Biotech Industries.

"It's not a chemical, friend. It's a microorganism that eats protein and turns it into the chemicals that make people come. And every time people check into one of your chambers, it spreads."

Rodrigues was pale and sweating. He pulled nervously at his collar.

"You know what the best part is? This little bug likes the human body so much that it multiplies. Pretty soon there are so many of them that you can't eat enough food to keep them happy. That's when they start eating *you*."

"No," Rodrigues said, trembling.

"Thank you for the help, Mr. Rodrigues."

Rodrigues sat unmoving, face ashen and eyes receding into his skull. Payne tugged at the door, walked out, and started down the hall, stepping out of the way of an amorous couple who were taking a chamber.

Another three steps and he heard a loud report. He couldn't place the noise, but it sounded as if there were a problem in one of the chambers. He ran back to Rodrigues's office.

The door was still open. He stepped in and caught a familiar, moist smell, spiked with something sharp and metallic. Rodrigues was nowhere to be seen. He pulled the door shut.

He walked around the desk and found Rodrigues on the floor, blood leaking from his ear and nose and mouth. He knelt beside him and checked for a pulse. Nothing.

Then he saw a gleam of metal in one of his hands, something of polished chrome and wood synths.

It couldn't be.

But there it was. Payne checked the desk and found a secret compartment that held three more.

Handguns.

He recognized them from old videos he had seen. None had been made since the end of the last century, yet here was Rodrigues with four of them. There was more to these rackets than had been let on. Thoughts raced through his head, each one contradicting what had gone before. He sat down and took deep breaths until things became clear.

How was this going to look to Smith? Here was his racket boss with a hole blown in his skull, and the last man to see him alive had been that meddling Payne. Smith wanted whoever was responsible for Honor's death, but it clearly was not Rodrigues's doing. The fate Rodrigues had inflicted upon himself was something that should have fallen on Kelce. This was going to mean trouble for everyone involved.

For now it was better that Smith not find out about this. Payne needed to get the goods on Kelce, turn it all over to the law, and watch them shut the place down. Then he could give them the gory details and let them worry about the body.

He rifled the items scattered across the desk. There was nothing of any use. Then he went back to the compartment in the desk. With Rodrigues dead, there was no telling what Smith would say about the situation caused by the house drug.

He looked the guns over carefully, then picked up the smallest one. It had a chrome finish, a snubbed tube where the bullet came out, and a small rotating cylinder. He bounced it in his hand, surprised at its weight. The handle must have been real wood, for it had a slick, tantalizing feel to it. It had the odor of some unrecognizable petrol synth and the same sharpness he had smelled earlier. It smelled like power.

He pulled his scarf off and wrapped it around the gun, running one end through the metal loop protecting the trigger. In the videos he had seen, men had walked the streets with these things strapped to their hips. He wouldn't dare do that now. He pulled up the leg of his jumpsuit and wrapped the scarf around his calf, knotting it tightly. He stood and smoothed out the leg. It looked natural enough, but he felt as if an anchor were attached to his ankle.

Payne pushed the door shut and secured it. A suicide in a room locked from the outside would look strange, but there was no time to debate the wisdom of the move. He checked the hall and walked away, stopping when he came to the desk.

"Have you seen Mr. Rodrigues?" he asked.

"No," the woman said. "I thought he was with you."

Payne gave her a dismayed look. "He was, but he stepped out. Said he had to confer with a man named Giles."

The woman shrugged. "He didn't come this way."

Payne thumbed his watch. "If you do see him, give him my regrets. I have another appointment to keep. Tell him I'll bring the samples in on Thursday."

She took note on a scrap of paper. "Certainly. Your name?"

He paused. "Winthrop."

"Very well, Mr. Winthrop, I'll see that he gets the message."

On his way out, he was stopped by Giles, who wanted to chat about his progress on the case. Payne lied his way through it. He tried to be brief but friendly, and before he could stop himself, he asked what kind of night the club was having.

"Rough," Giles replied. "They're dropping like flies in there."

"Who? The customers?"

He nodded. "Mostly women. I think something's wrong with the ventilation system. I've got the house techs working on it."

"How many are down?"

"Tonight? Six or seven, not counting the four you had taken out."

"Are they okay?"

"Oh, they're not dying or anything." He smirked. "I think it's the house drug. Part of it. I'm still looking into the vents, though, 'cause we did lose one guy."

Payne looked at his watch. "I hope the night goes better for you, Giles. If you'll excuse me, I've got to go."

He couldn't move away from that place fast enough. Every hour that passed, people packed in and the disease spread. He wondered how long after infection it took for the druggy effects of the organism to appear. It probably varied between deliberate and accidental infections. How was Kelce giving it? Probably by injection for a quick and efficient spread, although he might be trying to confine it to the stomach by giving it in capsules.

He took the streets slowly until he found an open grate to the city drainage system. Making sure he was unobserved, he dropped the key to Rodrigues's office and watched as it slipped through the iron bars and splashed into the murky water. He thought briefly about sending the gun as well, but his original impulse ruled, and he kept it.

He was dead tired by the time he reached his apartment. He fumbled the key into the lock and fought with it, finally getting the door to open. Slipping inside, he heard someone running up the stairs, calling his name. He went inside, quietly closing the door. He didn't want to be caught with Rodrigues's gun.

There was a knock on the door. "Payne! Hey, Payne!"

He looked through the peephole and saw Bailey. "One minute." He walked into the bedroom and removed the gun, wrapping it in his scarf and stashing it under his pillow. Once he smoothed out the pillow, he returned and opened the door.

"I hope you don't mind making it short. I'm exhausted."

"I need you to come down to my place," Bailey said.

"What for?"

Bailey looked at him helplessly.

"Can't it wait, Bailey?"

"Come to my apartment," Bailey insisted.

"Please. It's been a bad day." He tried to swing the door shut. Bailey caught it and held it open. Payne studied his face. "Is there something you're not telling me?"

Bailey shrugged. "Okay, I confess. I have a video you might like."

Payne thought. "British?"

"Australian."

Payne grabbed the keys from the table and walked out, locking the door.

"I promise you'll like this one," Bailey said as they

headed down the stairs. He brought out his ring of keys and unlocked his door with great production. It struck Payne as odd. For short jaunts up to Payne's place, Bailey never locked his door.

Bailey half bowed and extended his hand into the apartment. "After you."

Payne looked into Bailey's face. It looked sincere enough, but there was no way to tell for sure. Collecting reward money was as lucrative as having children.

"Bailey..."

"If you've never trusted me before, you've got to do it now. As a friend."

He stared.

"Payne, there were some rumors going around today. Something's going wrong with the club system. Something that is not good. A lot of people may be hurting."

"So?"

"So I think you know about it. In fact, I think you know quite a bit. Enough to warn me off of clubs."

"I was worried about your attitude."

"Whatever the excuse, you warned me. You may have saved my neck, and I owe you. I'm not going to sell you short."

Payne studied his face.

"Please."

Payne stepped inside. Bailey was right behind, closing and latching the door. The living room was cast in its usual blue, but there was a light on in one corner.

"This comedy had better be good," he grumbled.

"It's not a comedy," Bailey said. "It's a love story."

Payne was halfway to a chair when she came out of the kitchen.

"Trinina!"

"Payne," she said, and fell into his arms.

"You're okay?"

"I'm fine."

He kissed her and held her close. "How did you get here?"

"Bailey found me knocking on your door."

Payne winced. "That wasn't a good idea." He stepped away from her. "Bailey, do you have any idea why she's here?"

Bailey nodded. "Better to hide her here than your place. They're going to be looking."

"They are looking. Bailey, I love you like a rock."

"Save it for her," he said.

"Where's Nathan?"

Trinina tilted her head toward the bedroom. "Asleep."

Payne took her by the hand and led her away. Blue light was falling into the room from Bailey's video. Nathan was curled up in Bailey's bed. Payne knelt and gently ran his hand through the child's thick hair. Nathan stirred, and his eyes fluttered open. Trinina squeezed Payne's shoulder.

Nathan blinked and regarded Payne. "Who are you?" he asked in a groggy voice.

"I'm—" About to give him his name, he stopped. "I'm your father."

Nathan smiled. "Trinina says you're going to help us get away."

"Yes," Payne said. "I am." He reached out and patted the boy's bottom. "Now, go back to sleep."

"Okay." Nathan closed his eyes.

Payne rose, and Trinina led him out. He called for Bailey but got no answer save the sound from the video.

"He won't be here. He's doing the laundry."

"At this hour? Trinina..."

"He figured that you'd have a million questions."

"Only a thousand. I'll grant you the 'why.' That I can see."

Trinina nodded.

"Why is he so cooperative, though? He was almost glad to see me. They're taught to tolerate their parents but would hardly go along with something like this."

"He's hardly in love with Mother America. He's been

having some peer problems, and she's less than sympathetic."

"Peer problems?"

"He's not really like the other little boys. When they're on breaks, they run around and play mercenary. He stays inside and plays with the class Composition Board. They can't handle that, and neither can MA. She thinks he should be out with a stick counting coup with the others."

"That's how genius is unmade."

"And he's the runt of the litter. It's a double curse."

"Our son? Runt of the litter?"

She sat on the couch and pulled him down next to her. "I wasn't going to steal him, Payne, not at first. Then he told me stories about how his classmates treated him and how he wished he could stay with me." She started to break and fell into him.

"Easy."

"He wanted to meet you."

"I wanted to meet him. You're going to stay the night here?"

"Bailey's offered."

"A garland of fire roses for that boy. You're to stay here, then." He pointed to the fresh marks on his face. "The Feds have already paid me a visit, so you won't be safe upstairs. You came in the back way, I hope?"

"Yes." She sat up and wiped her nose, dabbed her eyes. "But something's wrong."

"Bailey?"

She shook her head. "If the Feds visited you, then the GCR is already after me. I arranged to have more of a head start."

"You've got one. Their little visit was only a few hours ago. Assuming you left Monday morning, you've had about thirty hours."

"Closer to forty-eight, but I should have had more. We left Sunday night. I packed a bag of essentials for myself and Nathan and took off. I left the door unlocked and had things set up to look like I'd just stepped out. I even left a pot of coffee on."

"I killed your head start," Payne confessed. "I went by your place Monday and locked your door. The Biotech agents have been going crazy because of that. They probably think you've absconded with the secrets of digestible cellulose."

Trinina smiled. "At least I kept the GCR away. I called them twice from a phone terminal on Monday to check Nathan in. You've only got twenty-four hours between the time you quit calling and they come looking, and I needed until midnight tomorrow. I had plans to be gone by the time they came looking for me."

"You've still got one advantage. Your apartment burned up. They couldn't check to see if any of your clothes were missing."

"It burned?"

"I locked the door, remember?"

Trinina smacked her forehead. "The coffeepot."

"I'm afraid so. Where have you been hiding?"

Trinina looked embarrassed. "I hadn't planned on using any traceable money, and I didn't dare stay with friends. I needed a place where the management wasn't really concerned with keeping records."

"You stayed at a chambers house?"

"In an S and M suite."

"Trinina!" Payne cried, outraged. "What about Nathan?"

"I went to a World Rescue Mission and shoplifted some men's clothing. Old stuff, real cloth and cloth synths. I dirtied his face and made him look like a midget."

"They swallowed it?"

"If you overpay enough, they don't even look you in the eye."

"But an S and M suite? You're going to corrupt our son."

"He had a great time, Payne. He thought it was some

kind of playroom. He was swinging from the chains in the—"

"Enough," Payne said. "As long as you're safe."

"Are you going to help me?"

"As long as my heart still beats."

"Thank you."

Payne stretched and yawned.

"You look tired," she said then.

"Dead."

"Supervisory that rough?"

"Supervisory's cake. I've been on a Thirty-first since Sunday morning."

"Anything serious?"

"It's going to have definite consequences." He rose from the couch. "But it'll keep until morning."

"Shouldn't we make plans?"

"That'll keep, too."

"What about the Federals?"

"They'll come to my place first. They can't possibly suspect Bailey, so you'll be safe here. Being safe from Bailey is another matter."

"He'll be on the couch. I'll be in with Nathan."

"I really must do something for the old boy."

"Like what?"

He thought of Karol. "I'll work on it." He leaned down and kissed her on the lips. "Good night, my dear."

"Good night."

Payne's apartment was mercifully empty when he returned. No bodies, no Myra, no bouncers from the Lancaster, no hoodlums in the guise of Federal Blue. He locked himself in and left his jumpsuit crumpled on the floor.

There was much to do. He needed to trap Kelce and force a confession and find out how the bloody stuff was spread. He needed a thorough documentation that would be turned over to Delgado. Most of all, he wanted to get back to supervisory. He wanted all this out of the way, and he wanted his E-7.

Then there was the problem of Trinina. She would need a meal ticket once she got to where she was going, something to get her established. It couldn't be the cellulose problem; that was the Biotech Challenge. It had to be something that could be finished right away. He would have to work on it.

There was one more thing, something that bothered him more than the problems that had gone before. It was unnamed, and though he attempted to force it out, there was no fighting it. It sat in the back of his brain and produced an eerie, nagging sense of doubt and doom.

He attributed it to exhaustion and crawled into bed. He would get some sleep. He would let his subconscious work on it.

His eyes opened wide in the middle of the night. He was awake and lucid. His subconscious had surfaced and brought with it a name to the worry he had taken to bed.

He pointed a finger and named it, then lay on his back and considered it. When he thought he had it worked through, he closed his eyes, but they wouldn't stay shut. They kept popping open. He tried to keep them closed by assuring himself that things were going to work out, but they started to burn and set the rest of him on fire.

He endured as long as he could, but he knew it was a lost cause. He pulled himself from the bed, put on a fresh suit, and slowly shuffled to the door. He put his hand to the knob. Already the fire was cooling.

Payne opened the door and smiled.

"I felt you calling," Trinina said.

Wednesday Morning

"Payne, can I ask you something?"
"Certainly."

Trinina moved to his side of the bed and put her arms around him. "Why did you ask all those questions when I came up last night?"

"Questions?"

"About our past. Meeting at the convention, the first time we made love, and the cologne you were wearing when we did. The words to our song."

"I wanted to see what the memories would do to you."

"What were they supposed to do?"

"Nothing."

She sat up. "That's not all of it. I know you too well. You can be romantic, but you're not nostalgic."

"You're right." He sighed. "Some of it *was* nostalgia, but the rest was something I'm working on."

"Anything you can talk about?"

"I'd rather not."

"Your Thirty-first?"

"Yes."

She went back to his chest. "You'll beat it."

"I already have."

They lay close, and Payne silently went over the last few days, piecing together what had happened and trying to make sense of Kelce's actions. Everything was in place except for the motive. Using Biotech labs and systems for personal gain was one of the strongest infractions of their corporate code. All work had to be done for the good of the human race and was superseded only by one other rule in Biotech's charter. Kelce had broken that one, too. He had released a malevolent culture into the outside world.

It still didn't figure. Kelce was a thorn in the side of his coworkers, but there couldn't have been a more loyal company man. He might do damn fool things in the lab but was usually restrained enough to keep within the boundaries of tact and common sense. Then again, he had nearly destroyed Winthrop's culture.

He perused this until it led him to the thought that had brought him out of a sound sleep. Even though he had it named, remembering it made him uncomfortable.

"What's wrong?" Trinina asked.

"You're leaving."

"I have to look after Nathan. I don't think that Bailey can—"

"You're leaving the country," he interrupted.

"Do I have any other choice?"

"No. I'd be doing the same thing."

She pulled away. "What's bothering you?"

"How are you going to get out?"

"Why should I tell you?"

"I can help."

"You're helping me already. You're keeping me safe. You can help more by not talking. The easiest way for you to do that is for me not to tell you any details."

"Australia."

"I won't say."

Payne sat up and grabbed her shoulders. "You'll tell me."

"I won't."

"Then you'll die trying to get out of the country." He stopped, realizing the strength in his grip on her. He slowly let go.

"I'll die?"

He nodded. "Something I discovered in my recent travels. Do you remember a British guy from Biotech, Lol Winthrop? Short, stocky, with long blond hair?"

She nodded.

"Last Saturday morning I was helping him with a project. Later that night he told me that he was shipping out for Australia. Monday I got word that he'd turned up dead. He was killed at the docks."

"Coincidence," Trinina said.

"A racket. He wasn't the first person to die under the same circumstances. There's a pattern, and he fit right in. It's possible that you do, too."

"You can't be serious."

"Deadly serious."

"How do I get out, then? I've gone too far to turn back now."

Payne smacked his forehead. "Racket."

"What?"

"That son of a bitch had to be lying to me." He turned to her. "I need to know something. How did you make arrangements to leave the country?"

"I hit a few clubs, a few bars, asked a lot of questions, passed a few bribes."

"What did you do with Nathan?"

"I left him in the room at the chambers house with instructions not to let anyone in but me. Give me some credit, Payne. I know I'm not the clubbing type, but I think I know enough to fake it."

"You don't have your letters of transit yet, do you?"

"How did you know?"

"How will you be picking them up?"

"Monday night I met this guy who said he'd fix me up. Last night I gave him an advance and was told to meet him tonight with the balance of the money."

"Where were you going to meet him?"

"I'm not telling."

"Do you want me to help or not?"

"Forget it, Payne." She sat up and planted her feet on the floor. "I got this far alone, didn't I?"

"Was it the club on Lancaster Boulevard?"

Trinina looked stunned. "How did you know?"

The color left Payne's face. "His name," he said quickly. "What's wrong?"

"I need the name of your contact."

"I didn't get it."

"A fine way to conduct a business transaction. What did he look like?"

"Latin. Short. Dark skin and eyes. Ruddy face."

"Rodrigues. What color scarf were you supposed to wear?"

"Scarf?"

"Weren't you supposed to make the exchange in one of the chambers?"

"Yes, but I was supposed to sit and wait at a certain table. He was to come and escort me back."

"You've fallen into an emigration racket," Payne said, "and fallen back out again."

"You're not making any sense."

"This Rodrigues managed the rackets for the Lancaster Club. You probably knew the place as Danse."

"Sounds right."

"You did see a reservation form for the ship?"

"Yes."

"I thought so. They've got to have something to show the victim. The next step would be the letters of transit. How they came onto them is beyond me. I'll bet they've only got two and have been selling them over and over."

"You're losing me, Payne."

"Sorry. Somehow, the people at the Lancaster got their hands on a pair of letters of transit. They get in touch with someone who wants out of the country, someone who hasn't family or friends to carry the Thirty-first for them."

"I have friends and family."

"But you broke the law. You've bolted with a kid, and the Feds are after you. If you turned up dead, your case wouldn't be put up for option. You're probably better than someone with no family because you've got a price on your head."

"So what happens when I show up?"

"When you go to the docks, someone would split your skull and take the papers from your corpse. They'd collect a reward for recovering Nathan and a refund by turning the reservations back after the ship has left. Then they do it all again the next day."

"That's cruel."

"Welcome to the world."

She looked at him, worried. "Back to my original question. How do I get out?"

"I think you're set. You don't have to worry about Rodrigues smashing you with a crowbar because he's dead."

"Someone catch on to him?"

"He caught on to himself. The biggest problem now is how to get into his office."

Trinina held his face in her hands. "You were carrying on for that English boy, weren't you?"

He took her hands. "The way things turned out, I might as well have been." He climbed out of bed and slipped into his robe.

"Where are you going?"

"To get breakfast."

"You want help?"

He shook his head. "I need the time to myself."

"What for?"

"To work on how to get into Rodrigues's office. I'd bet money that the papers are there. If you've got them and the reservations, all you need is money to pay for the passage."

"I don't have any money," Trinina said sheepishly.

He stared in disbelief. "How were you going to get the papers, then?"

She looked down.

"Damn you," he spat. "Why didn't you come to me?"

"You—"

"No. Forget it. I don't want to hear about it. I've got fifty K's coming that I wasn't expecting. That should get you to Australia with money to spare."

"You don't have to."

He kissed her. "I insist. I want you to raise Nathan happy and healthy and without an accent, okay?"

"But—"

"No buts. My mind is made up, the case is closed. The only thing left is a meal ticket."

"Meal ticket?"

"Something to get you started in Australia. Your F-1 will help, but you need something that will get you in the door."

"Like what?"

"After breakfast," he said, and left the room.

In the kitchen he examined Myra's job of restocking his pantry. There were lots of starchy foodstuffs and even more protein-heavy synthates, the thought of which turned his stomach. A search of the ice chest produced a fresh package of bacon and a half dozen real eggs. He put a pan over the Sterno heat and within minutes had something that could pass for breakfast. He called Trinina to the table, and they ate together in silence.

When they were done, Payne removed the dishes and placed them in a sink full of water. As he washed, Trinina excused herself and disappeared.

He had started drying when he heard a scream. He ran to the bedroom and found Trinina facing the bed, hand to her chest.

"What's wrong?"

"Scared me to death." She pointed at the bed.

He looked down. Bent chrome glimmered at him. He squatted down beside it. "This?"

"What are you doing with that?"

Payne wrapped the gun in his scarf and slid it under the bed. "I don't know."

"You didn't buy that thing, did you?"

He shook his head. "Nobody knows I've got it. I stole it from Rodrigues."

"*You stole it?*"

Payne licked his lips. "I guess I thought it would come in handy."

"For what?" Trinina was clearly distressed. "What would you ever do with one of those?"

"I don't know. I was acting on impulse."

"Your impulses are going to get you in trouble, Payne. You're looking at a capital offense."

"And harboring you isn't?"

"There's a difference between hanging and exile. What kind of trouble are you in that would make you steal a gun?"

Payne rubbed his face. "I thought I might need it when dealing with Kelce."

"Kelce. Derek Kelce?"

Payne nodded.

"What's he got to do with all of this?"

He closed his eyes and ran a hand through his hair. "He let something out of the lab. He had a dead-end malevolent culture whose waste product combines with memory triggers and stimulates the pleasure center. For some reason he's been selling it at the Lancaster. Your friend Rodrigues was in on it, too. He was taking a cut right off the top of the profits."

"How did you happen on to all of this?"

"Kelce had a girlfriend who was infected with the organism, and it killed her. He left her body in my apartment."

"Your Thirty-first?"

"Yeah."

"Have you told anyone about this stuff being out?"

"I told Rodrigues. He shot himself."

"And you took his gun? That was really smart, Payne. Why don't you turn your research in and let the law shut the club down?"

"It's not that simple. I think Kelce's bug has mutated from lab-safe status. Its characteristics are perfect for spreading by sexual contact."

"You'll have to compute a vector rate."

"Ninety-nine percent from a partially infected male." She looked at him.

"I broke into the program. I guessed your code and used it. I didn't think you'd mind."

"Why didn't you take it to somebody else?"

"They would have taken it out of my hands."

"Would that have been so bad?"

"You're right. I suppose I wasn't acting very rationally. This thing could destroy the club system if it goes unchecked. I guess I was just running scared."

"Do you have any figures on the rate of spread?"

"I didn't think of that. I did an informal survey of the Lancaster last night, but I was more interested in spotting cases through observation. I did find that the rate of infected women is three to one over men. That would indicate that the same handful of men are doing the infecting."

"Not necessarily," Trinina said. "You said this disease is a recreational drug. Would it be possible that women would have more of an interest in it than men?"

"What are you getting at?"

"Organism pathology. Pleasure."

"Of course," Payne said. "Women would tend to be drawn to it because their orgasms are more elusive."

"Generally speaking," Trinina corrected. "That was always one of your problems, Payne. Overgeneralization."

"If the spread is to be checked, users will have to be interviewed. We'll need listings of their sex partners," Payne continued.

"Don't forget that the Department of Health will have their own ideas on how to handle it."

"Of course they will, but they'd be fools not to take steps above and beyond the usual regimen of attempted containment. This isn't an old strain of the flu we're dealing with. We're talking major catastrophe if it got out of hand."

"What about spread to other countries?"

"Chances of that are almost nil. The people who spend their money on drugs are trying to make their escape that way."

"You're overgeneralizing again."

"It breeds optimism, which I need right now. Before you go I'll give you a complete rundown on the disease. You can get together with the ship's medical staff and run tests on the passengers."

"What if someone's infected?"

"I don't know. Toss them overboard, I guess."

Trinina giggled, but the smile from the laughter slowly melted into despair. "Assuming that I'll be on that boat."

"You will be."

"With my connection dead? Isn't that being a bit too optimistic?"

"I don't think so," Payne explained. "The club's owner has got to have a key to the office so he can check up on the rackets. All I have to do is convince him that something vitally important to my case is in that office."

"What makes you think he'll swallow that?"

"The dead girl in my apartment was his sister."

"You're going to bluff him?"

"Yes and no. Rodrigues must have kept some sort of records on what he was doing. He wouldn't be a professional if he didn't. I'm going to need that information to document my case against Kelce."

She looked away. "What do you think they'll do to him?"

"Hanging would be too good for him. They'd probably

turn him back over to Biotech as a P.V." He kissed her on the cheek and moved away.

"Where are you going?"

"Biotech. I need to finish my case so you'll have enough money to get to Australia."

"I thought you needed stuff from the club."

"Icing on the cake." He went into the bathroom and picked up his toothbrush. "I've got enough to do him in right now."

"I'm going," Trinina said flatly.

"No you're not. You've got to stay with Nathan." He looked at his watch. "Bailey will be going to work in a few minutes. You need to be there when he locks up."

"No, I don't," she said. "He gave me a key last night, in case you turned me out."

He shook his head and brushed his teeth. Bailey had done that to make her feel secure, knowing full well that she wouldn't have been turned out. He filled a glass with water and rinsed his mouth. "I'm turning you out now."

"You can't."

He wiped his face with a towel. "I've got to. You need to lie low until it's time to leave. This place will be crawling with Feds if they can't find you anywhere else. As much as I've enjoyed your company, you shouldn't have come."

"You can't make me leave."

"Yes, I can. Somebody's got to watch Nathan."

She blinked. "I suppose you're right."

He stepped away from the sink. "Do you need to get in here?"

She said nothing, but took his place in the room, locking the door.

Shaking his head, he walked into the living room and numbly looked through the reports on Kingman and Smith. He wished Trinina could come with him. She had already given him some new angles on the problem raised by Kelce, and he was sure there were others he had missed.

That was something he liked about Trinina—she made him think. Genius is contagious, she had always said.

Then he heard the scratching.

It was dry and metallic and came from the door. He froze in horror. The doorknob was twisting and rattling. He tried to swallow, but his mouth was dry. For a split second he thought about the possibilities. How long to dive into the bedroom, pull the gun from under the bed . . .

. . . and figure out how to work the damn thing.

Too late. The thought had taken too long. The door popped open.

"Hello." Myra smiled at him.

He fell onto the couch.

She rushed to his side, dropping a dozen shopping bags on the way. "Are you okay?"

"You scared the living hell out of me."

"Who did you think it was? The Feds?"

"Yes." Moisture returned to his mouth.

She hugged him. "Why would they be after you?"

"A girl bolted with one of my kids."

"And they think she's staying here? That shows you how the government works."

"How did you get in?"

Myra smiled and dangled a key. There was something different about her face, something he didn't quite understand. "This was in your dresser."

"You came to get your things?"

She looked confused. "Is there some reason I should?"

"After our last little episode, I thought that—"

"I knew I should have left a note."

"A note?" He had the feeling he wouldn't like what he was about to hear.

"I woke up yesterday morning and didn't feel all that great. You probably knew that was going to happen. You were dead asleep, so I had lots of time to think about what you said about being ladylike."

"You weren't supposed to remember any of that."

"I never get that drunk. Like I said, I really did some

thinking about what you'd told me. I even decided that
there was some truth behind it. You wouldn't take me to
bed because you didn't think I was enough of a lady."

"That's not entirely true—"

Myra held up her hand to stop him. "So I said to myself,
'What could I do to make myself more attractive?'"

Suddenly Payne realized what was different about her
face. "You went to a surgeon," he said hoarsely.

She smiled and turned profile. The scar was gone. The
side of her nose looked as clean as the day she was born.

"You didn't do that for me, I hope."

"Not entirely." She draped her arms around his neck.

He broke her grip and retreated. "Myra, I'm sorry."

"About what? The bill from the surgeon? The government's got it. I still had the original voucher for the work
to be done. I honestly don't know why I never had it
repaired. It didn't hurt, and I only had to stay overnight
to make sure the Healing Wax did its job."

He turned to face her. "Myra, you can't stay here."

"Why not?"

"I'm in love."

She smiled. "I'm not afraid of things getting too serious, Payne."

"You don't understand..."

There was a voice from behind them. Payne turned
and saw Trinina out of the corner of his eye. She was
wrapped in his big towel and was covered with sparkling
droplets of water. Her hair was wet and combed behind
her ears. She looked good. There was an agonizing, painful silence.

"I'm sorry," she said. "I didn't mean to interrupt."

Myra forced a smile. "You didn't."

Trinina politely nodded and disappeared.

"You're in love," Myra said.

"Yes."

"Is that—"

Payne nodded. "The one who bolted."

"I understand now."

"I'm sorry, Myra."

"Yes," she said, trying to stay calm. "I can see where you would be." She turned to the door.

"Do you want your things?"

She waved the key. "I'll come back when you're not here."

"Yes," he said.

Her hand fell on the doorknob. "She shouldn't stick around here, you know. She needs to get out."

"We're working on that."

"That's good. And you?"

He shook his head. "I'm staying."

She tried to smile past the hurt. "Maybe you'll look me up."

"Maybe."

She opened the door and left.

"Who was that?" Trinina called.

He remained frozen until she emerged from the bedroom dressed for the day, a sight for his tired eyes.

"You're still not going with me." He kissed her on the forehead.

"I'd resigned myself to that."

He went into the bathroom and showered. The process of cleaning himself was beginning to lose its therapeutic value. Each time he applied the soap, it took away less and less of the tired and the hurt and the confused ache from his brain.

Finally he was ready to go, although his lack of enthusiasm was beginning to show. He put his eye to the peephole. "I'm going to check the hall and see if any of our Federal friends are hanging around. If I'm not back in five minutes, get out, get Nathan, and don't come back."

"What if they find Bailey's apartment?"

"They won't. I'll lead them away. Which chambers house did you stay at?"

"The Wanderlust."

"I'll lead them there. Knowing them, they'll have someone double back to check here as an afterthought."

"Five minutes and I'll take the back way to Bailey's."

He checked the halls all the way to the street. On the way he thought of how futile his search actually was. They could be waiting anywhere. They could be in the apartment below, a hole drilled in the ceiling, a periscope stuck up beneath the coffee table. Maybe they had left a set of Ears in his place. Maybe a pair had occupied somebody's apartment, one man intimidating the residents while the other stared himself blind through the peephole.

Everything looked clear, so he turned back and darted up the stairs. He unlocked the door and called for Trinina, who was hiding in the bedroom. He took her by the hand and led her down to Bailey's, standing watch while she unlocked the door and went inside.

He walked out of the building and had made it to the end of the block, when he heard a familiar clicking. He stopped, afraid that it would be Myra. He shook off the fear and started across the street.

"That's okay. Leave me behind."

He stopped in the middle of the street and turned. "What do you think you're doing?"

Trinina caught up and took him by the arm, leading him to the sidewalk. "I'm coming along."

"Are you out of your mind? Who's watching Nathan?"

"Bailey's playing sick."

"With the phones down?"

"He said he'd face the consequences this once. For us." She looped her arm in his and pulled him toward Biotech.

"What about the GCR?"

"They'll be looking for me in the underground. I'm supposed to be in hiding, remember?"

"Flaunting yourself isn't going to help."

"It couldn't hurt. Did you ever read 'The Purloined Letter'?"

"The what?"

"Did you ever read any Poe?"

"Who?"

"Didn't you take any classes in early American literature?"

"I was too busy reading biology textbooks."

"What did you do for entertainment?"

"I've just told you. What's that got to do with a letter?"

Trinina shook her head. "Never mind."

He tried to get her to divulge the importance of the stolen letter, but she refused. They argued about it all the way to the Biotech building, and all Payne could think of was how good it felt to be arm in arm with her, how good it was to wake up in the morning and have her there, how good it was to be fighting with her again. It made it that much worse knowing that this would be the last time they would ever get to do this.

"Payne?"

He blinked and found himself staring at the Biotech building. He opened the door and escorted Trinina inside.

Billie looked up. "Trinina!" She started to smile, but it quickly faded.

"For her penance," Payne announced, "I'm going to have her check the work in my lab space."

"No," Billie said suddenly.

Payne laughed, but Trinina stopped. "What's wrong?"

"I can't let Payne in. He's been suspended."

"Suspended?" He was outraged. "What for?"

With trembling hands, Billie picked up her clipboard. "Two complaints from Kelce. Violation of Work Privacy and Abuse of Access."

"That can be contested. We're the same rank, so suspension shouldn't take effect unless the Lookover Committee orders it during a hearing."

"One more," Billie said. "From upstairs."

Payne threw his head back. "Son of a bitch!"

"What's going on?" Trinina asked.

"Let me guess," Payne said. "Breach of Limited-access Materials."

Billie nodded.

Payne repeated the curse and looked at Trinina. "I

accessed an Identiscan program so I could make a positive link to Kelce."

"I'm afraid there's more—" Billie started.

"Who pressed charges first?" Payne interrupted.

"It's not important," Trinina said.

"Yes, it is. Tell me, Billie."

She looked at her board. "Upstairs. Right after you left last night."

"And word was out this morning?"

Billie nodded.

"Kelce filed when he came in this morning?"

"He was here about half an hour before he did."

"What are you getting at?" Trinina asked.

"He's on to me," Payne said. "He knows I'm getting close. He had no real basis for pressing charges because I could turn them around. With the Lookover Committee breathing down my neck, there's suddenly more relevance to his charges."

"He's trying to get you fired."

"He's trying to make it look as bad as possible. And then, before the hearing, he'll get in touch and try to make a deal."

"You can beat him at the hearing," Trinina said.

"Even if I beat him now, both of us would lose our jobs. Only he'll be the one who hangs."

"You're not going to lose your job."

"I'm through here," Payne insisted. "Don't you realize what I've done? I've stumbled onto something major and didn't report it to my superiors. I overrode the computer and did the work on my own. They don't like that."

"If you come clean at the hearing, you may get an F rating out of it."

"But I screwed up." Payne grabbed her by the shoulders and shook her. "Don't you see? I let my ego get into this and got into a personal vendetta with Kelce. It should have been taken out of my hands, but now it's too late." He turned to Billie. "You've got to let me into that lab space."

"I'm sorry, I can't. They're having the E boards soon and—"

"And they're holding it over your head."

"They're holding it over the heads of everyone working the desk."

Payne cursed and gazed out the doors. Had he been looking at Trinina, he would have seen her eyes light up.

"Billie," she said. "What is the state of the work in Payne's lab space?"

"It's not good."

"Has the work been assigned for completion?"

"No, but—"

"Then I'm taking it."

Payne looked at her.

"Trinina, you don't understand," Billie said.

"Billie, if you don't give me appropriate forms for the work transfer, I'll do it myself."

"Forget it," Payne said. "Somebody's got to authorize you for the work."

She smiled confidently. "I can do it myself. I've got my F-2."

"But the computer said—"

"The computer's wrong. It won't be official until after they have the next boards, but I'm listed in Central as having all the rights and privileges of F-2." She turned to Billie. "Would you get Payne a visitor's clearance?"

Billie sighed resignedly. "Sure."

"I won't get it," Payne said.

"Yes, you will. Otherwise you couldn't get in for the hearing." Trinina signed the form and slid it to Billie. "Please get these on line as soon as you can."

Billie nodded quietly. Payne grabbed her arm to keep her from leaving. "You seem awfully cooperative."

Billie glared at him. "Well, what in hell am I supposed to do? Fight you?"

Trinina pulled him away from the desk. "Come on, Thomas. You're going to have to trust her."

He followed her up the stairs. "Why did you call me Thomas?"

"Ever read the Gospel of John?"

"Was he a contemporary of Poe?"

She let the question drop, placing her hand on the black square, flinching as light bathed it.

IDENTITY CONFIRMED.

ASHAHN-RUEBEN, TRININA.

RANK F-1.

"That's F-2," she complained.

YOU'RE LATE, TRININA.

17 HRS. 51 MIN. 09 SEC.

"Account," she said.

There was a long silence.

"It knows I'm with you," Payne said.

There was an angry buzz that made them jump.

TIME DEFICIT.

2 HRS. 16 MIN. 33 SEC.

Payne shivered with relief.

"Okay, fine," Trinina shouted. "Now let us in."

The hydraulics allowed them into the locker room. They silently went to their respective areas and climbed into uniform, not looking at each other until they stepped into the orange light.

Once on the fifth floor, they wound their way back to the lab space. Trinina complained about the fact that Payne had chosen one so small and out of the way. "You would have picked Doctor Tarr's torture dungeon," she said.

"Doctor Tarr?"

"More Poe." She pressed her thumb into the lock.

The door opened, and blood drained from Payne's head.

The inside of the lab had been completely gutted by flame, leaving it a blackened, tangled mess. The tables and shelves were chunks of carbon. The computer console was a hardened puddle. The scanning equipment and metal incubators were melted and twisted beyond recognition.

"No," he gasped, stepping inside. He sniffed and caught

the odor of liquid smoke. The carbonized lab crunched beneath his feet.

"This must be what Billie was talking about," Trinina said.

"Billie knew about this?"

"Didn't you listen to her? She was trying to tell us, and we didn't listen to her. Oh, Payne, I owe her an apology."

"No wonder she snapped at me," Payne said thickly.

"What did you do, leave something on?"

"I checked everything before I walked out," Payne said. "The Identiscan was off, and the incubators were all set within the range of the human body."

"No wonder the Lookover Committee is out to hang you."

"I'm dead. Dead and buried."

"I wonder what happened?"

Payne picked up a molten lump of glass from the floor and dropped it. He was surprised when it didn't break. "Kelce."

"You can't be serious."

"I am serious."

"You can't think that Kelce did this, too."

"I'm not a bloody fool, Trinina. When I left the lab yesterday, I secured it by the book."

"You've been under a lot of stress, Payne."

"I'll prove it," he said coldly. He stomped out of the destroyed lab space, grabbing Trinina's hand.

"Where are we going?"

He stalked to the floor desk, screaming for Errol. A short man came waddling toward them, a worried look on his face.

"What seems to be the problem?"

"My lab space burned. I want to know who checked and sealed it for hold status."

"Why, Security, of course."

"Which agent?"

Errol scratched at the hair that remained above his ears. "I don't recall."

"Do you have it written down?"

"As a matter of fact, I—"

Payne wheezed in exasperation. "Could you check it, please?"

Errol wobbled behind the desk and shuffled papers. "I didn't think you were the type of person to run off and leave an Electroscan on. Ah, here it is. A Mr. Wolzek from security and a subordinate secured the room."

"Which subordinate?"

"It doesn't say. It just lists Gregory Miller-Wolzek as having secured—"

"Thank you," Payne said, pulling Trinina to the elevators.

"What if you're wrong?" she protested. "What if it was your fault?"

"Not this time."

The elevator door opened.

He took her to the eighth floor and led her to Internal Security.

"I don't see what your hurry is," Trinina said. "If he's in, the twenty seconds you save won't mean that much."

"Point," Payne said, and slowed.

"What makes you so sure that Security is responsible?"

"Because it would explain how Kelce got the bug out of the archives without the Lookover Committee coming down on him. The organism he let out was abandoned because of its virulence."

"May I help you?" a receptionist asked.

"Gregory Miller-Wolzek, please."

"I'm sorry. He's asked not to be disturbed."

"Then I'll find him myself." Payne started into the maze of offices. The secretary was out from behind her desk, protesting.

"You might interrupt an interview," she cried.

"Then I suggest you tell me where to find him."

"He's—"

"In a meeting, I know. I've got some information that's vital to company security, and I don't care what I have to do to get it to him."

She pointed sheepishly. "Next corridor over. Last office on the right."

He broke away, Trinina in tow.

"I've never seen you like this," she said. "Did you have to be so rude?"

"This isn't a matter of manners. It's a matter of survival."

"And you're dragging me into it?"

"I'm afraid you've no choice in the matter."

Trinina stopped. "I'm afraid I do."

"Like the choice I had in helping you and Nathan? Tell me about that choice, Trinina."

"That's different."

"Of course it is. It affects you." He grabbed her hand again. "Tell you what. You help me pin this down, and I'll get you and the kid out of the country. Fair enough?"

"That's no choice."

"Of course it's not!" Payne shouted. "Do you think I wanted any of this to happen to me? Do you think I wanted to be the one to find out what's going on in the clubs?" He dropped her arm and continued toward Wolzek's office.

"Payne," she said, "it's not going to be that bad."

He didn't answer. He reached the end of the hall and knocked on the door.

"You said you almost had it figured. You'll stop it in time."

He knocked again. "And how will they show their thanks to me, Tree? By showing me the door."

She shook her head. "You'll make F without the boards. I'll see to it personally."

"No," he said. "I don't want it."

Trinina moved down the hall to his side. "What do you want?" she asked quietly.

"I want it all to stop," he answered. "I want it to be

quiet for a long time. I'd like to sleep and not have something lurking in my dreams."

"Open the door," she said.

He put pressure on the knob, and the door clicked. They walked in, and Payne closed the door. Wolzek was sitting slumped over at his desk, hands out front, fingers locked together. He lifted his head at the sound of the door and regarded his company. "Hello," he said hoarsely. "What can I do for you?"

"I was told you were busy," Payne said.

Wolzek smiled stupidly. "A lie," he croaked. "I'm feeling a little under the weather."

Trinina stepped toward the desk. Payne grabbed the neck of her jumpsuit and stopped her.

"You sealed the Payne lab space for the Lookover Committee."

Wolzek's eyes twitched. "That's correct."

"Who was your subordinate?"

He hunched his shoulders and shook his head as if someone had dropped an ice cube down his back.

"What was his name?"

Wolzek giggled. Trinina took another step.

"Don't," Payne said.

"He's sick."

"He's got it."

"How can you tell?"

"Watch."

Wolzek's eyes went moist. "Don't. Please don't."

Payne advanced. "What's wrong? Who are you to deny yourself a little pleasure?"

Wolzek trembled.

"There are outward symptoms," Payne told Trinina. "The pallor over the face. The bluish lips. Acetone breath. The hair looks bad, too. It doesn't look healthy. After all, it's only protein. The bug doesn't care if it's living or dead."

"It's good for a while," Wolzek said, weakly. "Real

nice. But—" He shuddered and grabbed at the desk. "You can't control it." He gasped for breath.

"I've seen these symptoms before," Trinina said.

"Where?"

"I don't know. I can't place them."

"You got a cure?" Wolzek said.

"I have a better question," Payne said. "Who was subordinate when you sealed the Payne lab space?"

Wolzek grimaced and lashed out for his desk top as if he were trying to keep from falling. *"Don't ask me questions!"*

"Did he give it to you before or after you did the lab space? Maybe he gave it to you for springing it from the archives."

"No!"

"Just tell me his name. That's all I want."

"No questions," he gasped. "Can't handle..."

Payne slammed his fists on the desk top. "Tell me," he whispered, "or I'll ask so many questions that it'll never stop."

Wolzek croaked.

"I don't even have to ask you questions. All I have to do is say something, and your brain will call it up. It's like the old grade-school game. *Don't think of a polar bear, Wolzek.*"

He cried out and slammed his head into the desk.

"Don't think of your access code."

He grunted.

"Do you want to smell the lady's perfume? It's a popular brand. Loaded with memories, I'm sure."

He pushed back in his chair and shook his head violently. "No," he cried. "No."

"I want the name of your subordinate."

"It hurts."

"It'll hurt more if you don't talk."

"Payne..." Trinina said.

Wolzek's eyes went wide. "You're Payne?"

Payne turned to Trinina. "Are you wearing perfume?"

"No!" Wolzek screamed. "No subordinate! No subordinate!"

"You did it yourself?"

He shook his head and squirmed in his chair. "No..."

"You're not making sense. Trinina—"

"He wasn't a subordinate!"

"What?"

Wolzek was trembling violently. He was bathed in sweat. "He just dressed like one. He said he had a cure."

"And who was it?"

"Was—" His muscles tightened, and his body twisted as if it had suddenly been palsied. His back arched out of the chair as the breath rushed from his lungs, squeaking through his vocal cords. Trinina rushed to help, but Payne shoved her away.

Wolzek cried out, desperation rising in his voice. "Won't stop."

"Name!" Payne shouted.

"Kelce!" he screamed. "It was Kelce! Kelce!" Wracked with sobs, he screamed the name one last time, drawing it out with the last bit of air in his lungs, then shuddered and went limp.

Trinina's hand went to her mouth. She grabbed the side of the desk and lowered herself to the floor.

"No need for apologies," Payne said. "You hadn't seen it before."

"Is he dead?"

"I don't know." He sighed and sat on the side of the desk. "To tell the truth, I don't care. If he is, he's lucky. I ran some calculations on the ways this stuff kills, and it's pretty grim."

She rose and moved around the desk.

"What are you doing?"

"I told you those symptoms look familiar. I want to take a look at him."

"Be careful."

"I won't touch him."

Payne took a seat at the computer terminal. He powered up and signed on, using Trinina's code. "I'm borrowing your identity again."

"What for?"

"Your meal ticket." He typed commands into the terminal and told her the story of Winthrop's cholesterol project and the stumbling block he had come up against. She listened with interest as she examined Wolzek's face, moving his head with the eraser end of a pencil. Payne went quiet as he found the program he needed and filled in the information needed to transfer the information in Winthrop's files to the other side of the world. "Are you going to transfer to Biotech Sydney or Biotech Perth?"

Combing through Wolzek's bookcase, she stopped. "Sydney, I guess."

Payne continued to type. Trinina scanned the bookcase again, and this time her eyes caught what she was looking for: a thick volume with a tattered blue cover and *Basic Molecular Biology* stamped in gold on the spine. She stretched and pulled the volume from the shelf. It was a high school textbook, and the copyright showed it fifteen years out of date, but it would contain what she was looking for.

The sound of her leafing through pages nibbled at his curiosity, but he didn't look up until he had the confirmation that Winthrop's work was now in memory at Sydney, Australia, waiting for Trinina to walk in and sign on. He powered down and turned to her.

"Checking on cholesterol structure?"

She shook her head gravely and stabbed a page with her fingers. "I was afraid of this."

"Something I overlooked?"

"Adrenaline toxemia. It looks like Adrenaline toxemia."

"But it's not."

"It's close enough." She ran her finger down an index and located the page number. "You were big on pathology. Tell me about it."

"Adrenaline toxemia? The Olympic disease?"

"Go on."

"Don't you remember?"

"I don't have time. I'm on to something."

"Simple enough. The Soviets kept getting blackballed at the Olympics because they kept filling their athletes with steroids. Their females were having problems with medical tests because they'd been given so many male hormones. So they hit on this idea and produced a synthetic adrenaline concentrate in little tabs that the athletes slipped under their tongues before each event. For the first three or four days their team cleaned up. By the end of the games, they'd all died."

"Not all of them."

"They might as well have been dead. What are you trying to tell me? That adrenaline kills the beast and the body kills itself by making more adrenaline than it can handle?"

"I wish it were that simple. I'm afraid it isn't." She stepped around the desk, textbook open to a page filled with sketches of molecular structures.

"I don't think I'm going to like this," Payne said.

"Remember high school MB? Did you have to draw all the chemicals manufactured by the body?"

"They're teaching it at high elementary level now, I know."

"How did you remember them for the exam?"

Payne went pale. "Building blocks."

"They all have the same base," Trinina said. "All you have to do is get the extremities of the molecule correct." She laid the book in his lap and pointed to the sketches. "This is adrenaline. This is your memory trigger."

Payne stared in disbelief. With the exception of an extra extremity on the adrenaline molecule, they were identical. "The girl's adrenal glands had collapsed," he whispered.

"Then it links with the organism's waste product," Trinina said. "And it may link more readily than the memory compound. All it would take is something to trigger the burst, like fright."

Payne said nothing. To Trinina, it looked as if he had seen a ghost.

"What's wrong?"

"You said the symptoms were similar."

"Very close."

"And all someone would have to do—"

"Is trigger it. Say, by being scared."

"By running, perhaps?"

"Or dancing."

Payne's lower jaw was trembling, and great dark circles appeared under his eyes. He was reliving the moment. He pushed it away and spoke in a thinning voice. "It still produces pleasure. But it would be different. More intense. Almost numbing."

"Pain might trigger adrenaline. Depends on the circumstances."

He closed his eyes. "One more situation. Something that would produce a lot."

"Sexual excitement?"

Payne shook his head. He could see the man, laughing at him, laughing at Myra, laughing at the fact that his own kneecap had been shattered.

"No," he said. "Trying to kill someone."

Wednesday Night

"**Y**ou expect me to believe this?"
"You've got to believe it."

Payne and Trinina were sitting in a small room in the Warax Substation, looking across a desk at Sergeant Delgado. They had notes and sketches of Kelce's work that had been liberated from the archives by forging Wolzek's name on a release order. They didn't have all of what they wanted but felt what they had was enough to get the point across.

Delgado was being difficult. He shuffled through the papers and the molecular biology textbook. "You'll forgive me if I don't follow all of this," he said, shaking his head. "I majored in law enforcement, not human mechanics."

"To put it in the simplest way possible," Payne said, "there are points in the human brain that produce chemicals. The organism that Derek Kelce engineered produces certain chemicals as a waste product. When this waste links with a certain one produced by the brain, it produces something very similar to an orgasm, only stronger, more intense."

"Where do the homicidal tendencies fit in?"

"The chemical also combines with adrenaline to produce another kind of pleasure, something that may be intensified by pain."

"Why would the victims be driven to homicide?"

"The organism itself doesn't cause them," Trinina said. "The victims would try it on their own. They would deliberately put themselves in such a situation in order to produce adrenaline. The glands that produce it are signaled by the brain. In order for the brain to to send it, it has to be in a high-stress situation, something requiring a little extra effort from the body. That's where adrenaline comes in. It gives you the strength."

"So victims would have superhuman strength?"

"No," said Payne. "The adrenaline produced would combine with the organism's chemicals to make the third compound."

"Do you have documentation of this?"

"The work was destroyed," Trinina said.

"There is one case," Payne said, "of the propensity for violence that victims might have. My assault case."

"The girl in your apartment?"

"No. She was a victim of the organism's primary symptoms. I mean the guy that attacked me on Saturday, the one you couldn't find. He kept attacking me even though I had shattered his kneecap."

"A lot of good that does us, Mr. Payne. You said yourself that we couldn't find him."

"I know who he is now. Mark Wilson-Kingman. His body should be in the morgue section. His case was taken by Andrew Lyndon-Smith, the owner of a club down on Lancaster Boulevard."

"How does the club fit into this?"

Payne said nothing.

"You've got to tell him," Trinina said.

"I need a guarantee," Payne said. "If I give you this information, you can't move on the clubs for twenty-four hours."

"I make no promises. The clubs are under the jurisdiction of the Federals. They ignore me and I try to ignore them."

Payne bit his lip and cursed.

Trinina spoke. "This organism is being sold out of the Lancaster Club as a recreational drug."

"*Trinina!*"

"He had to know."

"What you're telling me is nothing new," Delgado said. "The club system couldn't exist without drugs."

"This stuff is killing people!" Payne cried.

Delgado shook his head. "You're about to hear a speech I have to make three times a week to distraught people who, under the auspices of the Thirty-first Amendment, have figured out what you've just told me. When they hear it, they get hot under the collar and do strange things like bomb our offices or the telephone junctions. I don't think either of you would resort to that."

Payne shook his head.

"Go on," Trinina said.

"I know that drugs run out of the clubs. No matter what you do, they're always going to be there. Your company, Mr. Payne, they killed off all of the cannabis plants. Heroin addiction hasn't been a problem since the beginning of the century for similar reasons. It's been no big problem for the vice lords in this country. As soon as marijuana and heroin were on the way out, something else was taking their place. What your friend has done is nothing new. There's always some clever chemist trying to create something new, and more often than not it's impressively fatal."

"But this isn't merely a chemical!"

"May I finish?"

"Yes," Trinina said.

"If it was in my power, I would go after him. If I had anything to say about it, I would have the clubs shut down and the vice lords would all be living a primitive life in Micronesia. The truth is, the Feds won't touch the clubs."

"Why not?" Payne asked.

"They're necessary to keep the public pacified."

"Why do they need pacification?"

"There are a hell of a lot of reasons, Mr. Payne. Conditions aren't particularly grim right now, but they're hardly utopian. A hundred years ago you could drive a car somewhere far away if you got restless. You could book passage on a plane or a boat and get out of the country for a while. You can't do that anymore. You're lucky if you can get across town."

"Cultures change."

"So do environments. Russia owns the Eastern Hemisphere except for China and Australia. Japan's digging in because they know they're next. Half of South America is under a red flag. Do you think it's an accident that Canada and Mexico have closed their borders? They're not speaking to us. We've let too many friends down."

"We're gearing up for a war," Trinina said.

"That's my theory. Only the government doesn't want the public to know that yet. Take the Child Rearing Act. Do you think the government *wants* to raise kids? Do you think they're doing a good job of it? They're just freeing people from their responsibilities so they can get out and have a good time and forget about what's really going on."

"They're raising a generation of soldiers."

"It looks that way. When you've got a country that's coming unraveled, you look for things to blind the people to the obvious. You have Roman games or you exterminate Jews."

"Or let them go dancing."

Delgado looked at them cautiously. "It's at this point that I usually get slapped. People don't like bad news."

"We still have a problem," Payne said. "A health hazard."

"How can I convince you, Mr. Payne? If you could only see the casualty figures that come across my desk from bad chemical mixes..."

"I know it's difficult for you to understand, but we're not talking about chemicals here. This is a disease."

"But you said—"

"I know what I said. Look at the effects as symptoms. This disease has the unfortunate distinction of having pleasant symptoms while it's actually killing you."

"And people are taking this?"

"For the symptoms. They don't know that it's killing them."

"So you'd have to dry up all of the trafficking."

"No," Trinina said. "This is a disease, remember."

"So it can spread?"

"By sexual contact."

Delgado looked down at the papers. "You realize what this means?"

"I do," Payne said.

"This news won't be very welcome in some circles."

"It wasn't very pleasant for me to uncover."

Delgado rubbed his eyes. "You understand that I am bound by certain restrictions in drug cases involving clubs."

"It's not a drug."

"I understand that now, but the fact remains that the initial infections had their roots in drug culture. I'm afraid that's the way the Feds are going to see it, too."

"What are you saying?"

"I'll have to treat this like the usual drug case." He sighed and took some papers from a drawer. "The usual procedure is for the investigating party to sign a waiver which states they are not holding the club responsible in any way for the death of the victim. All you have to do is sign these and I'll do the final disposition. You have a choice: death by accidental drug overdose or suicide by intentional drug overdose."

Payne slammed his fist on the desk top. "That's not right! It's not true! Kelce is the one responsible! He brought the strain out of the lab!"

"The papers will be turned over to the Feds for investigation. All that's needed is the documentation of drug type, which can be done here since your work was destroyed. All you have to do is tell us what work needs to be done. The Feds will then make an evaluation of the drug's safety and take appropriate action."

"It'll take at least a month before that gets done," Payne said.

"At least."

"In the meantime, the disease will be running its course. The Feds will discover it for themselves if the death rate is high enough. By then there'll be no tracing which club it came from. It'll be all over."

"Are there any alternatives?" Trinina asked.

"Don't sign the papers, in which case the investigation is held until the draw time is up. After that it'll be handled by our agency."

"Nine months," Payne said.

"Or one."

Payne licked his lips. "May I speak with the lady in private?"

"Take as much time as you need."

Payne rose from his seat and took Trinina's hand, escorting her out. She walked a few meters and leaned against the wall as Payne closed the door.

"I know what you're thinking," she said.

"I didn't wait for an hour and a half to have him tell me that nobody's responsible."

She put her arms around his neck. "Kelce is responsible. The Feds will find that out."

"In a month," Payne said bitterly.

"Better than nine."

"It's not good enough. Last Friday I had one victim. Last night at the club I counted eighteen. If you can do math in your head, you can figure out what it's going to be at the end of a month."

"You're assuming a lot of things, Payne. There's a lot we don't know yet. How does the thing survive in the body, what's the incubation period, how does it multiply..."

"Unless she was taking massive doses of the suspension, the girl had it at least a month. Maybe this group I counted last night was in on the ground floor of Kelce's dealings."

"Think about what you've just said. If they've been infected for a month, there's no way to calculate the number of sex partners that have been involved."

"They can be traced through club records."

"For the Lancaster, yes. What about the other clubs? Is there any way to calculate the number of clubs that the eighteen and their sex partners have been to? And what about chambers houses? They have no records at all."

He looked at her with empty eyes.

"Don't you see, Payne? You're already too late. The epidemic you want to stop is already happening."

He said nothing. The only movement was that of his breathing.

"I realize what this has meant to you in terms of the challenge and the prestige in such a discovery, but it's out of your hands. Even if Kelce hadn't destroyed your work, it would have been taken away. From what Delgado's told us, the Feds would do the same thing. The only difference would be Biotech's obvious advantage in working out a cure."

"Listen to yourself. You're talking production time for a cure. You don't care about the people walking around with this stuff. What the hell would you care? You're leaving the country. All you want to do is to see me smile as I'm waving good-bye. You want me to go in and sign those damn papers."

"Perhaps you're right," she said, surprising him. "Maybe I've been working with microorganisms too long. I may be seeing this as a test case. I may have no feeling toward it other than the fact that I hope it doesn't find its way to Australia.

"And you're right about your other accusation. I do

want to see you smiling as you wave good-bye, but it's not as mercenary as you'd believe. You mean a lot to me, Payne. I could say that I love you and not feel guilty about it. I care about you, and what I'm seeing in you worries me.

"I do want you to go back and sign those papers, but it's not because I want to leave here with a clear conscience. It's because I'm thinking of your welfare."

"You think it's best for me to sign those papers?"

"It doesn't matter now. The way I see it, the plague is out, and one way or another, word is going to get around. You were probably the first to realize the full implications, but it's out of your hands, and there's no way you'll get it back this late in the game. The only option you have is whether you should give responsibility to the Feds or Biotech."

Payne kissed her on the cheek and hugged her, breathing in the scent of her skin. They turned and walked into Delgado's office.

"Come to a decision?"

"Yes," Payne said. "I'm going to sign Honor Lyndon-Smith over as a drug overdose."

"Accidental or intentional?"

"Accidental."

"A good choice. The Feds will be more likely to look into it that way."

With help from Delgado, it took fifteen minutes to get the papers in order. Payne had to sign his name on every page, and every half page on papers needed for completion of a case with no formal documentation. At the end of the session, Delgado gave carbons of the papers to Payne.

"This wraps things up," he said. "May I congratulate you? You're the fastest citizen investigator I've had in a long time. Anyone else would have taken a month to get this far."

After another twenty minutes Payne and Trinina walked out of the Warax Substation.

"You surprised me," Trinina said. "I thought for certain you'd throw the file on Kelce to Biotech. I'm sure they'd like to take care of him themselves."

"What's wrong with what I did?"

"Nothing, I guess. I just thought you'd have more company loyalty."

"After seeing the screwing I could have taken on the deal? I'm amazed that you'd even think that."

"Just curious."

"I suppose I am still loyal to them. After all, this is the only dark spot on my unexceptionable career. I think I'm tired of the work, that's all."

"If you're so loyal, why didn't you throw responsibility to them?"

Payne shuffled the new papers. "For these. They're going to get you out of the country."

Payne checked around the Plus Fours for signs of Federals while Trinina went into the building. He walked into the Handi-Mart and picked up a few meaningless items, waiting for Trinina to get inside. A short while later, he paid the clerk and left.

Inside, he dashed up to the fourth floor and gave his usual knock. He was eventually answered by Bailey, who was still wearing his political apron.

Bailey nodded. "Come on in."

Payne walked in to warm, friendly smells, nearly stepping on Nathan, who was pulling a toy boat on a string. There were wheels in the boat's bottom, and as they turned, the smokestacks moved up and down to the tune of "The Sailor's Hornpipe." Payne moved back into the archway and looked down at the boy.

"Hello."

Nathan looked up. He squinted, and his eyes lit with recognition. "You're Payne?"

"Yes."

"You're my father, then."

"Yes."

"You don't look like the school said you would."

"Is that good or bad?"

"I guess it's good." He didn't bother to elaborate but instead returned to the boat and ran it backward, fascinated by the reverse version of the hornpipe.

"That's some boat you've got there."

Nathan smiled, very pleased. "Trinina bought it for me while we were staying at the gym."

"What gym?"

"The place with the soft walls and the stuff that hangs from the roof."

Payne snickered.

"This is only a toy boat. I'm going to go on a real one. Trinina's going, too."

"I know. I'm going to help you get on the boat."

"Trinina said you would."

"Have you ever been on a boat before?"

"No."

"Are you scared about going on a real one?"

"No. Trinina says I don't have to. She said I'll get to see the whales."

"You will," Payne said.

"Are you going to come with us?"

Payne stared. The boy was going to look like his mother when he grew up. "No," he said softly. "I have to stay."

"Why?"

"There are only two tickets for the boat ride."

Nathan looked over his shoulder. Trinina emerged from Bailey's bedroom and ruffled Nathan's hair. "Have you washed for supper?"

Nathan shook his head.

"Better go to it if you want to eat."

"Can I take my boat?"

"Only if it doesn't eat much."

Nathan picked up the cord and hornpiped into the bathroom.

"What brings you here?" she asked.

"I need an excuse?" He rattled the bag stamped with

the Handi-Mart logo. "I thought Nathan might like one of these."

"A Chocoration Plus? Oh, Payne, hide it until later. If he sees that, he won't want his supper."

"For which you're welcome to stay," Bailey chimed from the kitchen.

"I don't want to put you short."

"Nonsense. I made extra. I figured you'd show up for the last meal."

"He's staying," Trinina insisted. She turned to Payne. "I'm glad you stopped by."

"It was a foolish thing to do. What if I—"

"Don't say it," she blurted.

"You're right. I should enjoy your company."

"You won't have it much longer."

"It's for the best."

A tear spilled from her eye. "I'm sorry."

"For what?"

"That you won't—" She choked. "Nathan."

He moved to her. Her head fell to his shoulder. He stroked her hair and held her close. "It's all right," he said, throat tightening.

They hugged until Bailey called them to the table for dinner. As they sat, they saw that what he had fixed was real. The smell was tremendous and lacked the fishy taint of the high-protein synths.

"You shouldn't have done this," Payne said. "It must have really set you back."

"Not really," Bailey said between mouthfuls. "I bought most of it on sale and kept it in the community chest. It's worth the charge to use their freezer so I can use my panels for the video."

"Still," Trinina said, "you should have saved this for yourself."

"Nonsense. I accumulated this for a special occasion, and this one is as good as any. I rarely entertain a group this size. It's usually myself and a lady friend."

"You still shouldn't have gone to the trouble."

"I'll have no complaining," Bailey ordered. "Final word belongs to the guest of honor. What do you say, Nathan?"

Nathan smiled. He had a mustache of white milk and a goatee of brown gravy. The corners of his mouth were flecked with whites and oranges and greens. He jabbed his fork at the roast. "Could I please have more meat?"

"Case closed," Bailey said, laying a forkful of beef on the boy's plate.

The four of them ate their fill, then sat for another hour to wind down. When Trinina disappeared into the kitchen with Nathan, Payne investigated and found them washing dishes. He ordered them out, stating that there were better ways to spend their last hours in America. She demanded to know what they were and was told to take a nap. The evening would be long, and it wasn't as if she could board the boat with Nathan in tow. He would have to figure out how to get the boy there without being seen. Time would also be spent at the Lancaster trying to get the papers from Rodrigues's office. She relented and took Nathan into Bailey's bedroom. Once they were gone, Payne took over the dishes.

"What do you think you're doing?" Bailey asked from the arch.

"Dishes."

"Unheard of. Get away from there."

"If you let them go, they'll get grotesque. Better to do them while the dirt is fresh."

"Can't let you do that, Payne."

"I have to pay you back somehow."

"Then pay my way into the Lancaster some time."

"You'll have a long wait before that happens."

"More rumors?"

"I was going to ask you. I haven't heard any, and you're the one who gets around."

"You're in the middle of it, I suspect."

"Let's say that things don't look too promising right now."

"Any advice?"

"Find a woman you trust and move her in. It's going to be a long, hot summer."

"That bad?"

"Worse." He rinsed a stack of plates.

"So what's the plan?" Bailey asked, picking up a dish and drying it.

Payne handed him a coffee cup. "I wish I knew. Getting Nathan to the boat is going to be a problem."

"You're not going to see a lot of six-year-olds out on the street in the middle of the night."

"Or the dead of morning. Trinina's boat leaves at 0400 hours."

"Don't they believe in keeping civil hours?"

"The boats come and go twenty-four hours a day. For every one leaving the dock, there's two waiting to get in."

Bailey put the coffee cups in the cupboard. "They should bring back air travel."

"They should bring back a lot of things."

"Do you have any ideas at all for the kid?" Bailey asked.

"I'm more worried about getting the papers right now."

"You're cutting things awfully close."

Payne handed Bailey the last of the dishes. "It's all happened so fast. I hope I don't screw anything up. It'd be a shame for her to lose it after getting this close."

"Agreed," said Bailey. "Listen, Payne. Trinina's not the only one looking at a long night. Why don't you catch some sleep, too? You look like you could use it. I've got the dishes under control."

"No," Payne said. "Too much to do."

Bailey ushered him out of the kitchen. "Tell you what. You let me worry about smuggling Nathan. I'll be baby-sitting him, so we can brainstorm."

Payne smiled wearily. "Okay."

"Can I tell you something?"

"As long as it's short. The prospect of sleep is starting to sound pretty good."

"I wanted to say that I think you're one hell of a guy.

Were it not for the obvious effect on their government checks, most men wouldn't give a tinker's damn if one of their women bolted. They'd just as soon turn them in as try to help out."

"Nathan's my future. I can't let it end at the Lancaster."

"What about Trinina?"

"She's the best part of my past. I've got to preserve that. The rough part will be letting go. There's a greedy part of me that's screaming for them to stay."

Bailey smiled, not out of pleasure but in confidence, in warm encouragement. "When the time comes," he said, "you'll do your part."

"Thank you, Bailey."

"Good night."

"Good night, friend."

Payne slipped into the bedroom, holding the door so the crack of light stayed away from the bed. Trinina was lying in a curve, and Nathan was tucked into the crook of her body in a fetal position. He moved to the other side of the bed and joined them. With Nathan nestled between, he embraced them. In less than a minute he was asleep.

Trinina woke him by gently running her finger down the bridge of his nose. He looked at her, trying to open his eyes beyond a squint, then shook his head and rubbed his eyes.

"I hated to wake you. You were sleeping so soundly."

"Yeah," he said groggily. "I feel pretty good. If I could only wake up now."

"Don't rush it. You'll ruin the effect."

Payne closed his eyes and felt sleep welling up inside. "What time is it?"

"2100."

That woke him. He threw off the covers and sat up. "2100? We've got to get moving."

"Relax."

"We've got a million things to do."

"I've handled it. I moved Nathan to the couch. Bailey's making leftovers into sandwiches for the trip."

"They'll feed you on the boat, I hope."

"Of course. This is just a precaution."

"I've got to go to the club. You need to pack your things."

"They're packed. All we've got are the clothes on our backs and a few essentials. You'll probably want to clean up before you go. I'm all ready."

"You can't go," Payne said emphatically.

"You're not going to start that again, are you? You have no choice in the matter. I'm the one who set up the ticket buy."

"That's no longer necessary. The papers are my problem."

"What's wrong with you? You've been terribly protective, and it's getting annoying. I'm a big girl, Payne. I got this far, and I didn't get hurt."

Payne sighed. "All right. But remember that this part of the show is mine. I'm calling the shots."

He rolled from the bed. In the bathroom he looked into Bailey's full-length mirror. His hair was askew, he needed to shave, and his jumpsuit showed that it had been slept in. He chastised himself for not thinking to take it off.

The solution was on the corner of Bailey's sink: a spray bottle waiting to be filled with water. He peeled the suit off, hung it over the shower curtain, and ironed it, taking the time to wash himself while it dried. By the time he emerged, he was awake and feeling the benefit of the sleep.

He left Trinina in the bedroom and walked into the kitchen, where Bailey was building sandwiches assembly-line style.

"You really don't have to do that, you know."

Bailey screwed the top on a mustard jar and set it aside. "I don't mind. To be frank, they're not getting all of these. Some of them are my carry-ins."

"You can keep them all if you want."

"Where would I keep them? It's too much trouble to take them down to the community chest. Let me be charitable, okay?"

"Sure."

He placed slices of meat across the bread and looked over his shoulder. "You have a plan yet?"

"I think so. You come up with anything for Nathan?"

"I think I've got an angle."

"Great. I've got to remember and get Trinina's money changed to Australian dollars as soon as possible."

"It's not going to happen here. If you do it'll be on the black market, and you're going to be looking at a ten for one exchange rate. Have her do it on board the ship once they're outside the two hundred fifty-mile jurisdiction."

"What will she do until then?"

"Eat sandwiches." He finished assembly and began to wrap them.

"Ready to go?"

They looked back. Trinina had completely changed her appearance by putting a scarf over her head and makeup on her face.

"You've got me outclassed," Payne said.

"It's 2115 right now. How long does it take to walk down there?"

"Fifteen, twenty minutes."

"Perfect."

Payne and Trinina linked arms and walked out, Bailey wishing them luck as they went. The walk to the Lancaster was uneventful. At the door, Payne showed the passcard and the clerk admitted them without batting an eye. Trinina entered first. When Payne followed through, he was stunned.

The lobby was almost deserted. A handful of people by the rest rooms and another by the concession stand made a total of eleven. The knockout brunette at the S and M counter was gone. A different girl was there, leaning on her elbow and staring into a college textbook. Payne put his arm around Trinina's waist and guided her over.

"Are Wednesday nights always this dead?"

The girl looked up from her book. She tilted her head at the double doors. "Why hang around out here? The action is in there."

"They pay you to say that," Trinina said icily.

Payne winced. He wanted to pull her away but didn't. The girl behind the counter dropped her fake smile, replacing it with a sincere one.

"But they don't pay me enough to keep it up," she said. "To tell you the truth, I don't know what the problem is. Our slow night is Thursday, but this looks worse than any Thursday I remember. Maybe somebody's come up with a better house drug. That's off the record, of course."

"Maybe somebody's come up with a safer house drug," Trinina snapped, walking away.

"That's off the record, too," Payne said, following.

"I hate it here," Trinina said as he caught up, venom showing in her voice. "I hate the clubs."

"Why?"

"Watch," she ordered, and walked into the ballroom.

Inside was the smoke and the noise and the people that he had come to expect. This crowd was smaller than the one he had seen on Monday, but there was a marked difference. There was dancing and banter and applause for the musical sets, but it all seemed forced. It was stiff and somber, as if Smith had hired a chapter of the American Chess Society to act as window dressing. That idea made him laugh. Trinina was a member of the ACS.

He looked at her and saw she was scowling at the dance floor. When he looked at the others on the floor, he realized that they all had the same expression.

"Something's wrong."

"There certainly is," Trinina hissed. "This is a disgusting place. All it's designed for is to manipulate people into buying drinks and making babies for the government. It's pornography."

"That's not it."

"You'd agree if you thought about it for any length of time."

"That's not what I'm talking about, Trinina. Look at the people. When you come to a place like this, you're supposed to have a good time. Nobody here is."

She studied the clientele, shaking her head.

"You don't see it."

"No," she said. "I'm here to get my papers and get out."

"Be glad you don't. It's scaring the hell out of me."

They took a booth and sat in silence, Trinina doing a slow burn and Payne trying to reason out the pallor over the audience. The barmaid came and asked if they needed a drink. Payne looked at Trinina, then waved the girl off.

Gradually, the crowd grew and spirits rose, but there was still something wrong. He couldn't keep track of any one person for more than five or ten minutes. He watched the doors and counted, noting what types were coming and what types were going and the number of couples heading for the chambers. Slowly it came to him. While the numbers in the club remained constant, they suffered a high turnover rate. People were coming in and dancing for a while, but when they went back to the chambers, they reemerged almost immediately.

The club was turning people away at the chambers.

When they came from being turned away, they danced for a song or two and then left. He watched the D.J. trying to grab people and hold them in the club. He tried fast sets, slow sets, fog, lasers, videos, and a quiet dance, which went over worst of all. The music went down and off, the lights dimmed, the fog rose, and the people rolled out the doors en masse.

"Well, Sherlock?"

"Sherlock?"

"Never mind. Have you figured out the big mystery?"

"The clientele is turning over about every twenty minutes."

"They've finally become bored with it all."

"Of dancing, yes. I think they've closed the chambers."

"What for?"

Payne thought of Rodrigues lying behind his desk, the back of his head blown out. "I wish I knew." He shifted uncomfortably in his seat. "What time do you have?"

Trinina thumbed her watch. "2330."

"Impossible. That can't be right. They play 'Danse' at the top of every hour."

"I don't think it's played since we've been here."

Payne rose. "Come on." He grabbed her by the arm and pulled her from the table. "We're going to see Smith."

She twisted her arm loose.

"If we don't go to Smith now, we're never going to get your papers."

Trinina stood firm for a moment and then relented, calmly following Payne's lead through the doors to the chambers. People were lined the entire length of the hallway, standing two and three abreast and milling toward the desk. As they cut ahead, there were jeers about keeping in line that didn't subside until Payne pulled his passcard and waved it, shouting about official GCR business. The crowd cooperated and stepped out of their way.

As they approached the desk, Payne dropped his hand from Trinina's waist and waved his card for the receptionist, who was looking over a Bill of Health.

"I need to see Smith."

"Piss off," said the man at the head of the line.

Payne stuck the card under his nose. "GCR. Official business."

"Then pull some bloody strings and get me into a chamber."

The receptionist shook her head.

"What's the problem?" Payne asked.

"I can't accept this Bill."

"I got it bloody yesterday!" the man protested.

"We can now only accept Bills of Health issued within

the past twelve hours." She spoke mechanically, as if she
had been reciting it all day. "A new directive from the
Department of Health."

"But this is unused!"

"I'm sorry. You'll have to take it up with the Department."

The man raked the desk top and sent papers and files
to the floor. "You can't do this!"

Payne grabbed the man by the back of the collar and
pushed him away from the desk. He slammed him into
the wall and held him. "You're making a scene."

He tore Payne's hands from his lapels. "You've no
jurisdiction. You're GCR."

"I'm sworn to uphold the law, and it's just been laid
down to you."

"But I'm clean. And I've been without for a week."

"If you're that desperate, go home and have one off
the wrist."

The man went red. "I'd go to a chambers house first."

"I'm not stopping you."

The man took a step forward. "No. I'll do it here. To
your arse if I have to."

"Do you have citizenship papers?" Payne asked quietly.

"What?"

"Do you have citizenship papers?"

"Who does?"

Payne motioned at the line. "Most of the people over
there were born into this country. You keep pushing this
horny sailor act, and I'll have to shut the line down. How
do you think they'll react to that?"

The man stared.

"Get out of here," Payne said, biting the ends from his
words. "Get out before I tell them myself."

The fight drained from the man's face, and he backed
away. He took six steps, turned his back to Payne, and
stalked down the hall. The line breathed a collective sigh
of relief, and the milling started again.

"Thanks," the receptionist said.

"What's with the sudden change in the health requirements?" Payne asked, gathering papers from the floor.

The receptionist shrugged. "Word came down at 1400 hours. It's not making anyone happy."

Payne stacked the last of the papers on the desk. "This came down from the Department of Health?"

The receptionist nodded.

"I'll have to ask Smith about it, if you don't mind." He showed her the card.

"For what you've done, I'd let you in without that." She opened the panel to the stairs.

"After you," he said to Trinina.

He followed, walking one step behind, hand on her waist. Hearing the door close, he asked,"What do you think?"

"About the new policy? Sounds like something's amiss."

"Kelce's bug?"

"Could be."

Payne carded the lock and allowed Trinina the first step into Smith's office. She was obviously impressed by the surroundings. Faces looked back as they entered, and Payne noticed that save for Giles, all were unfamiliar. He found Smith slumped at his desk, head in his hands. He led Trinina to within a meter of him and stopped.

Smith didn't move.

"Lyndon," Giles said. "You've got company."

Smith looked up. His face had aged fifteen years since their last meeting. His hands slid down his cheeks and flopped into a stack of papers.

"You've come at a very bad time, Mr. Payne."

"Bad house drug, Mr. Smith?"

Smith shook his head. His eyes looked distant and tired. "I don't know what the hell it is. Department of Health has put the squeeze to the testicles, and all the clubs kneeled. All because of that bastard Kitsch."

"I saw the lines downstairs," Payne said. "How is Kitsch involved?"

"Where have you been, Mr. Payne? It's been all over the media. The bastard dropped dead last night, so the lab boys cut him up, and guess what they found?"

Payne wondered if Louis had been the one behind the scalpel that had opened Kitsch from neck to groin.

"A chemical cocktail, Mr. Payne. Enough bloody drugs to sink a ship. You name it and he'd had a bit of it. He'd been through the lot, all right. His heart said, 'Enough already,' and stopped. His death is causing such a public uproar that it's forcing the Feds to do a reevaluation of the club system. A minor thing for them but a royal pain in the arse for us."

"Maybe the public is getting a little bit scared of you club owners."

"You couldn't be more wrong. We police ourselves, Mr. Payne, and we're damned proud of it. Most club owners like to run a tight ship, and I'm no exception. If there's a bad lot of Blueskies or Whiff going around, I'm not averse to stalling sales while someone finds the rat passing it and strings him up. We have to protect our interests or the Feds come in for a meddle."

"You're certainly in for one now."

"And nobody seems to know why." For the first time since their arrival, Smith's face was showing color, his voice charged with life. "All I know is that it's killing business. We're set up to push sex. The order of the music and the colors and the fog are subliminal messages. Even the drugs. We came up with the Quiet Dance because research said silence can be conducive to a mood if the lighting is right. I've spent a fortune making this the most successful breeding house on the coast, and some bastard with no stomach for drugs has come along and banged it all away."

Payne felt heat rising inside him. He felt embarrassed and used and angry. Of course Trinina was right. *Why weren't you smarter, Payne?* he could hear her saying. *Why didn't you catch what was going on and stay away?*

You would've been spared the grief you suffered with Myra.

That was the answer. That explained why he couldn't see what was going on. He had been caught in the club's spell, as were Bailey and Myra. He didn't notice because he was too busy being duped. The noise and the music and the smells and the fog and the lights and the motion all conspired to make him think he wanted Myra, and every time they came to this club, they fell in love all over again. He was bitter and hurt and disgusted, and the sudden knowledge made him want to vomit.

"You're sickening," Trinina spat. "You're a piece of filth. You're no better than a slave trader."

"My lady." Smith smiled, being his best English gentleman. "When I came here I was told that America was still the land of dreams and that anyone with the itch could still make a go of it, could rise above the blows dealt them and make a name for themselves. I didn't believe a word of it. Three years later *I am the word*."

"I want my money," Payne said, almost too suddenly. "I want my money and then I'm done with you."

Smith grinned sardonically. "You've let the lady sway your sentiments."

"Enough was done on my own."

"Very well. But I think you should keep up your part of the bargain."

Trinina looked at Payne uneasily. "Bargain?"

Smith laughed. "Oh, yes. He's had dealings with the devil."

"The money," Payne snapped.

Smith stood. "Who killed my sister?"

Payne dropped his eyes to the floor. "Not who. What. It was an accidental drug overdose."

"As your countrymen would say, you're handing me a line of shit."

"That's what the official report says."

"You know as well as I that those are a pack of lies!" Smith shouted. "Somebody had to be responsible for her death, and I demand to know who. I demand satisfaction, Mr. Payne!"

"You want an answer? Fine, I'll give it to you." He advanced on the desk and faced Smith down. "*You're* responsible, Smith. You're the one who runs the club. You're the one who approves the rackets. You're the one who has to have the best house drug. You were supposed to look after your sister, but you let her get strung out. And you let her take the special of the day. Only it wasn't a drug, Smith. It's a germ, a bacteria. You want to know why they've put the clamps on the chambers? *Because your house drug is spread by sexual contact!*"

The air left Smith's lungs, and he fell into his chair. "That was none of my doing. Rodrigues approved the drugs."

"But you approved of Rodrigues. And when he heard the news about Kelce's contribution, he blew his brains out. You didn't know that, did you? Right now he's lying on the floor of his office with a hole punched in his skull. Are guns a part of the rackets, too?"

Smith shook his head. "Too much."

"I want to know one thing. How did you corrupt Kelce?"

"Corrupt?"

"What did you have on him? Why did he bring the stuff out of the lab?"

Smith laughed weakly. "You make it sound like black-mail. It was nothing of the sort. He volunteered it. I had something he wanted very, very badly."

"Letters of transit," Trinina said.

Smith nodded.

Payne turned to Trinina, stunned. "How did you know?"

"Karol's pregnant."

"That's not possible. I've seen her—"

"But you haven't talked to her like I have. She's only about three months along."

"But they broke up. Karol said he was coming unglued so she broke things off."

"Coming unglued," Smith said, "because I wouldn't

let him have the papers." He rubbed his thumb over the tips of his fingers. "Somebody else came up with the money first. That upset him greatly."

"The emigration racket."

"Kelce had a valuable property to protect. He convinced Kingman to go and retrieve them by going into the chambers with him. Kingman was such a dear boy."

"And you kept on selling them."

"No. Rodrigues kept on selling them. He was no fool. He knew he was on to something good."

"And Kingman was killing the prospects."

"After the monies were paid and Kelce provided certain . . . favors."

"What about the drug?"

"Kelce was getting nervous. He was afraid the papers would get away. He went to Rodrigues with a counter-proposal. He promised delivery of a house drug with draw enough to offset the cost I'd spent in recovering the papers for him in the first place."

"Why didn't he run after he delivered?"

"There was a stipulation on the deal. He had to wait thirty days to see if the drug had fatal side effects." He smiled at Payne and dropped two plastic cards on the desk.

"There's a hundred thousand here, Mr. Payne. The extra is to buy your silence on this matter, as it seems you have given me what may be a good reason for the crackdown."

"That's it, then? Just like that?"

"You've done an excellent job of sleuthing, and I appreciate your help. You may consider the extra a bonus for work well done if the concept of hush money offends you."

Payne took the cards. The total of the two, after taxes, would be the amount Smith had quoted.

"What about the disease going around? You've got some responsibility for that."

"Mr. Kelce will be taken care of, I can assure you."

"You're going to kill him," Trinina said.

"I'd rather not go into that. It's in my hands now. He must be punished for my sister's death."

"What for?" Payne shouted. "What for? You knew it was coming. You weren't surprised to hear of her death. What gives you the right to clamor for blood, Smith? You didn't even care about her, other than the fact that you made some solemn vow to take care of her. You didn't even do that."

"She was beyond my control," he said solemnly.

"You believe that? You're wanting a scapegoat for your guilt, as if a little bloodletting would take the truth away. Why was she on drugs in the first place? You want to tell me about that? Why would a girl like your sister want to pollute herself like that?"

"He killed our parents," Giles said.

Payne's head turned so fast that the bones in his neck popped. "What did you say?"

"Giles, you ass."

Tears welled up in Giles's eyes. "He had to, Mr. Payne. You have to understand that he wasn't a criminal. He did it because he loved them."

"That's enough!" Smith barked.

"No, it's not!" Giles shouted. "You can't keep it dark, Andrew. You'll lose your mind. You've already lost Honor. You've got to talk!"

Payne looked back at Smith. "Is this true?"

Smith's face was stone, every muscle straining to hold back emotion.

"Our parents were a very proud lot," Giles said. "They were too old and sick to travel, but they didn't want to see England under a red flag."

"That's rubbish," Smith said.

"That's what you told me!" Giles bawled.

Smith gulped air and fought for composure. "My mother was a historian. My father worked for the government as a liaison between one of our agencies and one of your agencies—if you see what I'm saying.

"Both my parents knew what sort of stuff the Soviets are made of. Did you know that virtually every Russian soldier captured by the Germans during the Second World War and liberated at the end was sent to a death camp?"

"Erasing the taste of freedom," Payne said.

"My brother was correct to a point. They were too old to travel, and they were proud. Because of his line of work, my father knew that if the Soviets took England, there'd have been no peace for him. He knew they'd work on my mother to get him to break. So he kept me behind after Giles and Honor had left for the docks. He kept me long enough to give me his service weapon..." A single tear spilled down his cheek.

"He did it because he loved them," Giles said.

"And Honor found out."

"I broke and told Giles. She was eavesdropping. Things weren't the same after that." He removed two wrinkled papers from a drawer and held them out to Trinina.

"These are yours, I believe."

"How did you know?" she gasped.

"The liaison for emigrants was up here discussing Rodrigues's tardiness with me. As he had another... appointment, he gave these to me for safekeeping and pointed you out to me so I could see that they got to the right person." He rattled the papers. "You might as well take them. They're no good to me now. They're only money. That's one area in which I seem to have over-achieved."

Payne's nervous hands took the papers and gave them to Trinina. She turned them over in her hands and wept.

"Your ship leaves from Pier 21 at 0400 hours. The H.M.S. *Auckland*."

"Thank you," she choked. "Thank you."

"Get on the boat and don't come back," Smith ordered.

They backed out of the room. Payne carded the door, and they slipped out. "It's over," he said as the door closed. "It's over."

Thursday Morning

They hit the street as the midnight siren sounded. The weather had turned, misting the streets and bringing a starry look to the streetlamps. Payne sniffed and said he expected rain.

"A bad time to travel. You won't be able to stand on the deck and watch the lights fade."

"I have no desire for that," Trinina replied. "As soon as we get on that ship, we're finding our cabin and going to bed."

"You don't seem very partriotic." Payne laughed.

"If I was any kind of patriot, I would have turned myself in."

Payne watched her from the corner of his eye. She was scrutinizing the papers, running her fingers over their surface, rubbing a thumb across the printed lines and scratching them with a fingernail to see if they smeared or flaked. He noticed that they hadn't been filled out. He would do that so there would be no similarity between writings to arouse suspicions. Not that anyone would question the authority of the holder of such a document; the eagle on the letterhead and the Bureau of Emigration's seal stamped into the paper were very intimidating.

"Are they real?" he asked.

"What? The papers? I don't know. I've never seen this kind of document before."

"For having never seen one, what would you say?"

"I'd say they look very official." She handed him the papers. "I don't like it, you know. I think he gave them up much too easily."

"What else would he have done with them?"

"Left the country."

"He wouldn't leave. He's got too much going for him."

"So he's going to stay and watch it all come crashing down on his head. Sure."

"Maybe he did it to get me out of his way. After all, I know a bit more about him than he likes."

"I have no doubts that he wants you out of the way. What bothers me is that I'll be there when he tries to take you out."

"What makes you think he's going to do that?"

"Be serious, Payne. He admitted that Kingman was killing the people who bought the papers. Smith took you for a fool, and you played right along. If you're escorting us to the docks, you'd better bring along that gun you stole. You might need it."

"We're not going to need it."

"Not me. You. Smith's going to split your skull and save himself a fortune."

"Listen to me. Kingman's not going to kill us, because he's dead. The racket is over and done with. That's why Smith talked, and that's how we got the papers. If it makes you feel any better, the law is on to his emigration racket. If he got caught with these papers, he'd be in worse trouble than he is now. The only reason you'll get away is because you can legitimately say that you bought them."

"How do you know Kingman is dead?"

"After he killed Winthrop Saturday night, he went to my apartment to try and get the claim ticket on Smith's sister. Kelce had sent him to get it because he was afraid

I'd discover what he'd done to her. Kingman ended up attacking me, and I pushed him down the elevator shaft."

"Why did Kelce leave the girl in your apartment?"

"I don't know. That's what I've got to work out after you're on that boat."

"Drop me a line and let me know how things turn out."

"Maybe I'll open up a club."

"You wouldn't dare."

"I'd be smart about it. I wouldn't use every means at my disposal just because it was available."

"What do you mean?"

"It's what Smith said about being an overachiever. He had too much going, and that's why it's all coming back on him. He spread himself too thin. Kelce was the same way. Kingman's muscle was available, so he used it to try and get the ticket from me. If he hadn't done that, he never would have been caught."

"You weren't going to take the option?"

"I'd thrown the ticket away."

She shook her head. "What am I going to do with you?"

"Leave me."

When they knocked on Bailey's door, the peephole darkened, and the door opened to reveal Bailey, smiling at them through mole eyes.

"Glad to see you could make it," he said. "We needed two more for a rubber of bridge."

"Did we wake you?" Trinina asked apologetically.

"Don't worry. I had to get up to answer the door. Did you bring the groceries?"

Payne closed the door and held out the papers. Bailey whistled and held them under the light. "These must have set you back a piece."

"Lancaster's having a going out of business sale."

"Great. Any longer and I would have called the MP Bureau. I figure you should leave here at 0300. That should get you to the docks with plenty of time to check in."

"Two-thirty," Payne amended. "It's starting to look nasty out."

"Where's Nathan?" Trinina asked.

"Right where you left him."

She excused herself and left the room. Payne waved Bailey into the kitchen.

"I held up my part of the bargain. How's your end?"

"I'm on to something, I think." Bailey craned his head to check on Trinina. "How prepared are you to do this?"

"Do or die."

"You going to be ready for trouble?"

Payne thought of the gun under his bed. Trinina's words about carrying it were ringing in his ears. "Do you know something that I don't?"

"No, but I think you should be ready for the worst."

"Right." He walked into the living room, mind spinning. He had to get upstairs and get the gun. What if Trinina's suspicions were right and they ran into Smith at the pier? It would pay to be ready. All he needed was an excuse. If he left now, she would suspect. The last thing he wanted her to know was that he had broken down and gone for the weapon.

Trinina put her finger to her lips. Nathan was still on the couch, dead to the world. Payne ushered her into the bedroom and flicked on the lights.

"Have you got everything ready to go?"

She pointed to the bed. On it were her day bag and Nathan's government-issue suitcase, which Payne recognized by the shape. The fabric, a light tweed, he had never seen before. Suddenly he realized that Trinina had stapled cloth over its surface to conceal the Mother America logo.

"That's it? That's all you're taking?"

"Plus Bailey's sandwiches and what we're wearing."

"You need more than that."

"I wanted to travel light."

Payne took the money plates from his pocket and pressed them into her hand. "You're going to need this."

Trinina pushed them away.

"What's the matter? Too dirty?"

"Do you know how much this is? I can't take it all."

"What am I going to do with it? There won't be much to spend it on after you're gone. I'd rather see it go to good use."

She tried to hand them back. "It's yours. I don't know what you did for it, but you earned it. I'll make my way."

He closed her hand around them and pushed the fist back at her. "This money was for the three of us, Trinina. It was going to keep us together. That's not going to happen now, so it's got to go for the good of the majority— the two of you. If you're too proud to use it, then buy Nathan the nicest Composition Board you can find and put the rest away for his education."

Her eyes clouded. She slipped the cards into her pocket.

"And make sure that you tell him that his father bought him the board and that—" He swallowed hard. "I love him very much."

She slipped her arms around him and hugged. He clenched her as though he could never quite get her close enough. When the wave of emotion subsided, he opened his eyes. Two bags sat in the middle of Bailey's bed.

He had his excuse to go up to his apartment.

He broke the embrace. "It's going to be getting cold in Australia. You'll be going right into their winter."

"I'm aware of that."

"You're going to need more clothing."

"I'll buy some when I get there."

"You'll need them on the boat. Once you cross over the equator, you'll be heading into cold weather."

"What do you want me to do, see if there's a Fashion Mart that happens to have a rack of winter styles sitting around?"

"No. You remember the girl who came by my place this morning? She'd moved in, but we've since broken off. She left some clothes that might fit you. It's not winter issue, but it would give you a couple of extra layers."

"What about Nathan?"

"Get some scissors and do some customizing. You did a good enough job on his suitcase."

She looked away.

"It won't hurt to come look."

"Where am I going to carry them? My bag is full."

"I've got one you can take. Something to remember me by."

"If you insist."

He clasped her hand, and they walked out, stopping to tell Bailey their plans.

"If we're not back in an hour," Payne said, "start worrying."

They were out of breath by the time they reached the seventh floor. He found the key and tried it in the door. It jammed, and the door held tight.

Trinina watched Payne's face. "What's wrong?"

"The door."

"What about it?"

"It jammed like this before..."

"Before what?"

"Before I found the body."

"Do you think that—"

"No." He shook his head. "I'm being paranoid." He twisted the key to take it out, and the door popped open. "Look at that. I forgot to—"

But Trinina had stepped in and turned on the lights. When they came on, she froze in horror.

The apartment had been completely destroyed. The wallpaper had been peeled from the walls, and the couch had been turned over and gutted of its stuffing. The video set was dismantled, likewise the telephone, their parts strewn across the floor. The remains of the doorside table had been smashed beyond recognition.

"Payne, I'm sorry."

"That's how he got in," Payne said, his voice caught between fear and anger. "That's how he got her body in. Can you believe it? I left the door unlocked that night. I must have."

Trinina leaned against the door, hand over her mouth, hyperventilating. Payne's stomach knotted painfully. He slipped back to the door and closed it, clicking the deadbolt.

"Stay here," he ordered. "Don't move."

He made his way back to the kitchen, stepping around the wreckage of the living room. The carpet was soaked and squished under his feet. The stove had been torn and stripped, as had the refrigerator and faucets. Food had been opened and thrown against the walls.

"Who could have done this?" Trinina called. "Burglars?"

"They're fools if they did. Nothing seems to have been taken."

There was a shred of something floating in the water collecting on the floor. He moved part of the smashed plumbing aside and plucked it out. It was a shred of the slab shot of Honor Lyndon-Smith, her eyes shining dully with Solari. He crumpled it in his hand, wringing the water out of it.

Trinina screamed.

He was out like a shot, stumbling through the obstacle course that the living room had become. She wasn't at the door. He fumbled with the lock but stopped when he heard her again, this time giving a low, sick moan. He picked his way over to the bedroom.

A meter inside, Trinina was kneeling on the floor, head in her hands, gasping for breath. Shredded clothing was everywhere, punctuated with tufts of mattress ticking.

Payne moved forward. His feet sloshed in the water that ran from the bathroom. He looked around, eyes adjusting to the light filtering in from the living room. In one corner his eyes locked on what had made Trinina scream.

A human leg, twisted and bruised, toes pointed to the ceiling. He grabbed what was left of the mattress and tossed it aside.

A body, cut and battered.

Myra.

He moaned and fell to his knees beside her. Hair was missing by the handful. Blood from her flattened nose had run and caked in her ears. He reached a trembling hand for her neck. He found a pulse, and there was a moan, making him yelp and fall back.

She moaned again.

He crawled to her. Her bruised eyes opened to a narrow squint.

"Payne?" she slurred through split lips.

"Myra." He slid his hands under her shoulders and pulled her into his lap. Dots of cigarette burns ran down her torso. "Oh, Myra. I am so sorry."

"What I get," she whispered. "Breaking in."

He brushed hair from her eyes. "Who did this?"

She tried one sound and winced. She gasped for breath. "Blue," she said.

"Federals?"

He felt a slight nod.

"How long ago? Do you know?"

This time a shake.

His jaw was chattering. "Were they after the boy?"

Another weak nod. Her eyes teared. "Made me tell. So sorry. Didn't know much."

He held her close and shook.

"Told all." She coughed, and he tried to cushion her against it. "They wouldn't stop."

"I'm sorry," Payne babbled. "I am so sorry."

She tapped him with her left hand. Two fingers were missing nails. "Your girl. Gone?"

He blinked tears out of his eyes. "Soon."

"Get her out." The words came out so plain and clear that they frightened him.

"Yes," he said. "I will. I will."

She nodded, and her lips formed a pained smile. "Goodbye, Payne."

He drew her in close. "No," he said. "We're going to get you help."

She tapped him again. He looked into her face. There was calm beneath the bruises.

"Good-bye," she repeated.

He choked. "Good-bye, Myra."

She closed her eyes. Her left hand went limp and splashed to the floor.

He kissed her for the last time.

From the bedroom window came a flicker of pure, white light, followed by a low rumble that rose in intensity and shook the building. The air cooled, and there came the sound of rain hitting glass. Payne sat on the floor and rocked, tears falling and gently splashing Myra's face. His throat felt hard and tight, and his arms were weak as paper. He tried to push the blood from his face and became lost in each successive thunderclap.

Finally, a gentle hand rested on his shoulder.

"Payne, we can't stay here."

He bit his lower lip, and a last tear rolled from his cheek.

Trinina brushed his hair. "It's a miracle she held on this long. She must have thought a lot of you to do that."

"Yes," he choked out.

"She was very special, I'll bet."

He closed his eyes and saw her as she danced at the Lancaster. He stayed there for a moment, then told himself that she was dancing now, in some club where the music never stopped, and the nighttime crowds watched in awe and stepped out of her way to give her room to move and applauded warmly and sincerely when she was done.

He shook the thought away and sobered.

"Let's go." He gently laid Myra onto the wet carpet, then rummaged for a bed sheet to cover her with. The bedclothes had all been slashed, and it took three sheets to do an adequate job.

"Were there any clothes left?"

"No," Trinina said. "Everything's been destroyed, your clothes included."

"The landlord is going to have a fit over this. Those bastards did a great job. It'll take months to restore this."

Trinina was appalled. "You can't be serious about staying here."

"What do you want me to do? Move into a car?"

"Hasn't it occurred to you, Payne? You can't stay any more than I could. Didn't you hear what she said? They're on to you. If they catch you, you'll end up in Micronesia, providing you live long enough to be sentenced."

"What do you think I should do? You're the one who's done all of the planning. Did you ever stop to think that I'd be singled out because I'm Nathan's father? You didn't, did you?"

She didn't answer.

"Well, don't start worrying about it now. Our immediate problem is to get you and Nathan on that ship. Then I can worry about what to do."

He opened the door and let her out. He twisted the key to his apartment from the ring and flipped it inside. He set the lock on the door and slammed it, locking himself out forever.

Bailey's door was unlocked. They found him pacing the floor, and when he saw their faces, he knew something was wrong. "Are you all right?"

"Hit some snags," Payne said.

"The Feds are on to him," Trinina said. "They trashed his apartment."

Bailey went pale. "How did they find out?"

"Myra told them."

"That bitch. You shouldn't have trusted her, Payne."

"They beat it out of her, Bailey. She's dead."

Bailey's face fell. "I'm sorry, Payne. Forgive me."

"Forget it. Let's work on getting Trinina and Nathan to the pier."

"You've got to go, too," Bailey said.

"How?" Payne barked.

"The money," Trinina said. "You could wait for an opening."

"It wouldn't work. I'd be in queue with everyone else. People have stayed at the docks for months before getting out, no matter how rich they were. Besides, that'll be the first place that the Feds come looking."

"You've got to do something."

"Let's not worry about it!" Payne shouted. "I'm not the most important person here right now—it's Nathan. Let's get him taken care of first."

There was a slow, high-pitched wail from the living room.

"I'm sorry," Payne said quietly.

Trinina looked at him, face flushing. "It's okay. He needs to get up, anyway." She hurried out of the kitchen.

Payne turned to Bailey. "What have you got for the kid?"

Bailey tilted his head to the bedroom and walked away. Payne followed.

"I'm sorry, Payne. I'm stuck."

"You're stuck? There's only an hour left."

"I tried, Payne. I really did. I tried to shrink one of my old jumpsuits. It turned into soup. I don't have anything I could change his face with."

"At least you tried."

"And now you. What are we going to do? You could stay here if you want."

"Stop it," Payne ordered. "I don't want to put a crimp in your life. I'll work something out. Maybe I could defect to the Japanese. They still had an embassy here last I heard."

"What would you do in Japan?"

"Catch a boat to Australia."

"Too bad Trinina doesn't have another paper."

"Are you expecting one to fall from the sky?"

"In a way. I've been doing some thinking, Payne. They're not going to let Nathan on that boat, no matter what kind of paper Trinina has. The Feds could take the captain on a felony."

"That's not covered by international law."

"Do you think the government cares? So what if Australia stops speaking to us? They let Canada and Mexico stop, and they were neighbors. Do you think anyone's going to care?"

"Bailey, we're wasting time. We've got to find some way to smuggle that kid."

Bailey's face twitched.

Payne looked at him. Bailey's eyes were suddenly animated, as if new light were burning his brain.

"Bailey, what's wrong?"

"Yes," Bailey cried, his voice an octave higher than before. "Smuggle!" He yanked the closet door open and began tossing out boxes.

"What are you talking about?"

Bailey backed out of the closet with an armload of fiberwood slabs. Across one was stenciled "ICARUS INDUSTRIES SOLAR PANELS (3)." Below it in red were arrows and "THIS SIDE UP."

"Help me with these. They're a bear to move."

They weren't heavy, but they were large and cumbersome. Bailey was barking orders for Payne to hold or adjust, and raced around the form inserting slats and twisting cotter pins until they were standing around a small crate.

Payne looked at it, horrified. "It looks like a coffin."

"It's the only choice, Payne. Nathan would fit right inside, I'm sure. He won't have much room, but he'll be able to breathe. If they follow the directions on the crate, they'll keep this end up and he'll stay on his feet. Once he's on the boat, you can spring him. We'll pad it with some blankets and give him a sandwich and a canteen of water. Maybe a small can to pee in. The bottom's weighted, so it's not going to tip over. Most importantly, you'll have the extra paper for yourself. You've got to do it."

"No," Payne said flatly. "It's too dangerous."

Bailey stabbed the crate with a finger. He was pointing at the words "USE NO HOOKS."

"No," Payne repeated.

Bailey set his jaw and opened the bedroom door. "Trinina, would you step in here a moment?"

"What's wrong?"

Bailey pointed to the crate. "What do you think? It would free up a paper for Payne."

Payne watched her face. "It's too dangerous," he said.

"Quiet," Bailey ordered. "Let her make her own decision."

"It looks awfully rough," she said.

"We'll line it with blankets."

"We won't know how they'll move it or where it's going to end up," Payne said.

"They won't be using any hooks," Bailey looked at Trinina. "You've got the deciding vote."

She ran her hand across the inside of the crate. "I can't. We're going to let Nathan decide." She looked at Payne. "Agreed?"

Payne nodded.

Trinina disappeared and returned holding Nathan's hand. She led him to the edge of the crate, and the four of them stood around it. Payne studied the boy. He would fit inside with room to spare.

Trinina knelt and cupped her son's hands in hers. "Nathan." She spoke clearly and slowly. "We have a chance for something very good to happen. We can make it so your father can come to Australia with us. Would you like that?"

"Yes," he said.

"Okay. I want you to listen very carefully, because this is very important. Your father can come with us if you will hide in this box. It's just the right size for you."

"We'll give you food and water," Bailey said. "And a can to go to the bathroom in. You'll have blankets to keep warm."

Nathan considered this.

"It's going to be very dangerous," Payne said. "You're going to have to be a very brave little boy. The box might get bumped, and it might hurt, but you can't make any sounds. If you talk or sing or cry because you're hurt, you'll get caught and you'll have to go back to Mother America. They won't let you visit us anymore. You might be in that box for a long time, so it'll be very hard."

"Do I have to go in the box?"

"No," said Payne. "If you don't want to, we can do something else."

"Can you come if I don't go in the box?"

"No. I might be able to come later, but I might not be able to come at all."

"You'll have to be very brave, no matter what," Trinina said. "It'll be two different kinds of brave."

Nathan moved to the back of the box and looked in through one of the cracks. Bailey pulled the lid off and tilted it down so he could look in.

"Hello!" the boy shouted. Had it been any other time, the three of them would have laughed. When he emerged from the experiment, he looked around at them, his face locked with the firmness of a decision.

"I want to go in the box," he said.

There was no reaction from the grown-ups. He studied each individual face.

"Hey," he said. "Why is everybody crying?"

Payne ruffled his hair. "No reason. No reason at all."

Bailey produced a stapler from his bureau drawer and opened it so it could be used for tacking. He instructed Trinina to gather the thick wool synth blankets from the top of the closet to put around the inside of the crate. When she protested, he stated that he was planning on buying new ones in the fall. Under Nathan's supervision, Payne and Trinina began securing blankets to the inside of the box. Bailey went to the kitchen and returned with a large coffee can fitted with an airtight plastic lid.

"This is your bathroom, Nathan. There should be enough room in the box for you to use it, but do it only if you have to. If there's any way you can hold it, do that instead."

Nathan listened carefully and nodded gravely.

"We'll give you a couple of sandwiches in case you get hungry," Trinina said. "But try and save them, too."

"Can I take some toys with me?"

"No."

"Yes," Payne said. "One. What'll it be?"

Nathan smiled. "The ship."

"That'll be too noisy, dear," Trinina said. "You'll want something that doesn't make noise."

"The Soft Dog."

"The Soft Dog it is." She started for the door.

"We're just about done," Payne said, checking his watch. "Why don't you see that Nathan goes to the bathroom before we put him in?"

"I'm thirsty," Nathan said.

"Just a sip," Bailey said.

Trinina held out her hand. Nathan took it, and they left.

Bailey held the stapler against the blanket and slapped it with the palm of his hand. He stopped to admire his work and ran his hand around the inside of the crate. "Yeah. That's going to be real good."

Payne tucked an end of a blanket. "Put one here."

Bailey reached in with the stapler and slapped. "Can't have any loose ends."

"Right," Payne said. He stopped for a moment to think, wondering if he'd left any loose ends. He thought he had taken care of everything, yet there was something that bothered him. He looked at Bailey. "Listen, would you do me a favor?"

Bailey smirked. "Here it comes. The dreaded favor."

"This is strictly up to you. You don't have to do anything, but I'd like you to consider it. You seem to be fairly open-minded about things."

"This involves a woman."

"How did you know?"

"I can tell by your tone of voice."

"You'd have to be very tolerant. The guy she was living with is the reason for all of the rumors you've been hearing. It's only a matter of time before things come down on his head, so he'll be totally out of the picture."

"You want me to look in on her?"

"Consider it. She's had it rough, Bailey. She's pregnant by this guy, and she's a little messed up right now. She's going to need a good friend."

"What's her name?"

"Karol. She works days at Biotech, front desk."

"Can I tell her you sent me?"

"Absolutely."

They tossed Nathan's suitcase in the crate, then maneuvered it into the living room. Trinina was buttoning Nathan into thick flannel pajamas.

"I thought I'd put him in something warm, loose, and comfortable."

Payne picked him up and sat him on top of his shoulders. "Ready to go, space captain?"

"Ship's captain!" Nathan corrected. He walked to the crate, where Bailey had removed the baggage and was working on final preparations.

"All set," Bailey said.

"You're sure you want to do it this way?" Payne asked. "You can change your mind and nobody's going to be mad."

"Let's go!" Nathan said enthusiastically.

Payne lifted him from his shoulders and lowered him into the crate. The child ran his hands over the blankets and exclaimed how neat it was.

"Wiggle around. See how much room you have."

Nathan was able to turn all the way around and could lower into a crouch with his back against the wall, arms around his knees. He could stand by pushing his feet against the bottom of the box and squirming.

"This is it," Payne said, taking the lid in his hands.

"Inventory," Bailey said. He handed the coffee can to the boy. "Toilet."

"Check," Nathan said.

"Water."

"Check."

Payne reached into his pocket and pulled out the Chocoration bar. "Treat."

"Oh, boy!"

"Save it," Trinina warned.

"Sandwiches."

"Check."

"Pillow," Trinina said.

"Check."

"Soft Dog."

"Check."

"Extra blanket."

"Check."

"Room for everything?" Payne asked.

"I think so."

"We're going to seal you in, then." He started to fit the lid on, when there was an anguished wail from inside. He slipped it back off. "What's wrong?"

Nathan wiggled up, grabbed Payne's face, and planted a kiss on his cheek.

"Of course," Payne said, and kissed him back.

"Bailey, too."

Bailey moved over and received.

Finally there was Trinina. Nathan studied her face for a minute, watching the tears form in her eyes.

"It's okay," he said. "This is going to be fun."

They kissed, and she pulled him into a hug.

"It won't be long," she said.

Nathan wiggled into his domain and made a childish hand signal for the lid to be put on. Payne shoved it into place, and Bailey secured it with the slats.

"You okay in there?" Bailey asked.

The reply was muffled. "Yes."

"You two are going to carry this thing all the way to the docks?" Bailey asked.

Payne tilted the box. "It's not that heavy."

"It could get that way. It's a long walk."

"It's got to be done."

"I'll help you get it down the stairs."

"I won't have it. What if you're seen with us?"

"I'm in it enough already."

"But you haven't been caught." Payne extended his hand. "You've done enough. This is it."

They clasped and shook. Bailey's grip was strong and confident.

"I'll miss you," he said.

"Yeah," Payne said, trying to keep it short.

Trinina hugged Bailey and kissed him on the cheek. "I can't thank you enough for what you've done."

"Get to Australia, okay? Send me a postcard of the Alps."

Trinina looked embarrassed. "How about the Great Barrier Reef?"

"That'll be fine."

Trinina tilted the box back toward her.

"We're leaving now, Nathan," Payne said. "You'll have to be quiet from now until we get you out. Okay?"

"Okay."

Payne squatted, arms behind his back, and lifted the crate.

"Good-bye, Bailey."

Bailey said nothing. He guided them out the door, waved, then closed the apartment door and locked it.

Once they shifted the box into position, the going was easier. Nathan was lying against the height of the crate, so the weight was evenly distributed between the two of them. When they got to the stairs, Trinina balked.

"We can't do this," she said.

"Yes, we can. I'll go first. I'll have the weight of the box on my back. You can keep your end up high and steer."

"What about the bags?"

"Sling the bag around your shoulder. Put the suitcase on top of the crate and hold it in place with your chin."

Day bag around her neck, she hoisted the suitcase up, and they took the stairs slowly but surely. Without the

burden of weight, Trinina wanted to go faster. Payne cursed
and whispered instructions to her. By the time they reached
the second floor, Trinina knew what she was doing, and
the last flights went quickly.

Outside the Plus Fours, they propped the crate up and
leaned on it to catch their breath.

"I'm afraid Bailey was right," she said. "This is going
to be a trick."

"That was the worst of it. All we have to do now is
tote. Once we get to the docks, it'll be loaded for us."

"I don't want them to do it."

"Don't be a fool, Trinina. Let's go."

Payne took the day bag, and they tilted and lifted the
box sideways between them. Trinina freed a hand long
enough to load the suitcase, and they set off. They reached
a steady pace and held it, pausing only when negotiating
curbs. They made time, but both were beginning to worry.
After three blocks the weight of the crate and its contents
were starting to wear on them. Trinina, anxious to have
it all over with, kept speeding the pace. Payne barked at
her to keep it steady, and they started on their fourth
block.

"Payne," Trinina gasped. "How many blocks to a kilometer?"

"Don't ask," he grunted. "Not now."

"How far to the docks?"

"You don't want to know. Watch it. You're slowing
up."

"Can you reach your watch?"

"No!" he shouted, and stepped off the curb. He bent
his back, hitched the box against his shoulders, and plod-
ded across the asphalt, noting the steam rising from a
manhole cover.

"Step up coming."

"Payne— "

"Not now."

"Payne!"

"We'll rest up here."

He stepped up on the curb, and there was a scraping sound. Something struck him squarely between the shoulder blades and sent him staggering to his knees, the weight of the crate coming down on him. Nathan's suitcase slid neatly around his shoulder and arm and plunged to the sidewalk. A corner struck and the lock sprang, sending clothes across the concrete.

"I tried to tell you," Trinina snapped, shifting the box onto the sidewalk.

"I'm sorry," Payne said, trying to work the knot out of his shoulder.

Trinina rubbed her eyes. "This isn't going to work. This just isn't going to work."

"It's got to.'

"Do you see it working?"

"What else are we going to do? Do you have any great ideas?"

"Can one person carry the crate alone?"

"Empty, yes."

"Then we take Nathan out and let him walk. When we get within—" She added the number of blocks they had managed to walk. "—five blocks of the pier, we load him back in."

"No," Payne said. "Too risky. If anyone sees him, they'll report it. It'll be back to Mother America for him and separate parts of Micronesia for us."

"We'll have to risk it."

"We can't."

"We'll never make the boat."

Payne's patience was quickly fading. He opened his mouth to shout her down, when there was a crunching of stones on asphalt. There was the familiar sound of servos, and something rounded the corner where they stood and put them into the light.

"*No*—" Trinina's voice cracked.

Adrenaline filled Payne, but he was caught between fight and flight. He stood immobile, as if his feet had taken root in the concrete.

A shadowy figure moved out of the ElectriCart and moved behind the lights.

"Well, I'll be go to hell," it said.

Payne squinted against the lights and found a third, dimmer light, almost invisible because of its position behind the brighter headlights. It said TAXI.

"You!" Payne cried, flushed with relief.

"You do get around." The figure stepped into the lights. Payne laughed at the sight of him.

"You know this man?" Trinina quivered.

"In a professional sense." The driver removed his cap and bowed. "Citywide Taxi Service at your service." He scowled and straightened back up. "That didn't sound right, did it?"

"No matter," Payne said. "I hope you're for hire."

"Indeed. Looks like you're having some troubles."

"You don't know the half of it. How would you like to take us to the piers?"

"Love to." He scowled. "That crate going, too?"

"Of course," Trinina said.

"No way." He shook his head sadly. "I'd love to, but there's no way I could get you and that crate into my little machine here."

Trinina sighed in disappointment.

"What about the crate?" Payne said quickly.

"Huh?"

"Just the crate. Could you get it into the passenger's compartment?"

The driver scratched his beard and studied the scene. "I think so. Yeah, I think no problem. I'll have to charge extra, though. That thing might play hell with the seats."

"Help me get it in," Payne said. "The lady's tired."

The driver took an end. "You folks skipping the country?"

"There's a fifty percent gratuity in this for you," Trinina said.

"Like I said," the driver said, grinning, "folks do what they got to do, and it's none of my damn business."

Payne shoved on his end of the crate while the driver guided it across the surface of the seat, lifting the edges to keep it from snagging the fabric. Once the door was shut, the crate was held snugly in place.

Payne looked at Trinina. She tilted her head at the box. He nodded and called the driver over, threw his arm around his shoulders, and led him to a row of trash bins. He glanced over his shoulder and saw Trinina moving toward the cart.

"What do you need?"

"A favor."

"Name it."

"That box—" Trinina was leaning into the cart and whispering. "The lady's entire life is in that box. She's leaving the country under bad circumstances."

"Who isn't?"

"She couldn't get away with everything, so she only took what's most important. I want you to be careful while driving."

"Say no more."

"I want you to meet us down at Pier 21. The ship is the H.M.S. *Auckland*. We'll take the box from you there before the ship leaves."

"I could take it to the loading dock for you. Not that big of a deal. No extra charge."

Payne shook his head. Trinina was done. "No. She'll have to take it into the cabin with her. I know it seems senseless, but she's got to have something to hold on to. She's leaving all of her friends, the life-style . . ."

The driver nodded sympathetically. "You may have to bribe the purser."

"Leave that to me." He slapped the driver on the back and told him to get going. The driver saluted, climbed into the cart, and ground it into gear, lurching down the street until he had speed enough to move smoothly.

"What did you tell him?" Trinina asked.

"I told him you were a mental case and that you couldn't

live without that box. I told him that if he screwed up,
you'd claw him to death."

She slapped his arm.

"What did you tell Nathan?"

"I told him what was happening and to hold on tight.
And that we loved him."

Payne kissed her on the cheek. "Let's go."

They picked up the bags and started down the street,
watching the taillights shrink into the night. They finished
the block and were halfway down the next when Trinina
slowed and squinted.

"It stopped," she said.

"What's stopped?"

"The taxi." Fear was rising in her voice. "The taxi's
stopped." She pulled away.

"Trinina. *No!*"

It was too late. She had broken his grip and was running
down the sidewalk at full speed, heels slapping concrete
and echoing between the buildings. Over her running Payne
could hear grinding: servos, at least a half dozen of them,
the sound cascading down the street from where the cart
had stopped.

Suddenly pure white light stabbed at the taxi from a
score of places. A shriek broke from Trinina's throat.
From above the search beams came strobing reds and
blues and yellows.

Panic coated Payne's throat, and he pumped his legs,
his lungs pushing and pulling oxygen, almost catching fire
in the cool night air. Trinina was almost across the next
intersection when he caught her, an arm around her waist
and a hand over her mouth. His feet slammed and negotiated the asphalt and jarred when they hit the raised
concrete. A finger of light swept toward them from a
stopped cart. Payne twisted sideways and dove into a pile
of refuse, sending cans crashing to the ground and clattering into the street. The hand that sealed her mouth slid
to her hips and pushed her into an empty can. He twisted

and rolled, burying himself under a pile of decaying news-print.

"Payne," she sobbed.

"Shut up," he snapped in a coarse whisper. "Shut the hell up," he repeated, carefully enunciating every letter.

One set of servos stirred and got louder. He heard Trinina draw breath.

"Quiet!"

The sound peaked and stopped to idle less than ten meters from where they were. He tried to peek out and was blinded by light. He froze.

A latch snapped, and the sound of metal clicked against asphalt, tenuously at first, then slowly merging into a distinct rhythmic pattern. Someone was walking toward them.

The metal scraped and stopped. Payne clenched his teeth and squeezed his eyes shut. Except for the idling of the cart, all was silent. He couldn't hear Trinina's breathing, which made him terribly conscious of his own. He slowly sucked air and held it, thinking that the very sound of his heart was going to give them away.

There was a loud *pop*, and every muscle in his body tensed. It was followed by a sharp crack and the clattering of cans, the spray of papers on stone. There was a wild, high-pitched screech and a human voice blurting out an oath. The metal shuffled and clicked nervously.

A burst of static followed, an unintelligible noise beneath it, then another click and more scraping.

"What's that?" a voice croaked from the street.

There was more static and electronically scrambled speech.

"No," the voice said wearily. "No. Just a damn cat. Damn cat's all."

Static and voice and the clicking on asphalt mixed. The servos revved and ground down the street.

Trinina stirred. Payne snaked out an arm and held her still.

There were more servos, the remainder of the fleet,

revving and grinding and building to a crescendo, their
drone breaking and falling as they passed. Payne held fast,
his arms locked around Trinina until the sound of the carts
was a distant buzzing in their ears.

He retracted his arms and pushed up from the cement.
Bones cracked, and muscles signaled that they were raw
with abuse. He crawled to the edge of the bank of cans
and looked down the street.

"Where did they go?" Trinina's voice echoed from the
can.

"Stopped," Payne said hoarsely.

"Where?"

"Down. About six blocks."

"Not your place."

"Looks like it."

"Not Bailey," Trinina sobbed. "Not Bailey."

"I don't know. It's too far to tell. They're all lit up."

Trinina worked her way out of the can. "We've got to
help."

"No."

"We can't leave him like that."

"We don't know that it's him they're after," Payne
snarled. "If we go back now, we're dead. You saw what
they did to Myra. They're on a roll, and they're not going
to show much mercy."

"What about Bailey?"

"He can take care of himself. If it's him they're after,
he'd want us to get away."

"They may leave soon."

"We can't wait. If we do, we'll lose it all. We've got
to go, and we've got to do it now."

Trinina nodded, face streaked with tears. She made
her way to the sidewalk.

Payne stood and stretched, then took Trinina and moved
her close to the buildings.

"Our taxi's gone," Trinina said. "I hope it was just an
I.D. check."

"They didn't have it stopped long enough for an arrest."

They stayed in the shadows until they could no longer see the flickering overheads of the Federal carts, then moved onto the sidewalk and picked up the pace. After three blocks, Payne worked up his nerve and thumbed his watch. It was thirteen minutes after three.

"We've got to pick it up. We're running behind."

"I'm about to break into a run, Payne. If you want to carry me, fine."

"Five blocks and then we get a taxi. If we can find one."

"You carried me earlier." She looked at him coyly. "You swept me off my feet."

Any other time he would have played for the romantic potential. "I threw you."

They broke into a jog and moved onto the asphalt. They forced their breath into the night air, which was chilled enough to produce a cloud when they exhaled. The cool bit their noses and knuckles and reddened their cheeks. When they tired, they slowed to a steady walk. They alternated speeds until they saw the dock lights breaking from between the buildings.

"Almost there," Payne panted, stopping.

Trinina caught up and bent over, resting her hands on her knees. "This is a killer," she said. "That Kingman must have been made of iron."

Payne swallowed. "What makes you say that?"

"To kill Winthrop and then run to your place to get the ticket. Must have been a marathon runner."

"Or caught a taxi."

She straightened and gasped for air, looking back over her shoulder. "That's still a good way to go. At least five kilometers."

Payne checked his watch. "Screwing around considered, we did it in an hour twenty."

"Hardly a record."

"Someone in shape could do it much faster. Come on. Let's go."

"An hour, maybe?"

"Easily. You're not still worried, are you?"

"Kingman is dead. I know."

She took his hand, and they followed the lights to the docks. The closer they came, the brighter the lights grew, and the more their stomachs knotted in anticipation. There was electric excitement in the air, so crackling sharp that they could smell the ozone of it. When their nostrils twitched they picked up a hundred different scents: the heavy odor of the petrol synths, the prick of burning coal fuels, the salt of the sea, and the musk of human sweat. They could hear industrial sounds as well: the whirring of gears, the snapping of wood, curses from laborers. There were pulsating bass notes from engines revving, and the ambience was finished by the sounds of a crowd milling and waiting, biding time until opportunity came. The atmosphere was loaded, and it made them tremble.

"We've made it," Trinina cried.

"Not yet." Payne checked the streets. ElectriCarts in varying stages of decomposition shared the avenues with ancient pieces of loading equipment. People were in motion, some plodding, some scurrying, others merely wandering, clearly absent of mind. He spotted something mounted on a chain-link fence topped by concertina wire. Covered in graffiti-proof plastic was a large map marked with the words "YOU ARE HERE."

He ran his finger across the top of the map. "Pier Nineteen."

"Twenty-one," Trinina snapped nervously.

"Sorry." He held one finger over the "21" and used the other to trace a suitable path.

"Hurry."

"Be calm." He looked at her and smiled. Her face was pale. He didn't blame her. She was being chased out of the country and was harboring the notion that someone was going to rise from the dead to kill them.

In an hour? Sure. And Kingman was a big son of a bitch. He could do it and not even sweat. Sure.

"Home stretch." He smiled.

Kill Winthrop and beat it back to my place. Sure. Why not?

"Miles to go before we sleep," Trinina said.

"That book by John?"

"Forget it."

Payne navigated by sight, checking numbers on the warehouses, squinting and trying to remember the map, stepping around rusting drums that once held liquid and now held trash, stumbling over iron pipes and mechanical parts hidden in the squalor.

An hour. Sure. Maybe a little longer.

He jerked to a halt.

"Something wrong?"

"We've gone too far." He turned and backtracked. He caught the name of a warehouse that had been hidden from view and nodded. "This way," he said, and led her down a wooden boardwalk.

Wrong.

"What's the matter?" Trinina asked.

"Nerves," Payne said. "Nerves."

But the thought was back and wouldn't leave. *Wrong,* it said. *Kingman was on the stuff. If he ran, he might get an orgasm and be too numb to move after the first kilometer.*

Payne shook it off. *So he took a taxi, okay? He was no fool.*

There was a violent tug on his hand, and he stopped. He snapped out of thought and looked at the path ahead.

"What's the matter with you?" Trinina complained.

Across the boardwalk running from warehouse to warehouse was a large crane, charred and blackened by fire.

"We've got to go back. Go around." He didn't sound convinced. Something unpleasant was gnawing at the back of his head. It was a memory of a smiling face.

Winthrop. Poor Lol Winthrop.

They turned and retreated. Trinina checked her watch and gasped.

"How long?" Payne asked.

"Twenty minutes."

"We'll make it."

"If we don't get lost first."

"Over here," Payne said abruptly.

Trinina saw him heading for a concrete alley strewn with garbage and rotting crates. He negotiated the path between two narrow metal Quonset buildings opposite the warehouse.

"It'll save time," he urged.

She nodded and followed. His face looked vaguely troubled.

Poor Lol Winthrop, he was thinking. *Dead within an hour of the good news.*

Trinina stepped on a board, and something leaped out at her feet, squealing. Payne kicked the rat and routed it, sending it weaving out of the alley in search of a safer place to forage.

"A little farther," he said. "Stay to the concrete."

"I don't like it," she said. "I'm going around."

"There's nothing to be scared of. That's the only rat that'll mess with you, I promise."

She shook her head.

"I'll show you," he said, and stalked down the alley.

An hour. Assaulted at 2200. Winthrop dead at 2300.

He stopped short. "No."

He had been assaulted at 2200. Winthrop's meeting was at 2200. *Kingman was dead by 2300 . . .*

There was a shrill cry from Trinina and a clumsy rustling off to his right. He turned and ducked as something whistled over his head.

He took two steps back and looked into Kelce's face, slick with sweat. A crowbar was clenched in his hands.

"*No!*" Payne shouted, tossing Nathan's bag.

Kelce swung again, cleanly missing. He looked at Payne and froze in recognition. He opened his mouth to speak, and Payne jumped, hitting him at the waist and bowling them both to the concrete. The crowbar spun away from them, scraping on the ground.

They rolled, Kelce trying to land punches wherever he could. Payne was on the bottom when they stopped. He reached up and grabbed Kelce by the lapels and threw him off. Kelce rolled and grabbed for the crowbar. Payne kicked and snapped Kelce's hand at the wrist. Kelce slowed and looked at his hand, lips cocking into a wry smile.

Payne lunged again, grabbing him by the throat and crotch and slamming him into the corrugated metal building, sending peals of thunder down the alley. Kelce twisted and clumsily clawed with his hands. Payne ducked, then grabbed him by the shoulders and slammed him into the metal once, twice, three times.

"You son of a bitch!" he screamed. "You son of a bitch! You killed Winthrop!" His chest convulsed, and something hot was biting his eyes and spilling down his cheeks. He slammed Kelce again. "That's why Winthrop was butchered. He wasn't killed by a professional. It was you, you bastard!"

Kelce's head tilted, and his eyes crossed. His lip curled into a sneer. He turned to face Payne. His lips had been split, and dark fluid was oozing from one nostril.

"I had to, Payne," he said, gasping for breath. "He had my papers, and Kingman was after you. He couldn't do both, so I did Winthrop." He gasped for more air. "Because he could be taken from behind."

"Then you moved Kingman's body, too."

Kelce nodded. "When he didn't turn up, I expected the worst. When I went to Smith, he told me to go back and clean up my mess." He coughed in violent, wracking hacks. Breath escaped his lungs in bursts. He inhaled again, and there was a deep rasping as if something inside had been knocked loose. An unmistakable scent poured from his mouth.

"You've got it," Payne said.

Kelce nodded. "Smith. I think—" His neck stiffened,

his face the consistency of warming wax. "Can't remember. Too hard."

Payne tightened his grip. "Try."

"Smith," Kelce repeated. "The bitch slipped it to me. When I slept, I think."

"Did you screw her?"

Trinina put her hand on Payne's shoulder.

"This is important. Were you screwing her, Kelce?"

Kelce nodded.

"Then that's how you got it, friend."

Kelce's eyes rolled back in his head, and a moan slipped from his throat. It was cut off by a loud blast, a note that shook them down to their very souls.

"That's our boat," Trinina said. "We've got to get moving."

Kelce looked at them incredulously.

Trinina tugged. Payne turned to her and held up a finger. "One more thing."

"Make it fast."

He turned back to Kelce. "Why did you leave her in my apartment?"

Kelce blinked numbly. Payne slammed him again.

"Easy," Trinina cried.

"Why did you leave the body in my apartment?"

Kelce made a choking rattle that sounded as if his lungs were decomposing. "She was sick, Payne. I didn't know what the hell to do. We were walking to her place from the Lancaster, and she lost it. Her mind was gone." He licked his swollen lips and swallowed. "I had a pretty good idea of what it was, but I was scared. I couldn't think. I was really scared, Payne, and I knew you'd help me." He choked, and his eyes filled with tears. "I thought you'd help me."

Payne released his grip and watched him sink to the ground, pale and shaking. He looked up at them helplessly, sobbing.

"You're going to die," Payne said. He laid his hand on Trinina's neck, and they turned away.

"Eleven minutes," she said.

"We'll make it. It was just on the other side of that crane."

Their feet crunched disconcertingly on the concrete. Suddenly Payne felt very weary. Everything he had felt and stored up over the past week had deserted him, leaving his bare essence bobbing in the wake.

He turned to Trinina and there was an explosion of light and dark and he was gone, cast out and floating lost for a million years. He flew and floated until he heard a call for him to return. He cut loose from his wings and drifted back into his skull.

He was greeted by pain. His entire body was crying out in distress. His head was throbbing and alive with pain, feeling as if his skin had been peeled back to reveal his skull from forehead to the base of his neck, from temple to temple.

He stirred, and there was noise. He opened his eyes and was blinded by thick liquid. He rubbed them and his fingers came away red. He moved again and fell, scattering junk as he went. He discovered that he was sprawled in a line of garbage cans.

"No!"

He heard a familiar hissing. He pulled from the cans and checked the alley.

Trinina was on the ground, backing away on elbows and the balls of her feet, mouth frozen open. Kelce was standing over her, arms stretching out over his head and culminating in a hooked piece of iron.

"Kelce!" Payne screamed. *"Kelce. Let her go!"*

Kelce looked at him. His face was no longer human. He was being run by the bacteria now, and whatever had been sobbing on the ground a minute before had been suffocated. Their eyes locked. Kelce's mouth twisted into a bloody, sardonic grin, and he stretched back, the crowbar reaching back between his shoulder blades. He arched up on his toes, and the iron began a forward arc. Payne's mouth opened in a scream.

As the bar neared Trinina's head, a blossom appeared in the center of Kelce's chest and spat bright, foamy red. His legs kicked out, and the crowbar flipped harmlessly to one side. Kelce landed flat on his back, and his arms and legs clawed at the ground. His head tilted back, and he arched upward, trying to bend in half. A scream cleared his throat, a high-pitched banshee wail that ended in a panicked gargle. It stopped. What spirit remained left his body, and he collapsed.

Payne rolled and tried to crawl to Trinina. His arms and legs were numb, and he flopped to the ground. He called her name, but his head was spinning so badly that he couldn't tell if there had been a reply. He twisted and crawled, clawing into a sitting position, trying desperately to find her.

His head lolled back, and he found himself looking into a metal tube. A wisp of smoke drifted from inside and lodged in his nostrils. It was the same scent that had been left behind in Rodrigues's office after his suicide.

It was the smell of death.

"Mr. Payne?"

He looked up and blinked, not comprehending.

"Are you all right, Mr. Payne?"

Payne swallowed and squinted at the face. There was no malice to be seen.

"You?"

Giles lowered the revolver and zipped his suit down to his navel. "Sorry I was so late with the shot. I had to wait for the ship's whistle to blow. Didn't want to have the law come sniffing around."

Payne coughed. "Why am I so happy to see you?" He watched Giles work with the weapon. The barrel was at least twenty centimeters long, with a sighting device mounted on the top. Giles unclipped the sighting tube and slipped it into a leather pouch under his right arm.

"As far as I'm concerned, you didn't see me, okay?" He clicked a button on the gun and flipped a metal cylinder out. He spun it and removed a metal tube. "One shot." He grinned. "Nice to know I've still got the touch."

Trinina appeared with a torn strip of fabric and wrapped it around Payne's head.

"You might have a concussion," she said. "We'll have the ship's doctor look at you."

"What happened?"

Giles snapped the cylinder back into the revolver. "Never turn your back on a bastard like Kelce." He slipped the weapon into a sling under his left arm. "Even when you think he's out of it." He zipped his suit back up.

Payne's head throbbed. He cradled it in his hands. "Why did you kill him?"

"I couldn't let him kill your lady."

"You didn't have to save us."

"If you must know the truth, I almost didn't. Andrew told me to wait until he'd finished the two of you and then kill Kelce to get the papers back. His way of sealing Honor's crypt."

"Why did you save us?"

"I don't know. Maybe because you were fighting so bloody hard. And you did do us a favor, Mr. Payne. You warned us."

A third signal came from the ship.

"You'd better get a move on."

"Have him fill out the papers," Payne said. "Fast."

Trinina dug them out of her bag and handed them over with a pen. "You know the details?"

Giles nodded. "Unfortunately."

"What are you going to tell your brother when he asks for those?"

Giles mulled it over. "I'll tell him that they were folded into Kelce's breast pocket, along with the money cards. Much to my chagrin, I discovered that after I'd shot him."

"He might not buy it," Trinina warned.

Giles scowled, then with the flick of a wrist tore a corner from one of the papers. "Proof," he said.

"Better get some of Kelce's blood on it before you go."

"Good idea."

"That's ridiculous," Payne said.

Trinina shook her head. "It'll work. It's one of the oldest tricks in the book."

Giles gave the papers back to Trinina, then held his hand down for Payne and pulled him from the ground. He held the clasp, and they shook.

"Thanks," Payne said.

"Now, get out of here and live happily ever after."

Payne took Nathan's suitcase from Trinina. "You heard the man."

They set out at a dead run, finally clearing the alley and stumbling into view of the ship. It was a giant, majestic thing, towering above the structures on the docks.

Trinina looked at the people choking the pier. There were thousands of them, all swarming toward a roped-off path a meter wide leading up the boarding ramp to the ship.

"We'll never make it."

"Run."

They set off again, pumping their legs as hard as they could, Payne clutching his head to keep his senses from spilling out.

"Cut through!" Trinina cried.

"No!" he shouted. "Make for the path!"

She looked again. He was right. They would never make it through the crowd. Holding back the queues of people were men, larger than any of the bouncers at the Lancaster, arms interlocked, ax handles gripped tightly in their hands.

Ten meters from the path a figure jumped out and spread its arms, snagging them and pulling them to a stop. Payne grabbed him, startled. In a moment, understanding sank in.

"Where's the crate?" he shouted over the crowd.

"I didn't think you were going to make it!" the driver yelled back.

"Where the hell's her crate?"

"They gave final call for cargo," he explained. He started to say something else, but Trinina screamed for Payne and pointed. He followed the direction and saw the crate wrapped in a hemp net, suspended a hundred meters in the air, being carried by a shipboard crane.

Payne shook the driver with rage. *"I told you to hold it for us!"* He turned and waved Trinina on. "Go!"

"They're not using any hooks," the driver protested. "It says 'Use No Hooks'." He pointed at the airborne crate. "They're not. I made sure."

Payne swallowed and nodded. He dug into his pocket and pulled out a plastic card. Payday would have been next week, and it would have been recharged. Still, there was over four hundred dollars left in it. He pressed it into the driver's hand and spat out, "Thanks," then ran to catch Trinina.

"Hey," the driver shouted as he left, "do you realize how much this is?"

Payne caught up as a uniformed man with a megaphone announced that boarding was closing to check for last-minute cancellations. Trinina looked harried. The steward guarding the path looked stern.

He handed her Nathan's suitcase. "What's the problem?"

"He won't take this paper," Trinina sobbed.

"It's torn," the steward said in a thick accent. He studied Payne and cocked his head.

"You see this?" Payne shouted, touching the cloth around his head. "Somebody tried to kill us for these papers. You're telling me that she can't get on because somebody made off with the corner?"

"It's your paper," Trinina said weakly.

"Those are the rules," the steward said.

Payne put his hand between Trinina's shoulders and shoved her up the path. "Go!" he shouted. "Go!"

She looked at him, eyes wide.

"Go!"

"I love you, Payne."

"Go on! Get the hell out of here!"

She turned and ran up the path. The steward made a check on his clipboard, then reached for a gray metal box clipped to his belt and began keying a switch.

"I'd leave if I were you," he said. "I'm signaling that the ship's full. It'll get ugly around here when they announce it."

"I hope you realize what you've done," Payne said. He looked up the path and saw Trinina standing on the ship, waving her hands at a uniformed man and pointing to the steward.

"I certainly do," the steward replied. "It happens every time I come to this fucking country."

"Your attention please," a metallic voice boomed from the bullhorn. "Your attention please."

A roar went up from the crowd. It was hot and seething, as if they already knew what was going to be said.

"I regret to inform you—"

The roar pitched up into a panicked shriek. Payne saw that the man was still talking but could no longer be heard. The crowd began to push and crush in on the line of dockworkers, who pushed back and began to use their ax handles. Payne's stomach fell. This wave of people would crush anything in the way. He was going to die.

He heard a breaking noise and looked over the steward's shoulder. A member of the control line was falling back, his face laid open from forehead to chin. Above him, an arm angrily waved a green bottle, the blunt end fresh with blood. The assaulted worker hit the ground, and the line broke, moving his way. He took a panicked step up the path and heard the steward scream. He had been caught from behind by a hundred desperate arms, scratching and clawing and knotting around any part of him available. Their goal was what he held crumpled in his right hand, shoved high in the air in some senseless attempt to save it.

Payne's paper.

The steward screamed again, the sound cutting short.

The paper was still in the air even though his arm had been clawed to the bone.

The mob shifted again. Payne was now looking point blank into the steward's empty face. The hand began to fall, and with it the torn paper.

Payne reached and with two fingers plucked it from the dead hand.

The others cried in rage and released their grip on the steward's body. It tumbled into the crowd and was crushed underfoot.

Payne didn't see any of this. The paper held in his palm by a row of white knuckles, he ran up the path as it caved in behind him.

Trinina looked down and saw him, then reached out and called his name. Uniformed men scurried around her, tossing gas canisters into the crowd and picking up batons.

The ship's horn sounded as Payne made the stairs. He scrambled, pushing his feet against the metal, when a violent lurch knocked him back down to the foot.

The ship was moving away.

"Payne!"

He crawled to his feet and fought the stairs three at a time, collapsing when he reached the platform. He staggered to his feet and looked in dismay. He had two meters to get speed for the jump, and the distance from the jetty to the boat was growing by the second.

Trinina was leaning into the railing, looking helpless. He looked down the length of the ship, thinking there was another way. People were swarming the ropes that held the ship to the dock, climbing for all their lives were worth. Burly crewmen went methodically from one line to the next, severing them with axes and sending screamers into the oily waters.

He backed to the edge of the platform and took a weak first step. Strength coursed through him, and his legs pounded against the trembling metal. He made a short jump to the end of the jetty. He came down on the metal, and it bowed under the sudden weight. He crouched, and when the metal started to snap back, he pushed and kicked as if it was the last time he would ever use his legs.

Then he was flying. He stretched his arms out to the ship's siren call, unaware that breath was ripping from his lungs in a scream. For a brief, terrible moment he was hanging in midair watching the ship pull away, oblivious to his desperation.

He hit metal. He hit hard, and the landing knocked what breath he had left cleanly away. He started to fall and reached out with his left hand and grabbed. He jerked to a stop.

"He's got papers!"

Payne looked up in time to see a blue baton smash down on the knuckles of his left hand. He cried out, and the baton raised again.

"I said he's got papers!"

The man behind the baton turned for an instant, then pitched over the rail and down past Payne, splashing into the sea.

Trinina looked sheepishly over the side. She smiled and reached for him, taking his right arm and pulling. He put his feet against the side of the ship and kicked. When he was safe on the deck, he crawled to a wall and put his back to it, nursing his left hand.

"Broken?"

"At this point, I don't care."

A shadow fell over them. A man in uniform.

"What do you want?" Payne croaked.

The man tipped his hat. "I'm the chief purser. I believe this woman threw one of my crew overboard."

Payne raised his right hand and relaxed the grip on his papers. "It's all legal, I hope."

The purser held a tube to his eye and looked them over. "Genuine," he said, "but torn. And that doesn't explain why a man went over the side."

"He broke my knuckles," Payne said. "It was self-defense."

The purser handed the papers back.

"Put me away if you have to, but do it when we get to Sydney."

There was a change in the man's appearance, almost as if a smile had been hidden beneath the stoic face. "You two look like you've been through the mill."

They didn't move.

"I'm sure my man could swim. He's got his Australian Citizenship Card, so he can hop any freighter back. As for the sad condition of your paper, it's an infraction, but I fear we're too far from the docks now to put you over the side."

"Thank you."

"If you'll excuse me, then. I have other matters that need my attention."

"Of course," Trinina said. "Thank you."

The purser turned and walked away.

When he was out of sight, Payne struggled to his feet. Trinina tried to hold him down. "Rest."

"What about Nathan?"

"Nathan," she cried. "We've got to get him unpacked."

"In the cabin," Payne shouted. "He's got to stay hidden."

They wandered the deck, moving in and out of the swarms of people who were trying to become oriented. They rounded a corner and saw the crate that held Nathan, still wrapped in a net, being lowered through a hole in the upper deck. Trinina broke away and accosted a muscular figure in a torn shirt who was signaling the crane operator and cursing at him to go easy. He tried to brush her off, but she pulled on his arm. The crate disappeared into the hold, and the man made a quick slashing motion across his throat.

"What do you want, ma'am?"

Trinina pointed down into the hold. "That crate. I need to have it sent to my cabin. It's got some important things in it."

"I'm sorry, it's already in the hold."

"Isn't there something you can do?" Payne asked. "There are some very fragile things inside."

"I'd like to help, but it's an impossibility. We've got the hold full as it is, and we didn't have time to set the cargo up right, not with them storming the boat like they did. It gets worse every time we come back."

"You don't have to spare any of your crew. We can do it."

"Please," Trinina said.

The man looked down into the hold. Three crewmen had swarmed the crate and were freeing it from the netting. They swiveled it on one corner and attached it to a dolly.

He shook his head. "Sorry, ma'am. They've got it off the crane already, and if you look around, you'll see there's more to be done."

Trinina moved toward him. Payne caught her and held her back. "Please. You don't understand..."

The worker took a step back, looking them over very carefully. He studied their faces and their forlorn appearance, the dirty and frayed clothing, the fact that they had been bloodied on the way to the boat, and the odd baggage they carried. He looked into the hold and shouted.

"Ro-bert!"

One of the workers looked up. "Sir!"

"Put that one on L-2-X. Out front."

The man in the hold nodded. "Straightaway."

He turned back to Payne and Trinina. "I can't pull it from the hold, not in the state we're in right now. I'm having them put it in hold L-2, which is for passengers' excess luggage. It'll be easy to find there, but I recommend you wait until things calm down. You won't do much but get in the way right now. You're best off to wait it out in your cabin."

"Thank you," Trinina said.

"One more thing. You look a bit banged up. You might want to look up the ship's doctor."

"I'd planned on it," Payne said.

"Again, not right away. He'll be as busy as the rest of us until we're well out to sea. If you can live with your wounds, he could probably give you some pills to take the edge off the pain until he could tend you. These runs we make are a risky business now, and he'll be seeing worse than you for the next few hours."

"Thanks again."

The man turned and began cursing the crane operator. Trinina slipped her arm around Payne, and they walked away.

"What do we do now?" Trinina asked.

"Find our cabin," Payne said. "I think I'm going to be sick."

En-gland.

They slowly made their way across the deck, the sound of the ship cutting water hissing in their ears.

En-gland.

Their ears pricked as they caught the new sound. It was a high, sad chant, and it came again and again. They traced the source of the noise to the receding docks.

As they watched, they saw thousands who had come to find their way to a boat. They were queuing up on the Pier 21 jetty and lined the docks from horizon to horizon. Small fires began appearing from matches and lighters and candles and chemical torch-sticks. The orange light was caught by the rolling fog, giving an eerie glow to the coastline as the ship pulled away.

"En-gland," the crowd sang. "My England."

"Oh, Payne," Trinina said, tears spilling down her cheeks. "Look at them all."

The voices from the docks, having found the key and the pitch, turned the chant into song. The notes were crisp and clear in the still air and carried straight from the candlelit wharf to the departing ship.

"England, my England shall rise again,
And the lion shall rule the world,
Britannia shall rule the waves again,
With peace from shore to shore."

"How many do you think will make it?" Trinina asked.

"I don't want to know," Payne said quietly. "I don't want to know."

The two stood at the rail and watched until the fog enveloped the shore and extinguished the flames of salute and until the singing of the crowd could no longer be heard.